Return
to
Mandalay

Also by Rosanna Ley

Last Dance in Havana
Bay of Secrets
Her Mother's Secret
The Saffron Trail
The Villa
The Little Theater by the Sea

Rosanna Ley

Return
to
Mandalay

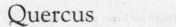

Quercus

First published in Great Britain in 2014
This paperback edition published in 2019 by

Quercus Editions Ltd
Carmelite House
50 Victoria Embankment
London EC4Y 0DZ

An Hachette UK company

A CIP catalogue record for this book is available
from the British Library.

PB ISBN 978 1 78747 169 6
EB ISBN 978 1 78747 170 2

10 9 8 7 6 5 4 3 2 1

Typeset by CC Book Production

Printed and bound in Great Britain by Clays Ltd, Elcograf S.p.A.

For Grey, with love.

And in memory of Peter Innes, John Sams
and all the men who fought in Burma.
Never forgotten.

CHAPTER I

'Could you come through to the office, Eva?' Jacqui Dryden's voice was, as always, cool and slightly irritated.

Eva was stooping over a Victorian dressing-table repairing the spring mechanism of a tiny drawer in the panelling. She straightened up. Ouch. Rubbed her back with the heel of her hand. It was a delicate job and she hadn't realised quite how long she'd been stuck in that position.

'Just coming,' she called back. Briefly, she touched the top of the walnut dressing-table with her fingertips as if promising her swift return.

Jacqui Dryden was standing staring out of the large bay window into the street below. It was a Thursday afternoon in late October and Bristol city centre was as busy as ever. The Bristol Antiques Emporium was well placed in a side street where rents were lower but there were still enough individual-looking shops to pull in passers-by. Vintage was in, business was brisk and Eva's boss should have been happy. She looked anything but. Her make-up was as flawless as ever, but there was something despairing in her blue eyes that Eva hadn't seen there before. Could it be anything to do with the raised voices she'd heard coming from the office this morning?

'Come in.' Jacqui turned towards her, the despairing expression vanished and Eva felt her scrutiny. Her boss had this way. She was a little over five feet tall, blonde and perfectly formed, and when she was around her, Eva invariably felt awkward, clumsy, too tall. She wasn't used to feeling like that. She brushed some sawdust from her jeans. Her hands were dusty too and she realised she had a splinter in her thumb. She kept her nails clipped short because of the nature of the job and at work wore jeans, a T-shirt and a pair of old Converse, tying her unruly dark hair back in a ponytail so that it wouldn't get in the way. She could imagine how she looked to Jackie, could see what she was thinking. She wasn't at her most glamorous. But this was work and Eva relished immersing herself in it.

Jacqui didn't invite her to sit down, didn't so much as smile. Several times over the past few months, Eva had been tempted to tap on her boss's shell, try and make it crack a little and take a peek inside. But she hadn't risked it – at least, not yet.

'I need you to go away on an assignment,' Jacqui said without preamble.

'Away?' Eva echoed. That was a first. 'What kind of assignment?'

She had worked at the Emporium for six months now. The job had attracted her because the company dealt mainly in Asian antiques. Thanks to her grandfather, as a child she had fallen in love with wood and with history; they were in her blood. At nineteen, she had left home in Dorset – a home that had splintered to pieces after her father's death when Eva was only six – and gone to university in Bristol to study antique furniture restoration with decorative arts. Specialist subject: Asian artefacts. And that was thanks to her grandfather, too. That was sixteen years ago now. But there was still so much, Eva reminded herself, to thank him for.

Jacqui didn't answer the question. Her partner, Leon – in business and life – hadn't answered her questions in the office this morning either. 'Why should you care? Tell me what's going on,' Jacqui had demanded. 'Or I walk out of here this minute.' But Leon hadn't and so Jacqui had. She had stalked out of her office in her pencil skirt and stilettos right past where Eva was busy repairing the scabbard of an old Japanese sword and pretending she hadn't heard what was being said.

'As you know,' Jacqui said to Eva now, 'our Asian stock is selling very well at the moment.'

'Yes.' Of course, she had noticed. The company were expanding that side of the business and soon perhaps Victorian walnut dressing-tables would be a thing of the past, so to speak. Many countries were opening up more than ever before and those in the Far East were in a position to take advantage of growing international interest in their colonial furniture, a legacy of days gone by, and in their cultural and religious artefacts too. Like their old stone Buddhas, for example – and they'd seen a few of those in the Emporium – often so badly eroded that they'd no doubt had new ones made by some local stonemason. The Bristol Antiques Emporium hadn't wasted any time in forging lucrative partnerships with Far East traders who wanted to sell.

3

'But there are problems.' Jacqui tucked back a strand of fine blonde hair that had dared escape the fifties' chignon she favoured. 'Too much stock is arriving badly damaged, for a start.'

'Which could certainly be avoided,' Eva agreed. She was the person who generally had to repair it. She had joined the Emporium hoping to make use of the expertise she'd gained doing her degree. At last, she'd thought. It had been thirteen years since she'd graduated, but none of her jobs had quite fulfilled her expectations. She'd worked in a second-hand furniture shop for a man who specialised in cold-calling with the express purpose of parting old ladies from family heirlooms with as little money changing hands as possible, until Eva could almost feel his smug smile destroying her soul. She'd worked in a museum shop, where she'd met her friend Leanne. And she'd spent over a year as a seamstress in vintage wedding hire. This was the time – she'd hoped – for her career to take off in the direction she wanted it to.

But the reality of the Emporium had proved another disappointment. Most of her time was spent doing run-of-the-mill repairs, cleaning, unpacking and often dealing with customers too. They might have formed a lucrative partnership, but the Bristol Antiques Emporium was under-staffed. Apart from Jacqui and Leon, there was only Lydia, who worked part-time in the antiques showroom above. And Eva who did just about everything else.

'If we can find a way of avoiding it, yes.' Jacqui frowned.

'Can't our contacts check the packaging before shipping?' Eva asked mildly. Many of the countries they dealt with packaged the goods poorly – often only with shredded newspaper. They didn't seem to appreciate the vulnerability of some of the more fragile pieces.

'And . . .' Jacqui dismissed this suggestion with a wave of her manicured hand. 'Our contact has come across some unusual items we may be interested in.'

'Unusual items?' Eva's interest flared.

'Statuettes, wooden furniture, eighteenth and nineteenth century – even earlier, some of it. Unique, primitive, just the sort of thing we're looking for.' For a second her eyes brightened with enthusiasm. 'But . . .' She hesitated. 'I don't fully trust our contact there.' She glanced at Eva as if to gauge her reaction.

Eva shrugged. She didn't need to ask why not. Firstly, six months working for Jacqui Dryden had shown her that her boss rarely trusted anyone, probably not even Leon, come to think of it. And secondly, she was aware that many of their contacts in the Far East had their own agenda. Why should they feel loyalty to their overseas dealers? Why shouldn't they look out first for their own families, their own countries, when so many of them had lived in poverty for so long?

'The provenance sounds more than plausible,' Jacqui told her. 'But they need to be authenticated.'

'Oh, I see.' Eva felt the fizz of anticipation. This was why she'd joined the company. Authentication, restoration, re-living history almost. And travelling too. That was an unexpected bonus. After the month she'd had, it sounded exactly what she needed.

'You could do that, couldn't you?'

'Of course.' It was what she'd been trained for. And this trip would give her the chance to prove her skills.

Once again, Jacqui frowned. 'You wouldn't object to going on your own?'

'Not at all.' Eva preferred to work independently. And it would be an adventure. 'I presume that you also want me to talk to our contact?'

'Yes.' Jacqui shot her an unfathomable glance. 'You'll need to reinforce our relationship with him.' She seemed to be choosing her words carefully. 'But it will need sensitive handling.'

'I understand.'

'And while you're there, you might also get the chance to look around.' Jacqui was still speaking cautiously, as if she wasn't sure how much to say.

'Look around?' Eva wanted to be clear. She twisted the ring she wore on her little finger. It was a cluster of diamonds shaped like a daisy and set in gold, a present from her grandfather on her twenty-first birthday and she wore it every day, work or no work.

'Explore other avenues. Go to some antique markets, chat to the dealers, make new contacts perhaps. Find some more items we may be interested in.'

Goodness. The thrill returned. Eva tried to hide her surprise. With so much at stake, why wasn't Jacqui going herself?

She couldn't be trying to get rid of her, surely? She'd only overheard an argument – although the embarrassment of that might be enough for someone like her boss. She was rather touchy, perhaps more so than usual.

'I'll be busy here.' Jacqui moved from the window to the large leather-topped mahogany desk that dominated the room, and pushed a pile of papers to one side as if to demonstrate just how busy she would be. 'There are some important shipments due to arrive.' Once again, she seemed to almost lose her drift. And then snapped out of it. 'I couldn't possibly get away at the moment.'

Leon, Eva thought. That was the real reason.

'These people won't wait forever. There'll be others interested, you can be sure. So there's nothing for it.' Jacqui sighed. 'You'll have to go. You're the only one there is.'

Praise indeed. Eva raised an eyebrow. 'And where exactly am I going?'

'Oh.' Jacqui plucked a piece of paper from her desk. 'Didn't I say? You're to leave next week if we can get you a visa sorted out by then. I'll book your flight and let you know the exact times. You'll have to bring your passport in tomorrow morning. I'll arrange for an agent to meet you at the airport and make the hotel reservations. Um . . .' With the tip of her forefinger – nail varnished deep plum – she traced a path along the paper. 'Yangon, Bagan and Mandalay,' she said. 'That's where you'll be going. Ten days should be long enough. You'll have to take internal flights. I'll give you all the details in advance, of course.'

Eva stared at her. She hadn't even dared hope . . . 'Burma?' she whispered. Her heart was hammering out an old tune, a familiar tune, the rhythm one that she had grown up with, that had become a part of her. She was going to Burma. She had heard so much about it. And now she was going to taste and experience it for herself. She wanted to fling open the window and shout it to the people down in the street below. There was a grin of pure delight bubbling inside and she wanted to let it out.

'Yes. But it's called Myanmar now, you know.'

'I know.' The grin emerged and Eva sent it Jacqui's way. What did it matter that Jacqui sometimes didn't seem to like her or felt threatened by her or whatever else it might be? What did it matter, when her boss clearly trusted her enough to give her this opportunity? What did it matter when Eva was going to Burma? She closed her eyes and felt the colours of the country flicker behind her eyelids. Blue and gold . . .

There wasn't much, she thought, that she didn't know about Burma. Her grandfather had spent some of his most formative years there. He had worked in the timber industry and he had fought against the Japanese. His life in Burma had touched them all in different ways. And the stories he had told Eva when she was a child had wound their way into her heart.

'You'll go, then?' Jacqui asked her. Though she didn't look as if she'd take no for an answer. 'I've printed out images of some of the things you'll be looking at because it's easier to have hard copy to hand. It's all here.'

8

'Oh, yes, I'll go,' Eva replied. She'd always known she'd visit Burma one day. How could she not? In her twenties and early thirties, holidays had been short, usually city breaks in Europe, since they gave her the best opportunity to explore antique markets and historic buildings. And during her now rather distant gap year she'd made it to Thailand, along with Jess, her friend from college. Burma was an expensive trip to fund herself but more than that, for a long time, the country had been a no-go area politically. Eva had read about the unrest among the hill tribes, the repressive government, and the house arrest of Aung San Suu Kyi, the woman they all adored, who had sacrificed her personal life in order to fight for democracy for her people. Eva knew about the sanctions and that although tourists had become welcome in Myanmar, money from tourism tended to go straight into the pockets of the military government. And she understood that to visit the country was to support them.

But things were different now. Aung San Suu Kyi had been freed, the political climate was changing and . . . Eva's childhood dream was about to come true.

Should she pinch herself to make sure she wasn't dreaming again? She moved closer to the desk. The image of a seated and clear-eyed Buddha, probably gilded teak, gazed serenely back at her. Nineteenth century, she'd estimate from the picture, which wasn't terribly clear. She peered closer, looking for tell-tale patches of wear on the gilding but she'd have to assess the condition more thoroughly when she was actually there. There were other figures she recognised from her studies too, some carved and painted, some gilded and inlaid, some possibly as old as seventeenth century. A delicately carved angel, a monk sitting on a lotus flower, spiritual guardians and nats. There was what looked like a carved teak scripture chest, an ancient wooden crib and a pair of highly decorative doors – most likely ancient temple doors, she realised with a jolt of excitement.

Eva glanced across at Jacqui and met her gaze head on. Jacqui would no doubt have more information about these artefacts and she'd be giving it all to Eva to study before she left. But her boss was right. From the pictures alone, she could see that there were some remarkable pieces here. And she was being given the chance to see them, examine them at close hand, authenticate them and bring them back to the UK.

'Thanks, Jacqui,' she said.

Her boss gave her a quizzical look.

'For having faith in me. I won't let you down.'

And she left the office and drifted back to the Victorian dressing-table, her mind already halfway to Burma. She could still hardly believe it. Would it live up to her expectations? Would it fill the gaps in her grandfather's story? And what on earth would he say when she told him? Going to Burma had changed his life. Eva couldn't help wondering if it would do the same to hers.

CHAPTER 2

Eva let herself into her flat and closed the door behind her. It had been quite a day. What she needed, she decided, was a large glass of wine and a hot bath – and then she'd phone him. He was the person she most wanted to tell. But first things first. She opened her laptop, located her music file and selected an album. *Japancakes*. The soft lilting melody of the first track 'Double Jointed' began to float through the room, rippling like water lilies on a lake.

The flat – the first floor of an Edwardian building on the outskirts of the city, hence the high ceilings, decorative coving and large bay windows – was relatively tidy, although she'd left in a rush that morning. As always, it had a rather transitory look about it, as if Eva might be about to gather up all her belongings and move out. Which was probably, she decided, down to her state of mind. She had stayed in Bristol because this was where the jobs were, as far as the West Country was concerned. But it was more than that. Since she was six years old, she'd lived in a world where something you loved could be snatched away from you and nothing in your life would be the same again. She didn't exactly love her flat, but it was practical, reasonable to rent and it suited her, for the moment.

There was only one bedroom, which housed her Chinese 'opium' bed, bought on a whim from eBay and a purchase she'd never regretted; every time she laid her head on the pillow, she imagined its possibly lurid history. It never gave her nightmares though, instead it seemed to be seeped in relaxation. But the living-room-cum-kitchen was a space easily large enough for one. Or even two, Eva thought ruefully, as she hung her autumn tweedy jacket on a peg and chucked her bag on the sofa. The music was building, the melody becoming more layered. Max's minimalist flat had been smarter but had less floor space and character. A bit, she thought, like Max himself. Or so it had turned out.

Eva owned only a few pieces of special furniture, acquired over the past thirteen years. Apart from the bed and a sprawling sofa, there was a hand-carved and sturdy Chinese camphor-wood trunk in the bay window, with cushions it made a perfect window seat; a hand-painted mango-wood cabinet from Rajasthan on the far side of the room, bought at auction a few years ago to house her novels and reference books from uni and beside that, her favourite piece, a Meiji-period Japanese red lacquered priest's chair that had turned up out of the blue in the Emporium only a month ago. She owned nothing from Burma yet. It was still early days for the country, which made it all the more exciting from Eva's point of view. What might she come back with for her own collection?

There was a Japanese print on the wall, and the kitchen cupboards held a motley selection of china, some Oriental, some English bone, so thin that when you held it up to the light you could almost see right through. Max would never have moved in here, Eva reminded herself. Their styles didn't match. They didn't match. She'd been fooling herself for two years, that was all.

Max. She poured that glass of wine, took a sip and went to run her bath. The sounds of *Japancakes* followed her through the flat, rising and falling, the perfect chill out music. She'd met him in a cinema queue. Someone in front of her had trodden on her toe, she'd taken a little jump back and managed to throw toffee popcorn all over Max, who was standing right behind her. It had proved to be quite an ice breaker. He had suggested they sit together, it had seemed natural to go for a drink afterwards to discuss the film, and the rest, she thought grimly, was history.

And now they were history too. Eva turned the hot tap and swirled in a generous dollop of her favourite bath oil. She wanted to lie back, relax, sip her wine and think about going to Burma. What did it matter that she hadn't yet met a man she wanted to spend her life with? What did it matter that she had spent two years with Max before she discovered his other agenda? If she were honest . . . Max had turned her head from the start. He was older, charming, sophisticated. He had not only taken her out to shows, events and to all the latest restaurants for dinner, but he'd often surprised her with gifts of jewellery and even weekends in Paris and Rome. Which was all very nice. Eva fetched her wine and began to peel off her dusty work clothes, piece by piece. The steam from the bath was already filling the room. She turned the tap and added some cold. But it wasn't really love, was it? Part of her had always known that.

And in two years their relationship had barely moved on. She began to hum as the track changed to 'Heaven or Las Vegas' – a good question, if it was one. Max had met her grandfather and she had met his formidable mother on one of the rare occasions when she'd swept through Bristol. But other than that . . . It was as if, she realised, they were still dating. They had often woken up together, but never discussed the future. They had given each other keys to their flats, but more as a matter of convenience, she suspected, than a wish to share their lives. Because they hadn't become close, at least not in the way that Eva imagined you became close with someone who was special. Apart from Lucas at uni – and that, she knew, had been more of a friendship than a love affair – Max was the nearest she had ever got to a full-time relationship with a man.

The water reached a perfect temperature and was as deep as Eva liked it. She lowered herself in, felt the liquid heat against her skin and smelled the neroli orange blossom rising from the essential oil. What would have happened, she wondered, if she hadn't gone round to his flat that afternoon one month ago? Would they still be together? Would she be thinking, even now, about where he would be taking her tonight, rather than contemplating a relaxing evening in alone?

It had been an unusual situation. Eva had stayed the night at Max's and the following day at work realised she didn't have her mobile and that she'd left it at his flat. She'd remembered a text that had come through; she must have left the phone on the coffee table after she'd answered it. She tried to call him, but his mobile was switched off; Max was a criminal lawyer so he was probably with a client. She'd nip round and get it at lunch-time, she decided. It wasn't far, he wouldn't mind . . .

Eva dipped her head back to soak her hair; she'd wash it under the shower later. She sank into the restful curve of the bath and had another sip of wine. From the moment she'd walked into the hall, she knew something was wrong. And she didn't have far to look. They were in the living room on the sofa, still adjusting their clothing, Max and some girl she'd never seen before, her make-up smudged over his pink shirt, her skirt still half way up her thighs. What a cliché. Eva hadn't hung around to witness their embarrassment or hear any pathetic excuses. She'd picked up her phone – still on the coffee table as she'd suspected, interesting that they hadn't even noticed it – and walked out, leaving his key on the hook by the door. Only afterwards did she remember the odd phone call which Max had left the room to take, once or twice when he'd cancelled their dates. The signs had been there, she supposed. She just hadn't let herself see.

More fool her. Eva began to soap her body, starting with her arms, generous with the lather. She'd been upset about Max, of course. But now . . . She was over him. She dipped under again. She'd reclaimed her life. And she was going to Burma.

When the water began to cool, she washed her hair and rinsed off under the shower and then climbed out, wrapping herself in a big white fluffy towel. He'd have finished his dinner by now. She paused the music. It was time to tell her grandfather.

He listened to the news without saying very much at first. Then, 'Well, Eva,' he said. 'My goodness. I can scarcely believe it. Burma. That's wonderful.' He drew in a shaky breath, perhaps remembering his own life there, she thought. 'Really wonderful.' He paused. 'Are you looking forward to it, my dear?'

Was she looking forward to it? 'I can't wait.'

'And when are you going?'

'Next week.' As soon as it could be arranged, she guessed. Jacqui didn't want any of those enticing antiques going anywhere other than to the Emporium. But there was a good deal of money at stake. Burmese traders, like any others, understood international markets: those artefacts wouldn't be going cheap.

'Next week!' He seemed quite shocked at this. 'So soon?'

'I think so.'

There was another long pause. What was he thinking? She imagined she could hear the cogs whirring. 'I wonder,' he said. 'I wonder.'

Eva smiled to herself. 'What do you wonder, Grandpa?'

She heard him take another breath. 'If you could possibly come here first, Eva?' he asked, his voice quavering just a little, the words coming out in a rush. 'Can you come to see me before you go?'

'Well . . .' She hadn't planned to. She adored her grandfather, of course, but this weekend would be quite a rush. Although it was tempting. Eva loved West Dorset and she still thought of it as home. Her mother no longer lived there . . . And Eva pushed that thought swiftly away. But her grandfather *was* her home – hadn't he always been?

'It's important, my dear,' he said. 'I wouldn't ask otherwise. I wouldn't expect it of you. Only . . .' His voice tailed off.

'Important?' Not just that he wanted to see her before she made the trip then? Eva hesitated.

'There's something that should have been done a long, long time ago,' he murmured. 'It's too late for me to do it now, of course. Perhaps I made a terrible mistake. I just don't know for sure. But if you . . .'

What was he talking about? Eva waited. She could hear his breath, thin and wheezy on the other end of the line. She didn't like the way he sounded. What should have been done a long time ago? What terrible mistake?

'It's such an opportunity, my darling,' he said, a sense of wonder in his old voice. 'For you and for me. Almost heaven-sent. But I'm wondering if it's too much to ask. And after all these years . . .'

'If what's too much to ask, Grandpa?' Eva was intrigued. 'What is it? Can you tell me?'

'Yes. I should tell you, Eva.' And just for a moment he didn't sound like her frail grandfather. Instead, Eva had a mental picture of him as a young man, before he went to Burma perhaps, when he was only seventeen.

'I'll come over tomorrow evening,' she said, making an instant decision. 'I'll stay the night.'

'Thank you, my darling.' He let out a breath as if he'd been holding it, waiting.

Eva was thoughtful as she ended the call and clicked on to her gmail. She re-started the music. It was a mystery, but she'd find out soon enough. At least her grandfather was pleased that she was going. It wouldn't be nearly so easy, she knew, to tell her mother.

18

Eva parked her ancient but much-loved red-and-black Citroen 2CV in the drive and got out. She pulled on her jacket, grabbed her overnight bag from the passenger seat, slammed the door sufficiently hard for it to shut properly and walked up the path to the front door. The yellow stone was pock-marked by sea winds and the green paint on the door was a little cracked and faded, but otherwise the house of her childhood looked much the same as always, the orange rose climbing from its pot by the bay window up to the black roof slates and beyond, still in full bloom. Eva bent to sniff the nearest blossom. The scent of tea-rose immediately whirled her back to childhood days, making rosewater perfume and picnics on the lawn in summer. Those were the good bits. It was different – everything was different – after her world fell apart. But she wouldn't dwell on that now, not when she had Burma to look forward to. Not to mention her grandfather's mystery.

She lifted the brass door-knocker and let it fall. Pulled her hair out from under her collar. Waited.

Her grandfather opened the door, beaming. 'Hello, dar-ling. Come in, come in.' He helped her with her bag, took her tweedy jacket and hung it on a hook by the door. 'How was your journey? I suppose the roads were busy? They always are these days.'

'The journey was fine,' Eva reassured him.

He turned to her. 'Let me look at you.'

Eva pulled down the sleeves of her lacy blouse and slipped the silk scarf she was wearing from her neck, tucking it next to her jacket. 'Let me look at *you*,' she said. Her grandfather had always been tall and lean. But was he a little more bent than the last time she'd seen him? Was his kind and familiar face more lined?

'You look as lovely as ever.' He smiled. 'How about a hug from my favourite girl?'

Eva stepped into his open arms and closed her eyes, just for a moment. His hair was fine wisps of snow-white. His fawn woollen cardigan smelt of eucalyptus and wood, a fragrance she seemed to have lived with all her life.

'Do you mind if we eat in the kitchen tonight, darling?' he asked, holding her at arm's length for a moment, his hands on her shoulders. 'It's so much more cosy now that the nights are drawing in.'

'Of course not.' Eva followed his slow passage along the L-shaped hall past the shelf of memorabilia that her grandfather had brought back to the UK after his Burmese days. She knew it all so well, but now she lingered, taking it all in as if for the first time: the wooden elephant bells, a souvenir of his work in forestry; the set of opium weights made in the image of Buddha; the Burmese flowered paper parasol and finally the Japanese flag in a bamboo case, the silk burned by shrapnel during the war. And soon, she reminded herself, she would be experiencing her own Burmese days.

In the farmhouse kitchen at the back of the house, the Aga's reassuring warmth filled the room and one of Mrs Briggs's stews bubbled on the hob, a rich fragrance emanating from the pan. Two places had been set at either end of the old pine table and a bottle of red wine had been uncorked but not poured. Thank goodness for Mrs Briggs. Now that he was on his own, Eva's grandfather needed her help with cooking and housework more than ever. Eva knew how much he valued his independence. And she couldn't see him anywhere else but here, in his own house, big, rambling and impractical as it was. It was part of him. It always had been.

Eva pulled off her laced leather ankle boots and left them in the corner next to her grandfather's green wellies. That was better. The ridges of the flagstone tiles felt reassuringly familiar, and warm from the heat of the Aga on her stockinged feet.

Her grandfather was watching her appraisingly. 'How about a drink?' he suggested. 'I've opened a particularly pleasant Burgundy I'd like you to try.' His faded blue eyes held a definite twinkle.

Eva smiled. Her grandfather was quite a wine buff these days. And since Eva's grandmother's death, he had allowed himself to pursue his hobby even more keenly. 'That sounds lovely, Grandpa.'

With a shaky hand, he poured them both half a glass. 'Lovely to see you, my dear.'

'And you, Grandpa.' Eva took a sip. The wine was as mellow and rich as antique velvet. 'That is very good.' She put the glass down and lifted the lid of the stewpot. 'Mmm. And this smells wonderful. What would we do without Mrs Briggs?' She wouldn't rush him. Let him tell her what he wanted her to do in his own good time.

'What, indeed?' He chuckled. 'It's ready when you are.' He steadied himself for a moment on the antique dresser.

'Let me.' Eva put down her glass and fetched the plates from the warming oven. She began to ladle out the beef stew.

'I expect you've been wondering why I asked you to come here this weekend, hmm?' Her grandfather eased himself down on the chair. 'Selfish old fool that I am.'

'Nonsense.' Eva brought the plates over to the table. 'You could never be selfish.'

'Ah, well.' He shook his head. 'You wait till you hear what I've got to say before you decide.'

Eva smiled. 'Eat up.'

He smiled back at her and picked up his fork. Took a mouthful and chewed slowly, watching her all the while. 'I don't want to take advantage of your situation, my darling. But when you said you were going to Burma . . . I saw immediately. It is what you might say, fortuitous.'

'Fortuitous?' Eva picked up her glass and took another sip of her wine. It was a strange choice of words. But she trusted

22

him. Her grandfather might be old and frail, but his mind was razor-sharp, it always had been.

He dabbed at his lips with his paper napkin. 'When you grow old, you have plenty of time to think,' he said.

'About Burma?' Eva guessed. She speared a potato and dipped it in the rich, fragrant gravy.

He nodded. 'And other things.'

'Such as?'

'Decisions that have been made, pathways that have been taken, wrongs that should have been made right.'

Eva reached across the table, which still bore the indentations of pens and pencils pressed a bit too hard during childhood crayoning sessions, and squeezed his hand. 'Everyone has regrets,' she said. It wasn't something reserved for the old.

'Even you, my dear?' He watched her sadly.

'Even me.' Eva thought of her mother. Too many regrets. Even at sixteen, you could make a decision that could snatch a person away from you. Was that what she had done? She wasn't sure though that she could have done it any differently.

He leaned forwards, those blue eyes as intelligent as ever and put his other hand over hers. 'But you're not talking about Max, I hope?'

'Oh, no.' He released her hand and Eva took another forkful of Mrs Briggs' beef stew. 'I'm not talking about Max.'

Her grandfather chuckled as he carefully topped up both their glasses. 'I'm glad to hear it. That man wasn't anywhere near good enough for my favourite girl.'

Eva smiled back at him. He'd never liked Max, and yet again, he'd been proved right. But she noticed that he'd pushed his plate away leaving most of the stew uneaten. 'Had enough?' she asked him. She didn't want to fuss, she knew that Mrs Briggs did enough fussing as it was. But she couldn't help worrying. He meant so much to her. He wasn't so much a grandparent as the life-force behind her childhood.

He nodded. 'My appetite isn't what it was, my dear.'

Head on one side, Eva regarded him. 'What is it that you regret, Grandpa?' she asked. She couldn't believe he'd done anything so very bad. Maybe things had happened in the war that had scared him or that he hated to think of, but he would never have willingly hurt anyone, not if he didn't have to.

He sighed. 'I kept something that didn't belong to me,' he said. 'I didn't find out the full truth when I should have done. And I never went back.' He heaved himself up, took the plates over to the kitchen sink and then slowly lowered himself down again into the old rocking chair.

Eva went over to him and took his hand. It was trembling. His skin felt paper-thin and it was threaded with blue veins and massed with liver spots from all those years of living in the tropics. 'You never went back to Burma?' she guessed. Did he mean after her grandmother had died? Why should he have gone back after all that time?

He nodded.

'And the truth?'

'That's what I would like you to find out, Eva, my dear,' he said.

She stared at him.

'I have an address.' There was a blue manila folder on the table next to the rocking chair, and from this he extracted two slips of paper. 'Two addresses,' he said, handing them to Eva.

She looked at the scraps of paper. He must have had them a long time. They were written in a younger man's handwriting and the paper was yellowing with age. *Daw Moe Mya*, she read. The same name, but a different address on each. Who was Daw Moe Mya?

'It's a long story, my dear,' he said.

Eva put the pieces of paper down on the table and moved over to the stove. 'I'll make us some tea.' She needed to keep a clear head. She filled her grandmother's ancient black kettle, her thoughts buzzing. A long story? Hadn't she heard all the stories about Burma?

She went back to sit by him. 'You'd better start at the beginning,' she said. 'And tell me exactly what it is that you want me to do.'

'I'm old, my dear,' he said. He leaned forwards and adjusted the red-tasselled cushion behind him. 'I've made mistakes. But perhaps it's not fair to ask you to help me. That's what your mother would say.' He shot her a look from under his bushy white eyebrows.

'I'm all grown up now, Grandpa.' Eva twisted her daisy ring. Thought of the email she'd sent to her mother last night. It was sad that these days they mostly communicated that way. More than sad, it was heart-breaking. But sometimes the fissures in a relationship only grew wider and deeper with time. And that's what seemed to have happened to theirs.

The kettle boiled and Eva got up to make the tea, using her grandmother's old floral patterned teapot. She assembled the porcelain cups and saucers and brought the tray over to the table by the rocking chair where he sat, went back to stack the dishwasher and put the pan in to soak, before returning to pour. She had the feeling that her grandfather needed a bit of thinking time. And so did she.

'What did you keep, Grandpa?' she asked gently as she placed a cup on the table next to him. 'What did you keep that didn't belong to you?'

'Get the chinthe,' he whispered.

'The chinthe?' Perhaps his mind was wandering after all? But Eva knew what he was referring to. The dark and shiny decorative teak chinthe – a sort of mythical lion-like creature, which always stood on her grandfather's bedside table – had been a feature of Eva's childhood, a feature of all those stories of Burma.

Eva had grown up sandwiched between her mother's flat and this yellow-stone, rambling house, between the gentleness of her grandfather's care and the brittle grief of Rosemary, her mother. Eva's grandmother Helen had been delicate, often tired, disliking noise and disruption. But her grandfather . . . He had picked her up from school and taken her on outings down to Chesil Beach and the Dorset sandstone cliffs, or off for muddy walks in the Vale. In the evenings they'd sat here in this kitchen and he'd made them mugs of hot chocolate and told her such stories . . . Tales of dark wood and darker mysteries. Of a land of scorching heat and drenching monsoons, of green paddy fields and golden temples, of wide lakes and steamy jungles. Those stories had become almost a part of her.

Eva went to fetch her grandfather's beloved chinthe from the bedroom. More than anything else, this symbolised his time in Burma, she supposed. She picked it up, looked for a moment into its iridescent, red glass eyes. It was a lovely piece, small and delicately carved in an eighteenth-century style, it looked a bit like a wild lion with a jagged tasselled mane and a fierce snarling face. It had a sturdy body and was made, she knew, of the rich burnished teak that her grandfather used to work with back in the days before the war, when he lived in the teak camps with elephants, sending the great logs that had been felled tumbling into the Irrawaddy River.

'Here he is.' She put the chinthe on the table next to the tea tray. Ran her finger across the carved mane. He was a proud animal and she'd always liked him despite his apparent ferocity. 'What is it that you want me to do, Grandpa?' she asked again.

Her grandfather stared at the little chinthe for a few moments and then looked back at Eva. 'It's a personal quest, my darling.' And to her horror his eyes filled with tears.

'Grandpa?'

'Those addresses I gave you,' he said. 'That's where she used to live, before the war, you know.'

'She?'

'The person I want you to look for,' he said. 'I need you to find out the truth of what happened.' He picked up the chinthe and held it gently in his hand. 'There's a promise I made many years ago, my darling Eva, that now I need you to keep.'

Rosemary Newman read her daughter's email with a growing sense of dread. Burma. Would that country never loosen the claw-like hold it seemed to have on her life? She shuddered. First her father, and now Eva. What was it about the place?

She slumped slightly in her seat, then straightened, clicked back to her inbox. She wouldn't delete it, couldn't delete it, and of course she'd answer it, later. Or maybe she'd phone Eva, which was much harder. Face to face had become harder still. Not that she'd ever intended it to be that way . . .

Her daughter had explained that her company were sending her over there, but Rosemary knew she was delighted to go. Her excitement was written between the lines as clearly as the words themselves. *It'll be so interesting to see the place after all Grandpa's stories* . . . Grandpa's stories indeed. And a lot he hadn't told her too.

Rosemary got to her feet and walked over to the window. She and Alec lived in Copenhagen, in a penthouse apartment in a residential borough just outside the old ramparts of the medieval city and the sweeping view of the city which was theirs to admire every day included the spires of Christiansborg Palace and City Hall. The people who lived here were justifiably proud of Copenhagen. It was a thriving and cultural city and it was kept immaculately clean. Heavens, thought Rosemary, the harbour was so unpolluted you could apparently swim in it, not that she had tried. The city boasted plenty of parks and green spaces, wide promenades and waterfronts, and the infrastructure of cycle lanes, metro and other social services helped maintain a pleasant lifestyle. Alec earned a good wage working as a project manager for a large financial institution, and although taxes were high, the rewards were good. Rosemary couldn't complain. And it was hardly Alec's fault that sometimes she wanted to scream . . .

The apartment was smartly furnished, modern, all clean lines and up-market furnishings. Stylish and tasteful. And, she thought, a million miles away from the house in which she'd grown up, in West Dorset. Her parents' house, rambling both inside and out with its cubby holes, inglenook fireplace, winding stairs and bay windows looking out into the untameable garden. Her mother, Helen, had tried to keep it in check; they had even employed a gardener for a while. Helen and wild gardens were not a match made in heaven. But that garden, with its climbing roses, meandering paths, blowsy hydrangea bushes and pond with water lilies and frog spawn, would always go its own way.

Like Eva. Rosemary put a hand to her hair and tucked a few strands behind one ear. She kept it in a short, shaped bob these days, smarter, easier to control. Her daughter had always been headstrong. But Burma . . . It was almost more than she could bear. How much did Eva know?

When Nick had been alive, they'd laughed about their wild daughter, teased one another about who she took after, as she climbed trees or galloped across the beach playing what she called 'horsacs', her thick dark hair streaming behind her in the wind. She was a proper tomboy, unable to sit still for a minute. More than anything she had loved to spend time with her grandfather up at the house, and he'd been a wild one too in his time. For a moment Rosemary felt the bitterness creeping up on her. But their closeness had been a blessing, she reminded herself, after it had happened.

Oh, Nick. When Nick was alive, Rosemary had been happy, blissfully happy. She used to laugh. Rosemary looked around the swish apartment, all chrome and beige, cream and leather. Original art from local exhibitions on the walls, cool wooden parquet flooring. She used to get up in the morning and sing while she was in the shower. If she sang in the shower now, Alec would probably think she'd lost her mind.

She went into the kitchen and plucked her navy blue apron from the drawer. It was such a nice kitchen and everything was where it should be. And she wasn't *unhappy*. How could she be unhappy when Alec was such a good man who tried so hard? And really, she had everything she could ever need. *Apart from your daughter,* a small voice whispered back to her. *Apart from your father. Apart from Nick.*

She slipped the apron over her head and tied it behind her and round. This was a new apricot silk blouse and she didn't want to get any stains on it.

31

It was just that back then it was a different sort of happiness. The sort that made you feel truly alive. The sort that had nothing to do with a comfortable home or money. And everything to do with love.

Rosemary reached up to get the Kilner jars down from the top cupboard, everything she didn't use too often was kept there.

Back then, she'd had a job she enjoyed, working as a legal secretary to a friendly bunch at their local solicitors. And she had a daughter she loved – they had wanted to have more children but it just hadn't happened for them. She lived close to the parents who had brought her into the world, with whom she got on well and who were always there for her. And she had a husband she adored.

On the drainer was a basket of sloes, small and plump from the rain. Rosemary had picked them this morning from the patch of wasteland behind their apartment building. It wasn't a garden and it certainly wasn't countryside. Even so, the white flowers were pretty in springtime and in autumn the berries clustered like bunches of tiny black grapes. More importantly, they reminded her of England. Of hedgerows and country lanes in Dorset. And inevitably of her life in Dorset, of Nick.

Rosemary sighed. The problem had been, of course, that Nick was her life. You couldn't love like that more than once in a lifetime. And so when she lost that . . . Her house of cards had simply come crashing down. Which was what life was like, of course. Just when everything was going well, just when you thought you could relax and enjoy what it had to offer, that's when life would hit you for six. *Ouf*. Rosemary could feel the pain right in her belly – just as she'd felt it that day.

'Nick?' She'd come home for lunch. Cheese on toast, she decided, as she was walking up the path. Then she'd clear up – she hadn't had time that morning – before heading down to the supermarket to get a few bits and pieces before she picked Eva up from school. She only worked mornings, which was ideal, and in the holidays her parents were more than happy to step in, especially Dad. He adored his granddaughter, he seemed to have bucket-loads of patience and time for her. And Rosemary tried not to feel resentful. It was different when you were a grandparent, she reminded herself. You weren't working, you welcomed the chance to give your grand-children the time you hadn't given your own kids. Perhaps she'd be the same . . .

'Nick?' He always came back for lunch unless he was seeing a client who lived some distance away. Nick's workshop was only a few minutes round the corner. He designed and made stained glass for doors, windows, churches even. Beautiful stained glass that could recreate a bygone era, that could send an echo of the twenties or thirties in Art Nouveau or Deco geometrics and curves, that could send a warm amber glow into a hallway when the sun shone, a shaft of blue like a summer's day, or even a spark of fire.

She went into the kitchen. 'Nick?' Dropped her bag.

33

He was lying, crumpled on the floor. He'd fallen. He was unconscious. 'Christ, Nick.'

She could still see it, see him; the image was branded on her memory. Rosemary picked one of the berries up and rolled it between her forefinger and thumb. She still had a few spines lodged in her fingers – blackthorns were not kind to predators and she supposed she was a predator in a way. And they weren't pleasant to eat raw, the taste was bitter and dry. But in gin . . . Sloe Gin at Christmas was Alec's favourite. The longer you steeped the berries, the richer the drink; Rosemary still had some left from three years ago. By now, it would taste of almonds on the tongue.

She closed her eyes. Nick had died from a blood clot which stopped the flow of oxygen to his brain. He'd had a massive stroke. He wasn't even forty. And Rosemary was left alone.

She realised that she was gripping the basket of sloes, white-knuckled. *Breathe, Rosemary*. The horror of it had never gone away. She had moved, unknowing, into some sort of dark place where she could survive, and she didn't even know, now, where that place was, how she had got there or what had happened to the people around her.

Rosemary took her large colander from the low cupboard left of the sink and shook in the sloes, ensuring that all the fruit was good, that she removed anything that was beginning to rot. She turned on the tap to wash them.

She came out of that dark place when her father grabbed her by the arm one day when she'd come to pick up Eva. Rosemary worked full time now. They needed the money

34

and, besides, work was a distraction. When she was typing up a legal document or speaking to clients on the phone, she didn't have to think about what had happened. That she was now Rosemary Gatsby, widow. That her husband was dead. That, really, life should not have gone on.

'What?' Rosemary waited. Eva was still playing outside.

'She's just a child,' her father said.

'What do you mean? I know she's a child.' She frowned.

'I mean that you've got to pull yourself together, Rosie.' He put a hand on her arm. He was pleading with her.

She tried to tug her arm away, but he held fast. How could he possibly understand? How could anyone? Her world had no foundations anymore, no anchor. 'All very well for you to say,' she snapped. 'Do you ever think what it's like for me?'

He sighed, let her go. 'All the time,' he said. 'All the time. But you're her mother. It's your job to think what it's like for her.'

'I don't think I can do that job,' she had told him. 'Not anymore.' At least not in the way he expected her to. Since the cards had fallen, there seemed to be little reason to do anything. Why bother to get up in the morning when there was no one beside you to turn to? Why bother to clean the house? Make dinner? Pay the bills? Eva was the only reason Rosemary dragged herself out of bed at seven-thirty. The reason she shopped and cooked. The reason she forced herself to function.

'You've got to move on, Rosie,' he told her, his blue eyes burning with the need to get it through to her. 'It's not easy.

I know it's not easy. But you've got to do it,– for her sake, if not for your own.'

Rosemary tried. But Eva was not a comfort. She was a responsibility, a worry, one that was no longer shared and enjoyed with the man she loved. How could Rosemary hope to give her a balanced and positive upbringing after this? How could she do it alone? The task, even with her parents to help her, seemed insurmountable, a mountain with only a goat-track to follow. And at the top? All she could see was a very long drop down to rock bottom.

The berries had drained and now Rosemary prepared the Kilner jars; they must be sterilised with boiling water. She filled the kettle and switched it on. Pressed her weight against the counter.

Eva was tearful and needy and this had stretched her jangled nerves to the absolute limit. Of course the child had lost her father. *Yes, Rosemary,* she told herself sternly, *she's lost something too.* And at a vulnerable age when no one should have to experience such a loss, such a heart break, one she might never recover from, too. *And she needs you.* That was the thing, the certainty that hit her like an axe in the guts when she awoke from a fitful sleep every morning at dawn. She had to be two parents for Eva now. And the more her father reminded her of this fact, the more she cringed away from it. It was weak of her, she knew, but she simply couldn't think where to begin.

The kettle boiled and Rosemary poured the water into the tall jars quickly, feeling the hot steam licking like flames at her hands, her wrists, dampening the cuffs of her silk blouse. When Eva hurt herself and ran to her . . . Rosemary felt herself pulling back, her arms half-lifting and then falling impotent to her sides. She shrank from holding her own daughter. Why? Was she scared of loving her too much? When Eva woke up at night and her tears pulled Rosemary away from her dreams and her memories – the only things that seemed to keep her sane – she bitterly resented the intrusion. She wanted to shout at her: *Go to sleep. Let me be.* Did these things make her a bad mother? She loved her daughter and yet she couldn't love her, didn't dare to love her, couldn't risk being hurt that badly again.

Rosemary held everything back. She kept her distance. If she needed to, she walked away. And all that had become a part of her. She was now that woman. She couldn't hold her own daughter and she couldn't tell her she was safe. Because she wasn't safe. Neither of them were safe. The cards had fallen. Their anchor was gone. Where was there for them to run? Not to each other, it seemed. Eva turned more and more to her grandfather for her hugs and kisses. And Rosemary? She simply battled on alone.

She pricked the ripe sloes with a fork to release the flavour and weighed them out equally, tipping them into the jars. She weighed out the sugar too and added that. Measured the gin. Sealed the jars. And so . . . Eva was going to Burma – of all places.

Rosemary shook the jars, one by one. She shook them to dissolve the sugar but she felt as if she were shaking something out from deep inside of her. She shook them and shook them and then finally, she put them on a tray and carried them to the cupboard under the stairs. Placed them on the shelf in the dark. All she had to do now was wait.

She sat down on the cream leather sofa. It gave gently under her, cushioning and comforting. But cold, Rosemary thought. As she had been cold.

The fact was, that when Nick died, something had died in Rosemary too. After his death, she was only half living. And since then, she had never been able to get it back. Perhaps she never would. But so much, she realised, was lost when you only lived half a life. And the other people she had tried to love: her father, Alec, Eva. Would they ever find it possible to forgive?

CHAPTER 5

Eva woke up from a restless doze, the kind you have on a long-haul flight, still conscious of those around you, sensitive to your neighbour needing to squeeze past or the stewardess nudging you awake with a *sorry to disturb you, madam, but did you want breakfast/lunch/a snack/coffee,* whatever, each long hour was punctuated by something.

She'd been dreaming about her mother. She was five years old and her mother was reading her a bedtime story about Mister Fox; she could see that fox with his red waistcoat and bushy tail so clearly in her mind's eye. And hear her mother's voice, low, sing-song, her laughter that seemed to bubble up inside and tip from her like fizzy lemonade. She could feel her too, her warmth and her kisses better, she could even smell her scent, of springtime. Eva focused in hard. There were other sounds, her parents' banter and the rhythm of their voices, her father's booming: *What d'you reckon then, love? Don't give me that!* And then she was being swung between them. *One, two, three, up she goes.* The security of a hand being held.

Was she still dreaming? Somewhere inside, Eva knew she was in that strange state between sleeping and waking. She heard his voice again. Her father. Her memories were sketchy at times and at others clear as glass. He had taught her to swim in the sea, which she loved to do, even now. *Don't tense up, love. Let yourself go* . . . The water cool on her skin, the wave rising. *Ride with the swell. That's the way. You can't fight it.*

Eva couldn't fight it when she lost him. One day he was there, the next gone. No chance to say goodbye.

She blinked as her memory skittered back. She remembered that first day, that dark day. Grandpa picking her up from school. A hop, a skip and a jump. 'Where's Mummy?'

'She's busy. You'll see her soon.'

Eva didn't mind. She loved the secret games she always played in her grandparents' garden. But it was different today. Her grandparents were talking in hushed voices, watching her. Her grandmother turned to her in that too bright, bird-like way she had. 'How about a special treat for tea, Eva, dear?' Something was wrong.

When her mother arrived, she walked down the path very slowly. Her eyes were blank and red and when Eva shrieked, 'Mummy!' and ran towards her, she hardly seemed to hear or see. 'Mummy!'

It was as if her mother weren't there. She glanced at Eva and she seemed to look right through. Were neither of them there? Eva was scared.

'Hello, darling.' Absently, her mother touched her hair. She didn't lift her up and spin her around, she didn't hold her tight, she didn't kneel down and look her in the eyes, pulling a funny-mummy face. She just touched her hair. Eva knew that something was very, very wrong.

Every hour they were nearer to reaching their destination. Eva shifted in her seat. It had been a long journey, broken up in Doha for just an hour and a half before they were re-boarding. Fourteen hours in all, and the little sleep she'd had was fitful and crammed with these scenes from her past. How reliable were these memories? What she knew for sure was that life without her father had been as different as life could be. There was so much missing: his voice, his laughter, the presence of him. Even the house became silent and brooding, a house that had lost somebody. But at least there was still her mother. She had that to cling to.

Eva waited for her mother to come back to her. She waited for the stories, for the warmth of her arms, for the bubble of her laughter. But they never came. Her mother might still be there. But as the months went by, Eva finally learned the truth. There was something missing. Her mother had lost the heart of her. And so Eva had lost her mother too.

She stared out of the window at the blanket of cloud below and thought of what her grandfather had told her in the kitchen a week ago. Everything was a lot clearer now. She'd always known how much Burma meant to him, but this new story was different from any of the others. It was about the decorative teak chinthe that even now was tucked safely away in her cabin bag, protected by her bottle-green silk wrap. And it was about the woman whose address was written on the slips of paper in her purse.

'Take him back to Burma for me, Eva,' he'd said to her,

handing her the little wooden animal. 'Take him back to her family. Where he belongs.'

Her family . . . The family of the woman called Daw Moe Mya, or Maya, as he called her. This story was about what her grandfather had lost, and what he wanted to return to its rightful place.

'There is another chinthe,' he'd said, his faded gaze drifting off beyond Eva and the farmhouse kitchen in Dorset, back to the past and a far off place. 'This is one of a pair.'

'Yes.' She supposed it must be. They always came in pairs. They were guardians of temples and pagodas and were a feature of many Asian cultures, sometimes with animal, sometimes human faces and made of stone, wood and even bronze. Eva sipped the mineral water that the stewardess had just given her. She was so looking forward to seeing them in situ, particularly the famous fourteenth-century bronze Angkor Chinthe in Mandalay. She'd only seen a picture but open-mouthed and snarling, he looked satisfyingly ferocious.

'They need to be together, my darling,' her grandfather had said. 'To restore harmony.' But that was only the half of it. 'I should never have brought it back to England,' he murmured. 'It wasn't the right thing to do.'

Eva scrutinised the progression of the flight path of the Boeing on the screen in front of her. They were only forty minutes from touching down in Yangon. Her heart seemed to skip a beat. She peered through the window, anxious to catch her first glimpse of the place, longing to see what

42

her grandfather had seen, feel what he had felt. She could make out the land mass already. The cloud was breaking, but with uncertainty, as if at any second it might fold into a blanket of leaden grey and unleash its contents on to the ground below. She felt the rush of adrenalin. It wouldn't be long . . .

'I loved her, you see.' Her grandfather spoke softly, tenderly, the memories lights in his eyes.

Eva wasn't even surprised. It was a moment when things from her childhood suddenly made sense, a jigsaw slotting into place. The way her grandparents always were with each other: his patience, her sadness, the polite distance between them. Eva had taken his hand in hers and squeezed it gently. A warm shiver spread through her. Her grandfather had come back to Dorset, and he had married her grandmother Helen. But . . . And she thought she was beginning to understand. No wonder her mother and grandmother had never been interested in his life in Burma.

'I have always loved her,' he said.

It was there in his face. All the answers were there. He had always loved her. She had forever usurped Eva's grandmother Helen in his affections, no matter how hard he must have tried for it to be otherwise.

'Then, why did you leave her?'

'It's a good question, my darling Eva,' he said. But he didn't give her the answer.

'And what makes you think she's still alive?' How old would she be? In her early nineties, Eva guessed.

Her grandfather nodded. He seemed very sure. 'If she were no longer alive,' he said, 'I think that I would know it.'

Now, as she watched, the dark sky lightened into streaks of pink and blue and began to give way to a misty dawn. The morning sun illuminated the crenellated tips of turrets of cloud. And there it was. Burma. What was it Kipling was supposed to have said? *It is quite unlike any place you know about*. Eva didn't doubt it. It was spread out there below her, kite-shaped, surprisingly green – but why not? The rains had barely finished. And the string of the kite was that winding river. She could see its many branches and the delta below. She checked the map in front of her, pushed her seat to an upright position, so she'd feel more ready for it all. The Irrawaddy, muddy brown in the milky morning light. It was another world.

Since her grandmother Helen had died . . . Eva frowned at this sobering thought, the rift between her grandfather and Eva's mother had grown. And she had to face it - the rift between Eva and her mother had done the same, as if moving in a perfect parallel. Did Rosemary blame her father for not making her mother happy? And if so, was it true? Eva gazed out of the window at the place that had perhaps been part of it, at the place that might give her the answers. But her grandfather was a good man. Whether it was true or not, Eva believed that he had done his best.

The stewardess brought round hot flannels and Eva held her hair up with one hand and let the scented towel rest on the back of her neck for a moment. She closed her eyes. Her mother's reply to her email had been brief and non-committal, like most of her communications, Eva thought. *Don't give anything away, Mother . . .*

Take care, Eva, she'd written. *Have a good time.* A few lines of news about Alec's company and what long hours he was working; in the world of computer technology everything moved so fast, there was a lot of pressure not to get left behind. And that was it. Nothing about Rosemary herself or when she might be coming over to visit. The word 'love', easy to write. A single kiss. But what did Eva expect? Especially now.

This was a work trip, yes, and she was looking forward to seeing lots of interesting antiques and artefacts, to have the chance to obtain some for the Emporium, to examine and authenticate. But that wasn't all. When she'd heard what her grandfather had to say, Eva had realised she couldn't do this in ten days. She couldn't do justice to Myanmar, to her work commitments, to her grandfather's request in such a short time.

'I've some holiday owing that I have to take before the end of the year,' she had said to Jacqui on the Monday morning after she'd visited her grandfather in Dorset. 'And so I was wondering . . .' Her grandfather had offered to help fund the trip, Eva had some savings. Financially it wouldn't be a problem, if Jacqui was prepared to be flexible. Eva was aware that her trip would take a huge chunk out of the Emporium's profits, though presumably the riches to be found in Myanmar must make it potentially worthwhile.

'How long do you want to stay?' Jacqui asked her when

Eva had explained a little of her family's connection to the place.

'Three weeks?'

Jacqui came to a quick decision. 'Why not?' she said. 'It could be useful. As long as you maintain email contact with me throughout, Eva.'

'Of course.'

Eva exhaled and let her shoulders release the tensions of the flight, of her tiredness, of her apprehensions. She was going to look for her grandfather's other life, the life that had excluded his wife and his daughter. She didn't know what she would find, but her mother wouldn't like it. She was going to a country that would be strange and unfamiliar in every way possible and she was doing it alone, apart from the slightly dubious contacts that Jacqui had arranged for her.

Eva opened her eyes and peered down at the great river looping its way over the marshland, dividing as if about to take some new path and then winding back again to join forces. Stronger together than alone. It had never been like that for Eva and her mother after Eva's father had died. Neither of them had been strong. Eva had been too young then to understand, but she'd had a long, long time to think about it ever since.

Eva had turned to her grandfather. But what she had always understood was that her mother had preferred to be alone.

'Not long to go now.' The man in the seat beside her spoke. He was a journalist and had been a pleasant enough companion. They'd had one or two brief conversations during the flight, which was all Eva had wanted with so much to think about.

Eva smiled. 'Can't wait,' she said.

The seat belt signs had been on for a few minutes. Now, the pilot put the air brakes on, the flaps went down on the wing. The land was becoming more cultivated, there were paddy fields, and in the half-light of the dawn Eva could see how much rain there had been. She could see rectangular shacks now too, randomly built on the river bank. Some kind of small settlement maybe; she was only too aware of Burmese poverty, although she knew about the riches to be found in this country too. There were clumps of palm trees and a very long straight road.

The plane banked as it turned into the wind, ready to make its final descent and Eva's head lurched with dizziness. Just tiredness or disorientation probably. And yet there was a familiarity to the land too. It didn't look as alien as she had expected. What *had* she been expecting? She wasn't really sure. She could feel the excitement though, it was tingling through her fingers and her toes, making her heart beat faster.

'Cabin crew, take your seats for landing, please.' The voice came over the tannoy.

And then she saw a golden pagoda, glinting in the sunlight. Its tapering spire stretched up towards the heavens, the cone of its body shimmered in the morning sun. This was Burma. Her journey lay ahead of her like the path of the winding Irrawaddy itself. She had arrived.

CHAPTER 6

The first time ever he saw her face.

Lawrence glanced at his bedside table, just for a second before he put out the light. Or to be more accurate, he glanced at the space on the table that the chinthe no longer occupied, though Lawrence could see it still in his mind's eye. *Watching over you.* He'd always kept it there, perhaps he thought it lessened the betrayal if he had even a part of her closest to him while he slept. Yes, or perhaps he was a fanciful old man. The truth was just touching the wood could take him back there. And then he looked at the clock, frowned, tried to work out if Eva would have landed. He must get it right. He wanted to arrive there as she arrived there, at least in his head.

He couldn't read, not tonight. When Helen was alive, she had loathed him reading in bed. 'Aren't you tired?' she would sigh as if it were his fault for not doing enough during the day to make him ready for sleep. And so then he would read maybe a paragraph or two of his book and leave it at that. Why upset her? It wasn't her fault, none of it was her fault. But now that he was alone . . . Now that he had the opportunity to read entire books if he wanted to, with no one to say

48

a word about it . . . Well, his eyes just weren't up to it. He was tired in a way he had never been tired before.

The first time ever he saw her face.

There was a song, wasn't there, but he hadn't heard it back then when he was first in Burma. It hadn't even been written in 1937, though she could have been the reason why such a song had ever been born. He felt afterwards that he hadn't heard anything till then. Hadn't lived.

Mandalay, 1937

They were walking through the market, he and Scottie. There were market traders selling fish, vegetables and beans; many of the men and some of the women smoking Burmese cheroots or chewing betel and there were food stalls where people sat to eat under the shelter of a bamboo-walled hut crammed on wooden benches like pilchards in a tin. Steaming tureens of noodles and soup bubbled on open fires tended by proprietors in stained *aingyis*. It was hot, and a heavy humidity hung in the air like a quilt of mist. People milled around: Burmese and Indian in the main, though also a few Europeans, the men mostly dressed in thin jackets and *longyis*, the long wrap-around skirt worn by both men and women; the women's *longyis* tucked into the waist band, rather than knotted like the men's, and worn with bright colourful blouses, or in saris, draped elegantly around head and shoulders, falling to the dusty ground. Rain, Lawrence thought to himself. That was what they all needed.

'Was it what you were expecting?' Scottie had asked him when he first arrived at the chummery. Was it?

For a long time, Lawrence had craved adventure. Not just danger or girls, but travelling too. He'd wanted to see the world, at least as much of it as possible.

'What's wrong with us?' his father had demanded when Lawrence had finally plucked up the courage to tell them his intention. He'd meant, of course, the family firm. The shadow of Fox and Forster had loomed over Lawrence's childhood, a security and yet a threat. 'Why do you need to go anywhere, eh? We need you here.'

'He'll be back,' his mother had said. She was a diplomat, every glamorous inch of her from the top of her fair coiffured head to her immaculate shoes and stockings. 'Let him go and he'll come back.' She knew how to keep them both happy. It wasn't even a tightrope for her. All her life she'd twisted her father round her elegant little finger; it had become second nature to do the same with her husband and son.

Lawrence's father had grumped and growled and reached for the whisky decanter. But his mother had understood and so his father had let him go. He could never refuse her anything, all she had to do was allow a tear to creep into her blue eyes and he'd bluster his way back to getting a smile out of her. *Very well, my dear, if it will make you happy* were words Lawrence had heard frequently during his childhood and beyond. If Mother was happy then so was Pa. Simple. It was an equation that worked. But for himself, in whatever life he carved out for himself with a woman, Lawrence knew he'd want more.

Elizabeth had rumpled her son's hair affectionately. 'He'll

come back to us when he's needed,' she reassured them all. 'When he's got it out of his system. And be all the better for it. He wants to live a little, that's all. It'll do him good.'

Had it? Lawrence wasn't so sure. It had made him dissatisfied, he knew that much. But that was when he came back. As for the rest, she was right. Life was about seeing new places, wasn't it? Experiencing new things. Not sticking to what you knew and who you knew and staying in London working as a stockbroker in the family firm. There were worlds out there that others had explored and conquered. The British Empire was vast and he wanted to experience some of it. How could working in the family firm satisfy him? How could Helen? But he wouldn't think of Helen.

'Plenty of time for that,' his mother had told him, a gleam of satisfaction in her diplomat's eye. 'Plenty of time, my darling, for you to spread your wings a little.'

And fly, he thought. And fly.

Some of it, some of Burma, this land of dark-skinned people, overwhelming heat and golden temples, had been exactly as he had expected. It was different, it was exotic, it had a colour and a heady fragrance that made him dizzy. And it had its hard side too. It could be rough and uncomfortable. The heat could be unbearable. So could the mosquitos. There was poverty and hardship. One couldn't – or shouldn't – take Western comforts for granted.

Work had been a revelation. When he signed up at the company, Lawrence had given hardly a thought for the conditions he'd work under in the teak camps, for the labour he would be commanding in all weathers under pressure, getting as many good logs as humanly possible into the river and on their way down the raging Irrawaddy to Rangoon. Although in the end, humans didn't have as much to do with it as elephants.

And the people . . .

'They look up to us,' Scottie had said, trying to explain how things worked, how the system of the British clubs with their unquestioned luxuries, whist drives, cocktail parties and dances operated in apparently comfortable harmony with the poverty often seen on the streets, women begging, men in ragged clothes desperate to do a deal, children stealing scraps from the market in order to survive.

He seemed so sure. And yes, the Europeans were the undisputed masters, no doubt of that; the last Burmese dynasty had burned itself out in the previous century. Burned itself out, or been burned out by the British Empire, which had no qualms in using its superior weapons, knowledge and experience to get what it wanted. Or so some said. Scottie had all the stories. His father had been a witness to it all. Scottie and the rest of his family were bound up in the colonial web of imperialism more securely than anyone Lawrence had ever met. And that was good, because it was Scottie who had shown him the ropes and Scottie knew all the rules.

Lawrence had seen his fair share since he'd been here. He'd got into the rhythm of the weather, the heat and the rains which ruled everything, and he'd grown accustomed to the food, which wasn't so bad if you liked curry and rice. From February to May was the worst time, the hottest, when your shirt would stick to your back five minutes after you'd put it on and the white glare of the heat could drive you half-mad if you let it. In July and August the rains came with hardly a break in the monsoon, and this was when the real work was done with the timber, when the race was on to get the logs down the rivers and safely to the company's timber yard at Rangoon. Then the rains would tail off, ending with a final squall in October. The fields would dry up and there would be, at last, a wonderful short winter, when the breeze was mild instead of burning, when wild flowers reminiscent of those in English meadows grew in the rural areas, when the paddy grew and ripened into yellow and the nights and mornings could even be cold in the upper reaches of the country, with a cooling mist that filled the valleys and hung over the hills.

The company was generous in giving leave, perhaps it knew that it had to be in order to keep its young blood healthy and content, relatively speaking, at least. Like the rest of them, Lawrence enjoyed visits to Rangoon, going to the English bookshop to stock up on reading material for those long evenings alone in camp, out to sample steak dinners with as many G and Ts and as much ice as you wanted (there was no running out of ice in Rangoon . . .). He enjoyed his regular bouts of R and R up at the hill-station too and the easy camaraderie of the chummery there at Pine Rise in Maymyo, the guesthouse owned by the company and used as bachelor quarters for the single male employees. But there was something about the British clubs that left him cold.

They know who are the masters, Scottie had said. But sometimes Lawrence wondered. *Us and them.* Was it that simple? He thought not. It was a careless racism that was little more than an assumption. Could it be right to make such an assumption? It seemed to Lawrence that there was something in their eyes . . .

There was something in her eyes. She was standing by a stall and he could see her in profile. Small, neat, self-assured. And when she looked up . . .

The stall holder, an Indian, was selling hand woven rugs and blankets. The girl was inspecting a piece of cloth. She held it lightly between her fingers. She wore a *longyi* of bright orange and yellow like the streak of a sunset and her hair hung down past her shoulders as dark and glossy as a bird's wing slicked in oil. Her nails were pale pink, almost white, her lips a kind of bruised plum. And there was the slightest pucker of a frown on her brow. She was perfection, in miniature.

Scottie followed his gaze. He leaned closer to Lawrence. 'I know what you're thinking, old man.'

Lawrence ignored his grin.

'She's a stunner.'

But it wasn't that. Lawrence moved towards the stall, couldn't help himself. She was attractive, yes, but lots of girls were attractive. Helen was attractive – she was a beauty – or so his parents kept reminding him, a fragile, very English kind of beauty. And more significantly, she was the only daughter of his father's business partner and closest friend. But the look of this woman wasn't just striking, she'd walloped him right in the pit of his chest.

'Yes, sir?' The stallholder was quick to notice his interest. 'You like a nice new rug, sir? What colour is it to be? Red, blue, yellow? What size, sir?'

'A blanket.' Lawrence addressed him but looked at the girl.

She glanced up as he spoke, but immediately glanced down again. The Burmese were like that. They weren't meek, but they were self-effacing, the opposite, he thought now, of women like his mother, like Helen. *They know their station*, Scottie would say. Lawrence suspected they knew rather more than that. And no doubt were careful not to show it.

'What kind of blanket, sir? Wool? Cotton? Silk? I have very good collection. What colour? Red? Yellow? Brown?' Deftly, he swept first one blanket, then another, then another down from the display, flourishing each in front of Lawrence for his approval. Pretty soon the stall was in complete disarray, swathed in fabrics of every material and hue.

Scottie stood to one side and languidly lit a cigarette.

The girl seemed about to move away.

'That one,' Lawrence said quickly, indicating the blanket she still held lightly between her fingers. 'Let me see that one.'

'Indeed, sir, a fine choice.' The stallholder whisked it away from her.

She blinked and took a graceful step backwards. Lawrence noticed her feet which were tiny and clad in red silk slippers.

55

'Excuse me.' Lawrence addressed her. 'You were here first.'

She shook her head, took another step backwards.

Would she speak English, he wondered. Many of them did, and Hindustani too. Scottie spoke fluent Burmese. If she didn't speak English, would he act as interpreter? Lawrence hadn't had time to get to grips with the language yet.

'Really. Please. So rude of me.' Lawrence grabbed the blanket, which was made of a soft and fine wool. He handed it to her. 'It is a good blanket, is it not?' His voice to his own ears sounded tender, and this was a surprise.

She looked up at him. Her dark eyes were calm, but he saw in them a curl of humour that gave him hope. He'd been right. This wasn't some poor and lowly Burmese servant girl. This was a young woman of class. She understood him, he could tell.

'It is very fine,' she conceded in perfect English. Her voice was soft and gentle, it seemed to stroke his senses. And as he continued to hold the blanket out to her, she reached out her hand and again held the fabric, smoothing it with her finger-tips.

'Lawrence Fox.' He gave a little bow. 'Please excuse my bad manners. Blame the heat, it must be affecting me.' A weak attempt at humour, he knew. But it was all he could strum up at the present time.

Scottie cleared his throat. 'Jimmy Scott,' he said.

'We are both at your service.' Lawrence smiled.

She nodded her head in acknowledgement but made no attempt to reciprocate their introductions.

What next? Lawrence had always considered himself pretty expert at chatting up the girls. Warming them up with a compliment and a joke, making them laugh, moving in for the thaw, that sort of thing. Not that he had a wealth of experience to draw on. But somehow, knowing he was destined for Helen Forster had freed him to playing fast and loose whenever he had the chance. Cross that bridge when he came to it. But this girl wasn't like any of the other girls. She wasn't British for a start. He had no idea what to bloody do.

'And may I enquire your name?' he said, quietly so as not to intimidate her. At least she hadn't walked away.

'Moe Mya,' she said.

'Moe Mya,' he repeated. The short syllables were small and neat like her. And yet, as he looked into those eyes, he'd like to bet she could let go. Not in the way Scottie and the others in the club might joke about it, but . . . Well, in the real meaning of letting go.

She nodded. 'Some call me Maya,' she said. Her lips pursed together slightly.

I want to kiss them, he thought. *Jesus*. He felt an ache, almost a pain, in his groin. What was the matter with him?

He offered what he hoped was a suave, confident but reassuring smile. 'And you live here in Mandalay?' he asked.

'I live with my father, yes,' she said. 'Most of the time.'

'And the rest of the time?' Was there a man in the picture? Lawrence desperately needed to know.

'Sometimes we stay in Maymyo. My father has a house there.'

Lawrence acknowledged this with a nod. The hill station of Maymyo was situated at a higher altitude than Mandalay and was cooler and restful. Some said it was like England with its grass and neat manicured gardens, its road names reminiscent of his homeland, such as Downing Street and Forest Road. And Lawrence knew that its Englishness was confusing to the Burmese – even the notion of a garden planted with flowers was confusing, since wild flowers were so abundant, why would one plant one's own? But it wasn't just the British who went there. Any Burmese family in Mandalay who had money would generally also have a place in Maymyo for holidays and weekends. Her admission had reinforced his previous impression. She was not a poor native girl. She was, for Burma, a class act.

'And I have an aunt who lives in Sinbo. It is a small village on the Irrawaddy near Myitkyina.' She looked down at her feet in the red silk slippers. 'She lives alone and sometimes needs me to help her.'

'Indeed.' That was even more interesting. Because Lawrence was working in the jungle up near Myitkyina and her aunt's village was only a few miles away.

She looked back up at him from under her eyelids. Was she flirting with him? It wasn't the kind of flirting he was used to, but there was something, some dark knowledge in her eyes that drew him forward. He saw Scottie grind his cigarette under the heel of his boot, noticed that he was getting restless.

'See you back at the club, old man?' he asked with a wink.

'Yes. Perhaps . . .' What was the etiquette? Would she be welcomed in the bar there? Should he invite her? Lawrence wasn't sure of the form. He wasn't sure of anything anymore. 'You could tell me more?' he asked her, instead of what he had been going to say.

'More?' Her eyes were innocent and yet knowing.

'About Mandalay. About your life here.' Not the club, he decided. She didn't belong there, he wouldn't insult her.

She gave a little shrug as if Europeans waylaid her regularly to ask her such questions.

'You must know the city well?'

'My family has always lived here,' she said. 'My grand-mother was a servant girl to the Queen.' Her slim back was already straight, but as she spoke these words she seemed to stand straighter still.

'Really? I say . . .' Lawrence was brave enough to take her arm. Scottie had already strolled off. He only had one chance with this girl and he wasn't going to chuck it away.

'Yes,' said Moe Mya. 'It is true.'

'About the blanket, sir?' The stallholder complained. 'You like the blanket, yes?'

'Shall we walk for a while?' Lawrence asked her.

She looked doubtfully around. And it was true that there wasn't really anywhere to walk to.

'To the Palace moat? It isn't far.' He could hear the reck-lessness in his own voice. But there was something. Perhaps she felt it too.

'The blanket . . . ?'

'I'll take it.' Lawrence reached for his wallet.

She drew back, shocked. 'You have not even agreed a price,' she said.

Lawrence grinned. 'How much?' he asked the stallholder. 'Name your figure and don't be greedy or I might change my mind.'

He could see the cogs spinning. *How much would lose the sale? How unpredictable might a man like Lawrence be?* By this stage Lawrence didn't even know the answers himself.

The stallholder named his price.

Moe Mya replied in Burmese. Lawrence had no idea what she said – he really must make more of an effort – but something must have been agreed because the stallholder argued briefly, then shrugged, nodded and began to fold the blanket into a neat square.

Lawrence passed over some money, tried not to feel that the initiative had somehow smoothly been taken out of his hands.

She passed him the blanket. 'They will not respect you if you let them cheat you,' she said softly.

He could feel her warm breath on his neck as she leaned closer. She smelt of coconut oil. This was the first time she had somehow separated herself from her people. Had she aligned herself with him? *Us and them.* Lawrence didn't understand it, but for him he felt it was no bad thing.

'You must barter. It is part of the game.'

The game . . . 'Thank you,' he said. 'And now?'

'We will walk towards the moat of the Royal Palace,' she said, as if it had been her idea all along. 'And I will tell you about Mandalay.'

CHAPTER 7

'Do you mind if I join you?'

Eva looked up from her guidebook to see a tall blond stranger smiling down on her. For a moment she was almost blinded by the reflection of the sun on his hair. 'Oh. Well . . .'

'Only there are no empty tables.' He indicated the café terrace around them and it was true, it was lunchtime and the place was heaving.

'Of course I don't mind, that's fine.' Eva was sorry for her initial hesitation.

She looked over at the busy street on the other side of the terrace. The people of Yangon were going about their business in the sweltering heat. Men and women in *longyis*, often carrying their wares on top of their heads in wide baskets as they elegantly threaded their way through the crowded streets. Different races, Sikhs, Shan, Indian, Thai, doing business on street corners. Street sellers and food-stalls, motor bikes and scooters with girls in *longyis* riding side-saddle, open-air trucks and trishaws . . . It was a riot of noise and colour. Eva had almost had heart failure when her taxi from the airport had hit a traffic jam. The driver had given a cursory glance at the road ahead and simply continued, driving on the other side. No one had seemed to care.

There still weren't many Westerners around in Yangon. And so when you saw one you tended to gravitate towards them to discuss local sights and the best places to eat. In other words, this blond stranger wasn't coming on to her, he just wanted to have lunch.

'Thank you. I appreciate that,' he said, as he perused the menu.

She could tell from his accent that he wasn't British. German, she guessed. His English was excellent though. And, like her, he seemed to be travelling alone. This was unusual. Most of the Westerners she'd spotted clustered in small groups with their tour guides as if Myanmar might otherwise taint them, though with what, she wasn't sure.

'*Min-ga-laba*. Welcome.' A young Burmese waiter appeared. Like many of the Burmese he kept grinning and saying hello to tourists all the time. She'd had no reason so far to worry about travelling alone. The people in this city were the friendliest and most helpful she'd ever come across.

Earlier today, Eva had taken a taxi to the randomly placed gilded stupa of *Sule Playa*, at forty-eight metres high and positively glowing in the sunlight, it sat slap bang in the middle of the British-constructed grid system that made up downtown Yangon. And then, thinking of her grandfather, she'd got out, paid the driver and walked on to the grand colonial buildings on the waterfront. Already, the heat was all-consuming, the pavements baking and the Burmese were using umbrellas as sunshades as they walked down the street. Her grandfather had told her what it was like arriving at Yangon on the steamer and, standing there, Eva could imagine. Stepping on to the jetty, walking on to the wide waterfront, faced by the Victorian High Court building, which could have been plucked from London's Embankment, and the classic Strand Hotel. If *Sule Playa* reminded her that even in bustling downtown Yangon she was still in the land of golden temples, then these colonial architectural masterpieces were an equally resonant echo of the grandness of Imperial Britain.

Her grandfather had stayed in the Strand and so Eva stepped into its cool, air-conditioned interior, admired the luscious creaminess of the walls which set off to perfection the teak staircase, gallery and furnishings in the high-ceilinged foyer. It was pure, understated luxury. But her grandfather hadn't strolled through hallways of precious Burmese art and jewellery as Eva was now doing. He would have stayed in a mosquito-infested room cooled by an electric paddle fan in those days. Even so, even before all its renovations, from what he'd told her, the colonial life in the Strand Hotel and elsewhere had been lavish and comfortable. At least compared to what most of the native Burmese had to endure.

After a restorative G & T in the plush bar, Eva had retraced her steps to the Indian and Chinese quarters where the locals squatted on their haunches among sacks of rice, lentils, heaps of noodles and, yes, definitely fried locusts. She grimaced. They chatted and laughed, their children playing nearby, as bicycles and trishaws careered along the narrow pot-holed streets, and as they cooked Burmese curries in huge cauldrons on top of braziers, the scents of spices, dried fish and nut oil hanging ripe and heavy in the air.

She laughingly refused a trishaw ride, a rejection which inspired the driver to spit betel juice forcefully on to the road. A nasty habit, she thought, noting his gory, red-stained teeth. The trishaw looked ancient and possibly dangerous, its saddles supported by two rusty springs and the driver himself was bow-legged and certainly no spring chicken. He rattled his money pouch enticingly at her, but she decided not to dice with death on Yangon's busy highway. Instead, she bought a bag of oranges and a pancake for her lunch and stood in the shade for a moment to take it all in. It was as if she'd moved from one side of the world to the other. A G and T in the Strand Hotel at one end and a Burmese pancake cooked in peanut oil at the other – the price of said G and T enough to buy dinner for six at the local open-air eatery.

Before coming here for lunch, Eva had visited Bogyoke Aung San market, where she purchased two *longyis* made to measure, one in magenta silk and one in indigo batik; two embroidered white cotton blouses and a pair of black velvety Burmese slippers, flip flops really, but made of softer fabric and clearly *de rigeur* in Yangon. And she'd enjoyed the shopping trip; the Burmese liked to barter, but it seemed it was just for fun. 'I am happy; you are happy,' more than one of the stallholders had said to her when they'd agreed a price. And they were right. Eva was glad that she had come here with some room in her suitcase, as her grandfather had advised.

Her companion, probably in his early forties, she guessed, had taken his time before ordering Myanmar beer and a Burmese noodle soup. There was a cultured look about him, in the suave confidence of his voice and manner, in the clothes he wore, which were casual but expensive. Was he a tourist? He looked as though he knew his way around.

He glanced across at her, friendly enough. 'It is your first visit here?' he asked.

She must have it stamped on her forehead under her wide-brimmed straw hat. An innocent abroad. 'Yes,' she admitted. 'I only arrived yesterday.'

Yesterday, the agent from MyanTravel had met her at the airport and accompanied her in the taxi to the Agency Offices housed in a huge old colonial building where she had been given green tea and slices of juicy watermelon. She would have the morning to settle in, he'd told her and then she would be meeting with her company's contact in Yangon who would collect her from her hotel at 3 p.m.

At three on the dot he had appeared in the hotel foyer. 'I, Thein Thein,' he said. 'Now, I take you to the showroom.' They had driven miles, finally arriving at a building that looked more like a shack than a showroom. The man who let them in looked rather shady too and already Eva was having doubts about what she was here to do.

The friendly little waiter brought the *kauk-sweh* soup, a thin broth with vegetables and stringy noodles.

'How about you?' Eva asked her companion. 'It's not your first trip, is it?'

'No, it is not. I have been here many times,' he told her. 'The first in 1999.'

'The city must have changed a lot since then.' Eva poured herself more jasmine tea. The hotels seemed full and although all visitors must still bring only pristine US dollars to the country and there were few ATMs and internet cafés, she could see that other changes wouldn't be long coming.

'It has, yes. And you are travelling for pleasure, is that so?'

'Yes and no. I've wanted to come here most of my life,' she admitted. 'But I'm here on behalf of the company I work for. I'm hoping to authenticate some antique pieces and arrange for them to be shipped back to the UK.'

'Indeed?' He took another spoonful of his soup. 'You work for an antique dealer? You are an expert, perhaps?' His blue eyes were twinkling and he had an open smile that she liked.

She tried to look modest. 'It's what I do,' she said.

'And what have you seen so far?' He called over the waiter and ordered more beer for himself and tea for Eva. 'If you do not mind me asking? I might even . . .' He leaned forwards confidentially, '. . . be able to help you, if you are looking for contacts, that is.'

Eva remembered what Jacqui had said about looking around for more stock. 'It's possible that I might be,' she said. He seemed nice enough and it was good to have some company for a change. Why not tell him what had happened?

'It was a bit of a disappointment, I'm afraid,' she said.

'Oh?'

'I can't possibly examine them in this light,' she had told Thein Thein. 'It's far too dim.'

A lengthy discussion followed between Thein Thein and the man in the shack. Voices had grown more and more heated but no one was actually doing anything.

'Come on.' Eva picked up one end of what she hoped was a nineteenth century scripture chest. 'Give me a hand. Let's get it outside.'

Eventually, amidst much grumbling, Thein Thein helped her and they heaved it into the open air. It was weighty enough to be solid teak . . . But there was a lot of damage, as she could now see. She ran her finger over the wood carving. It almost looked like termite damage, but teak was generally very resistant because it was so rich in natural oils. She examined the piece all over for colour consistency and patination. It had been extensively repaired, although the top was sound. But there was a muddy look to the wood grain that made her suspect it had been treated with something. 'What are you asking for this one?' She checked her paperwork. It would need considerable restoration.

Thein Thein translated. The Burmese dealer looked her up and down briefly as if to assess her wealth. Eva sighed. Hadn't it been explained to him who she was and what she was doing? He named a figure.

It didn't correspond to what was on the paperwork and Eva pointed this out to Thein Thein. He shrugged. 'He want to barter,' he said.

'Well, he can forget it.' Eva put her hands on her hips. 'We're not interested.'

'You do not think it genuine?' Thein Thein took off his battered straw hat, he seemed so shocked.

How could she explain to him? Authenticity was a blurred subject. How much an old piece had been worked on – restored, repaired, whatever you wanted to call it – could affect whether it was considered genuine or not. How much reconstitution was permitted before an item ceased to be an authentic antique? And how it had been repaired would certainly affect the price that could be obtained for it. Everyone had to make a profit, after all, this was a business.

The dealer burst out in a spate of outraged Burmese.

'He say it came from a sacred temple.'

Eva nodded. It might well have done.

'He say it has been protected by a special guardian, a nat, and that it once held holy scriptures on parchment.'

'Is there any documentation?' Eva asked. Not that she would understand it, but Thein Thein would presumably be able to translate.

Both men looked blank.

'Come on then,' she said. 'Let's look at the rest.' Experience had shown her that in every scrap heap there could be a pearl, and if it were here, she would find it. Otherwise Jacqui Dryden would certainly have something to say.

Eva gave her companion a condensed version of the story. She didn't want to say too much to someone who was

69

virtually a complete stranger, but on the other hand he might be a useful person to know.

'And what about the rest of the pieces?' he asked. 'Was there anything interesting?'

'Not really.' She pulled a face. On behalf of the Emporium, she had purchased an old circular lacquer table, a carved teak screen and a few bits of colonial furniture that she knew would be highly saleable. But nothing that had made her heart beat faster. Still, onwards and upwards as they say. There were still Bagan and Mandalay. And she had also been able to talk to Thein Thein about the packaging and shipping damage that Jacqui had complained about. In fact she'd arranged an inspection the following morning of a shipment that was due out this week. She'd caught it just in time.

Thein Thein was doubtful about her conclusions. 'I am surprised that your company not want these special goods I have found,' he said. 'Very surprised they not want to take advantage.'

He could raise his eyebrows and widen his eyes as much as he liked, Eva thought. It wouldn't affect her judgement.

'You are likely to find better items in Mandalay,' her companion now told her.

'That's good,' said Eva, 'I'm going there next.' She eyed him curiously. 'And what about you?' she asked. 'Are you over here on business?'

'I am.'

She raised a questioning eyebrow.

'I have various interests,' he admitted. He sipped his beer

and regarded her appraisingly. 'I help to run a German charity which supports an orphanage in Mandalay.'

'That's nice.'

He sipped his beer, still watching her. 'And I like to buy gemstones.'

'Ah.' Eva's gaze was drawn to the signet ring he wore. 'From here?' she asked.

He nodded. 'A small Burmese ruby.' He smiled warmly. 'I'm sure a connoisseur such as yourself, knows that Burma is very famous for her rubies.'

Eva twisted her own diamond daisy ring. It was the only jewellery she was wearing. In this heat she had decided to dress light, in a simple white sleeveless cotton blouse and a flowery wrap-around skirt; she wanted to fit into the culture as far as possible and it was the best thing to wear to preserve the required modesty and to keep relatively cool. 'Hardly a connoisseur,' she protested. 'Especially not of jewellery.'

'Ah.' He smiled. 'Every beautiful woman is a connoisseur of jewellery, is that not so?'

'Perhaps. But tell me . . .' She leaned a little closer. 'How do you know the stones are genuine?' Her guidebook had advised not to purchase unless you could truly identify the real thing. And Eva had seen the jade and the rubies in the jewellery shops and on market stalls, there were so many, you couldn't help but. If they weren't genuine, then they were very clever imitations.

He touched his nose. 'Contacts,' he said. 'For those who

are interested in buying good stones, they must make contacts who can be relied on. It is like furniture, I think.'

'So it's all about who you know?'

'In Myanmar, yes.' He frowned. 'The government here is very strict about the export of gemstones. There are disreputable dealers. You must find a dealer you can trust.'

Disreputable dealers . . . Eva thought of the pieces she'd seen so far and the reaction of their contact Thein Thein. How trustworthy was he? He had seemed disappointed about the amount she had purchased and yet he must have seen for himself that some of the pieces were of dubious quality.

She looked thoughtfully at her companion, who seemed pretty knowledgeable about such things. Eva had gone into this business because she loved old artefacts and the history they could tell. But in the end, how could you make people really care that a diamond was a real diamond and not a piece of glass, or that an intricately carved teak Buddha painstakingly made by hand hundreds of years ago was still in its original condition?

'It is the price, of course,' her companion said when she put this to him. 'Look at the buses.'

'The buses?'

He was pointing towards the busy wide road. Two buses were creaking and hurtling down the street as if they were on fire, people hanging tightly on to the handrails. 'Why do you think they drive so fast?'

She shrugged. 'Because they're running late?'

He laughed. 'Because they are paid by the number of

passengers on board. So they race and overtake each other to get to the next stop first.'

She laughed with him. 'Really?'

'For sure.' He nodded. 'Always, everything is about money.'

Eva pulled a face. That wasn't what she wanted to hear, or believe. 'Not always,' she said. 'It's about history too. It's about the original source. The value of a genuine artefact. Its story.'

She realised that he was giving her that appraising look again.

'Your passion does you credit,' he said. 'But you should take care in this country when you say what you think.'

'About politics?' She had read that one shouldn't engage the Burmese in conversations about politics or their government – a loose tongue could get them into trouble.

He spread both hands. 'About many things,' he said. 'We take free speech for granted in Europe. The Burmese do not.'

Eva sat back in her chair, chastened. It was true though. She plunged in, whether to conversation or to love, and then considered the wisdom of it later.

'My name, by the way, is Klaus Weber,' he said.

She smiled at the fact that they hadn't yet even exchanged names. 'Eva Gatsby.' And shook his outstretched hand.

'And tonight?' he said smoothly. 'What plans do you have?'

Eva checked her watch to give herself thinking time. Had she really been talking to this man for almost two hours? And more to the point, did she want to spend any more time with him? She certainly wasn't looking for romance. But on the other hand, he had been very easy to talk to.

He shrugged. 'We are both travelling alone,' he said. 'I am staying at The Traders Hotel just down the road here. If you like, we could meet there for a drink and share a taxi to see the Shwedagon Pagoda at sunset. You have not yet seen it, I think? And it is the best time of day to experience its splendour.'

'No, I haven't.' Though she had seen the pagoda from a distance, of course, gilded and graceful, rising above the city like a halo. And the temple was apparently a 'must see'. She'd have to go tonight; tomorrow afternoon she was flying to Mandalay.

Mandalay. The next leg of her journey. Where she would be examining more antiques but also looking for a woman who might not even be there, who might be long dead in fact, for all she knew. And if she was dead? She had to find this woman's family then, if they existed, so that she could return her grandfather's chinthe to its proper home with its twin, in order to restore harmony. Not only that, but she had to try and discover the truth. Would she find Maya? And if she did, how would Eva feel about her?

'We could have dinner afterwards,' said Klaus.

'Well . . .' He was friendly and interesting and would be a lot more amusing over dinner than her guide book had proved to be.

He held up his hands and shot her again that open grin. 'No pressure. No ulterior motive. You are quite safe.'

Eva laughed. His attempt at humour had convinced her. 'Why not?' she said. Max was long gone. And anyway, this was just companionship and just for one evening. What harm could it possibly do?

CHAPTER 8

'You're early.' Rosemary looked up at the sound of Alec's key in the door. This was unusual. She knew that he was heavily involved in a project and that usually meant a late one.

'Uh huh.' He came closer, bent and kissed the top of her head.

Rosemary half-smiled, distracted. She'd been thinking about Eva. Eva in Burma.

'I'm just going to have a quick shower.' He was heading for the bathroom already. 'And then I thought maybe we could go for a walk.'

'A walk?' Mentally Rosemary calculated how long it would take to cook supper. 'Is there something wrong?' she asked him. It had rained earlier and already the light was fading.

'No.' His voice was muffled and then she heard the water coming through. 'Nothing wrong,' he called. 'I just need some fresh air. Want to clear my head.'

'OK.' But she knew there was more to it than that.

They walked along the promenade at Nyhaven, the seventeenth-century waterfront, one of their favourite strolls, where you could admire the brightly painted townhouses and the historic wooden boats moored in the canal. There were plenty of bars and restaurants too, but Rosemary could tell that Alec wanted to walk – and talk.

'I've been thinking,' he said, as they strolled along the wide walkway. 'It's been a long time since you saw Eva and your father.'

She glanced at him. *Was that it?* 'I know.' Almost a year to be precise.

Alec stuffed his hands in his pockets. 'Any reason?' He sounded casual, but Rosemary wasn't fooled.

'Not really,' she said. Other than the fact that during her last visit her father had been defensive and Eva more distant than ever. The truth was, it hurt. She wanted to see them both, of course she did. It was just that it was so hard. And surprisingly easy to lose yourself in a different life and not remember. Or at least to try. Alec wouldn't push it, he never did. Alec's parents had died several years ago and since then there was little reason for him to go back to the UK, apart from with Rosemary. He had one brother who was living in Australia and he'd lost touch with most of his British friends. It had happened to Rosemary too. Easier to bury yourself, easier to let them go.

They walked in silence for a moment. There had been a slight drizzle in the air and the sky was November-grey and dimming into dusk. The colour of the canal was a dull olive. Like the winter sea back in Dorset, thought Rosemary.

'Eva's in Burma,' she said, after a while.

'Burma?' he repeated. He pushed up his glasses which had slipped down his nose. 'Isn't that where—?'

'Yes.' She wasn't prepared to make any more connections at the moment. Eva had gone on a work trip. Whatever else she was doing there, Rosemary wasn't sure she wanted to know. 'She needs to authenticate some antiques.'

'Right.' Alec made to reach for her hand, she noticed the gesture but didn't respond. 'Rosemary?'

She felt his gaze upon her, the question in his eyes. Always the same question. *What's going on with you? What's going on inside?*

And she shot him a quick smile. It was her usual smile, the smile she'd perfected over the years which meant everything was OK, when it wasn't. That there was nothing to worry about, when there was. Which meant, which begged him, to let it be.

They passed the oldest house, number 9, built in 1661 she'd heard, painted blue and a different shape from most of the others. On the other side of the canal were the more lavish mansions, including the Charlottenborg Palace on the corner.

Alec didn't say anything else. And that was why they were together, Rosemary thought. Because he let her be. He accepted the distance which had become a part of her. And so she'd been able to let him get closer, in a way she had been unable to let her father or her daughter, because, unlike them, she knew he'd never get too close. Self-preservation. It was the most necessary thing in life. That was what Nick's death had taught her.

Rosemary had met Alec almost ten years after Nick had

died. Some might say it was a long time not to be involved with a man, but Rosemary didn't see it that way. It was more incredible that she had ever managed to be involved with a man again.

There was a female solicitor at the practice in Dorset called Selina, who had become something of a friend; her husband was a keen golfer and so Selina found herself with free time at the weekends which she sometimes spent with Rosemary if she was at a loose end. It suited them both.

'Come to dinner on Saturday,' Selina had urged her one Monday morning. 'One of Jon's friends will be there, and Jon's sister and her pal. It's just a casual get-together.'

'You're not matchmaking?' Rosemary was hesitant.

'Course not.'

But as a matter of fact, Rosemary had liked Alec from the first. Tall, thin and be-spectacled, with an obvious distaste for small talk, he was about as poles apart from creative, outgoing Nick as any man could be. But he wasn't just a computer science geek, he liked walking and he was into music. Turned out he was a bit of a foodie too and their conversation ranged from his love of Led Zeppelin, to walks along the South West Coast Path, to the menu of a particularly good local restaurant that had opened up in town. When they had a quiet moment to themselves, just before Rosemary said goodnight, he invited her there the following evening. And to her surprise, she heard herself accept.

'I can't believe it,' Selina had said. 'The first man you look at since Nick and he lives in Copenhagen.' She looked apprais-ingly at Rosemary. 'I suppose that makes him safe.'

'Maybe it does,' Rosemary conceded. But it was a step, wasn't it? She was still only thirty-seven. But not ready to run the mile.

Alec did work in Copenhagen but he was back for a month to see his parents and to carry out some program-ming research, and so Rosemary saw quite a bit of him. And she liked what she saw. He didn't expect too much of her. In fact he seemed to expect nothing. They could walk and talk, or they could walk in silence, it didn't matter to him. He liked her when she dressed up for dinner and he liked her just as much after a morning's gardening when she was wearing wellies and jeans. He didn't try to get her to talk about Nick (she was more than a little fed up with the 'better out than in' brigade), but once, when she did want to talk about Nick and even had a bit of a weep, he hadn't minded a jot. He met Eva and was nice to her, but he didn't pretend he wanted to adopt her or become her best friend. Some people might have said he wasn't very emotional. But that was what Rosemary liked most about him.

Two days before Alec returned to Copenhagen, Rose-mary's mother, Helen, was diagnosed with a virulent form of cancer. It was a shock and yet hardly a surprise. She'd been getting paler and weaker for some time and her debilitating migraines had become more and more frequent. Rosemary was devastated. All she could think was, *another loss*. She had always adored her mother even though she was the first to admit that Helen wasn't easy. The trouble with her mother was that she'd always wanted everything to be perfect. Sometimes she had crackled with the pure tension of it. And what was perfect? What could be perfect? Certainly not life, which was ragged and raw and full of snakes and ladders around every corner which would always take you by surprise.

It was Alec who comforted her when she cried, who held her in his arms and eventually made love to her. And briefly, wonderfully, Rosemary found herself wanting it again, this closeness, this intimacy with another human being. It had been missing from her life for so long. She'd thought that it was another part of her that she would never find again.

'Will you come and visit me?' he asked her on the day he left. 'Copenhagen's a beautiful city. And it's only a short flight away. You could stay as long as you like.'

Rosemary wasn't sure exactly what he was asking. Was he proposing a long-distance relationship? She couldn't see herself flying out to Denmark every other weekend. Or was he suggesting something more permanent? What about work? What about her family? 'I can't leave my parents,' she said. 'My mother . . .' And then, of course, there was Eva. What sort of a proposition was she with a teenage daughter like Eva? She wasn't easy, she never had been easy and Rosemary's relationship with her was fraught at best. She was working towards her GCSEs and eventually she'd go on to university, or so Rosemary hoped. But what did Eva feel? Rosemary hadn't a clue. And worse still, she wasn't sure how it had ever got that way.

'You'd like it over there,' Alec said. 'It could be a new start.'

Magical words. If there was anything Rosemary needed, it was a new start.

'About Burma,' Alec said now. He paused to look at one of the old boats moored in the canal, but Rosemary had the feeling he wasn't looking at it at all.

'Yes?' She re-wound her soft pashmina scarf and tucked it back into the collar of her jacket. But she was mildly surprised. It wasn't like him to delve.

'Couldn't you put it behind you now?'

Could she? Rosemary thought of the day she'd made her discovery.

Alec had returned to Copenhagen and within months her mother had died. Her father had grieved for her, but there was something else. Relief, perhaps? Her parents were very different, she reminded herself, maybe over the years they'd even grown apart. But they'd been happy, hadn't they, in their own way?

The letters were tucked in his bedside cabinet and Rosemary only found them because she was sorting out some of her mother's stuff and had discovered a couple of pairs of her father's socks in Helen's drawer. The letters were tied with a red ribbon and her first thought was: love letters. And she felt a streak of happiness. Because this meant they had loved one another after all. They had written love letters and her father had kept every one.

She soon realised her mistake. She flicked through them.

Each envelope was written in her father's hand, but they weren't addressed to her mother. They were addressed to someone called Daw Moe Mya who lived in Burma. And they hadn't been sent.

Rosemary held them in her hands for several minutes. What did it mean? Who was this Daw Moe Mya? Why hadn't he sent any of these letters to her? What had he wanted to say, but not said? She was intrigued. And her father was out of the house.

Curiously, she eased open the first envelope that he hadn't even sealed, just folded.

My dearest Maya,

she read.

> *Will I ever send this? Or will I simply read the words over and over again? That, if I cannot talk to you, I need to do. So I doubt I will post this letter, my love. You see, sometimes it is enough just to write the words I want to say to you. It somehow loosens the constriction I have around my heart . . .*

Rosemary gasped. She put a hand to her mouth. She checked the date. It was written only two years ago.

Constriction around my heart . . . That phrase had an awfully familiar ring. Rosemary knew exactly how that felt.

She rummaged through the letters then, read every one, about thirty in total. Love letters, yes. But written to a woman in Burma. And when she'd finished reading. Well, then she understood.

Her father had never really loved her mother. Through no fault of her own, Helen had always been second best. He had met this woman in Burma, and he'd never stopped loving her since. The dishonesty . . . Rosemary could hardly credit it. It left her with a bitter feeling, a taste in her throat of bile. He had come back to England and married Rosemary's mother, allowing her to think she was his chosen one, his special girl, the woman he wanted to marry.

But she wasn't. She never had been. And she must surely have known. No wonder he had never given Rosemary his time when she was a child and then a woman, no wonder her mother had always longed for everything to be perfect and had often looked so sad. No wonder that he was relieved now that he could stop pretending. He had always been in love with Maya, this woman from Burma. And his marriage, his English life with Helen, with Rosemary and, yes, even with Eva. It had all been a sham.

'The thing is, Rosemary . . .'

It took her a moment to realise that Alec was still talking.

'It doesn't matter too much to me because I've got no one left.'

She stared at him. No one left?

'But for you. You've got your father and you've got Eva.'

Had she though? Rosemary put a hand to her brow. He was really confusing her now.

'At first, I wasn't sure I needed another new challenge at my age,' Alec went on. 'I'm still not completely convinced.' He let out a short laugh.

He was walking more quickly now and Rosemary had to pick up her pace to keep up with him. She almost took his arm to slow him down, but they weren't really like that, she and Alec. They didn't link arms and they didn't hold hands, not usually.

'Convinced about what, Alec?' she asked him.

He glanced at her, distracted. He brushed back his thinning sandy hair. 'I mean it's nice that they're interested, of course. Flattering, you know.'

'Convinced about what?' Rosemary stopped walking.

He stopped too, put his hands on her shoulders and she felt the pressure through her leather jacket. 'I've been asked to join a different company, Rosemary,' he said. 'It means a promotion, more money, a complete change in fact.'

'A complete change?' she echoed. What did he mean, a complete change? Had he been head-hunted then? Was that it?

'Yes.' He relaxed his grip. She searched his expression, still waiting.

'It's in Seattle,' he said.

CHAPTER 9

The Shwedagon was so much more than Eva had expected. The pagoda was bigger, grander and more golden. The mosaiced glass of the walls and pillars glittered and the ornate teak carving around shrines and pavilions simply took her breath away. Eva was in awe. 'Did they really use sixty tons of gold to build this place?' she asked Klaus. Not to mention the diamonds decorating the top of the spire.

'I believe so.' He smiled. He seemed to be enjoying her reaction to the most famous temple of Myanmar.

Eva decided to get that information later from her guide book. For now, it was more important to absorb the atmosphere, to stare up at the golden stupa rising over 300 feet above her head, to absorb the wafting fragrance of incense sticks lit for various Buddhas and nats, the spirits of the place who must be appeased, and to listen to the soft chanting of men and women praying and meditating, sitting cross-legged, bowing forwards reverentially on the worn matting of the temple. None of her studies, none of her grandfather's stories had prepared her for this, the reality.

'You must take off your shoes at the bottom of the steps,' Klaus had told her, indicating where she should leave them.

But no sooner had she set them down than they were seized upon by two doe-eyed, raggedy children and carried triumphantly back to their stall. It seemed that they stored captured shoes and gave them back to their owners in return for a small donation.

Klaus clicked his tongue at them. 'No, no,' he said. 'Bring the shoes back here.'

But Eva just smiled. 'It's alright, really,' she said.

'They take advantage,' he told her. 'You should not encourage or this will become another culture of beggars rather than people trying to be independent.' But from his tolerant expression, she guessed that he understood how she felt on this, her first trip.

Because the children were being enterprising, surely? Eva was keen to support the community. And she didn't care a bit if they were taking advantage. Five hundred kyatts might do something significant for them, but for her it was less than fifty pence.

'It is traditional to visit the planetary post dedicated to your birth day,' Klaus told her as they commenced their walk around the stupa. 'Which day is it?'

'Saturday.' As in Saturday's child has to work for a living, thought Eva.

'*Naga*. It is the dragon, I think.' Klaus raised an eyebrow and took her to the post where people were strewing the Buddha with offerings of flowers and pouring water over him from a gilded cup, as was the custom. 'Astrology is very important to Buddhists,' Klaus told her. 'The day of the week when you were born, the position of the planets. They are considered to have great significance.'

They continued to wander barefoot around the stupa in a clockwise direction, pausing to admire anything that took Eva's fancy, a pavilion containing four teak Buddhas, house martins darting and diving in and out of the castellations of a temple, a group of black-haired children striking a big, golden bell. Klaus seemed quite happy to go wherever she wanted and Eva couldn't stop taking photos. She knew she was behaving like any other tourist, but how could she help it? There was so much to see, so much to capture. The dusty ceramic tiles were smooth under her feet and the air was warm, soft and fragrant, filled with that rhythmic prayer and chanting.

But when she put her camera to one side . . . That was when she felt it. The real and gentle spirituality of the place and the people. The sense of stillness. The shimmer of the gold and the warmth of the teak, the smoky incense and the fading light as the sun dipped and began to slowly set behind the greenery on the far side of the temple. It cast a shaft of red light that mellowed the pagoda into burnished amber and made it seem richer than ever. Darkness softly fell around them like a blanket. And the golden stupa, now bejewelled with lights, was outlined against the indigo sky, pinpricked by stars and cradled by the crescent moon.

'I am glad that you like the Shwedagon,' Klaus said to her. 'It is the glory of Myanmar, I think.'

She nodded. 'And perhaps it has its spirit too.'

He bowed his head in acquiescence. 'But now, you are ready to go?'

Most people had left the temple, but Eva and Klaus lingered to watch a procession of pink-robed, shaven-headed novice monks holding strings of jasmine flowers and paper parasols. They were just children, not more than nine or ten years old, and they were accompanied by members of their family dressed in their best *longyis* and most colourful shawls.

'It is the most important moment in the life of a young Burmese boy,' Klaus told her. 'His initiation.' He seemed thoughtful. 'It is when he becomes a proper and dignified part of the human race.'

'But will these boys stay monks for the rest of their lives?' she asked.

'No. Some do, of course. There are many *phongyis* who dedicate their entire life to the scriptures. But most of them simply withdraw from the secular world for a period of time in order to seek enlightenment, just as the Buddha did.' He shrugged. 'Or so they believe.'

But what did he believe? Eva liked him, but she guessed that there was more to him than met the eye. She sneaked a look at him as they proceeded down the marble steps and into the long aisle lined with handicraft stalls. He seemed cool and perfectly in control but she sensed that he was as deeply affected by this place as she was.

As they approached a small group sitting on the steps, Eva saw one of the Burmese men glance towards them. He got to his feet, re-knotted his green and red checked *longyi* and came a few steps closer.

Klaus saw him too. His brow clouded. Swiftly, he bent towards Eva. 'Excuse me for a moment, please, Eva,' he said. 'Will you wait here?'

'Of course.' He had indicated the doorway of one of the shops, which sold thin sandalwood fans and beaded purses and, although Eva was tempted to take a closer look at the goods on offer, instead she watched Klaus as he approached the man in the *longyi*. Who was that man? And what was he up to? She was curious.

Klaus and the Burmese man were soon deep in conversation. They moved round the corner and out of sight.

Eva frowned. She edged towards a nearby pillar. At first, there was no sign of them on the other side. But then she spotted the two figures standing in the shadows. They were talking animatedly, gesticulating with their hands. She studied the body language. The Burmese man, smaller and shorter than Klaus, seemed to be asking for something, hands outstretched. Klaus shrugged, peeled off some notes from his wallet and passed them over.

What was that all about? As Klaus looked over in her direction, Eva dodged out of sight behind the pillar and, somewhat unsettled, drifted back to the place where he'd left her. A souvenir seller materialised ahead. Her little cards had pictures made from black and gold bamboo, and Eva bought some, choosing at random, silhouettes of stilt houses, boats and palm trees, a big gold moon in the centre. She put them in her bag.

A few minutes later, Klaus appeared and took her arm. 'Sorry, Eva, that was a contact of mine. He was giving me some information, but not as much as I would have liked.' He smiled ruefully.

Eva relaxed. She was seeing drama where there was none, she decided. Klaus had business in Myanmar with some of the people who lived here. Nothing more, nothing less. He had moved away to shield her from what might have held a hint of unpleasantness, that was all. It was nothing. He was a nice man, but she must remember, he was still almost a stranger.

They had dinner in a small but smartish local eatery nearby and Klaus proved to be an entertaining companion. She was tempted to ask him about the Burmese man at the Shwedagon, but something stopped her. After tonight she'd probably never see Klaus again. So, what did it matter?

But in the taxi on the way back to her hotel, he withdrew a leather diary from his jacket pocket. 'I am staying at The Mandalay Royal. Are you?' he asked her. 'Most foreigners stay there so perhaps we can meet up again? I will see if one of those contacts I mentioned has something you might be interested in.'

'I am, yes.' Eva nodded. It would certainly be useful from a professional point of view.

He made a note. 'Then I hope I will see you, Eva, in Mandalay.'

They had arrived at her hotel and he got out to open the car door for her.

'Goodbye, Klaus.'

He dropped a platonic kiss on her cheek. '*Auf Wiedersehen*.'

She gave him a wave and watched as his blond head ducked back into the car and then disappeared out of sight. She'd had a lovely evening. But how well could you possibly know someone you'd just met?

At the desk, the receptionist handed her the room key. 'There is a telephone message,' she said. 'From England.'

'From England?' Eva felt a dip of panic.

'It is from the Bristol Antiques Emporium.' The girl read slowly from a notebook. 'Please telephone. Urgent.'

Urgent? Eva checked her watch. It would be around 6.30 p.m. in the UK. She'd switched off her mobile phone. Global roaming didn't work here in Myanmar and it wasn't easy for a tourist to buy a local SIM card, or so she had heard. Internet connections were awfully slow too. Jacqui had told her to call from a hotel if she needed to, but at over five US dollars a minute she'd be mostly on her own.

'Here is the number.' The girl handed her a slip of paper. It wasn't the office number though, it was one she didn't recognise. 'I dial, yes?'

'Yes, please.' Eva waited. It was painstakingly slow.

At last the girl spoke and handed the receiver to Eva. 'Hello?'

'It's Leon.'

Eva was surprised. Leon had never had much to do with

her side of the business, she'd always dealt with Jacqui. 'Is Jacqui alright?'

'She's fine,' Leon said. 'She asked me to call because she's a bit tied up tonight. Anyway, it's about the shipment that's due to go out. The one you wanted to check over.'

'Oh, I see.' Leon dealt with that side of things, deliveries, shipping and so on. 'What's the problem?'

'No problem,' Leon said. 'Not really. I just wanted to let you know that you don't need to check it. We only intended you to have a word with the people over there. We don't want to upset them, make them feel they're not doing their job properly. Do you see what I mean?'

'I suppose so. I just thought that as I'm here and it's about to go out . . . That it would be a good opportunity to check that packaging.'

'Best not to.' Leon sounded breezy. Clearly, he'd got over whatever had upset him before Eva left Bristol. 'There's too much red tape, to be honest with you, Eva. The shipment's already packed and ready to go. We can't afford any delays at this stage.'

'Oh, alright then. If you're sure . . .' It wasn't up to her, was it?

'We're sure.' Leon hesitated. 'And, like I said, it's a delicate matter, dealing with these people. OK?'

'Alright.' Though Eva felt snubbed. Didn't Leon and Jacqui realise that she could be tactful and diplomatic? She was hardly likely to go in there all guns blazing.

'And you can call me on this number if you have any more queries.'

'Fine.'

'Happy hunting.' And he rang off.

Eva stared at the phone. No enquiries about how she was getting on alone here in Burma, if everything was alright, if she had any problems . . .

'Thank you, madam.' The girl took the receiver back and made a note. Counting up the dollars, no doubt.

Had she misunderstood her role here? Eva didn't think so. Leon had always been difficult and she didn't envy Jacqui one bit. But she was faintly relieved that her duties in Yangon appeared to be over. She was thoughtful as she went up to her room. She draped her silk wrap on the chair and slipped off her leather sandals. She padded over to the window and looked out at the lights and night life that were Yangon, the golden stupa of the Shwedagon still glimmering in the distance against the night sky. Why should she bother about Leon? Tomorrow she'd be in Mandalay and there'd be more artefacts to examine. And lots of other things to keep her occupied too. Such as her grandfather's story and her promise to return the chinthe still nestling in her cabin bag at the bottom of her wardrobe, safe from the prying eyes of any chambermaids. Such as her mother's disapproval. And such as the elusive Maya who could, her grandfather had promised, tell her much more and who she might or might not find in Mandalay.

CHAPTER 10

Quite often, Lawrence found that he'd fallen asleep during the day. He'd be sitting quietly, watching the sparrows and blue tits on the bird feeder, a cup of tea on the side table. And then he'd let his mind drift. Next thing, he'd wake up with the sound of Mrs Briggs or the postman at the front door, the tea stone cold and his head full of the place. Couldn't think where the hell he was for a minute or two. Old age, he supposed. Not that he'd ever stopped thinking about Maya entirely. But his life had been full enough. For many years there had been his work and Helen, then later Rosemary and Eva . . . But now. Well, his darling granddaughter, Eva, was in Burma and it was as if Lawrence had gone back there too, at least in his mind.

Mandalay, 1937

Back at the club, Lawrence couldn't stop thinking about her.

After meeting in the market, they had walked one quarter of the way around the still and calm waters of the moat, which was one mile, she told him, along a cool and wide walkway shaded by trees. The city within its confines, where the club was also located, had once housed the famous Royal Palace and Lawrence felt a swamp of shame when he remembered what Scottie had told him – how the British had ousted the last of the Burmese dynasty at this very place. Why had they done this? Was it purely a matter of greed?

They walked side by side, Lawrence conscious of her small body gently swaying with the rhythm of her steps and as they walked Moe Mya told him what there was to see in the city, the stone carvers and furniture makers, the Shwenandaw Kyaung gilded teak monastery, the Mahamuni, a golden Buddha on which men laid gold leaf in homage to the Great One and the U Bein teak footbridge across the River Irrawaddy.

'I want to see it all,' he told her.

She smiled at his enthusiasm. 'Then perhaps you will,' she said.

After their walk, Lawrence didn't want to let her go, so he took her to a tearoom where green tea was served in tall pots painted with flowers and bamboo and she talked of her family. Of her father who had commercial interests as a broker in the rice business, of her aunt, her mother's sister, who lived near Myitkyina and of her grandmother, Suu Kyi, who had been a servant-girl to Queen Supayalat back in 1885 when the King and Queen had been ousted from their thrones in the Palace and taken into exile.

'Where were they taken?' he asked her, trying not to be distracted by the rich purple of the high-necked blouse she wore, elegantly draped over her *longyi*. It wasn't so much the blouse, it was the metallic sheen of the purple against her burnished skin.

'Madras in India,' she said. 'It was considered to be a place of safety.'

'So far away?' Lawrence was surprised. He knew little of Burmese history, he realised. He had come to this land knowing it was different, but all the differences he had experienced to date concerned the countryside, the people and the culture. Scottie had told him stories, but they were always told by the voice of imperialism rather than the voice of the people. He realised that now. 'Were the King and Queen in so much danger then, to need a place of safety?' He was confused.

'The safety the British were thinking of was their own,' Moe Mya pointed out dryly. 'More tea?'

'Please.' He pushed his cup closer and she lifted the tall and decorative teapot once again. 'What were the British so worried about?' Though he could guess. And he realised that at this moment there was nothing he wanted more than to separate himself from those whom he called the British. He had always been a patriot, but it had been unthinking. Now, he was beginning to wonder.

'An uprising,' she said. 'Even peaceful people like the Burmese have such moments.'

He frowned. 'But the King and Queen were not harmed?'

She shook her head. 'No, they were not,' she said. 'There was a British Protectorate, to ensure that they were well looked after.' She passed him back his cup, now filled with the hot green liquid.

'And to ensure that they stayed put and didn't try to get back to Burma,' he added. It wasn't hard to work this out. How much support had the royal couple had among the Burmese people? It might have been possible for them to regain power. But the British clearly weren't going to take that chance.

'Precisely.'

Out of sight, out of mind. And now Lawrence felt more than shame, he felt guilt, for being British, for being part of imperialism, for the rout which must have affected so many, including Moe Mya's family.

'And what happened to your mother?' he asked her gently, for so far she had only talked of the aunt in Myitkyina and of her father and the close bond between them.

She bowed her head, but not before he had seen the tears fill her dark eyes. 'She died when I was a child.'

Moved, Lawrence reached for her hand, which was still resting on the handle of the teapot. It seemed so small next to his own and he marvelled at the tiny fingernails. 'I'm sorry,' he said.

She acknowledged this. She looked at his hand too although she did not attempt to take hers away. 'My father is a good man,' she said. 'If you like, you can meet him.'

'Of course.' Lawrence spoke automatically, though he was a bit surprised. After all she and he had only just met themselves. But he must see it as an honour and naturally he could not object. Damn it, he didn't want to object. He wanted to know all there was to know about her. 'I'd be delighted,' he added.

She smiled then and extracted her hand from his. 'It will not be easy,' she warned. She lifted her cup to her lips and he followed suit, watching her over the rim.

'Because he's very protective of you?' Lawrence would be protective of her too if he had the chance.

'Because you are British.'

Ah. Another reminder of the unpleasant fact that not all the Burmese were friendly and hospitable to their imperial masters. That some indeed would rather be free. 'I see.' He nodded. But he would still meet him. There was a lot, he realised, that he would do, for a chance to spend more time with this woman.

'Tell me about your work,' she said to him.

'Well . . .' The teak camp had not prepared Lawrence for any such notion of Burmese freedom. Every man who worked for him seemed loyal and accepting of his place. They had to be, otherwise the logging could not run smoothly. 'We are a team,' he said simply. And it was tough, demanding work. 'We have to be resilient.' It meant living for long periods in the teak camps away from civilisation and spending a lot of time in the jungle, along with the leeches, mosquitoes and the rest. And in a heat and humidity that could sap every ounce of energy from a man. But she would know all that, he realised.

'Why did you choose such a job?' Her eyes were wide. To her, such a choice must seem very strange for an Englishman.

'I often wonder.' Especially when the rains didn't come to take the logs off down the river, or when they lost an elephant to disease or accident. It was such bloody hard work. 'I like to be close to the earth, to the soil, to nature,' he told her, and perhaps this was what had first attracted him. He relished the rasping sound of the saw as the timber was felled, the creak of the complaining tree and the explosion as it fell, crushing everything in the forest within reach. He loved the sweet scent of the wood that could fill the hot, heavy air, and he had nothing but admiration for the elephant handlers who guided the great beasts, tied chains and fastened harnesses, so that the logs could be dragged to the banks of the *chaungs*, the wild and rushing mountain streams.

'You have taught us how to use the power of the river,' said Moe Mya. 'And to harness the power of the elephants too.' Although even as she acknowledged this, her small smile seemed to suggest that it was, after all, an insignificant thing.

What was not insignificant, thought Lawrence, was the way that with a boom and a crash, the logs would tumble downstream. And those logs could move. They'd hurtle singly or in packs, colliding into each other and everything in their path with a reverberation that could be felt all along the river bank. Or a log could get caught in rapids or heavy debris and in the blink of an eye there'd be a massive dam of the things until the force and weight of them made the obstacle give and a tidal wave of water carrying logs like missiles would pour down the mountainside. If you got in the way, you'd be a dead man.

'It's not all hard work, though,' he acknowledged. There were terrific cold-weather days too in Upper Burma when you could go on a jungle-shoot for fowl, geese or even bison. And there were the Forest Headquarter hill-stations like Maymyo where you could take leave to play tennis and enjoy a whisky in the club and plain home-cooked food and British camaraderie in the chummery or simply rest and recuperate before returning to camp. Even in camp, there were compensations; there were men who specialised in ferrying supplies and luxuries out there. You could more or less order anything you wanted: cigars, whisky, cans of meat or sardines. You just didn't know when it would arrive. 'You never know what will happen next,' he told her. 'That's what's so exciting. You're at the mercy of the elements. And you're living – do you see? Really living.' It was about as far from a desk job in the UK, working in the family stock-broking firm, as you could get.

'You have great passion,' she said, 'for your work.'

And he supposed this was true. He'd come to Burma to escape duty and the desk and he'd discovered the world of nature, the world of wood and a landscape and people that had already crept into his heart. It was indeed a different life.

Forestry was an old trade. Teak had been shipped from Burma to India as far back as the early eighteenth century though Lawrence's company had only acquired the forest leases, the elephant herds and the logging staff at the turn of this century when others had looked to the railways for their living. And the legislation was strict. Every teak tree in Burma belonged to the government and the Forest Department supervised which trees were chosen for felling. They must be mature, they must be dried out for at least three years and seasoned so that they could float. There was a hell of a lot of forest in Burma, but the amount of trees in any given area that were allowed to be felled was inconsistent and the terrain was tough. This made Lawrence's job still harder.

He quickly learnt to recognise unsound trees, to take into account irregularities of shape. The trees were felled by saw at ground level and that's when Lawrence and his crew would visit each one, to measure and hammer-mark it to indicate the points at which it would later be made into logs. It was indeed a trade dependant on nature: on the earth, on the trees, on animals and on the seasons. They needed the rainy season to move the logs down the rivers and they needed the elephants to haul them there. It was quite a spectacle. And the terrain was far too hilly and broken by *chaungs*, the spread of the extractable trees far too random to use mechanical haulage means. He explained some of this to Moe Mya.

She seemed interested, watching his face as he spoke, occasionally nodding or pouring more tea. 'And you like our elephants?' she teased. 'They work well for you, yes?'

'Oh, yes. Without them we couldn't do what we do,' he said. He worked closely with the forest assistant to look after these sagacious beasts and he got to know them individually, you couldn't help but. They were quirky and they had their likes and dislikes – which side they were approached from, for example (if you got it wrong, you'd get swiped from the swishing tail and that was no joke, as Lawrence had found out to his cost) and the spot from which they liked to feed. They were sensitive too and had to be protected from sores and disease. Anthrax was the worst; you could lose an entire working herd of a hundred in a matter of days. And they needed lots of food, sleep and baths in order to perform at their best.

Their working day might be only six hours – by noon they'd had enough – but by God did they put the work in. Lawrence was in awe. Between May and October during the rains, unharnessed elephants would follow the logs downstream, breaking up the jams of wood that tended to occur in the feeder streams and tributaries until they reached the main swollen river and the point where villagers could retrieve the logs (not a job Lawrence would care to undertake himself) and make up the raft. It was a bloody long and hazardous journey.

'I have seen the rafts many times,' Moe Mya told him. 'They are so big, yes?'

'They are. They need to be. They even have grass huts to accommodate the raftsmen, their families and possessions.' The whole family were involved with the retrieval of the logs, they would move location according to where was the best position to be stationed, children would keep lookout for the timber, skilled retrievers would bring in the logs which must be anchored, moored and then bound to make a raft of the size decreed by the timber company. But it was dangerous work. Men could die.

'How strange it all seems,' she murmured.

'It can take a long time to get to Rangoon by river,' he explained to her. 'Weeks, sometimes months. One has to take everything one will need.' The rafts were powered by the current of the river and guided by oars.

'And when they get there? What will they do then?' She was teasing him now, that spark in her dark eyes that he had noticed at the market, that meant that she understood him, even that she was laughing at him perhaps. Not that he minded. As long as she was there.

'The company gives them rail tickets to return to their villages,' he told her, keeping his back straight and proud. They weren't so bad, were they? It wasn't such an unsatisfactory job. What else would they do? 'And they stay there until the next rains.'

'Perfect.' She laughed.

The cycle of the seasons, the cycle of life. It was something that perhaps Britain had lost somehow with its city ways and industry. But it was here, Lawrence thought now. It was here.

'And when will you go back to camp?' Moe Mya asked him, her face serene. Was she wondering when she would see him again? Did she want to see him again?

'Just before the rains,' he said. There was no sign as yet, but it couldn't be long. All the extractions had been completed, the logs were arranged instream and the *ounging* herds were patiently waiting . . . It was a frustrating time. There was a sense of achievement but they needed that rain. And the heat went on.

'They will come soon,' she said. 'And now, I must go.' She rose to her feet. 'Please excuse me.'

'Oh.' He almost stumbled as he too got up from the chair. They had been sitting there for so long and he had quite lost track of time.

She shivered as they stepped outside, though to Lawrence the heat still seemed to hang heavy in the darkness that had now fallen.

'May I?' He put the blanket he was still holding gently around her shoulders. 'It is yours,' he said.

'Thank you.' She looked suddenly vulnerable as she stood there on the street with the thin blanket around her.

On impulse, he bent down and very gently brushed her lips with his. She didn't flinch as he'd thought she might, but neither did she respond. 'I can see you again?' He tried not to make it sound too much like a question – that way, she could refuse.

She bowed her head. 'Of course.'

'Good.' He came to a sudden decision. 'And I too will call you Maya,' he said.

Eva walked out on to the wooden verandah at Pine Rise in Pyin Oo Lwin, previously known as Maymyo. The goods she had come to see in Mandalay weren't ready to be inspected. She had emailed Jacqui who didn't seem overly concerned and who had agreed that Eva could take a few days of her leave here. There would be plenty for her to see, Jacqui had confirmed, when she returned to the city.

After the stifling heat, the hustle and bustle and traffic spilling in all directions in downtown Mandalay: rundown cars, scooters, trishaws, bicycles weaving around one other, signalling their intent with sharp bursts of the hooter or rings of the bell, this was an oasis of calm. And so it must have seemed to her grandfather when he stayed here. Eva took a deep breath of the clean air. A taste of paradise. The wide and dusty teak verandah felt solid and reassuring under her feet and there was a freshness in the air and a lushness to the planting that felt like silk on her somewhat frazzled senses.

In Mandalay, Eva had braved the city madness and taken a hair-raising taxi ride on the back of a scooter to the first address her grandfather had given her. She'd plucked up the courage to knock on the door of the rather smart traditional

Burmese house and wondered. *Could this be where she would find her?* But the young girl with ebony hair and a big smile who said, 'Hello, hello,' to Eva as if she were a long lost friend had not been able to help her.

'Gone ten year,' she'd said, holding up both hands.

'Do you know where?' Eva had gesticulated to try and get her meaning across.

The girl shook her head sadly.

'OK. Thanks.' But now she knew. The family, or some of them, had survived the war. They had lived in this house until ten years ago. And Eva still had address number two.

The address written on the second slip of paper was here in Pyin Oo Lwin.

As soon as she received Jacqui's email, Eva had checked out of her hotel in Mandalay and booked herself back in again for two days' time. Then she'd made a reservation at Pine Rise. Her need to follow the trail was all-consuming. It was easy to get a driver and she'd enjoyed the journey this morning as they drove from the broad plain of the Irrawaddy towards the old hill-station of Maymyo. Already the landscape had changed. The earth was a rich red and the vegetation more abundant; oleander and tall bamboo, poinsettia and mimosa lining the way with red and yellow and bursts of shocking purple.

Pyin Oo Lwin itself was an elegant and leafy town with avenues of eucalyptus trees hiding mock-Tudor houses, grand red-bricked villas and white bungalows positively shimmering in the sun. The houses were set far apart and in extensive grounds, their background, pine woodland and, in the distance, rolling hills of oak. They passed the Purcell Tower which her grandfather had told her housed a clock that used to chime with the same sound as Big Ben – how English was that?! – and a vibrant flower market. And finally, there it was. Pine Rise. Airy and light. All polished teak, clotted cream walls and glass chandeliers. Eva loved it on sight.

Her grandfather had spent a lot of time here, in the colonial guesthouse once owned by the company he worked for, now a hotel. It had provided rest and recuperation after a session working up in the jungle. It was a place in which to unwind, relax, recharge the batteries along with other company colleagues, before plunging back into the fray. He'd also spent time here recuperating from a bout of malaria.

Eva looked out over the lawn, where a carpet of yellow celandine-like flowers was just opening into bloom and, in the centre, a hexagonal wooden bench with a pergola above. Maya's family had also owned a weekend- and holiday-retreat here, hence the address written in her grandfather's hand in Eva's purse. Apparently, many of the well-off Burmese still did. It was two hours' drive from Mandalay, but at a higher altitude and so refreshingly cooler.

Eva trailed her fingers along the handrail. Her grandfather had stood here, perhaps even touching the same piece of wood, staring out at the same tropical gardens, which must have seemed a million miles away from the busy cities and steamy jungles he'd been working in. He, too, had climbed the highly polished teak staircase, which rose elegantly from the foyer to open out at the top like a tulip, forming a gallery from which you could promenade all the way around and gaze down into the foyer, where there was a Victorian fireplace twice as tall as Eva. He had stayed in one of these high-ceilinged rooms with disused fireplaces, maybe her room? The thought made her spine tingle. She didn't think she had ever felt so close to him. And the little chinthe was still safely tucked in her bag. He was on quite a journey too, though it wasn't his first. She thought of her grandfather in the jungle. Had he carried the chinthe with him when he went to war?

It was 2 p.m. She returned to her room, picked up her wide-brimmed hat and her new colourful Shan bag and left the hotel, the slip of paper in her hand, along with a road map provided at reception. The house that had been Maya's family retreat was less than ten minutes' walk away, the receptionist had told her, and now she was so close, Eva wanted to take it slowly.

She found the house on a dusty road at the top of a slight incline, its entrance framed by bamboo fencing wound with frangipani. She paused just for a moment to drink in the scent, which was so rich she almost felt dizzy, and made her way up the wide driveway. It was another traditional house but grander than the one in Mandalay. Built of teak and intricately patterned bamboo, it was made up of two storeys, the upper having a wide verandah which swept right around the house. There was so much wood. Even the roof was constructed with wooden tiles and the panelled door was framed by bougainvillea, which the Burmese called the paper tree, as her driver had informed her this morning on the way here.

Deep breath. Eva lifted the brass door knocker and let it fall. The sound seemed to reverberate around the walls of the house, shattering the air of tranquillity. In more ways than one, she thought ruefully.

A man opened the door. He was in his mid-thirties, with the dark hair of the Burmese, but with the features and height – he must be six feet tall – of a Westerner. Anglo-Burmese perhaps; Myanmar was a country of mixed races and influences: Japan, China, Thailand, India and Britain, for starters. He was clean-shaven, his skin a shade of dark olive.

Eva licked her dry lips. 'Hello.' She smiled. 'Do you speak English?'

'Of course.' He smiled back at her and his rather sharp-boned features were transformed. His accent was European, his tone soft and low.

She straightened her shoulders. 'I'm looking for the family of Daw Moe Mya,' she said. 'Do they live here, by any chance?'

He eyed her curiously, with just a hint of suspicion now. 'Why are you looking for them?'

A question for a question. Fair enough, she supposed. 'I have a message,' she said. 'For Daw Moe Mya, if she is still alive.' It still seemed so unlikely, but somehow Eva couldn't help trusting her grandfather's intuition; he had rarely been proved wrong.

The man frowned, calmly scrutinising her from hat to toe.

He seemed relaxed, she found herself thinking, but ready to pounce if necessary.

Eva fidgeted uncomfortably under his gaze. 'Does she live here?' she repeated. 'May I speak with her?'

He bowed his head slightly. 'My grandmother is old,' he said.

So she was alive! Grandpa, bless him, had been right. Eva wished she could tell him this instant. See the expression on his face when he heard the news . . . 'That's wonderful!' She beamed at the man in the doorway.

He raised dark eyebrows at her, a threat of a smile now touching the corners of his full mouth. 'It is?'

'Yes, it is. Not that she's old, of course, but that she's still . . .' She trailed off under his stare. 'I've come a long way,' she explained. 'From England.'

'England?' He blinked at her as if he expected her to break into a song-and-dance routine. He was wearing a short-sleeved, dove-grey shirt, and the traditional male *longyi* in a sage green and black check knotted at the front. And it was funny, but, as she'd already observed since she'd arrived in Myanmar, the effect was surprisingly macho.

'Yes. And I've come especially to see her.' Eva stood her ground.

'And who . . .' he said, 'are you?'

Ah. Here we go, she thought. Another deep breath. 'I'm the granddaughter of Lawrence Fox,' she said.

His eyes flickered. She realised that he had heard the name. Unlike most of the Burmese whose eyes were dark brown, sometimes almost black, his eyes were green, and with his dark hair and skin the effect was quite dramatic. But if he was surprised at her disclosure, he hid it well. He hesitated but then seemed to come to a decision. 'You may come in,' he said, his tone more guarded. 'I will see if my grandmother wishes to speak with you. But you must not stay long. Please,' and his eyes met hers, 'she is very frail.'

Alleluia, she thought. She was in and, 'I won't tire her,' she promised. But she wondered, was he just being protective? Or did he know their grandparents' story and resent what had happened between them all those years ago? What was more important, and rather scary, was that she was about to meet her, at last. Maya, the woman her grandfather had always loved.

The white entrance hall was open and airy and according to the custom, Eva slipped off her black Burmese slippers before following him into the next room. In the centre was a magnificent polished teak table. Eva couldn't help but reach out to touch its smooth and glossy surface, though as she did so, she caught him casting a probing glance her way. Around the table were several ladder-backed chairs, also beautifully made. On the far side of the room was a platform with blue-tiled walls and a shrine, placed high on the far wall. On it, looking down on the room below, was a small intricately carved Buddha and a vase of fresh flowers, their scent drifting through the air.

'Wait here,' he said. 'Please sit.' He gave her another assessing glance and in one fluid movement, turned and was gone from the room.

Eva sat. On the side wall were some photographs and she strained to see. A couple – presumably a King and Queen – seated on royal thrones. They looked very grand.

A few moments later, she heard the lightest of footsteps. She looked up. An old Burmese lady stood framed in the doorway. She was very tiny and her hair was white, but still, she held herself erect.

Maya.

Eva jumped to her feet. How would she be received? She hesitated for a moment, but Maya was already moving towards her, arms outstretched, her brown milky eyes filled with an expression of excitement and disbelief.

'Lawrence's granddaughter?' she breathed. 'But, yes. Look at you. You must be.' She seemed quite overcome.

'Yes. My name is Eva.'

Her grandson materialised from behind his grandmother and offered his arm, but the old lady grasped Eva's arms instead and pulled her into a close embrace. 'Eva . . .' she murmured. 'Eva.'

She smelt of oil and coconut and her grip was intense for such an old lady. *My grandfather's lover*, Eva thought, closing her eyes for a second. His Burmese lover. She didn't know why, but she was surprised that Maya spoke such fluent English. She'd known that the family were well-educated, cultured and well-off by Burmese standards. Even so . . .

Maya drew away and looked into her face, deep into her eyes as if she could look much further. With dry fingertips she traced a pattern over Eva's cheekbones. 'The shape of your face,' she murmured. 'It makes me remember . . .'

My grandfather. Eva had never thought they looked alike, but the family resemblance must be there, reminding Maya of what she had lost. But had she lost him? Or had she chosen to give him up? That, among other things, was what Eva intended to discover.

At last, Maya released her. 'Bring tea.' She clapped her hands. 'We must sit.'

Her grandson called out to someone in the far reaches of the house and Maya indicated to Eva that she should sit down again. The old lady was still smiling. There was no doubt that she was pleased to see her. Eva felt the relief wash over her. She wouldn't think about her mother and her grandmother, Helen, and whatever loyalties she should feel towards them, not now. First, she wanted to understand.

'You have come from England to see us?' Maya asked, her old eyes incredulous in her creased face. 'After all these years?'

'Yes. My grandfather asked me to bring something here for you.' Eva fumbled in her bag.

'He is still alive?' Maya's face lit up and for a moment she looked as eager as a girl. 'Lawrence is still alive?' She was holding on tight to the sides of her chair, her tiny body tense as a coiled spring. Slowly, she relaxed. 'I thought so,' she murmured. 'But I could not be sure.'

Just like Grandpa, Eva thought. They were as intuitive as each other. 'He certainly is.' With a flourish, Eva produced the decorative teak chinthe from her bag. She had wrapped him in tissue paper but his head and mane had escaped its confines. 'And he thought it was about time this little one came home.' Gently, she unwrapped the rest of him. Placed him on the table in front of her.

Maya and her grandson gasped simultaneously as they stared at the chinthe. The sight of it seemed to have an extraordinary effect on them both.

'Ah!' Maya's eyes filled with tears and she murmured something in Burmese. 'Lawrence,' she said softly. 'I knew, I knew.'

Eva was moved. She wasn't sure precisely what it was that Maya knew, but it was blindingly obvious that this woman had felt the same about her grandfather as he had felt about her. But if so . . . It seemed so wrong that they hadn't stayed together. What could be the reason? Eva glanced at Maya's grandson but he continued to stare at the chinthe as if still in shock. Had he known of its existence? She assumed so. Was he simply surprised that she had brought it back?

Maya must have married after Eva's grandfather had left Burma, Eva realised. She'd had a child, the mother or father of this man, her grandson. And that child must have married a Westerner for him to look as he did. Tall, green-eyed . . . A wing of his dark hair kept flopping on to his forehead, and he swept it away in an irritated gesture with the back of his hand. Did he know how Lawrence and Maya had felt about one another? How could anyone not know when the emotions were written so clearly on his grandmother's face?

He reached forwards, scooped up the chinthe in one brown

hand and frowned, turning it from left to right to examine it. She noticed his long fingers and short square nails. 'It seems undamaged,' he said. 'I do not think it has been tampered with.' With a swift glance at his grandmother, he got to his feet and took the chinthe to the other side of the room, where he got something out of a drawer.

He had his back to her, so Eva couldn't see. But . . . Tampered with? She bridled. 'My grandfather has looked after it.' She addressed Maya. 'He cherished your gift,' she assured her.

'Of course.' Maya bowed her head. 'Thank you, my dear child. Ramon . . .' she remonstrated.

With a nod, he came back, replaced the chinthe on the table. But he didn't sit down.

'So now he can be reunited with his twin.' Eva looked around the room. Where did they keep the other one? She would have expected it to be guarding the shrine. 'To restore harmony.' That was what her grandfather had wanted. That was how he had said it must be.

Maya and her grandson exchanged a look.

'Isn't that the belief?' Eva asked.

'Yes, it is.' Maya laid a gentle hand on her arm. Her skin was thin and papery but her hand was warm. 'But you see, Eva, it is not so simple.'

Her grandson muttered what sounded like a curse in his native language. He paced over to the other side of the room and then turned back to her. 'You brought this in your luggage from England?' he demanded.

'Yes. In my cabin bag.'

116

He shook his head. 'Incredible,' he muttered. 'Impossible.'

Eva was confused. 'Why isn't it so simple?' she asked Maya.

Maya sighed. Tenderly, she took the chinthe from the table, gazed into its red glass eyes. She shook her head sadly, running her fingertips over the carving of the face and mane Eva had always admired so much. 'Because,' she said, 'I no longer have the other.'

'Oh.' Eva hadn't even considered that possibility, and she suspected her grandfather hadn't either. 'Where is it?' she asked. 'Do you know?' But it had been a long time. Perhaps it had been naive of them to imagine that the chinthe's twin would have survived the war and its turbulent aftermath.

'It was stolen,' Maya's grandson said. He shot her another look. He still seemed angry. Perhaps that was his default emotion, Eva found herself thinking.

'Really?' She looked again at the little chinthe. It was a beautiful piece of carving, but, although old, she didn't think it would mean much to anyone other than the family who owned it. Why would it be stolen? 'Who by?'

'It is a long story.' Maya nodded and laid her hand again on Eva's arm. 'Do you know anything about the origin of Burmese chinthes, Eva?'

'A bit.'

'It is linked to our Buddhist philosophy,' she said.

'In what way?' Eva was intrigued.

'It is said that once, many moons ago, a princess was married to a lion and had a son by him,' Maya said, her voice slow, almost hypnotic. 'But later she abandoned this lion. He was

enraged and set out on a pathway of terror through the lands.'
She paused. 'The son went out to slay the terrorising lion.
Three times he shot an arrow at him. But so great was the
lion's love for his son that three times the arrow rebounded
from his brow.' Maya sighed. 'But the fourth time the lion
grew angry and the arrow killed him. Thus the lion lost his
life because he had lost his self-possession and allowed wrath
to invade his heart.'

'And what happened to the son?' Eva asked.

'He returned home to his mother who told him that he had
killed his father. The son then constructed a statue of the lion
as a guardian of a temple to atone for his sin.'

And the lion was the chinthe. Eva reached out to touch it
as she had done so often in her childhood. This was like listening to her grandfather's stories all over again. Burma must
be a land full of them. Myths, perhaps, but myths that had a
way of resonating and revealing some inner truth.

A young girl appeared with a tray of tea things and laid
them on the table next to Maya. The old lady picked up the
teapot, lifting it high and accurately pouring the stream of
green-gold liquid into three tiny cups.

'So, can you tell me what happened to your chinthe?' Eva
asked. She had come all this way. She wanted to know the
whole story and so, of course, would her grandfather.

Maya's grandson spoke swiftly to his grandmother in Burmese. It didn't take much imagination to guess that he was
warning Maya not to tell.

Maya nodded. 'What you say is true, Ramon,' she told

him. 'But she is Lawrence's granddaughter and she deserves to know.'

'We have a tradition in our country to pass stories from generation to generation.' She turned to Eva. 'Drink your tea, my dear,' she said. 'And I will tell you what happened.'

CHAPTER 12

Mandalay, 1885.

For Suu Kyi, the Royal Palace in Mandalay in the centre of the walled city, a spread-eagled complex of red-roofed pavilions, towers and lush Royal Gardens, had always been the safest place in her world. She was an orphan, from the Shan states, and had been rescued and brought here to serve the Queen, purchased by the Queen's agents and brought up at the Palace, as was Nanda Li, another young maidservant of her own age. She could barely remember living anywhere else. The Royal Palace itself had been transported here and rebuilt thirty years ago, long before Suu Kyi was born. Four walls surrounded the citadel, and a moat deep and still. Their position seemed impenetrable.

Many were afraid of Queen Supayalat; she was small but had a fierce temper and there were those who said she had only become Queen because she had seen to it that all the rivals to her husband, King Thibaw's throne, seventy-nine princes all told, were wrapped in carpets to prevent the spillage of royal blood, bludgeoned to death and thrown in the nearest river. Perhaps this was true. But she loved the King, Suu Kyi could see that, and this impressed her greatly. She herself was slightly afraid of him; he looked very handsome in his royal sash and golden slippers, though she was aware that he was half-Shan which accounted for his high cheekbones and fine eyes. Mostly though, she kept her eyes downcast when he entered the room. Suu Kyi was humble and she was happy simply to serve. Most especially she loved to serve the two princesses aged one year and three. Suu Kyi was proud that no one else – and especially not Nanda Li – could deal with the Second Princess's paroxysms of rage as well as she could. And now the Queen was in her eighth month of pregnancy and there would be a third child. No one could be more delighted than she.

But even Suu Kyi was aware that something was changing. Although their palace was guarded at all four corners by sentries of the King's bodyguard, and uniformed soldiers were all around, the Queen was jittery. And besides, Suu Kyi could hear the guns, the distant boom and grumble of cannon.

They all knew the origin of the problem; it had been much talked-of. There had been a dispute with a British timber company about the amount of duty that was being paid (Queen Supayalat insisted they were trying to avoid paying duty altogether) and the company had complained to the British Governor in Rangoon. The Queen was in favour of levying a substantial fine on the company. They must not think that they could behave as they liked, that they were in charge of this country, she said to her maidservants, to the King, to the Court and to anyone else who would listen. But the King's ministers had advised otherwise. A line should be drawn under the entire affair and the matter of paying duty on the timber should be forgotten, to ensure that the British allowed the King and Queen to remain on the throne. *Allowed* them to remain on the throne? The Queen had ranted and railed. Who did they think they were? She refused to give in and the King had followed her lead as he always did. And now . . .

Suu Kyi knew that the British had crossed the border; they all knew. But every time the King or the Queen asked for news, they were told that all was going well for the Burmese soldiers, that, indeed, there had been another victory and that there was no reason to worry. Even so, they all were worrying, the Second Princess was being even more difficult than usual and did not want to play five stones with rubies with her sister. Because they had all heard what the Queen had said. 'Those are not our guns. And they are getting closer and closer.'

It wasn't long before they found out the truth. The Burmese army had, in fact, disintegrated and fled to the hills, the war had lasted only fourteen days, the Royal Family were now being kept here as prisoners by ministers thinking only of their own personal gain and the British would be arriving very soon, to take them into captivity. Suu Kyi was shocked. How could this be? Who were these British who seemed to have so much power that even the might of the Burmese Army could do nothing against them?

'They have superior weapons,' Nanda Li said. 'I overheard the King talking to one of his men. There are thousands of them, not just British but Indian too, many Indians. They have big guns and cannon. We can do nothing against such a force.'

Indians too, thought Suu Kyi. And yet there were so many Indians living here in Mandalay, she had seen them. How was it, she wondered, that they came to fight for another side?

Nanda Li rolled her eyes. 'India is part of the British Empire,' she snapped. 'Do you never hear anything? Do you know even less?'

Sure enough, only a day later, the British soldiers came to the fort and they began to loot it, leaving the gates of the citadel unguarded when they left. There was so much, they could not take everything. The Queen seemed to go into a trance, as if the looting of her palace and her possessions was not real, as if it could not be happening. And it was up to Suu Kyi to care for the princesses, to shield them from harm, to prevent them from seeing the worst of it.

But more was to come. When they saw the soldiers leave . . . When they saw the citadel unguarded for the very first time . . . Then the people came. Suu Kyi saw their faces. At first, they must have been surprised that it was possible, since entering the palace unbidden would normally be punished by execution. Then they became greedy. They arrived in a jumble and a frenzy. They ran bare-footed, clutching their *longyis* close to them, right into the women's quarters where the Queen, the princesses, Suu Kyi and the few other maid-servants who had not run away remained, bewildered and confused.

The princesses were both crying. Suu Kyi was trying to comfort them. The Queen, who because of her condition was supposed to be resting, simply lay on her royal couch and Nanda Li stood staring out of the window as if contemplating her next move.

Occasionally she shot a look of derision in Suu Kyi's direction. 'Why do you bother?' she hissed, when she could see the Queen was not listening. 'They are finished. Do you not see?'

But it was second nature to Suu Kyi. She loved the princesses and she would protect them with her life. Indeed, she could not imagine life without them, nor without Queen Supayalat for that matter, tyrannical and selfish though she could be. And besides, she, like Nanda Li, had no other family to go to. What choice did they have?

The noise from the mob increased until they could ignore it no longer. A man, a Burmese man, one of their people, had grabbed a rock and was trying to knock out the jewels from the jade-studded panels of the doors, someone else was throwing an offering box on the marble floor in an attempt to dislodge the gems within. And it was not all Burmese. There were many other nationalities apart from Indian living in the city of Mandalay and Suu Kyi could see some of Chinese and Thai origin also here in the chamber. But nationality was immaterial. They were all out for themselves. A woman was trying to dig jewels from the floor with the heel of her shoe, a child was even attempting to bite the rubies from the lid of a large, golden betel box with a lacquered dragon stand. People were grabbing what small objects they could, from decorated candelabra to jewelled hand mirrors, from filigree caskets to golden pitchers, using makeshift tools of rock or wood to gouge out the jewels from others. They were squabbling and fighting in the stifling heat, tearing things from each other's grasp. The beautiful wooden furniture, intricately carved cabinets and chests studded with precious jewels whose drawer handles were delicately moulded in the shape of elephant trunks and dragon tails, was being hacked to pieces. The walls of the chamber were tiled with clear and green glass and an oil lamp flamed, illuminating the carnage.

At first, the Queen continued to do nothing. She and the rest of them stayed in their candle-lit antechamber, and they listened helplessly to the raucous frenzy going on outside. Suu Kyi saw the Queen come out of the trance and begin to grind her teeth and look frantically from left to right. She knew that the Queen was not afraid; her face was purple with rage under the ivory *thanaka* face powder she wore.

She arose from her royal couch, made of teak and gold and studded with diamonds. And she stood in the doorway, next to the glass mosaic jade screen, her silk robes billowing around her. She was like a great ship in full sail. 'Get out!' she shrieked. 'How dare you come here like this? Go away! Get out!' And she shook her fist.

But what could she do against such a mob? Suu Kyi tried to hide the terrible sight from the princesses. Some of the looters had noticed Supayalat, some were clearly shocked to recognise their queen, and were bending and bowing into the reverential *shiko* that must always be afforded to royalty, some so low it looked like they were walking backwards. But even as they did this, others were dragging up the mat of silver and continuing to loot and steal from the Queen's chamber. Their supposed homage and respect meant nothing.

Before she had really thought about what she was doing, Suu Kyi leapt past the Queen and into the chamber where the people were rampaging and looting. 'The soldiers are coming back!' she yelled to the mob. 'Quick! Run! Soldiers are coming!'

Terror flamed briefly on the people's faces. They looked over their shoulders and then they ran. Fast and furious, they tumbled out of the glass-walled chamber as quickly as they had arrived, pushing and shoving to get through the tiny doorway, even dropping some of their booty in their haste.

The Second Princess was bawling. Her tiny bejewelled body was rigid and her fists were closed tight.

'Hush now.' Suu Kyi ran to her. She picked her up and held her close. 'Hush little one, for we shall be safe.' She crooned to her, she sang softly as if everything was not disintegrating around them. And she tried not to look at Nanda Li and the nasty sneer that seemed fixed on her arrogant face.

When the child was sleeping once more, Suu Kyi looked up to see the Queen standing beside her.

'Thank you, Suu Kyi,' she said, her eyes still angry. 'You have been very brave. But we cannot stop them. If these riches do not go to the people, then they will go to the British who are taking us prisoner.'

Suu Kyi nodded. She understood. She knew too that their

country housed the richest gem mines in the whole world and that the King and Queen were in possession, or had been, of a huge fortune in gemstones alone. It was their Royal Right and had been so throughout the Burmese dynasty.

'But we can gather up some things of our own.' With some difficulty the Queen reached down to a bag she was filling with her own personal jewels, necklaces of rubies and jade, rings of diamonds and gold and her own gold jewellery box with a lock and key. 'And these are for you.' From the bag she pulled two decorative chinthes. They were of the finest teak carving and their eyes shone.

'For me?' Suu Kyi could hardly speak. The Queen had never given her a gift before.

'For looking after the Second Princess so valiantly,' the Queen said. 'And for what you have done for us here today.' She nodded and bent as low as she was able. 'See here.' She demonstrated how skilfully they had been constructed. 'Look after these beasts and be careful who you choose to give them to,' she said. 'They may prove to be your security and your fortune. Use them well.'

Suu Kyi bowed as deeply as she could whilst still holding the sleeping princess. And it was when she arose that she saw it. The look on Nanda Li's face. It was a look of pure hatred and it made her shudder inside.

CHAPTER 13

Seattle.

'Seattle?' she'd echoed. 'But that's . . .'

'A long way away, yes,' he said grimly.

The United States. America.

'What did you tell them?' she'd asked him later, after they'd finished dinner, cleared up and gone to bed. It was king size, the duvet, goose-down, the sheets Egyptian cotton. Both of them were staring up at the ceiling. They were lying at least a foot apart. What would happen, Rosemary wondered, if she were to reach out for him?

'That I need time to think about it.' He glanced across at her. Without his glasses on he seemed naked, despite the cotton pyjamas he was wearing. 'To discuss it with my wife.'

'I see,' she murmured. All she could think was it seemed so far away.

Alex hiked himself up on one elbow. 'Rosemary, you hardly see your family,' he said.

'I know.'

'It's a great opportunity. I didn't think I'd ever get it at this stage.'

At this stage in his career, he meant. He was still only in his early fifties. But it was a young man's game.

'I know.'

He sighed. 'What do you want to do?'

That was three days ago and Rosemary wasn't any closer to giving him an answer. She filled the percolator with water and reached for the coffee beans. Did he want to go to Seattle? Did he want to uproot them and move to the US? She supposed that he did. Alec had always been ambitious, and she knew he'd always hoped to further advance his career, to be given a higher role in the company, to be a solution architect and actually in charge of designing interactive software rather than a senior developer. But she also knew that Alec was giving her some sort of choice. She had gone with him before, left the UK, moved to Copenhagen, followed that promise of a new start.

Rosemary switched on the grinder. She felt something painful in her chest. Was it regret?

She had never intended to leave her daughter behind. She had assumed – of course she had assumed – that when she decided to marry Alec and move to Copenhagen, Eva would come too. She was still only sixteen. Her place was with her mother. She could take her GCSEs in England and then finish her schooling in Copenhagen. And why shouldn't Rosemary marry Alec? After Nick's and then her mother's death, she was finally seizing a chance of some sort of happiness. And she had longed to get away. She had always loved West

Dorset. But now it stood for her marriage to Nick, her husband's death, the loss of her mother. As for her father . . . She was finding it hard to forgive him for those letters, for what had happened in Burma all those years ago before she was even born. She didn't want to be living in Dorset. Not anymore.

Rosemary switched off the machine and transferred the freshly ground coffee to the percolator, breathing in the rich, mellow fragrance that would always remind her of her honeymoon with Nick in the Cinque Terre of Italy; of the narrow streets and tall, colourful houses in the five mountainside villages; the scent of roasted coffee beans spilling out on to shady walkways and café terraces.

But there was also Eva. Transplanting her sixteen-year-old into a different lifestyle, with new opportunities, could only do her good, could only go some way towards healing the rift between them. That, at least, was what she had thought.

Rosemary screwed on the lid of the percolator and switched on the hob. She would never forget the day she came home from work and found Eva hunched and crying in her room.

'I don't want to go,' she had wept. 'I don't want to go.' Her dark hair tumbled, unruly as ever, over her shoulders. Her eyes were red and her lips swollen from her tears.

'To Copenhagen? But Eva, you'll soon make new friends. You'll go to a fantastic sixth-form college, have a great life, a much better time—'

'I've been talking to Grandpa.' Eva sniffed and hiccoughed. 'He says if I want to, I can go and live with him instead.'

Rosemary stared at her. Her mind was a blank. Where had she gone wrong? 'You don't want to come with me to Copenhagen?' she whispered.

'No.' And Eva had looked up at her with sad, dark eyes that were such an echo of Nick's, it almost broke her heart.

'You're sixteen,' she heard herself saying in a cool voice she hated. 'It's your decision. It's up to you.'

Rosemary had never forgiven her father for giving Eva the option. It hadn't been his place to. First Burma and now this, she had thought. Of course he'd been thinking of himself, as he always did. He didn't want to be apart from his precious granddaughter, he couldn't bear the thought of her living in another country. So why not stop it from happening? Rosemary was shocked at how bitter she felt towards him.

She stood by the stove and waited for the coffee to brew. She could have still changed her mind, of course; she didn't have to go. But she didn't. She told herself Eva would change *her* mind, but she hadn't. Once Eva had taken her GCSEs and it became clear that she was staying in Dorset whatever her mother did, then Rosemary had married Alec and moved to Copenhagen.

'It's not so far,' Alec had reassured her. 'We can come back for weekends as often as you like.'

And they had, at first. Rosemary had even wondered if they had more chance of rediscovering some mother and daughter bond if she was away. But that hadn't happened either. Wishful thinking, she supposed.

The coffee began to percolate and Rosemary put some

milk on to heat. She had to face it. As every year went by, she and Eva had become more and more estranged. Until it seemed to be too late.

By the time Alec came in from work, Rosemary had made a decision.

When they'd first moved here, she'd looked for a job as a legal secretary; that was what she knew, but the system was very different in Denmark and instead, she'd surprised herself by taking a part-time job in a local bookshop. She often used to drift in there to pick up copies of paperbacks and she had got to know the owner. But after a while, he admitted that he couldn't afford to keep her on, and so she left, feeling slightly guilty.

Alec had suggested that she take a break from the workplace. He earned more than enough for the both of them, he reminded her. She'd had a hard life working full time as a single parent, losing her husband so young. 'I want to spoil you a little,' he'd said. 'I want you to relax and take a rest. Have some me-time.'

And so she had. Over the years she'd got involved with various voluntary organisations: Stroke Awareness, in memory of Nick; Copenhagen Youth Project Support for disadvantaged kids and the Library Foundation. It took time and energy, but gave Rosemary a sense of self-worth. She was doing something. But now . . .

'I'm going back home for a while,' she told Alec. She

poured him out a bourbon with ice so that she wouldn't have to look at him as she said it.

She felt him exhale. 'Home?' And she heard the desolation in his voice.

'I need to see them both,' she said. She handed him the drink. Eva was in Burma but she would be back in a couple of weeks.

He downed it in one, never taking his eyes from her face. 'And America?'

'I don't know, Alec.' How much time did her father have left? She needed to make her peace with him.

'You don't know about me?' he asked her. He took off his glasses and rubbed his tired eyes. It made him seem so vulnerable somehow. 'Or you don't know about America?'

Rosemary didn't reply. She closed her eyes. All she knew for sure, at this moment in time, was that she must go back to where she had begun.

CHAPTER 14

'But that is only part of the story.' Maya took a deep and shuddering breath that seemed to come from the core of her tiny body.

Immediately, her grandson Ramon laid a gentle hand on hers. He spoke softly in Burmese, all his anger seeming to have evaporated. Eva was surprised at his tenderness. This was a different side to the man, one she hadn't expected, and she was glad that Maya had him there to look after her.

But as he turned to Eva, his gaze hardened. 'My grandmother, she is tired,' he said. 'She must rest.'

'Of course.' Though Eva was aching to know the rest of the story. She had hoped to discover the heart of the Burmese tales from her childhood, the force behind them that seemed to have been absorbed into her very being. And she hadn't been disappointed. This story of Maya's was of routs and British imperialism, of precious jewels and royal shenanigans going right back to the final Burmese dynasty. Did her grandfather know all this? If not, Eva couldn't wait to tell him. Though he would be devastated to hear that the other chinthe had been stolen. She looked again at the photographs on the wall. 'The King and Queen?' she asked.

Maya nodded. 'Thibaw and Supayalat,' she said. 'And that is the Lion Throne.'

Eva got up to take a closer look. Unless she was very much mistaken, the throne was made entirely of gold. She looked at the other photograph. It was of an elderly woman sitting very upright in her chair, her eyes fixed with a great sense of stillness on the camera taking the picture.

'My grandmother, Suu Kyi,' Maya murmured. 'Servant-girl to the Queen. She told me the story when she gave me the two chinthes.' She turned to speak to her grandson in Burmese.

'She says I should take you to the National Kandawgyi Gardens for sunset,' he said. 'It is two-hundred-and-forty acres of botanical gardens and forest reserves. It is very beautiful there. Meanwhile, she will rest.'

'There's really no need for you to do that,' Eva said stiffly, since he hardly seemed enamoured at the prospect. And that was an awful lot of acres. 'I don't expect you to organise my sightseeing for me.' This came out more harshly than she'd intended and she noted the flicker of surprise and what might have been amusement cross his features.

'It has been decided.' He bowed his head. 'Then we will return here for dinner.'

'I see.' They seemed to have all her movements planned. Her first instinct was to refuse, to make her own arrangements. For a moment she thought of her mother's remarriage and the decision she'd made to stay in Dorset. Was that the reason they had grown apart? It would have meant leaving all her friends and her beloved grandfather. She couldn't do it, hadn't wanted to do it. Not even for the mother she had lost so many years before.

But this was Burma. Eva must respect their hospitality. She would be gracious and hopefully she'd then hear the rest of the story. 'That sounds lovely,' she said. 'Thank you.'

Maya beamed and rose to her feet. 'Ramon will look after you,' she said.

Eva glanced across at him doubtfully. But as Maya clasped Eva's hands in hers, she felt again the intensity of the old lady's emotion. 'I will see you in a few hours,' she said. She looked deep into her eyes, and Eva felt the potency of her gaze, her spirituality, she supposed. And she could imagine her as a young woman, as her grandfather must first have seen her. She could perfectly understand how they had come to fall in love.

On the drive to Kandawgyi Gardens, Ramon provided her with water and fruit magicked up by one of the girls in the house. Eva longed to ask about them all, find out who was who, but Ramon kept up a polite, detailed and impersonal commentary on Pyin Oo Lwin and their surroundings as he drove smoothly and confidently along the leafy roads, and so she didn't get the chance. He was clearly just doing his duty. And to find out anything more personal, she'd have to wait till later.

'When did Burma become known as Myanmar?' she asked him as he turned the car into the sweeping entrance to the gardens. 'Was it part of the move forward, of independence?'

'1989,' he said. 'Though it is more of a return to our cultural roots. It was the name originally given to our country by Marco Polo. It dates from the thirteenth century. Before that . . .' He raised a dark eyebrow. 'It is more complicated.'

Eva could well imagine. She had read something of the Indian and Cambodian tribes, the influx of early Thai and Tibetan people on the country. And later there were Britain, China and Japan, all getting in on the act. Even now, the hill tribes were separate and independent and there was much infighting. Which all explained the eclectic mix of races and nationalities on the streets of Myanmar. And some of the troubles that the country had been through, she supposed.

Eva looked around her as they drove towards the parking area. On the one hand, the planting was very British: pansies, petunias and roses arranged in neat rectangular beds. But on the other hand, the vast, rolling landscape of the park had retained its oriental feel, with bamboo thickets, palm trees and red pagodas.

Ramon pulled up in a parking bay and they got out of the car. He was only an inch or two taller than her, Eva realised, as they stood side by side for a moment, his body lean with not an ounce of spare fat. And he had an air of self-possession about him that intrigued her. Was he as calm and collected as he seemed? Or was he just good at pretending? She sensed he didn't want to be here, sensed he resented her intrusion into their lives. And yet . . .

'The pagodas house many collections,' he informed her, as he strode towards the lake. 'We will see the orchids. There are three hundred different varieties. And all collected from Myanmar forests.'

Goodness. She followed more slowly, not wanting to be hurried.

The orchids were stunning, row upon row of every stock and colour imaginable, each one with a glorious scent of honey. Eva took lots of photos, even managing to snatch a shot of Ramon bending to examine a vivid purple flower with an appreciative look in his eyes. He clearly enjoyed the beauty of nature. He glanced up at her though with a glower of irritation.

'You don't like the British very much, do you?' she asked him at last. Unless it was just her. Elsewhere, any mention of being English had created huge excitement among the Burmese. They immediately asked a multitude of questions about London, blithely assuming that anyone British must live there, and, rather bizarrely, premiership football, over which they became as animated as they did at any mention of 'our lady', Aung San Suu Kyi.

Ramon shot her an unfathomable look from under his dark brows. 'That is not so,' he said. He squared his shoulders. 'My father was English, of course.'

'Of course.' She looked at his face, the fullness of his lips, the unexpected green of his eyes. She'd thought as much. And she noted the tense he had used. *Was*. Well, she knew how that felt. 'Your father . . . ?' She trod carefully.

'Is dead.' He swung down the next path and, again, Eva had to hurry to catch up with him. He was so . . . well, blunt.

'I'm sorry,' she said. 'What happened to him?'

He was ahead of her and so she couldn't see his expression. 'He was a strong man.' His voice was bitter. 'But he died very suddenly. A massive heart attack, they said.'

'I see.' He was clearly very upset and she felt the impulse to reach out to him, but he was walking much too fast and she didn't think he'd appreciate it somehow.

They had left the orchids and now were heading back towards the lake, passing flower beds of petunias and yellow phlox. The scent of blackcurrant and freshly mown grass seemed to waft on the air. Very British, Eva thought. And as for Ramon's father, a strong man he might have been, but, unlike her own father, he was living in a country only a few steps away from being regarded as third world, one which had not yet benefited from advances in medical technology. Not only did it lack good hospitals but there was extreme poverty and hardship. Thanks to Western sanctions. Thanks to the repressive government. But hopefully, things were now changing.

'My father died when I was young as well,' she told him as they walked under the thicket of stripy bamboo.

He paused and stared at her, a sudden compassion in his eyes. 'I am sorry,' he said.

So was Eva. She had always wondered what it would be like to have a father who took you out bicycling in summer or tobogganing in the snow. Who was always available with a listening ear or a hug, or a lift back home when you'd stayed out late. She was lucky though, she'd had her grandfather.

Without him . . . Well, she couldn't think about where she would be without him.

'What about your mother?' she asked Ramon. Maya's daughter. They had reached the wooden bridge and at last he slowed and stood looking down into the water. She followed his gaze. Brightly spotted koi carp were meandering through the gentle ripples, every so often coming to the surface, mouths gaping open for food. Eva looked back at him. He seemed miles away. And he still hadn't answered her question.

'She died two years ago,' he said at last. 'She had leukaemia. It was a great sadness to us all.'

This time Eva touched his arm in a gesture of condolence. So he had lost his mother too . . . She thought of her own mother, just as lost in her own way. And now, by coming here, had she damaged their relationship still further? Or could she somehow find a way to become close to her again?

'Was your mother Maya's eldest daughter?' Eva asked gently. Maya must have married after the war, sometime after Lawrence had left the country. Had she known that Lawrence wasn't coming back?

But Ramon was eying her rather strangely. 'My mother was the only child my grandparents had,' he said at last.

And she had married Ramon's father. Like her mother before her, she had fallen in love with an Englishman. As if, Eva thought, it were in the genes. It was ironic. So the British had stayed, as it were, in the family, despite the fact that Lawrence had left them.

In the distance, Eva saw a pair of black swans with red beaks make their graceful way from the other side of the lake, gliding effortlessly side by side. A thought came randomly into her head. Wasn't it swans who mated for life? It hadn't been like that for Lawrence and Maya though, had it?

'You want the truth?' Ramon suddenly swung around to face her.

She jumped. 'Well, yes.'

'The truth is that I envy you,' he said.

'Me?'

'I envy the British and all you Westerners.' He turned away to stare back at the lake. His slick, dark hair hung in a wing across his forehead and he flicked it roughly back with his fingers.

'For what?' Although she could guess.

'For your freedom,' he said. 'It is so easy for you to come and go. To Europe, to America, to Asia. To trade, to speak your mind, to follow your beliefs.'

'But things are changing here,' Eva said gently. She was aware how hard it had been. The restrictions, the endless bureaucracy, the lack of civil and human rights. And she could only imagine what it must have been like to grow up in Myanmar with constant fear, intimidation and poverty.

'It is a slow process.' He met her gaze. 'And sometimes much slower than our government would have people believe.' He led the way from the bridge and back to the main path, easing off the pace, walking now in a more leisurely rhythm.

'You'd like to travel then?' she asked him.

'It is what I have always dreamed of.' His words were simple. But they said so much.

'Then you will,' Eva assured him.

He shrugged. 'I am one of the more fortunate ones,' he said. 'I come from a privileged family. For others . . .' He let this thought trail.

'But we should not talk of such things,' Eva murmured. Klaus had warned her about talking politics to the Burmese. They could get into trouble if anyone were to find out; the government still did all they could to limit what they called unnecessary contact between foreigners and the Burmese people. And apparently everyone was watched at some time while they were in Myanmar. Could that be true? It was hard to believe, here in these lush and well-manicured gardens. But the journalist she'd met on the plane coming over had told her he'd called himself a teacher on his visa application. Writers, he had said with a wry smile, are considered rather dangerous. So maybe it was true after all.

Ramon said nothing, just looked away towards the distant trees. They walked on beside the lake.

'And my grandfather?' Eva asked him.

'What about him?' But she could see that she'd touched a raw nerve.

'You think that he just left your grandmother after the war, don't you? You think he just went back to England without a second thought. That he didn't care.'

Ramon seemed about to say something. But he stopped himself. 'It was a long time ago,' he said instead.

'But he did care.' It was important to Eva that he believed her. 'There were repercussions for both our families. But whatever happened between them, he did care.'

Ramon held her gaze for a long moment before finally he looked away. 'We must find a place to watch the sunset,' he said. 'Or my grandmother will never forgive me.'

As the sun dipped lower in the sky, he led the way to a stylish café made entirely from teak, where they sat on the open terrace with a view of the lake and gardens. To their left, a group of students lounged under a broad leafed horse-chestnut tree and one of them started strumming his guitar. A couple of the girls sang softly as he accompanied them. It was a Bob Dylan song, 'Most Likely You Go Your Way', Eva recognised it; her mother had often played it and, for a second, she was transported from this landscape and back to Dorset, England and her mother's grief. 'Most Likely You Go Your Way'. Despite the heat, Eva shivered.

Ramon ordered soft drinks, which turned out to be a delicious cocktail of pineapple, ginger and lime, and they sat, more amicably now, watching the sky deepen from pale blue into dark grey and orange as the sun dropped laconically behind the distant forest of silver oaks. In the distance, a peacock strutted proudly towards his mate and some golden pheasants flew up into the trees.

'Where is it that you want to go?' Eva asked him, thinking of the lyrics of the Dylan song and of what he'd already told her.

'Many places.' He sipped his drink. 'I intend to expand my

business and increase my exports. It is not just a question of survival. I want to be successful.' He looked at her suddenly, sharply. 'Many of my countrymen, they are not ambitious. But me, I want to travel and I want to experience my father's world.'

Eva thought of her own father, the man she had hardly known. She had inherited his dark hair and eyes. But not the shape of his face, according to Maya. Eva sipped her fruit cocktail. She had a photograph of him taken by her grandfather when she was a child. He was sitting on a wooden bench in the garden. It was late springtime, the yellow forsythia was in bloom behind him and the roses on the trellis were tight orange buds. But what Eva loved about the photo was his expression, he was clearly unaware the photo was being taken and he was staring towards the lawn with such a look of contentment. That told Eva a lot about him and his life. Their life. Because her grandfather had told her what he was looking at – his wife and daughter sitting on the lawn making a daisy chain, and Eva had that photograph too. They were a pair. Whatever else had happened in her world, those photographs said it all.

With some effort, Eva brought herself back to the present. 'And what is your business?' she asked Ramon. She could see why he had been a little hostile at first. He had been through a lot and he felt protective towards his grandmother; there was nothing wrong with that. She had seen another side of him at Maya's house and the lakeside and she felt a bond with him because they had both, in different ways, lost their parents. And she liked the fact that he wanted more.

'I make furniture.' He sat up straighter, with pride. 'Quality furniture. From teak wood. The business was begun by my father when he first came to Myanmar. Everything is handcrafted. We are very proud of that.'

'Teak?' Eva's senses tingled. Could that be just a coincidence? Although she supposed it wasn't so strange. Her grandfather had come here to Burma to work in the teak industry because teak was something the country was rich in. And Ramon's father had no doubt come here for the same reasons. Both men had met a Burmese woman and fallen in love. But Eva's grandfather had left and Ramon's father had stayed.

As they finished their drinks, they watched the sun reddening, strands of pink and amber threading the sky around. Sunset in Asia. What could be more stunning?

'There she goes.' Ramon turned to her as the sun finally dipped behind the trees. 'Shall we leave, too?'

She smiled and took the hand he offered to help her to her feet. A craftsman's hand, she thought. Well shaped, slightly calloused from working with wood. 'Thanks for bringing me here,' she said. 'I don't have long to look around. Tomorrow, I have to get back to Mandalay.'

'Tomorrow is another day,' he said. And again, he gave her such a straightforward and thoughtful look that she struggled to understand. 'Do you think you were right to come here, Eva?'

She stared back at him. Right? What did he mean, right? Of course, he knew nothing about her job here. He hadn't asked. He had assumed, no doubt that she was just another tourist. 'Are you worried about me upsetting your grand-mother?' she asked. Though she had the feeling that despite appearances, Maya was mentally very strong.

'It is not just my grandmother to think of.'

'Then who?' she asked. Or what?

But he just shook his dark head. 'The past is long gone,' he said. 'And is it right to open the box? That is what you must ask yourself.'

'The box is already open, Ramon,' Eva said. 'It's too late.'

Lawrence replaced the telephone receiver. He was rather confused, what with all this coming and going. He wasn't sure
what was happening. But it would all come clear. It usually
did.

Had Eva found her, his Maya? Was she still alive, as he
hoped? He had just wanted her to know. It was all such a
long time ago and of course there was no need to send any of
those letters. There never had been any need, they were for
Lawrence and his peace of mind. But he wanted her to know
what he still felt for her, what he had never stopped feeling
for her, and the chinthe would tell her that more than words.
Maya and Burma. They were entwined in his heart, always
had been. He'd never been able to separate the two.

Mandalay, 1937.
Lawrence tried to tell Maya something of what he felt for
Burma when they met again the following afternoon. They
were walking along the downtown streets of Mandalay to her
father's house. She had invited him there for dinner and he
appreciated that this was an honour. He didn't tell anyone at
the club where he was going, though Scottie probably sus-

pected. He didn't want to hear any of the jokes about native tarts and all the rest of it. It was commonplace to have a Burmese mistress, whether a man was married or no; Burma still wasn't as comfortable for colonial wives as India, with its longstanding *Memsahib* tradition. But Lawrence didn't care about all that. All he knew was that he didn't have long. Tomorrow, he must return to camp.

'You think we are a very simple race,' she teased. 'Living so much of our time outside and close to nature. Lacking many material things.'

'Is that so bad?' He did think that. But he'd tried to express it in a positive way. Spiritual contentment, people with smiles on their faces, with warmth. And now, once again, she was laughing at him.

She gave him a look. 'Wait till you meet my father,' she said.

Lawrence had been expecting their house to be quite basic – nearly all the houses he'd seen here had been quite basic – but in fact it was not. It was simple in construction, yes, but made of wood and bamboo with a wide verandah and a charming carved wooden frieze dividing ground and first floor to the eye from the outside. It was beautifully furnished too with cushions, embroidered tapestries and silk hangings, cane furniture and vibrant rugs strewn on the floor. The windows and doors, shaded with bamboo blinds and wooden shutters, which led into the front living room had all been flung open and a man in his mid-forties, or thereabouts, was lounging on a bamboo reclining chair, his dark head resting on a red satin pillow. There was, surprisingly, a black piano by the far wall. And the scent of burning incense oil wafted through the room.

Maya addressed him in Burmese. Then she turned back towards Lawrence. 'This is my father,' she said. 'And this is Lawrence.' And then she disappeared to prepare the food.

Her father got to his feet and nodded. 'How are you?' he asked. 'I can offer you a drink, perhaps?' He was polite, but not warm.

Lawrence accepted a beer but then felt embarrassed when his host only drank the tea Maya brought out for him a few minutes later. Of course, Buddhists didn't drink and Lawrence had already noted the shrine, the image of the Buddha, the fresh flowers in the room. Somehow, drinking when they weren't similarly indulging, made him feel a bit of a fool. It was that sense, again, that the Burmese always knew more and felt more than they'd let on. What did they really think about it all? He had a feeling he was about to find out.

But it wasn't until after they had eaten a simple meal of river fish, rice and a thin but spicy consommé that Maya's father finally opened up.

'Why did you come to Burma?' he asked Lawrence. And then before he could reply, 'I am not talking about the business you are in, I know about that. What I want to know is: do you mean to make it your home?'

'I don't know, sir.' Lawrence decided honesty was the best policy with this man. 'I wanted to see something of the world, I suppose. And I love your country, you can be sure of that.'

'You love the country?' he asked. His black eyes shone. 'Or you love being a master in our country?'

Lawrence considered this. Once again, Maya had disappeared, leaving them to talk. He guessed that she'd known what would be said. Maybe it was even a test. She had said it wouldn't be easy and talking to her yesterday about the last King and Queen of Burma had at least given him a taste of what might be to come. 'I see your point,' he said. 'Though in every job there's at least one master and at least one worker, isn't that so?' Maya had told him that her father worked as a broker in the rice business, and that his business was successful. Lawrence knew too that he had dealings with the British from time to time.

Maya's father nodded. 'This is true,' he said. 'But do not underestimate us. We know who is really in charge. And there is an old Burmese proverb: wise man's anger never comes out.'

Lawrence shrugged. Of course there must be resentment. But the situation in this country was hardly his fault. 'The legacy of the British Empire is not my responsibility,' he said. It sounded more pompous than he'd intended. He wanted the man to like him, but he had to be honest.

'But you are part of it,' the other man shot in.

'I am.' And proud to be British, Lawrence thought, despite everything he'd seen here. He'd talked to Scottie last night about the imperialist rout and now he knew that although the row had to all intents and purposes been about teak, the facts were more complicated. For many years the Burmese dynasty had simply been unable to keep control over its warring factions. Some might say (and Scottie did, rather loudly after several whiskies) that the British had been compelled to step in. That it had been almost a favour for them to take control out of the hands of those who simply couldn't cut the mustard. 'And then, of course,' he'd said to Scottie, 'there was the wealth we were taking from Burma – the jewels, the teak . . .' 'Ah yes,' Scottie had replied. 'Well, no man will do something for nothing, old chap. Fair dos.'

'The work's hard,' Lawrence told Maya's father. He hadn't signed up for this job to get rich quick. It was not a job for an ambitious man, far from it. 'And believe me, I'm not afraid to get my hands dirty.'

Maya's father smiled for the first time. 'I believe that you are not,' he conceded. 'And you must excuse me for speaking my mind.'

He continued speaking his mind for the next hour and a half. He talked of what he wanted for Burma: independence and personal freedom for the people. Yes, he knew that there had been considerable unrest between the hill tribes for centuries; yes, he understood that the British Empire was not a tyrannical master. But it was still a master.

'The British have brought some progress to your country, surely?' Lawrence asked. He was thinking of the law and order, the schools, the roads, the hospitals. It wasn't all bad. Even Maya had admitted that before the British came, the Burmese had had no idea of how to manage the elephants and the logging industry.

Maya's father took a cigarette from a lacquered box on the table and offered the box to Lawrence. 'Perhaps they have,' he conceded. 'But did we ask for such modern progress? Did we want it? Or was the giver thinking more of the people from your country who now live here? They would insist, I am sure, on not living in a slum. They are, I believe, the ones who benefit most from the progress you mention.' His lip curled. 'When you give without being asked,' he added, 'should you always expect gratitude and thanks? Should you expect some sort of payment too? Change is not always a good thing.'

Lawrence couldn't answer this question. He had never looked at it that way before.

'So what *has* our country paid? What have we given in exchange for this progress?'

Lawrence considered, but he wasn't sure what to say. Did he mean the teak? Did he mean the rice paddy fields? Both were a rich source of income for British companies, such as the one which employed Lawrence. Was that what he meant by payment?

'We have given our culture.' Maya's father nodded. 'We have given our freedom. Our natural riches. And we have given away our right to rule our own country.'

Lawrence wasn't sure that he could deny this. He almost

wished Scottie were here to make it all plain. 'I understand what you are saying,' he said. 'But—'

'And there are many much younger and more energetic than me,' Maya's father went on, 'who are determined to see some change of their own.'

'How will they go about it?' Lawrence enquired mildly, wondering what he was getting into. And where the hell was Maya?

'I am sure that they will try the peaceful way first,' he said. He inhaled deeply, blowing out the smoke in a perfect ring. 'After that, who knows?'

When Maya eventually re-entered the room, the talk turned to other things and very soon her father said goodnight and left them. But when he did, Lawrence was heartened by the warmth with which he shook his hand. Although British and a foreigner, perhaps he had, after all, passed that test.

'Your father's house is very fine,' Lawrence said to her. He indicated the silk hangings and the vibrant tapestries.

'Thank you,' she said. 'I embroidered the tapestries myself.'

'Did you, by Jove?' Lawrence took a closer look at the silver, gold and red threaded silk on black velvet. There was a depiction of a dragon and another which was a landscape with a river, a sampan and a house built on stilts. But the one that really caught his eye was of a golden temple with two silver chinthes guarding the gate, their eyes glowing red like fire. The tapestries were the work of a skilled needlewoman, he realised. The touch was so delicate.

Maya came to stand very close to him. He could smell the scent of coconut oil, feel the warmth permeating from her skin. 'So, do you still wish to know the daughter,' she said softly, 'now that you have met the father?'

He smiled. 'I do.'

'Then would you like to stay the night?' she asked.

He blinked in surprise. 'Here?'

'Yes.'

'With you?'

'Of course.'

'Maya . . .' He wanted it more than he could say. But . . . 'I can't promise you anything,' he said. Though the words stuck in his throat. Because he wanted to promise her things. Things that he had promised no woman. Already, he wanted to promise her the earth.

'I am not asking for your promises,' she said.

'And your father?'

She smiled. 'He does not want them either.'

That wasn't quite what he had meant. 'But—'

'Ssh.' She put her finger to his lips. 'My father is not like other men. You will discover.'

'Then . . .'

She wound her arms around his neck. They felt warm and surprisingly strong. She lifted her face to his. Her sleek black hair fell back from her face, revealing tiny and perfect ear lobes. 'Sometimes, there is no need for words,' she whispered.

And as she led him to her bedroom, as she untied her *longyi* and allowed the scarlet fabric to fall around her feet, as she came to him and he held her in his arms, slender, supple and warmer than he could ever have dreamt . . . Lawrence realised that she was right.

CHAPTER 16

By the time they returned from the Gardens, Maya was rested and dinner had been prepared by a few of the younger women, under Maya's direction. She wanted to give Eva something simple but traditional, so she had chosen her special fish curry, the chicken with peanuts and a refreshing and spicy salad. She would serve these with *hin-jo*, *balachaung* and other accompaniments.

'What happened to your grandmother after the rout?' Eva asked her as they ate. 'Did she stay with the King and Queen?'

Maya smiled at her enthusiasm for the story. This girl could not wait, could she, to find out everything? She served her some of the curry and salad and thought back to her grandmother's old, brown face, her liquid eyes, her gentle voice as she told Maya what had happened all those years ago. She thought of other things too, of her grandmother's dark coiled hair which smelled of the coconut oil she poured over it once a month to keep it glossy and supple, a tradition Maya had continued with her own. Her grandmother, Suu Kyi, had washed Maya's hair too, when her mother was sick, washed it with tree bark, lemon and tamarind rind to create a giant lather and hair that was squeaky clean and smelled of the garden of paradise. Her grandmother's hands massaging her scalp, the scent of the spices . . . Maya could close her eyes and still smell it to this day. She sighed. 'Yes, she stayed with them.'

'And were they kept prisoner by the British?' Eva seemed outraged. She was looking very pretty tonight, Maya thought, tall and elegant in her simple blouse and long skirt, her skin slightly flushed from the heat and fresh air. Her hair too was dark and thick and it hung loose over her slim shoulders.

Maya tasted a little of the chicken. She remembered the details of the story very clearly for it had had a profound effect on her. Her grandmother had told her that the King had tried to sell certain jewels and possessions and that the British guards had found out, insisted he was being cheated and promptly appropriated everything of value that the Royal Family owned. But perhaps she should not tell the girl all these things. 'They were taken to India,' she said. 'And it is true that they were not free to come and go.'

'And your grandmother, Suu Kyi? Did she go to India too?' Her eyes were dark, not like Lawrence's eyes of clear sky-blue. Nevertheless, she had the shape of his face, the slant of his cheekbones. Maya had seen it, felt it. She had a certain look about her. And an honesty. Maya liked that.

'Yes, she did. Later, she was told she could return here . . .' Maya laid down her fork. These days she did not eat so much; her appetite was small. She was often tired too, she lacked the energy for long conversations and she needed help to prepare meals such as this one which once she would have loved to cook alone. 'But she did not return, not then.' She was loyal to the Queen and to the princesses. They had lost so much already.

'It must have been so hard for the King and Queen,' Eva murmured. 'After what they had been used to.'

'It was.' The girl was imaginative too. And Maya remembered making exactly the same observation to her grandmother. 'The Queen expected the old Burmese ways to still be part of her life,' she said. 'The reverence, the *shiko-ing*, the respect. But everything changed and most people in the royal entourage left before very long.'

Ramon dished out more food to Eva and offered some to his grandmother. She shook her head. But she accepted the glass of water he poured for her.

'What about the other servant girl?' Eva asked as Maya had known she would. 'What about Nanda Li? Did she leave too?'

'Not at first.' Maya frowned so as to remember more clearly every detail of what she had been told. 'But Queen Supayalat continued to prefer Suu Kyi and Nanda Li grew very bitter. She was lazy too. Often, she refused to serve her Queen and one day, the Queen simply sent her away.'

'And that was the last Suu Kyi saw of her?' Eva asked. She had a healthy appetite. Lawrence too had always eaten well; his job had been physically demanding of course. Maya had often wondered how he had managed during the war. Some of the men she saw after it was over had lost much weight. They were so thin, you could see their protruding bones.

'If only,' growled Ramon.

Maya saw Eva look across at him, surprised. There was some tension between these two, she could feel it, though she did not know the cause. Ramon was stubborn of course, very loyal and sometimes prickly like a wild bush on the plain. And Lawrence's granddaughter did not know the whole truth. Should she tell her? Maya had not yet decided. To tell Eva was to tell Lawrence. She did not have so much time left. But she would have to give it more thought.

'No, it was not the last time,' she said. 'The Royal Family were moved to Ratnagiri, many miles south of Bombay. They remained in exile, stripped of all power. But the people who looked after their interests were not always unkind.' She remembered what her grandmother had told her of the official's wife who had befriended her grandmother and made it her business to try and find a husband for Suu Kyi. She hadn't succeeded, but she had eventually persuaded her to return to Burma. There were new servants now, the Queen had become cantankerous and difficult, the princesses had grown and no longer needed her. The official's wife was of Indian origin but she had family in Rangoon who would give Suu Kyi work. 'I am giving you a chance of freedom,' she had urged her. 'You must take it.'

Suu Kyi had gone to the Queen and asked for her blessing. 'Go,' the Queen had told her. 'Go while you can. I would go myself, if I could. And, please God, my daughters will return to Burma themselves one day.'

Maya told Eva this part of the story.

'So she returned here,' murmured Eva.

'Yes, she did. The family she worked for moved to Mandalay,' Maya told her. 'My grandmother met my grandfather there, and she also met again with Nanda Li.'

The two families had had little contact. Maya remembered as a girl seeing Nanda Li's son and his wife in the bazaar, her mother ushering her quickly away. And she remembered the man's dark scheming eyes too, eyes that he had passed on to his own children, Maya's contemporaries, and on even beyond this. The family had grown in power and wealth, but their reputation went before them.

'One day, when I was a girl of sixteen,' Maya said, 'my grandmother gave me the pair of chinthes. And she told me the story of the rout of the last King and Queen of Burma, just as I have told it to you, my child.' She nodded. 'She told me to treasure them, and she warned me to keep them together for the sake of spiritual harmony. She told me that they would keep me safe and that the gift was the most special gift, that I should remember that.'

'But you gave one of them to my grandfather.'

The girl, Eva, looked so innocent sitting there. Maya's heart went out to her. 'Yes, I gave one to your grandfather,' she said. 'When he was about to go to war.'

'Before you leave, I have something I must give you.' That is what she had told him. And she had withdrawn the teak chinthe from the faded red Shan bag she carried over her shoulder. She passed it, almost reverentially, to him. It meant so much.

'What's this, my love?'

But she could tell that he knew. Everyone who had lived in her country knew the role played by the chinthes. They protected, they guarded, they kept from harm. Traditionally, they guarded the temple. But they had been given to Maya's grandmother because she had guarded the princesses. And now their strength was needed again. 'It is all I can give you.'

'And yet I have brought you nothing.' He frowned.

With her eyes, she told him that no, he was mistaken, he had given her everything.

He held the chinthe up to the lamp and looked into its red eyes. 'And where is his partner?' he asked softly.

'I will keep that one with me.' She bowed her head. 'They belong together. I hope and pray that he will bring you back to me.' It was the first time she had said this. No promises. That was what she had always said before. Nothing about belonging. Nothing about forever.

He dropped the chinthe into his backpack. 'I will take him with me wherever I go.'

Maya smiled to herself. If only he knew. But better he did not know perhaps.

'Many people in Burma bury their treasures,' she said. 'It may be that when you go to war, you will have to bury him too. If you do . . .' she smiled. 'You must remember where and mark the spot, my love.'

Gently, he held her face between his two hands. 'But I will never bury our love, Maya,' he said.

'Nor I.' She looked into his blue eyes. 'I will remember it for all of my days.'

He stroked her hair. 'I will come back.'

She put a finger to his lips. 'Whatever you do, my love,' she said. 'I will understand.'

She watched him go with his precious cargo slung over one shoulder. 'Keep him safe for me,' she whispered to the chinthe.

Later that night, after dinner, her father had grasped hold of her arm. 'Mya?'

'Father?'

'Where is the other chinthe?' He pointed up at the shrine where one lonely animal guarded the image of the Buddha who was, as he should be, placed higher than anything else in the room on top of a sandalwood box.

'I have given it away,' she said.

'Given it away?' He let out a curse. 'How could you give it away? We may need that, when . . . when . . .'

She put her arms around him. She knew that her father, for all his bravado, was frightened too. The war was getting closer. They were all in danger. But she would far rather have the chinthe guarding Lawrence, than have the pair confiscated by the Chinese or Japanese.

'He needs it more,' she whispered.

'So.' He looked mournful. 'You have given it to your Englishman?'

'I have.'

'Then you are a fool.' He sighed, ran his fingers through his hair.

'It was mine to give,' Maya remonstrated softly. 'My grandmother gave me the pair.'

'I know. But still, it is a family legacy.'

'I have respected the manner in which it should be given,' she told him, love giving her a stubbornness she hadn't known she possessed. 'And I believe that it will come back to our family one day.'

He looked up at the shrine. Shook his head. 'Does he know what it is?'

'No. But he knows what it means.'

He patted her shoulder. 'You must really love this man, my daughter,' he said. 'He must be your life.'

'He is,' said Maya. And that was the truth.

The rest of them were quiet as they listened to the remainder of her story. Maya wiped a tear from her eye.

'And what happened after the war?' Eva asked softly.

Maya could see that the girl was deeply moved. 'After the war, I kept my chinthe safe in the shrine in the house in Mandalay,' she said. 'I always felt that the other would return.' She smiled at Eva. 'One way or another.' Though she had never dreamt that it would be like this. That Lawrence's granddaughter would come from England and bring it back to her. It meant so much to her that he had done this. And it told her a great deal. If only her dear father had known that giving the chinthe to Lawrence before he went away to war, had in fact guaranteed the safety of them both . . .

'But one day,' she continued with the story. This girl,

bless her, was curious and wanted to know it all. And perhaps she too had in some way been sent? Perhaps she too could help? 'I returned from our house here in Maymyo with Ramon's mother to find that someone had broken in. They had smashed the windows to gain entry. And yet only one thing was taken.' She sighed, recalling the dread she had felt in the pit of her stomach. And with it had been the sense of inevitability, that one day . . . 'We always knew who was responsible. She had never forgiven my grandmother, you see, and neither had her family.' If both chinthes had been there, of course they would have taken the pair. What use was one without the other?

'Bitterness breeds bitterness,' she said sadly. 'Greed multiplies. They feel it all as if it were yesterday.'

CHAPTER 17

Even in the darkness, the yellow-stoned house looked as familiar as ever, but tired. Rosemary knew the feeling. Once she'd decided to come here, she'd acted quickly. She'd booked the next possible flight from Copenhagen and cancelled arrangements she'd made for the next couple of weeks. She didn't book the return flight. She wasn't sure how long this would take.

Alec had said very little. She just hoped he'd understand why she had to do this, and why she had to do it alone. It wasn't just a question of coming back to West Dorset, of seeing her father and Eva. But he'd probably know that too.

She trundled her case up the flagstones to the front door. The house seemed to be in darkness, but the lights were probably just on in the back. He'd always been conscious of saving electricity; his generation were. He'd be in the kitchen, probably, reading a paper and staying close to the Aga. Her father lived in that kitchen in winter months. Rosemary smiled at the thought. She'd missed him. But it was hard to admit that, even to herself. Anyway, she'd phoned, so he'd be expecting her.

At the front door, she hesitated. It was her childhood home

and she still had a key. But how would she feel, if——? No, she wouldn't barge in. She lifted the brass knocker and let it fall. Heard the sound echo as if the house were full of empty rooms. Along with the darkness, it gave her an uncomfortable sensation.

She pulled off her leather gloves and rubbed her hands together. It was chillier than it had been in Denmark. An English November. She thought of Bonfire Night, her father lighting Roman candles in the back garden. Rosemary holding sparklers in her gloved hands, shouting with delight, waving them round and making glitzy patterns of fire in the night air. The Catherine wheels he nailed to the fence that never spun properly, stopping halfway; the rockets spurting from an old milk bottle.

Rosemary sniffed. The shrubs hadn't been pruned, but her father wouldn't have noticed. And the paintwork on the door was starting to peel. She'd take a good look around and discuss it all with him, she decided, make a list of maintenance jobs for the spring. They mustn't let the place go to rack and ruin.

The phone call between them had been brief. 'Dad?' she'd said. 'I'm coming back for a visit. Is that alright?'

'Rosemary?' He had sounded vague and confused. She hated it when he sounded confused. And she noticed he never called her Rosie any more. When had he stopped?

'Yes. Can I stay at the house?'

'Of course, of course.' He paused. 'Will you want picking up at the station? The airport?'

'I'll arrange it all this end,' she reassured him. She told him when she would be arriving. 'I'll see you then.'

Alec had taken her to the airport. 'Take care, Rosemary,' he said when she got out of the car. 'Say hello to your Dad for me. And to Eva, when she gets back.'

'I will.' It was the first time she'd gone back to the UK without Alec. It felt very strange.

She knocked again. Still no answer. What on earth was he up to? She supposed that he couldn't hear her. He probably had the radio or the TV on and his hearing wasn't what it was.

After waiting for a minute or two, Rosemary groped in her bag for the house key. It slotted into the lock but the door held fast. She opened it with a good shove of the shoulder. That door could do with a plane. Draft proofing was all very well but you had to be able to open and shut the thing. Another one for the list.

'Dad?' she called. 'Hello!' She left her suitcase in the hall and after a quick glance into the lounge, went straight down the end into the kitchen. She switched on the light. Everything was scrupulously clean and tidy, the Aga as warming and cosy as ever, her father's rocking chair with the red tasselled cushion neat but unoccupied.

Silence.

'Dad?' Rosemary felt the panic stir, low in her chest. Had he forgotten she was coming? Gone out? But where on earth would he go out to on a cold November evening? 'Dad?'

Nothing. She pushed down the panic, retraced her steps and stood at the bottom of the stairs. Had he gone to bed, perhaps? That would explain why the whole house was so dark and quiet. She started up the stairs, heading for her parents' old bedroom. And then she remembered Eva telling her that he'd moved downstairs a few months ago; he couldn't manage the stairs like he used to.

She should have thought. 'Dad?' Rosemary hurried back to the downstairs bedroom next to the lounge. It was an en suite. 'Dad, it's me.' She spoke more quietly now. If he were asleep, she didn't want to wake him.

But she could see immediately in the light coming from the hall. The bed was made up and there was a glass of water on the bedside table, a towel hanging on the chair. But he wasn't here.

Now she was scared.

And then she realised that the light was on in the bathroom adjoining.

She rushed in. He was lying on the floor face down in his checked pyjamas and tartan dressing gown. 'Dad!' Rosemary put her hand to her mouth. It was an awful replay of the moment she had discovered Nick dead on the kitchen floor all those years ago. 'No,' she whispered.

She knelt beside him and she eased his face from the floor, frantically feeling for warmth, for a pulse. No, she was thinking. Not her father. Not now. Not like this. Please God. She couldn't go through this again.

CHAPTER 18

'But I don't understand,' said Eva. 'Can't you just report them to the police? The chinthe belonged to you and your family after all.' And if the Li family thought they had the right to steal one of them . . . She looked over at the little animal standing sturdily at the front of the shrine. Would they not also think they had the right to steal the other?

It was just 9 p.m. The rest of the family must have eaten earlier; only Maya, Ramon and Eva were sitting around the circular wooden dining table. And finally Maya had finished telling her story. Or had she finished? From the significant glances now passing between her and Ramon it seemed there might be more to come.

It had been quite a feast. Rice was at the core of most Myanmar cuisine but what Eva loved most were the side dishes that accompanied the curries, the spicy salads, with lime juice, peanuts and tamarind; the tart leaf-based soup known as *hin-jo*, Ramon had informed her; and *balachaung*, a pungent combination of chillies, garlic and dried shrimp fried in oil.

'It is not so easy here in Myanmar.' With his fork, Ramon deftly plucked a slice of papaya from the dessert of fresh fruit which sat in a simple white dish at the centre of the table. 'That family have connections.' His dark expression was the only indication as to what sort of connections these might be.

'And we have no papers to say that the chinthe is ours,' Maya agreed.

'Do *they*?'

Ramon shrugged. 'Probably. Forged ones, of course.'

'Why do you think it took them so long to steal it?' Eva wondered aloud.

'We used to take it with us when we travelled,' Maya admitted. 'This was perhaps the first time we left it in the house.'

But how would they have known that? Eva was indignant. She hadn't come all this way to fulfil her grandfather's last wishes, to return his chinthe to the place where it belonged, with its twin in the house of this family, to give up quite so easily. Nothing she had heard so far had convinced her it couldn't be done, the opposite in fact. Now that she knew the true provenance of the little animal . . . It made it even more important to get the other one back. 'But it isn't right,' she said.

'Many things are not right,' Ramon replied. 'It may not be right that we still do not have a full freedom of speech, or that those who we elect to government never have enough power. It may not be right that workers are paid so little for doing so much. Or that there are those in our country who still suffer.' He took a deep breath. 'Because it is not right, does not mean it does not happen.'

It was quite a speech. 'I appreciate what you're saying.' And she agreed with him too. 'But the fact that so many other things aren't right, doesn't mean we should take this lying down.'

'Lying down?' Ramon frowned.

'Accept it.'

He held her gaze. She recognised the passion there, and something else she couldn't define. 'No one is accepting it,' he murmured.

Maya intervened, laying a gentle hand on Eva's arm. 'It is not good to worry over things we cannot change,' she advised. 'All will come to those who have a clean heart.' She nodded sagely.

Was it her Buddhist faith that made her feel like this? Or was it living under a repressive regime for most of her life that had created such a sense of acceptance? But Eva was surprised at Ramon. He'd said he hadn't accepted it, but what was he actually doing? How long was it since the chinthe had first been stolen? It made her blood boil that this Li family could steal someone else's property and be allowed to get away with it.

'Who are these people anyway?' she asked. 'Where do they live?'

'What difference does it make where they live?' Ramon smiled grimly.

'Because if you know they've stolen the chinthe and if you know where they live, why couldn't we just steal it back again?'

Ramon let out a snort of laughter. 'Brave words,' he said. 'But you have no idea how dangerous that would be.'

Only if they found out who had taken it, Eva thought.

But Maya shook her head. 'Two wrongs do not make a right,' she said. 'It is wrong to steal and it will lead to no merit in the end.'

Eva sat back in her chair. Karma. But they must be able to do something. She looked Ramon straight in the eyes. 'So what *will* you do?' she asked.

He raised an eyebrow. 'Softly, softly,' he said.

Maya gave him a beatific smile. She reached for the teapot and poured out more tea. 'You must take care,' she warned.

Eva took the tiny cup that was offered to her. What was 'softly, softly' supposed to mean? Did Ramon have his own plan of trying to get the chinthe back? She hoped so. 'But the other thing I don't quite see . . .' She frowned. 'Is why they want it so badly.'

Maya and Ramon exchanged a look. Maya smiled and gave a small nod. Ramon shrugged.

'What?'

Ramon helped himself to more papaya, offering the fruit first to his grandmother and then to Eva. Maya shook her head, but Eva took a slice of watermelon, red and juicy. 'It is an important piece of history,' he said.

'Yes, of course.' The chinthes were originally the property of the last Queen of Burma. Eva looked across at the little animal she had brought all the way from Dorset. He had pride of place just below the Buddha in the shrine. He stood on guard, but Eva couldn't help thinking he still looked a little lonely.

'The decorative teak chinthes were among the treasures of the Royal Palace,' Ramon went on. His eyes were gleaming as he casually helped himself to more fruit. He bit into the dripping flesh of the watermelon, never taking his eyes from her face. 'And the Royal Palace was full of precious things,' he said. 'Teak carvings, golden images of our sacred Buddha, lacquer-work studded with gems. Even the walls were made of glass or decorated with jade and topaz.' He raised a dark eyebrow.

'Yes, I know.' But Eva still didn't quite understand. Naturally, the provenance of the chinthe gave it significance and value. It was what she had always believed: the story of an artefact was the one vital element that made it unique and special.

Ramon and his grandmother exchanged more significant looks.

What had she missed?

Lazily, Ramon got to his feet, stretched up to retrieve the chinthe from the shrine. He placed it carefully on the table between them. Watched her.

Eva smiled. The little chinthe was special. She would miss him. She ran her fingertip over the carving. 'Designed and carved by a royal master-craftsman?' she guessed.

'Of course. And?'

'And?'

He turned the chinthe to face her.

Eva looked into its red glass eyes as she had done so many times before. 'You might expect his eyes to be rubies,' she said. 'When you know the provenance. The fact that they're cheap glass, makes you think that the little beast isn't worth . . .' And then the penny dropped. 'That's the idea?' she breathed.

'That is the idea,' Ramon confirmed. He gave a grim smile. 'When you turned up with it earlier I checked all was in place. I could hardly believe it. But it was so.'

'All was in . . . ?'

Ramon picked up the little chinthe and, very gently, between his thumb and forefinger, he twisted its tail. In response, the head of the animal moved backwards to reveal a secret cavity inside.

Eva's eyes widened as she leaned closer. Of course, in her work, she had come across many antique wooden pieces with hidden compartments and sliding panels. But this was so delicate, so unexpected.

And inside . . . Ramon removed first one, then another from a nest of cotton padding. Two jewels sat in the palm of his hand.

Eva gasped.

The large rubies seemed to blink up at the light after the long period of darkness. Ramon held them out for her to see. They were dark red, almost purple in this light. Intense and passionate with a deep lustre and a blade that shimmered down the centre of each like an iris.

Rubies . . . She was speechless.

'Burmese Mogok Rubies,' he said. 'We call them pigeon-blood rubies, because of their colour.'

Eva was transfixed. They were stunning in both colour and luminosity.

'Would you like to take a closer look?'

Eva met his gaze, realised that for the first time today, he trusted her. Maybe he resented her grandfather and Westerners in general for the freedoms they took for granted. Maybe he didn't want her to open up the box of the past. But he and Maya were trusting her with something very special.

'Yes, please,' she whispered.

She held out her hand and he dropped one of the stones into her palm. She held it up to the light. There was a reflection that was like the sheen from a spool of silk. Why hadn't she guessed? But then again, why on earth should she have guessed? Ramon was right, red glass eyes, too obviously bright and glittering, had de-valued the piece. No one would guess. Unless they knew.

'And the other chinthe?' she asked.

'The same.'

'So . . . ?'

'The four Burmese Mogok rubies are very rare,' Ramon said. 'Suu Kyi suspected their value from what the Queen had told her and she knew of the existence of the secret compartments and of the mechanism with which to open it. It was then a simple matter for our family to have a master craftsman remove the rubies and insert the glass instead. The rubies must be kept in place for good luck, of course. But in front of them, for all to see, would be . . .'

'The red glass eyes,' Eva said.

'Yes.'

'And Nanda Li?'

Maya bowed her head. 'Of course, she, too, knew of the Mogok rubies, perhaps even of the secret compartment. She was there on that day with the Queen and Suu Kyi. She would have told her family. They would have known.'

Ramon glanced at his grandmother and murmured something softly in Burmese. 'They are a national treasure. It was illegal to take them out of the country.'

Maya nodded and smiled, patted his hand. She turned to Eva. 'But your grandfather did not know that,' she said.

'Illegal?' Eva echoed. So, she'd blithely transported an artefact of national importance and worth a small fortune from Britain to Myanmar, whisked it through security and deposited it back where it belonged, with hardly a second thought. No wonder they had both been so shocked. Eva had assumed it was the emotional trauma for Maya of the chinthe she'd given Lawrence being returned to her after all these years. Maybe it was that too, but it was so much more.

'The chinthe has always been a very special gift.' Again, Ramon looked at his grandmother. Maya nodded.

'And so my family thanks you from the bottom of its heart.'

Eva appreciated these words. But her mind was still spinning. Maya had said that her grandfather had not known he was not allowed to take the chinthe out of the country. What else had he known – or not known? Of course there would have been few checks during the aftermath of war. She thought of how dearly he had treasured the little beast. Could he possibly have known its value? For a moment Eva felt a flare of doubt. But he couldn't have known. He treasured it because it was a gift from the woman he loved. Her grandfather would never knowingly have placed her in danger.

Maya rose to her feet, which seemed to be a signal that the evening was at an end. Ramon got up too and so did Eva.

'But shouldn't you keep it under lock and key,' Eva said. 'If it's so valuable. I mean . . .'

Maya shook her head. 'What will be,' she said. 'We must trust him to do his job, to protect. We must trust him to be seen. And perhaps one day our missing chinthe will be drawn to return. If the Lord Buddha wills it.'

Eva nodded. She hoped she was right. But some sort of human intervention might be necessary too.

'We do not value either of the chinthes because of their material wealth,' Maya said softly. 'Nor even for their traditional symbolism. The ruby represents leadership and self-esteem and will bring wealth, good health and wisdom to its owner.' She smiled. 'We hope that this is so. But we value them for their history. For what each one represents and the spirit in which it was given.' She bowed her head and when she raised it again, there were tears in her dark eyes. 'But for others it is not the same. Which is why it would be such a dangerous task to try to reunite the two.'

'I understand.' Eva took Maya's outstretched hand. She respected what she was saying. But didn't everything that the chinthes represented make it even more important to reunite them? 'I've brought some photographs with me,' she said. 'Can I bring them to show you, tomorrow, before I leave for Mandalay?'

'Oh, yes. Please do.'

They said their goodbyes.

'Ramon will accompany you back to Pine Rise,' Maya said. And held up her hand when Eva was about to demur. 'I insist.'

'Very well.'

He held the door open for her and she slipped on her sandals before stepping out into the night air. Did Ramon really have a plan to get back the other chinthe? And if so, what was it? Eva decided that before she left Pyin Oo Lwin, she would make it her business to find out.

CHAPTER 19

Eva's mind was still back in the time of the final Burmese dynasty as they walked towards Pine Rise. In contrast, though, the night was silent and still, even the cicadas had been quiet since nightfall, the only other movement the faintest trembling of the velvety flowers which looked almost ghostly in the darkness, their scent more magnified than in the stark light of day. Eva's English life felt so far away, almost as if it belonged to someone else.

But she'd been wondering. She glanced at Ramon walking beside her. 'What happened to the other treasures from the Royal Palace?' she asked him. He had been subdued since they left the house; perhaps he, too, had a lot to think about. And now she sensed rather than saw his frown.

'Some are in the National Museum in Yangon,' he said. 'But most were plundered at the time of the exile.'

Plundered . . . Eva shivered, although the night air was still so warm she didn't even need a wrap. What had the King and Queen of Burma felt when they knew they had lost everything? And what had all that reverential bowing from their subjects really meant? Very little, it seemed, when there were riches to be had, beyond their wildest dreams. 'But where is it now?' she murmured. The ground was dry and hard under her thin sandals, still dusty from the heat of the day. They had taken the same route back to Pine Rise that she had taken earlier to get to Maya's. The lane was narrow but they were walking along the pathway that ran beside it.

'Sold many years ago and long gone,' he said. 'By now it will be in China, India, Britain, who knows?' But she wasn't fooled by the casual tone of his voice. Ramon cared. It was his country, she knew that he cared.

Eva paused to stare up at the canopy of the night sky. The whole galaxy seemed laid out before them. The sky was clear, never before had she seen so many stars. 'It was a sad end to the dynasty,' she said softly.

He followed her gaze. 'It was.' And he seemed to soften slightly.

'And what happened to the Royal Palace itself?' She refocused on the path ahead, allowed her hand to trail over the foliage of a eucalyptus tree as they passed by, its leaves glimmering blue in the light of the crescent moon.

'It was taken over by the British.' Once again, she heard the note of bitterness and Ramon's pace seemed to quicken as if he wanted this walk to be over.

'What did they do with it?' Though Eva could guess.

'The West Wing was converted into a club. The Queen's Audience Hall became a billiard room. The gardens were dug up to build polo fields and tennis courts.' His voice rang out in the darkness. He had moved ahead of her, but now he stopped for a moment to allow her to catch up with him.

'I see.' That didn't seem very respectful. She almost felt she should apologise.

'The Burmese, they call this period in our history, "The English time", he added, as the path narrowed and they moved once more into single file. 'Look around you at this town.' He waved his arms in an expansive gesture. 'It is full of the British legacy. It was even named after one of your Colonels. A Colonel May.'

'Really?' Eva hadn't known that, but she wasn't surprised. It was certainly true that Pyin Oo Lwin still looked very British, at least in the suburbs. But if the Burmese people had resented the 'English time', then why did they seem to like the British so much, she wondered. They were all so friendly, so eager to talk to her.

'And in the Second World War, the Palace was destroyed by fire,' Ramon continued. He glanced back at her, clearly expecting a reaction.

Also caused by the British, no doubt. Sometimes Eva felt more than a little ashamed of her heritage. But Ramon had an English father too, she reminded herself. Was he also ashamed? It didn't appear so. Hadn't he said that he wanted to go to the UK, to travel, to experience his father's world?

'And now?' she asked as she drew level with him. She had seen the wide moat that surrounded the old citadel. 'What's happened to the Palace now?'

'It has been reconstructed,' he said crisply.

'Oh?' It was hard to see the path ahead and Eva almost stumbled over a tree root. He heard the sound and turned to make sure she was alright, but she'd just lost her footing for a moment and she was fine. Ramon didn't seem to find their night walk such a problem. He could obviously see in the dark, she thought, like a cat.

'Perhaps you will visit the Palace when you return to Mandalay,' he said.

That sounded rather as if he couldn't wait for her to be gone. And once again he had become distant, that moment of trust back at the house when he'd shown her the rubies had disappeared. 'I will,' she told him. After what she'd heard tonight, it would be high on her list of must-sees.

The scent of the frangipani, rich and intoxicating in the night air, seemed to pull them along the road towards Pine Rise. Sometimes, Eva thought, it was almost too much, too cloying, too heavy. Even so, part of her longed to linger a little, to take her time dawdling and absorbing the sweet warmth of the night, which seemed so gentle on the senses. But Ramon clearly had other ideas and again, she had to hurry to keep up with him.

'Your country has many riches,' Eva observed, slightly out of breath as she thought again of those rubies. But it wasn't just the rubies and other jewels. There was also teak and oil, as well as rice, of course; she'd seen lots of paddy fields since she'd been here. No wonder the British and the Japanese had wanted a slice of everything.

'This is true.' He glanced across at her again and slowed his pace for a moment. 'But not many of our people are rich.'

She knew that too. Hadn't she seen them? Living in what

were little more than makeshift shacks? Begging by the road-side?

But, 'You have restored something of our family's heritage to us, Eva,' he said. His voice was surprisingly tender and, for a moment, Eva was aware of the proximity of him, tall and lithe just ahead of her in the darkness. 'We are very happy for that. And there is someone else, who will also be happy.'

'Your grandmother?' She heard the shrill cry of a bird or a bat from high above them. But she'd be happier still if the family had both chinthes, and the rubies, restored to them, Eva thought. She had read the mixed emotions in Maya's dark eyes. Bitter-sweet. And although her grandmother, Helen, had died and Maya's husband too, Eva knew that Lawrence and Maya would never be reunited – it would never be possible. Her grandfather was too frail to come here to Myanmar and Maya would never leave her country. For them, it was too late.

Ramon did not answer her. He was looking beyond her into the night. For the moment, she realised, she had lost him. 'And will you tell me your plan to get back the other chinthe?' she whispered.

'It is not your concern.' In a millisecond, he was back in the present and on red alert. And his voice had changed again. It sliced through the darkness.

No room for further discussion then, she thought. For now. 'Do you remember Maya's husband, your grandfather?' she asked. She was curious about the man who had stepped into the breach left by her own grandfather.

'Yes, I do.' He paused, seemed to rein himself back. 'He was a good man, a kind man.'

'And you had a happy childhood?'

He laughed. Perhaps he was amused by her questions. 'We survived very well,' he said. 'We were fortunate, compared to many of our countrymen.' He glanced back at her as if knowing what she were thinking. 'And if my grandmother ever missed your grandfather, then I never knew about it.'

Touché, thought Eva. 'But you always resented him.'

In the darkness she couldn't read his expression this time. 'Some might say that many Burmese women were taken advantage of by British men living in our country,' he said. He spoke clearly and there was no mistaking his meaning. 'They were not given the respect or the position that they deserved.'

Was that what had happened with her grandfather? 'Is that what your grandmother says?' Eva asked him.

He straightened and walked on. 'My grandmother is the most loyal woman I know.'

Which was, she knew, his way of answering the question. Maya would never criticise Lawrence. But Eva was sure it hadn't been like that. Theirs was a love story in a million. Her grandfather would never have left her if . . . But Eva stopped there. She didn't know the end of their story, not yet.

'Are you married, Ramon?' she asked him. He hadn't mentioned a wife. She wondered if they could ever be friends. He seemed to blow hot and cold and she never really knew where she was with him. Even so . . .

'No, I am not married,' he said. As he walked, he flipped his dark hair back from his forehead with that flick of his fingers, the gesture she'd noticed before, unconscious and unstudied. 'It is wrong to marry when I have so many plans.'

'That's very practical of you.' Though not terribly romantic. Eva recalled what he'd said before. 'You mean your plans to leave Myanmar?' She ducked to avoid a low branch.

'Perhaps.' He shot her a quick glance. 'And you?'

She shook her head. 'A couple of near misses,' she said. Though in truth they hadn't even been that. She thought of Max. Felt for the first time a sense of relief. She wouldn't have to try so hard anymore to be what he wanted her to be. She could just be herself.

Once again, she drew level with him. 'You will know when the right man comes along,' he said, the hint of a smile in his voice.

'Maybe I will.'

Now, he seemed to move a little closer to her as they walked along the path. She felt a sudden strand of tension between them, seeming to pull them closer still. It took her by surprise. In another time, she thought. In another place. But not here. And not with a man like this.

He pushed aside another branch hanging low over the path, so that she could walk through, and as she did so, her arm brushed against his. The jolt she felt almost stopped her in her tracks. Where had that come from?

'Eva?' he said.

'Yes?' She glanced up at him. His dark hair had once again

fallen across his forehead and he was looking at her intently. He wasn't moving. He stood perfectly still, as if he were waiting.

For her? Eva felt herself hovering on the edge. She felt as though she could move just a few centimetres closer and her body would be touching his. What would happen then? Would he kiss her? Did she want him to? If he did, she had the odd feeling that there would be no going back.

Once again, the thick, cloying fragrance of the frangipani wafted towards her, filled her senses like a drug. What was she thinking of? He was attractive, yes. Was it just that? Or was it the seductive scent of the flowers, the smooth darkness of the night?

She moved on, deliberately stepping away from him and he let the branch fall behind them. The moment was gone. And gone so completely that she half thought she'd imagined it. But she knew she hadn't. And she knew why she hadn't taken that extra step. It might mean nothing to him, but for her, there would be far too many complications. Her experience with Max was still fresh in her mind. She wasn't interested in any kind of one-night stand, and that was all it could ever be.

Their footsteps crunched on the gravel as they turned into the sweeping driveway of Pine Rise.

'Why did you come here, Eva?'

Had he felt it too? She had no idea. If he had, nothing in his voice, manner or body language betrayed the fact. His emotions seemed to be fully under control.

'To find out the truth of my grandfather's story.' She

looked up at Pine Rise gleaming at her in the moonlight. 'To see this country for myself. And to do my job, of course.'

'Your job?' He folded his arms and looked at her.

'I'm an antique dealer,' she told him. 'My company buys from your country.'

His lip curled. 'So the plundering continues,' he said.

'Well, hardly . . .' But before she could say more, he had already begun to walk away.

'Goodnight, Eva,' he called. And in seconds he was gone, swallowed up by the night.

It isn't like that, she wanted to say. They didn't take items of cultural or religious significance from the country. They were careful to check provenance. It was all above board. But . . . Eva sighed. For the first time, she felt a needle-prick of doubt. About her job, about what she was doing here.

She needed a good night's sleep, she decided. And she needed to get *her* emotions under control. In the meantime . . . She was left alone with only the soft sound of his footsteps on the gravel fading into the distance, the heady intoxicating scent of the frangipani and a long, pale sliver of moonlight.

Back inside Pine Rise she collected her key from reception. 'Is it possible to make an international call?' she asked. 'To the UK?'

'Yes, madam.' The girl lifted the telephone receiver and spoke to the operator. She looked back at Eva. 'The number, please?'

Eva told her. She waited.

'There is no answer,' the girl said at last.

'Are you sure?' Eva made a quick calculation. It would be around 7 p.m. Her grandfather was always home at this time. He would have just had his dinner. 'Can you try again?'

'Of course, madam.' Again, she went through the motions. Nothing.

'Thank you.' Eva walked away. It was probably nothing to worry about. Maybe he just hadn't heard the phone ring. She'd try again tomorrow. And if not . . . But she pushed the 'if not' away. Tomorrow, as Ramon had told her earlier, was another day.

that her conversation drives you to drink. Do you want to study philosophy?

But he persisted and asked again. Then at least we met he had begun to understand how the world works.

CHAPTER 20

Lawrence could smell something metallic and unfamiliar. The bed he was lying on was narrow and hard and the sheets seemed to be clamped tightly to his body as if he were in danger of falling out. It wasn't his bed, which must mean that he wasn't at home.

Earlier someone had given him water and he'd drunk it through a straw. Was he in hospital? He hoped not. Everyone knew the food was bloody awful and the nurses woke you up every five minutes to take your temperature or your blood pressure or ask you if you needed to empty your bladder. But he had the feeling that someone had mentioned something about hospital.

What had happened? His head hurt when he tried to think about it. Had he collapsed? Had a heart attack? Was he dying, was that it? He hoped someone would tell Mrs Briggs. She'd be worrying if she came in to clean and he wasn't even there.

This thought almost made him chuckle but the chuckle turned into a cough and suddenly he couldn't breathe. That was it then. He'd choke to death. In a bloody hospital.

But she was there. Someone was there and she lifted him

slightly, enough to clear his lungs. 'Do you want to sit up?' she whispered.

But he was too tired to sit up. Too tired even to answer her. So instead he thought of Helen.

There had never been that spark between them, though they had been together for so long, shared good times and bad times and had a child together. They had rubbed along, one might say, and for most of his life with her, Lawrence had been contented enough. Contentment though, was flat, like a plateau. It didn't flow like the mountain streams of Burma in which ran both force and passion.

Lawrence also knew that he had not tried hard enough to forget, that Helen knew his thoughts and his heart lived elsewhere, in a country very far away. Many times he had tried to get close to Helen, to make some recompense perhaps, or to discover with her something that was more precious, more intimate than what they already shared. But he could not. She protected herself against him with the armours of prudery and convention, with the conservatism which grew more and more brittle inside her, until he felt she might break rather than let herself go.

Of course it was his fault. If he had been strong, Helen would have attached herself to some other man who would have made her so much happier. But it was too late for such regrets. He had done what he had done, rightly or wrongly. And he respected Helen, as both a wife and a mother. He believed that she too had tried her best. And even that was a sadness to him.

When Rosemary was born, it was almost a relief to hand the reins for his daughter's emotional welfare to Helen. Rosemary could give Helen what Lawrence could not. Helen could have all of Rosemary; he wanted her to have it all. He took a back seat and focused on making a living to provide for them, to give them a good life. Lawrence loved his daughter and would have liked to give her more. But he would not. He watched from the wings.

Now, he tried to remember when he had first felt an obligation to Helen, which was hard, because he felt as if it had always been there. Was it when his mother began hinting and his father began to slap him on the back as if he were a friend and contemporary, rather than a son? Was it when Helen's parents fussed over him and treated him as if he were one of their own? Or was it even earlier?

Helen was twelve the first time he kissed her. Or, he should say, the first time she kissed him. Lawrence was just thirteen.

His family had gone to a weekend lunch party at her house and it had drifted into late afternoon. They had a small swimming pool and even a tennis court; the family had money then, both families had money. Unlike others, they had benefited from the financial recession of the thirties; they had made some canny investments at the right time and now they were reaping the benefits.

Lawrence and Helen had been swimming in the pool, length after short length, racing each other and laughing and splashing and when they'd got out, she had taken his hand and pulled him towards the summer house. 'Come on. I want to show you something.'

It was a perfect summer's day, cloudless and blue, the way summer days often were in England back then, no breeze, bees idly buzzing around the clumps of lavender bordering the path. They sat on the decking of the summer house, which was hot from the sun, and stretched out their bare legs already dried from the pool. Helen's blonde hair was dripping on the bleached boards of the decking, the water almost sizzling as it landed. She moved close to him as if she might whisper in his ear and then shook her hair like a dog.

He laughed. 'What do you want to show me, Helen?'

'This.' And she'd pulled him close, put her lips against his and kissed him. Not just on the mouth, but prising his lips apart with hers until he felt her tongue, warm and moist on his.

He felt the stirring in his groin. 'Give over, Helen.' He half pushed her away, his hands on her shoulders, her wet hair trailing over his fingers.

'Why?' Dreamily, she looked up at him, batting wet eyelashes. Kissed him again, lightly this time. Her lips tasted of chlorine.

'Because.' He lay down and stared up at the sky, through the corrugated leaves of the apple tree next to the summer house, into the blue. Truth was, he didn't know why.

'One day we'll be doing this all the time.' She licked her finger and traced a path across his forehead.

'Doing what?' He grabbed her hand, held it pinned down by his side.

How stupid was he? Not to realise they had his whole life mapped out for him. His parents. Her parents. Helen.

'You and me,' she said.

'You and me?' He let go of her hand, leant up on one elbow and watched her. She'd picked a blade of grass and was dissecting it with her fingernail. He understood how it felt. She was a pretty girl. But he'd grown up with Helen. He knew her, warts and all. She was more like a sister.

'Don't you know?' she said, tickling his face with the grass. 'Don't you feel it?'

'Feel what?' He was scared of what might happen if she kept kissing him that way. Which was precisely why he had to stop her kissing him that way. It didn't feel right.

'Me and you,' she said again. 'We'll be married one day. We'll live in a big house. Maybe this house.' She waved vaguely towards where all the grown-ups were sitting outside, out of sight: his parents, her parents – colleagues and best friends – eating and drinking and planning someone else's future.

'Oh, yes?' He laughed. She was just a girl. What did she know?

'We'll have lots of furniture,' she said. 'And children.'

He laughed again, wondering if she'd detected the note of panic.

'And we'll have parties just like this one.'

Her parents' life, he thought. That was what Helen wanted.

'What makes you so sure?' he teased. He was still more curious than worried. It was just Helen's fantasy, it wasn't real.

She tilted her head towards him. Screwed her eyes up against the sun. 'It's what they want,' she said. 'So it'll happen.'

And Helen had been right. It had happened.

CHAPTER 21

The next morning, Eva took the photographs she'd brought from home to show Maya. It was too early to phone her grandfather again, but she'd try later, before she headed back to Mandalay. Fascinating though this trip to Pyin Oo Lwin had been, she mustn't forget that her contact would be waiting and that she had a job to do, whatever Ramon might think of it.

Eva handed her the first photo. 'My grandfather.' As he must have been when Maya first knew him. Had she had a picture of her lover back then? Possibly not. Certainly, her eyes filled.

'Lawrence,' she whispered. She held it carefully, as if it were so brittle it might snap.

'It was taken just before the war,' Eva said. It had *1939* scrawled on the back in her grandfather's hand. And he had told her that at the time he'd been on leave from camp.

'Yes. It was here in Maymyo,' Maya said. 'I remember that day.' She traced a fingertip over the picture. 'At Pine Rise.'

'Oh, yes, of course.' Eva recognised the carvings around the front door behind where he was standing. Now, she had seen them with her own eyes, run her fingers over that same wood . . .

Her grandfather was standing, legs akimbo, staring straight at the camera. He was wearing khaki shorts and a short-sleeved shirt. His eyes were pale and unblinking in the faded black-and-white shot. A young man ready to go to war. Had he known that? Had he been at all prepared for what he was about to go through? Eva doubted it.

'And this is Grandpa in the early nineteen fifties.' She produced the next, an early colour shot. Her grandfather was sitting in the window-seat at home, looking towards the garden, which was long and backed on to the Nature Reserve and the cliffs. The garden had a small pond with a yellow water lily, irises and carp and an old-fashioned crazy-paving path that meandered from the bench up to the vegetable patch. To Eva, it had always been a secret garden, because of the narrow paths that wound behind the sprawling hydrangea bushes, and the many places to hide behind the trellises of sweet peas and raspberry canes. The photo must have been taken less than ten years after he had left Burma. He looked wistful and, yes, a little lonely.

Maya nodded. 'It is a beautiful garden,' she said. 'And Lawrence looks just as I imagined.'

How many times had she pictured him, Eva wondered, thinking of what Ramon had said last night. Maya smiled, but again Eva could see the sadness in her dark eyes. How had she felt when this man whom she loved had gone off to war? Had she known she would never see him again? And how had she felt when he never returned? She seemed to have known that he had gone back to the UK rather than been a casualty and she must have accepted it long ago. But Eva wondered, nevertheless, how much had she suffered at losing him? She had married and she'd had a daughter. But so had Eva's grandfather. And yet he'd never stopped loving this woman sitting beside her now.

'It was taken not long before my mother was born,' she told Maya. Maya, too, must have been married by then. She and Eva's grandfather had been desperately in love. But they had parted. They had both moved on.

'Ah.' Maya held the photograph to her breast. 'What was she like, your grandmother? Did she make him happy?'

'Well . . .' Eva wasn't sure how to answer this. She didn't want to betray anyone, but she felt she must be honest with this woman who had already lost so much. 'He was content, I think,' she said. 'My grandmother loved him.' Which kind of said it all.

'Good.' Maya nodded. 'I am glad.' And her eyes were wise. 'It is good to be content, I think. Ramon . . .'

'Yes?' Though Eva wasn't sure she wanted to discuss Ramon, not after last night.

'He is not content. He is troubled. I know it.' Maya let out a small sigh and Eva could see the tension in the stiffness of her narrow shoulders.

Eva thought about what he'd said yesterday in the Gardens. 'He cares very deeply about things,' she said cautiously.

'He is political.' Maya took her hand. 'Just like my father. In this country, it is impossible to be content if you are a political animal.' She sighed. 'Could you talk to him, Eva, my child? He would listen to you. He is drawn to you, I can see.'

'I really don't think—' Eva began.

'He imagines he protects me. But I worry . . .' She tailed off. 'Soon, I will no longer be here to worry.'

'I'll try.' Eva felt she had to be honest. 'But I'm not sure he would listen to me.' She was probably the last person he'd listen to, in fact. 'And I'm so sorry, but I must leave this afternoon. I have to return to Mandalay.' She changed the subject by producing the next photograph.

'Here's Grandpa with my mother.' This photo was very different. Her grandfather was holding her mother's hand and her mother, five or six years old perhaps, her hair a mop of blonde curls, eyes as blue as her father's, looked up at him with trust and love. And he gazed down at her adoringly. The photograph never failed to make Eva sad. What had happened between these two? Because once – and the evidence was here – they had been so close. But now . . . The rift between them seemed an insurmountable one. Copenhagen wasn't far away, but it was a while since her mother's last visit. And any meaningful reconnection between father and daughter would take a lot more than an email or a phone call.

Again, Maya nodded and took her time examining the photo. If anything, she seemed even more moved by this one than she had by the previous two. She clicked her tongue and murmured in Burmese. She peered at the photo, moving it closer to the light. 'Yes,' she said. 'His daughter. Yes, I see.'

Eva showed her some more photographs, one from each

decade, some of him alone, some with Rosemary, some with Eva. And Maya gave them all equal time, attention and care. Fortunately, the subject of Ramon appeared to have been dropped.

The very last photo Eva had taken herself last week before she left, printing it out so that she had a complete set. Lawrence here looked old and more fragile, his hair snow-white but his eyes as intelligent as ever. 'And as he is now,' she told Maya.

Maya let out a choked sob when she saw it. 'Look at us both,' she whispered, touching the face on the photograph. 'We are old . . . We have taken our chosen paths.' And then in a lower voice, 'Each without the other.'

Eva waited a moment for her to collect her emotions. Had she been right to bring this catalogue of memories with her? Her mother wouldn't like it. She would say that this was their life, that it had nothing to do with Maya. But it had seemed so important to Eva to show Maya the pictures of their family. And she was glad now that she had. 'Would you like to keep them?' she asked her.

Maya stared at her. Her hands were trembling. 'Truly?'

Eva was moved. She took her hand. 'I brought them for you.'

Maya bowed her head. 'Thank you, Eva,' she said. 'If only . . .'

But Eva never found out her 'if only' because at that moment, the door opened and Ramon strode in.

'Eva,' he said. 'Good morning. Did you sleep well?' His

gaze was distant as it swept over her. He was dressed as usual in short-sleeved shirt and *longyi*, in navy blue today, and was barefoot.

'Very well, thank you,' she said smoothly. Though she hadn't. She had tossed and turned half the night until a pale pink dawn had crept through the crack in the curtains. She was worried about her grandfather. And she had decided to steer well clear. Of moonlight, the scent of frangipani and Ramon.

'And when are you returning to Mandalay?' he asked, again.

'I've booked a driver for this afternoon.'

'You do not need a driver,' Maya said. 'Ramon is also returning to Mandalay this afternoon.'

'Oh?'

'I am needed at work,' he said. 'The city of Mandalay is where my business is located, of course.'

'Of course,' she echoed. She hadn't considered that. Not that it mattered. She needn't see him when she was in Mandalay. He would be busy and so would she. She was sorry not to be able to help Maya, but Ramon would never listen to her. And anyway, what should she say?

'Ramon will take you back with him,' said Maya.

'That's very kind ...' Of Maya; the suggestion hadn't come from Ramon after all. Perhaps she was hoping the long drive would inspire confidences. 'But, as I said, I've already booked my driver.'

Maya got to her feet. 'We will cancel the driver,' she said regally.

Eva couldn't help smiling. Serene, but with a core of steel, she thought. 'But—'

'He will understand. Ramon will take you back to Mandalay. It is decided.'

Eva took a deep breath. 'Very well,' she said. 'Thank you.' The journey might have been more relaxing with a different driver. But she was an independent woman who could find her way around the world. What threat could a man like Ramon possibly pose for her peace of mind?

'How soon can you be ready?' Ramon glanced at his watch.

'In an hour?' She just had to pack a few things and make that phone call. She was eager now to get back to Mandalay. Work would distract her, it always did.

'And in a few days I, too, will be there.' Maya held out her arms and embraced her.

'Will you? I'll look forward to that.' Eva kissed her gently on both papery cheeks. She didn't want to betray anyone, and she knew her mother wouldn't approve, but she liked Maya. She appreciated her sense of calm, her strength, her connection to the grandfather Eva adored.

Maya nodded. 'There is more that I must tell you.'

'Oh?' And more that I should ask you, thought Eva.

Maya put a finger to her lips. 'When the time is right,' she said softly. She turned to Ramon. 'And in the meantime,' she said, 'you need have no worries and no problems. You will be perfectly safe. Because in Mandalay, Ramon will take care of you.'

*

Eva hurried back to Pine Rise.

At reception, the girl put her call through. Again, it was painstakingly slow. Finally, she handed the receiver to Eva.

'Hello? Grandpa?' she said.

'Eva?'

The voice was one she recognised. But it wasn't her grandfather. 'Mother?'

'Yes, darling, it's me.'

She sounded breathless but familiar, and Eva was surprised how glad she felt to hear her voice. But, 'What are you doing in England, Mother? There's nothing wrong, is there?' She felt a sudden churning in her belly. Grandpa?

'Everything's fine.' She heard her mother take a deep breath. 'I came over for a visit on the spur of the moment . . .'

While *she* was in Burma, Eva couldn't help thinking.

'And I found your Grandpa . . .'

'Found him what? Where?'

'He'd collapsed.' Another deep breath. 'But you mustn't worry. He spent last night in hospital and he's feeling much better now.'

He was feeling better. The churning subsided. He was alright. And her mother was with him. 'What happened?' she whispered. 'Was it a heart attack?'

'No, no.' Her mother's voice came across clear and reassuring. 'We think he just fainted. The doctor said he'd recently adjusted the pills he takes for high blood pressure. We think that's all it was.'

'Should I come home?' Eva found that she was clutching

the receiver close to her. Thank God her mother had turned up when she had. Supposing he'd been alone?

'There's absolutely no need.' Her mother sounded so in control, it was a huge relief. 'I'll stay here and look after him.'

'Can I speak to him? He's OK to talk, is he?' Suddenly Eva knew she had to tell him as soon as she could.

'I'll take you through. He's in bed, just resting.'

Eva heard her footsteps. 'Are you alright, Mother?' she asked.

'I'm fine, darling. What about you? How is everything?'

Everything. So much had been happening, Eva could hardly believe she'd been in Myanmar for only a week. 'It's going very well,' she managed to say. 'So far, so good.'

'It's Eva.' She heard her mother's voice. 'Calling from Burma.'

'Eva.' And here was her grandfather, sounding even more frail than usual. Perhaps it was the distance that separated them. She hoped so. 'Is that really you, Eva, darling? How are you? How's Burma?'

She chuckled. 'It's wonderful. And I'm very well too. But how are you, Grandpa?'

'Oh, I'm not so bad. Plenty of life in the old dog yet.' He laughed. 'Where are you, exactly, my dear?'

'Maymyo.'

He paused. 'And have you found her?'

Eva heard the emotion, the shaky exhalation of breath. She imagined him clutching the receiver closer too, just as she was clutching this old-fashioned black Bakelite receiver to her ear. 'Yes,' she said. 'I have.'

'What?'

'Yes!' She almost shouted. 'I've found her. She's well. Living here in Maymyo. I just wanted to let you know.'

'Thank you, my dear. Oh, thank you.' She heard in his voice a sweet relief that moved her so deeply. 'Thank you, darling Eva.'

'I'll tell you the rest of the news when I get back,' she said.

'You take care, my darling,' he wheezed.

'And you. I just wanted you to know . . .' The line had gone dead. But it didn't matter. She'd told him and he was alright. Her mother was there looking after him. Well . . .

'Could you make up my bill?' she asked the girl on reception. 'I'm almost ready to check out.'

'Yes, madam, of course.'

Eva took her key and went up to her room to finish packing a few bits and pieces. She could only imagine how that news had made him feel.

CHAPTER 22

Rosemary was building the fire in the living room. The kitchen was fine for eating in but it wasn't comfortable enough. He needed to be lying down and he wouldn't be wanting to stay in bed all day. If she made up the fire he could lie on the sofa and be warm. And it gave her something to do.

She started with scrunched up newspaper and old egg boxes. It was a long time since she'd been down on her hands and knees in front of a grate getting her hands dirty. The thought made her chuckle. It was a long way from the sleek radiators of their apartment in Copenhagen. She paused and sank back on to her heels for a moment. And how was Alec? He hadn't phoned since she'd left. But then again, neither had she.

Her father was asleep but she had her ears open for the moment he woke up. She hadn't lied to Eva, but on the other hand neither had she been scrupulously honest. They were so close and she didn't want to worry her, not while she was away in Burma. He wasn't well. He seemed to be . . . as Mrs Briggs had put it when she tried to explain to Rosemary this morning, *not quite with it*. Which itself seemed a bit of a betrayal. Her father had always been such an intelligent man, she'd been proud of that. And not only that, but according to Mrs Briggs, this wasn't the first time he'd had a fall. 'He asked me not to say,' she confided. 'I'm sorry. I wasn't sure what to do for the best.'

Rosemary began to build a little pyramid of kindling around the newspaper. Like a bivouac. Somewhere to hide, to shelter. But it was true, he wasn't with it, it was as if he were somewhere else.

That wasn't the reason he'd collapsed though. Rosemary shivered and thought back to the moment she'd arrived at the house, the moment she'd found him there, passed out on the bathroom floor. She'd found a pulse straightaway. Thank God. And she'd turned him into the recovery position. Talked to him, gently, tried to bring him round. At the same time, she'd groped for her mobile in her bag and dialled 999. He needed to be taken to hospital, now. She wasn't taking any chances.

In the ambulance she'd held his hand and he'd come round.

'Eva?' he'd muttered. He struggled to sit up. 'Eva, is that you?'

'It's Rosemary.' She had repressed a sigh and squeezed his hand. Even now he could upset her so easily 'Don't worry about a thing, Dad. You had a fall. We're on our way to hospital.'

'Hospital?' He pulled a face and the paramedic had laughed.

'Don't reckon you're too delighted about that then, Lawrence,' he remarked.

Rosemary leaned closer. He was so thin, so pale. His skin

was as pouched and creased as old paper, criss-crossed with lines she didn't even remember. He smelt of shaving cream and something vaguely medicinal which she couldn't quite place. She had left this visit far too long, she realised. But she'd make up for it now. 'Don't worry, Dad,' she whispered. 'You'll be fine.'

At the hospital he had shifted in and out of his usual sharp awareness. They had done lots of tests and concluded that there was nothing seriously wrong and that they could go home. No doubt he was taking up a bed needed by someone more ill. They would contact his GP, they told Rosemary, and tell him what had happened and he would probably make a home visit. Doubtless, it was the change in his prescription that had done it. Blood pressure could be hard to balance, not too high to risk a stroke, not too low to get dizzy and faint. But in the meantime, she should stay with him.

As if I'm going anywhere, she had muttered under her breath. He was her father. She should never have left him. It wasn't fair for him to be alone.

Rosemary picked up the matches and lit one, the scent of sulphur hitting her nostrils like some far off memory. She held it to the newspaper, it caught and she carefully added more kindling, building it around. She didn't let herself think about what he'd said to Eva on the phone, she was pretending she hadn't even heard. But at least Eva was well and it was good that she'd phoned, that Rosemary had been able to talk to her and fill her in on what had happened.

By the time she heard him stir, the fire was lit and blazing with life. It reminded Rosemary, more than anything, of her childhood growing up in this rambling house, of Christmas Day and a log fire burning. The tree in the corner decorated so carefully by her mother. She always allowed Rosemary to help, but Rosemary soon noticed that the bits she did would more often than not be done again by her mother. Made perfect. She sighed. How do you mend a broken marriage though? How do you mend a marriage that had never been perfect, not even in the beginning?

She put a couple of logs in position and placed the guard in front of the growing blaze.

'Hello, love.' He was already sitting up and reaching for his glass of water. He seemed a bit brighter.

'Let me.' She passed it to him. Then she fussed with his pillows for a bit, to make him more comfortable. 'I've lit a fire,' she said. 'We'll give it half an hour to warm up and then I'll take you in there if you like.'

He was watching her. 'It's grand to see you, love,' he murmured. 'I never said. But it's grand to see you.'

'You too. How are you feeling after your nap?' She smoothed his fine white hair from his brow. Soft as baby hair, she thought, and something stirred inside her. She felt her eyes fill with tears. What on earth was the matter with her? Whatever she did, she mustn't let him see her cry.

'Cock a hoop,' he whispered.

She took his hand and gently patted it.

'Why did you come, Rosie? Why the sudden visit, eh?'

She was relieved to see a spark of animation in his pale blue eyes. How much could he see? 'I came to see you, didn't I?' And lucky I did, she thought.

He frowned. 'I'm not about to kick the bucket, am I, love?'

'Stop it.' She squeezed gently. 'Of course you're not. I just wanted to see you.' And she realised that it was true. She'd been so angry with him, hadn't she, over the years. But seeing him now, like this . . .

'I wanted to see you too,' he said. 'So that's alright then, isn't it?'

'That's alright,' she agreed. She was the woman who kept things at a distance, who had found it easier to bury herself in a new life in Copenhagen and to let the old life go. But this was her father and for a moment there she had thought she'd lost him. And she realised she didn't want to let him go.

She got to her feet. 'Fancy a cuppa?'

'Thought you'd never ask.' He grinned.

CHAPTER 23

Rather to her surprise, Eva found herself confiding in Ramon on the journey to Mandalay. She told him about the phone call and that her grandfather was far from well.

'I know you feel that he behaved badly,' she added. 'But it meant everything to my grandfather that I brought the chinthe back here to your family, that I found Maya and that she's still alive.'

Ramon glanced across at her. 'Perhaps I misjudged him,' he admitted. He swung the car out to overtake a smoke-belching truck that must have been fifty years old, full of local villagers squatting on pink plastic crates of live chickens and huge watermelons.

Health and safety hadn't made much impact on Myanmar, Eva noted and not for the first time.

'Or perhaps you do not know the full story.'

'It's possible,' she conceded.

He drummed long brown fingers on the steering wheel. 'Why, for example, did he never come back here? It has been many years since the war ended.'

Eva considered. 'Because he was married to my grand-mother,' she said. 'And then maybe he felt it was too late.'

'Too late to again disrupt my grandmother's life?' he asked.

'I think so.' She would have been married by that time. 'And your country was very isolated then,' she reminded him. 'It wasn't easy to get here. Politically—'

'Yes, that is also true.' He frowned. 'And I am sorry he is not well.'

So was she. They had left behind the leafy suburbs of Pyin Oo Lwin and were now descending towards the plains. The road to Mandalay, Eva thought nostalgically, lined with yellow mimosa. There was no sign of any tension from the night before and slowly Eva allowed herself to unwind and enjoy the journey through the red-earthed hills and lush vegetation. She leaned back in the seat. She had worn her hair up to keep cool but of course the car had air-con so she was perfectly comfortable. She closed her eyes for a moment, enjoying the sensation of the chill air on her skin. She had come to Pyin Oo Lwin not knowing if she would find Maya. And she had not only found her, but she had heard yet another story, one that had got her thinking and planning. Because there must be a way, mustn't there, to get that little chinthe back?

She stretched out her legs. She was wearing green linen cropped trousers and a sleeveless embroidered top and had already slipped off her leather-thonged sandals. 'It's been so lovely to meet your family,' she said.

He laughed. 'And you'll meet even more of them in Mandalay.'

Eva had a vision of more cousins, second cousins and

assorted ebony-haired children who seemed to belong to everyone. And she realised that it was assumed she would continue to see the family in Mandalay. It was a pleasant thought.

'Tell me some more about your furniture company,' Eva prompted, sneaking a look at him as he drove. He was a confident driver. Both hands rested languidly on the steering wheel, he looked casual but in charge. She'd like to know him a bit better, she decided, find out what made him tick.

'My father began the business in Myanmar,' Ramon said, 'but his father's family, the English side . . .' And she heard the pride in his voice. 'Were master craftsmen and furniture makers in Britain for more than four generations before that.'

'Really?' She'd find out the name, she decided, and look them up. 'So why did your father move here in the first place?'

'He was an explorer.' He looked swiftly across at her and then back to the road ahead. They were passing one of the many scatterings of shacks and dwellings with fruit and vegetable carts, children playing on the roadside, chickens pecking in the dust. 'At that time he was not sure his father's business was for him. He came out here at twenty-five, met my mother and decided to settle in this country.'

Again, Eva was reminded of her grandfather. He too had left England because he was an explorer and because he didn't want to join the family firm. But in his case, the war had changed everything. He had returned to Dorset when it was over and tried to rescue Fox and Forsters, but although he'd had some degree of success and the company had recovered to fight another day, Eva knew for a fact that her grandfather's heart had never been in it. He had left his heart, she supposed, in Burma.

'But your father became a furniture maker anyway?' she asked Ramon.

'Yes.' He nodded and swung the steering wheel to the left to follow the bend in the road. 'He had trained in London and always loved to work with wood. Very soon, he formed a Burmese furniture company with the same ethics as his father's.'

'Which were?'

'We pride ourselves on being environmentally conscious,' he said. He paused and accelerated smoothly to overtake a small truck. The journey was taking no time, already they were descending towards Mandalay, the sun low in the sky, visible through the trees to the west. 'We use only the best teak wood sourced from conscientious dealers with legitimate concessions.'

Eva was impressed. His words struck a chord with her own thoughts and values. 'But what happened to the business when your father—'

'Died?' He glanced across at her. 'My father had a loyal manager who has only recently left us to retire. He trained me and taught me the skills necessary to take over. From when I was only a young boy, it was always expected that I would grow up and take charge of the company.'

'And you did,' murmured Eva.

'And I did.' He braked at the junction and took the turning to the city. 'Each generation has a responsibility,' he continued. 'To develop the business as he sees fit, but to also remain loyal to the original ethos of producing high quality and hand-crafted furniture. To move forwards, but gradually and faithfully.' Once again, he glanced across at her. 'It is our way.'

'And your method is through expansion?' She recalled what he'd told her before, his dream of exporting his furniture to the UK and elsewhere.

'Not just expansion.' He shook his head. 'That is important, yes. But I have my own ideas too. You will see if you visit the factory.'

'I'd like to.' Eva was intrigued. 'Did your father try to merge his company with your grandfather's in the UK?' Had that been a possibility back then?

Ramon shook his head. 'They never had the chance to try,' he said. 'My English grandfather died only a year after my father arrived here. His heart, too, was not strong. There was, what do you say?'

'A family history?'

'Exactly.' He nodded. 'The company in Britain was terminated. It was even more important then for my father to make our business a success. He must continue his father's work. Now he was doing it for him and for his new family too, for us. And I must do the same.'

'I see.' She was certainly beginning to understand where Ramon's ambition came from and why the furniture company was so important to him. It was a legacy, a family tradition.

'And you?' Ramon asked as they entered the suburbs of the

city. 'You have antiques to view in Mandalay?' His voice was a little cooler, but thankfully he was less antagonistic than before.

'I have.' She watched him negotiate the busy road. 'But we're not depriving your country of anything iconic or culturally significant, you know,' she said. She twisted her daisy ring around her little finger as she spoke.

'Is that so?' He flicked back the wing of dark hair from his forehead. 'But who is to say? You?' He swerved to avoid a cyclist and sounded the horn of the car. 'Forgive me, Eva, but you are not Burmese, even though you may be an expert.'

'We are taking what the Burmese wish to sell,' she insisted. 'And we only buy from the legal owners. What's wrong with that?' Eva tried to control her rising anger. He was questioning her integrity, which she prided herself on more than anything.

Ramon braked sharply as a pedestrian loaded with watermelons stepped into the road. He swore under his breath. 'But why do they want to sell? Have you asked yourself that? Have you thought that perhaps they need to sell because they are desperate? Why not leave things where they are sometimes?'

'You can't take away people's right to sell their own possessions.' Though Eva knew it wasn't quite as simple as that. 'And anyway, lots of the things we buy came originally from the British.'

'Ah, the British.' His lip curled. 'Well, that is your history, Eva.'

'Your father was British too,' she said.

'Yes, and my mother was Burmese.'

Eva sighed. He was quite impossible. 'We are at least bringing money into your country.'

Ramon conceded this with a small nod. 'And we are grateful,' he said with some sarcasm. 'Just as we are grateful that the US has been good enough to lift some of the harmful sanctions against us.'

'Ramon—'

The tyres squealed as they drew up outside her hotel.

Eva didn't wait for him to open her door. She got out and practically dragged her suitcase out behind her.

'I apologise.' Ramon was standing in front of her, blocking her pathway to the hotel's swing door, long-limbed and with a determined look in his green eyes. 'It is your business. I must not interfere.'

'It's alright.' Eva had to concede that he had a point. And she would do what she could to ensure that everything she accepted for the Emporium had been checked and deemed appropriate for export.

'Perhaps in a day or two, you will be free to do some sight-seeing,' he suggested.

'I hope so.' Eva watched as he picked up her case and took it into the foyer, went in after him and gave her name to reception.

'Ah, madam, you have two messages,' the receptionist told her, checking a pigeon-hole. She handed Eva two slips of paper.

One was written neatly and signed *Klaus*, she'd read that

later. The other was from her contact in Mandalay, giving a phone number and the words: *it is ready for the view.*

'It looks as if you will be busy tomorrow,' Ramon murmured.

'Yes.' She smiled up at him. 'But thanks for bringing me back to Mandalay. I'm very grateful.'

'It was nothing.' He handed her case over to the porter. 'And at the weekend?'

'The weekend?'

'I can take you to visit Sagaing and Inwa, if you wish,' he said. 'They are special places. You must see more of our country to fully understand.'

Eva hesitated. Had his grandmother dictated that this was how he should behave? Or did it come from the heart? 'I'm sure you're very busy,' she hedged.

'Not really.' He shrugged. 'I would like to take you, to show you,' he said. He certainly seemed sincere. And again, he fixed her with that long, considering look of his.

'Then, yes. Thank you. I should be free at the weekend.' It would give her the chance to find out more about the location of the missing chinthe, and what exactly Ramon was planning to do to get it back. It would fulfil her promise to Maya to try and discover what was troubling her grandson. And it would help her to get to know this country even better. Which, more than anything, was what Eva wanted to do.

CHAPTER 24

She had found her. Eva had found her.

Lawrence watched his daughter bustle around the bedroom, tidying up things that really didn't need tidying up. They had Mrs Briggs for that.

But, 'Take a few days off, Mrs B,' Rosemary had said to her yesterday. 'I'll look after everything here.'

Him, she meant. Look after him. It made Lawrence feel like standing on top of the bed and shouting. *I'm here, don't you know? I can look after myself. I always used to look after you.*

But that was then. How could he look after anyone now? How could he even stand on top of the bed, come to that? It was as much as he could do to get out of bed and get to the bathroom.

'Leave it, Dad,' Rosemary said when he tried to do anything. 'Let me.'

He'd only be tidying a book away or hanging up his dressing gown. Nothing really. But he realised that she wanted to do those things, it was important to her. She wanted to feel useful. So he let her.

She wouldn't stay, though. He knew she wouldn't stay because she didn't live here anymore. He was sure of that, but for a moment it had slipped his mind where she had gone to.

And then Eva had telephoned from Burma. She had found her and Maya was alive and well. Lawrence had sunk his head back into his pillows that night and he was back there. Simple. He was back there and he could smell once more the jasmine in the porch outside her father's house, the coconut oil in her hair.

Upper Burma, 1937

Lawrence had returned to the camp. It wasn't much more than a forest clearing, a few huts with bamboo screens and thatched roofs for the timbermen surrounding the rear of the *tai*, a wooden house erected on a wooden platform and built on stilts, where, as Forest Assistant in charge of the camp, Lawrence lived. But he couldn't get her out of his head. Maya. She was the lightest of shadows in his daytime and his compelling silhouette after dark. And he could have stayed longer in Mandalay, because still the rains didn't come.

It had only been one night but their love-making had been a revelation. She had kept a lamp burning low and she had made him wait while she massaged his neck and shoulders with oil and kissed a trail from his lips down to his belly.

At last, with a groan, he could stand it no more and he had held her tightly and entered her with a passion he could barely control. The connection between them was immediate, electric.

'Touch me with your lips,' she said. And Lawrence remembered something Scottie had said to him, *there's no Burmese word for 'kiss'*.

So he kissed her throat, her hair, her mouth. Deep liquid kisses such as he had never experienced before. Lawrence had shuddered as he held her and he had felt her shudder too.

Later, he watched her sleep and it seemed her whole body was bathed in peace. Already he wanted her again and she opened her eyes as if she knew. Lazily, she arched her back like a sleek cat, moved towards him, her gaze fixed on his face.

'Maya,' he whispered.

Before Lawrence had left Mandalay, he had tried again to tell Maya about his life in England and Helen, about what was expected of him. He didn't want to pretend with her, he didn't want to simply leave one day and for her father to say: *I told you so. He never meant to stay. He just wants to seize all our country's riches and then leave, like all the rest*.

She turned on him, almost fierce. 'You owe me nothing,' she said. 'Nor I, you.'

'But Maya—' That wasn't what he had been trying to say.

'We have lain together in my bed,' she said. 'And we have talked. That is all.'

He took her arm. 'That is not all.'

She acknowledged this with a small nod. 'We are from different lives,' she said. 'And we do not have to say that we will always be together. We are together now. That is all that matters.'

'Are we together now?' He felt eager like a child. Because

he could hardly bear to have her like this and then leave. 'Are we? Can we be together again?'

'I will come to my aunt's house in Sinbo,' she said. 'Do not fear.'

Do not fear. With her, he had no fear. Better than that. With her he had a hope, more than he had ever known.

Now, Lawrence paced the *tai* and he walked around the camp. He climbed up the ladder and stood on his verandah, which gave him a very good view of the surrounding area, shaded by the vines grown around the structure for that purpose. As the sun set across the distant valley, he poured himself a whisky, sat on his chair outside, lit a cigarette and tried to relax. But he could not.

Desperate for something to take his mind off his need for her and his need for rain, he decided to visit a small village upstream from the camp where the logging of next season's out-turn was going on. He would go tomorrow to check on progress. Why not? There was nothing he could do here for now. And he was on a knife-edge just waiting.

He arrived the following day to find that the logging there was going to schedule. It was soothing to discover this, despite the heaviness of the heat and the tension of anticipation.

'The rain comes,' one of his men told him.

What was so different about tonight, he wondered. It was hot, as usual. The insects were persistent, as ever. There was no cloud to be seen, just a haze of heat that lifted only at sunset. And what a sunset. Even Lawrence, with so much on his mind, had to admit that the view was glorious. The darkening sky seemed shot with gold and amber as the blush filled the entire heavens over the forest. He sat there with his whisky long after he should.

And then he felt something change. There was a weightlessness in the air, a sharpening of the senses and he knew what this meant. His man had been right. Lawrence was impressed. He went inside as the sky grew black, the wind blew and he could hear the thunder beginning to rumble. At last. Lawrence went to bed, still with the ache that he'd felt since meeting Maya, but at least feeling optimistic. And the rains came.

Even as he was falling asleep, he heard it. Rain, welcome rain, pattering at first on the roofs, getting louder and louder, sending him off into a deep sleep which included dreams of great rivers rising, logs tumbling and crashing downstream. And Maya.

In the morning the coolness of the temperature was another welcome relief after the heavy oppression of the past weeks. But now Lawrence had to get back to camp urgently. The paddy fields were awash and the two men he had sent ahead rushed back to tell him the news. There was flash flooding. The road back to camp was already impassable. Bloody hell. The rains had remained ferocious all through the night and even now they hadn't eased. Talk about one extreme to the other. The men were saying that the rivers had risen quicker than they'd ever known before.

He waited another day, but the rains didn't even stop to

catch breath. The incessant croaking of the bullfrogs was unnerving him. Lawrence took stock. He only had stores for a few days, but he mustn't panic. Still, the bungalow was built on low-lying ground and reports were already reaching him that all streams were in full spate so that not even elephants could ford them and that houses were being washed away, so great were the sudden floods. It was looking serious. Was he going to be marooned here? Or was the very water that he'd longed for going to snatch everything away? Nothing else for it. They had to get back – and fast.

The usual way back to camp involved crossing two large streams and it was clear this would be impossible. They'd have to go the long way round. There were still *chaungs*, but they were small ones, at least for the moment.

Not so small, it turned out. The first one was almost waist deep as they waded across and the current was swift. But they did it. The second fazed even the elephants. They screeched and bellowed at the sight of the raging torrent which was already uprooting trees and crashing them into the banks. Jesus. Lawrence shouted the order to the *oozies*, the elephant handlers, and the others to move upstream, though it was hard to even make himself heard with all the racket going on, and eventually they found a safer place to cross.

It was still hairy and there was only one way to do it. Halfway across, clinging on to his elephant, hoping they could avoid the debris being flung by the wild waters of the river into their path and praying they'd make it across, the elephant stumbled and Lawrence slipped and almost fell from its back. The driving rain was in his face, in his eyes, in his ears. He could barely see and all he could hear was the thundering of the river, all he could feel was the ponderous movement of the great beast on whom his life depended, trudging through the mud and waters of the *chaung*. Lawrence clung on with wet, numb fingers, regained his position on the elephant's back, thought of Maya's father. He was going to get his hands dirty today, alright. And more.

But at last they were over. Luck had been on their side that day. They stopped for breakfast, completely done in. They scraped the leeches off their legs since the puttees hadn't stopped the buggers getting through. But they had no choice. They had to go on. And on they went. At times the path wasn't visible and there was a lot more wading to be done before they eventually arrived back at the camp, wet through and exhausted.

Only then could Lawrence relax. He thought of Maya. She would be coming up to Myitkyina to her aunt's house in Sinbo in a few days and he would see her again. She seemed to want that as much as he. And then perhaps, he told himself, the ache would go away.

CHAPTER 25

The Emporium's contact in Mandalay was the main agent for all their dealings in Myanmar; his other men in Yangon and Bagan were apparently answerable to him. This, Eva found out within five minutes of arriving at his 'office', a dusty shack in downtown Mandalay on Eighty-fourth Street near the stone carvers' workshops in Kyauksittan. His name was Myint Maw, he talked very fast and he was extremely full of his own importance. Jacqui had warned Eva in her latest email. *You can be firm with him . . . But don't push him too far. If he gets at all funny with you, just walk away.* Funny with her? It sounded to Eva as if Jacqui were expecting her to walk a tightrope as far as diplomacy and tact were concerned.

'Now, what I can show you? What I can show you?' He shuffled through the heap of papers on his desk. 'What we have? What is to view?'

He seemed very disorganised. 'This is what I am expecting to see,' Eva said resolutely, consulting her own paperwork. 'Figures and statues, carved and painted.' She showed him the pictures of the delicately carved angel, the nats, the monk sitting on a lotus flower and the Buddhas.

225

'Ah.' He pressed his skinny hands together. 'So special, yes?'

'I hope so.' Eva picked up her bag. 'Shall we go?' She was determined to be businesslike and, with this in mind, had worn loose linen trousers and a smart silk jacket for the encounter. But she was getting awfully hot already.

The goods turned out to be in a storeroom several doors along. Between them the stone-carvers, their workshops so small that they worked by the roadside, sculpted Buddhas and other iconic images up to three metres high, working in white stone, marble and even jade for the smaller pieces. Men in *longyis* scurried around fetching and carrying and the noise of angle grinders and drilling throbbed dull and monotonous in the hot and dusty air.

'Who are their customers?' Eva asked.

Myint Maw dismissed customers and stone-carvers with a wave of his hand. 'Local business people,' he said. 'And foreign buyers perhaps.' He leaned towards her, so that Eva had a too-close-for-comfort view of the hairy mole on his chin. 'But as you know, most money in the old, not the new.'

Last night Eva had been happy enough to chill out at her hotel and take a walk alongside the Palace moat before finding first the nearest internet café and then a restaurant in the evening for dinner. She had tried to call the number Klaus had left for her. *Dear Eva, Sorry to miss you. Give me a call when you return to Mandalay* . . . But it wasn't available and there had been no sign of him at the hotel. It didn't matter. When you travelled alone, you grew accustomed to eating on your own. And after everything that had happened over the last few days, it was actually quite a relief to be alone with her thoughts and have an early night.

She'd also made an appointment with Myint Maw for 11.30 a.m. and so before coming here she'd taken the opportunity of visiting the silk weavers, where she watched, fascinated, as the Burmese women worked the looms, deftly threading the different colours of silk from their spools into intricate patterns with nimble fingers whilst working the pedals with their feet. They were so fast. Eva had moved from the factory at the back to the front of the shop and it hadn't taken much persuasion for her to add a silk scarf in delicate lavender to her growing collection of Myanmar souvenirs. Her mother, she'd decided, would just have to love it.

Now, they arrived at their destination and Myint Maw showed her into the storeroom. There were wooden objects crammed on to every dusty shelf and they were not, she saw immediately, quality goods.

'What's all this?' she asked.

But he hurried her through. 'This not for you,' he said. 'No, no.'

'Is it yours?' He seemed a little edgy. Eva paused to take a closer look but he pulled at her arm and she was forced to follow.

'No, not mine,' he said. 'It is shared storeroom. Do not worry. Come with me now, please.'

And that was a relief because it looked like cheap tat, very far from the sort of pieces she and the Emporium were interested in.

'Here.' Myint Maw led the way into a smaller room. He got a large box down from a shelf. 'This what you are here to view.' He nodded energetically. 'Yes, yes. I remember. I know. This is what you must see. Please.'

Eva took the first figure from the box. It was about thirty centimetres high, a female nat statue carved from wood with painted headdress, red lips and porcelain eyes, her expression regal but sad. Eva examined it carefully, using her eyeglass. The patina on the face was extraordinary, the glaze so cracked that it made her look like a very old lady indeed.

'Nan Karaing Mei Daw,' Myint Maw told her. 'Yes, yes. Beautiful nat, yes?'

'Part human, part buffalo.' Eva had done her homework. She knew the history. This particular nat destroyed her enemies when given offerings of fried fish. Like most of the other Burmese nats – there were thirty-seven in total – she had suffered a violent death and had become the Burmese equivalent of a martyr.

'You like?' Myint Maw rubbed those skinny hands together.

'I like.' It was nineteenth century, in excellent condition and perfectly genuine in Eva's opinion. Jacqui would love it.

Slightly taller was the seated Bhumisparsha Buddha in lacquered teak. As Eva knew from her studies, the style of Buddha images, from Mon to Taungoo and beyond, differed according to date and dynasty. This Buddha was, she recognised, from the Mandalay period with his youthful and innocent face, the hair tightly curled, the robes decoratively folded, the hand making the *mudra* gesture of touching the earth.

There was the angel, the *deva*, carved intricately in teak, and the rather gorgeous monk sitting on a lotus flower, lacquered teak with a gilded and glass inlay. She wasn't disappointed, although she did wish Myint Maw didn't feel compelled to keep up such a high speed commentary on everything she looked at. His English wasn't the best and it was distracting to say the least. He seemed nervous too, constantly checking his watch and looking towards the doorway as if they were about to be disturbed. But this was important and Eva was determined to take her time.

An hour later, she surveyed the collection of antique nats, Buddhas and other artefacts. It was impressive and she'd been able to confidently authenticate every one. She was so excited, she couldn't wait to see them in the Emporium. 'Prices have been agreed?' she checked with Myint Maw. That was her understanding; she didn't want to get into haggling.

Maw shrugged. 'Prices? Now, what you say?'

Oh dear. Once again, Eva produced her paperwork. And then she remembered Ramon. 'And where did all these pieces come from?' she asked the contact. 'Can you tell me?'

'Come from?'

'Where did you buy?' She included the statues in a wide gesture. Spread her hands into a question.

'All over,' he said. 'Private houses, monasteries, temples . . .'

'Monasteries?' That didn't sound right. 'Why are they selling?'

'They not want old things,' he said. 'They need the money. They want new.'

'And temples?'

'You go to Bagan?' he asked.

'Not yet.' But she would be going. And she knew there were hundreds of temples there.

He made a flicking gesture with his hand. 'When you go, you will see,' he said. 'Too many temples, much destroyed. Too many statues. Nowhere for them to go. But they want money. You see.'

Oh, dear. How could you balance the need for money with the need to keep iconic pieces in their original environment? It was a tricky question. 'And do you have the paperwork?' she persevered. She tried not to look at the mole and the long dark hair that sprouted from it. 'For the sales?' She wanted to at least check they had been paid for.

Myint Maw clutched his chest. 'You not trust? You think these things are stolen?' He seemed nothing less than devastated.

'Yes,' said Eva. 'No. That is . . .' She shrugged. 'My employer wants me to check.' Which wasn't quite true, but was good enough for the moment.

Maw seemed incredulous now. 'You joke?'

'No.' She shook her head but she wasn't sure they were getting anywhere.

'I show you other stuff,' he said. 'I know.'

Eva frowned. What was he talking about now? 'What other stuff?'

'I know,' he said. 'Why you care?'

Eva thought of what had happened in Yangon. 'Do you mean another shipment? Are there more goods being sent out to us?' She was confused. Why did she keep getting the feeling that everyone else knew a lot more than she did? She was the one inspecting all the artefacts, but there seemed to be another agenda. She liked transparency in her business dealings, with a mutual respect. Here, in both Yangon and Mandalay, dealings seemed to be decidedly muddy.

'You have no need to worry,' he assured her. She could feel him swiftly back-tracking. 'It is all good. Price is right. There will be no questions asked.'

But *was* that a good thing? Eva thought of all the roughly made wooden objects she'd seen in the other room and she thought of what Ramon had said. *Plundering* . . . Burma might be opening up to trade and to tourism. But who was benefiting? And she was pretty sure the answer was not the ordinary Burmese people.

CHAPTER 26

The doctor came in the afternoon. Rosemary felt that she'd known him forever; she had, more or less, he had been their family doctor since she was about ten years old and had looked after her mother when she was ill.

'Dr Martyn.' Warmly, she shook his hand.

'Rosemary. It's been a long time. How are you?' He looked much the same. Worn leather briefcase, scuffed shoes, green tweed jacket, his hair a bit thinner on top. Rosemary supposed that he'd be retiring soon.

'I'm alright,' she said. 'But Dad . . .' She told the doctor how she'd found him. 'And he did say his prescription had changed.'

'Mmm.' He frowned, pulled some notes from the briefcase. 'His blood pressure was getting a little high. We were trying to bring it down.'

'And he seems different,' Rosemary added in a low voice that she hoped wouldn't carry to the downstairs bedroom.

'Different?'

'A bit vague. Muddled.' She'd tried to explain to Alec on the phone last night too, but it was hard to put it into words.

'Do you want me to come over, Rosemary?' he had asked her. 'Give you a hand?'

'No.' And they both knew she had said it too quickly. 'I'm fine,' she told him. 'Thank you. I need this time with him.'

'Of course.' But he had rung off soon afterwards, saying he had a lot of work to get through, and she knew she'd let him down. *Sorry, Alec*, she whispered, in her head.

'Muddled, yes.' Dr Martyn nodded in that avuncular way that she remembered. But somehow it wasn't as reassuring as it used to be. 'A touch of dementia,' he said. 'But he's managing quite well, given his age.'

'Is it dementia, though?' she asked. 'He seems so clear about some things.' She frowned. 'And will it get worse?'

He raised bushy eyebrows. 'It might do, my dear. Or it might not.'

'I see.' She supposed it was a bit like asking if he would get older.

He took her to one side and put a reassuring hand on her shoulder. 'It's all part of the ageing process,' he explained in a low voice. 'Confusion, dementia, call it what you will. It's not uncommon, you know. And sometimes the long-lost past is a whole lot clearer than what happened yesterday.'

Rosemary nodded. 'Yes, that makes sense.' She forced a smile.

'So, where's the patient?' He rubbed his hands together. 'I'll look him over. My goodness, I remember your father from when I was first qualified.' He shook his head as if wondering where all the years had gone.

'Come through then.' Rosemary took him to the bedroom where her father was resting after lunch. Not a very substantial lunch, but she supposed a few spoonfuls of chicken broth and half a slice of bread was better than nothing.

She opened the door wider. 'Dad, Dr Martyn's here.'

'Now then, young feller me lad,' the doctor said. 'What have you been up to?'

Rosemary left them to it.

He emerged ten minutes later. 'His heart's tickety boo,' he said. 'Blood pressure fine. But I've adjusted the prescription slightly given what's happened. Here.' He handed her the new one. 'He's pretty stable, I'd say. For now.'

'Good.' Rosemary moved towards the front door. 'And we should check his blood pressure again once the new pills kick in, shouldn't we?'

He nodded. 'Ring the surgery in a week or so,' he said. 'I'll pop in again, no problem.'

'Thanks, Doctor.'

She opened the front door. 'And I was wondering . . .' She lowered her voice. 'Is there anything else we should be doing? Do you have any advice?'

'Let him rest,' he said. 'Plenty of fluids. Keep an eye on him.'

'Is that all?'

'And think of the future.' He fixed her with a penetrating gaze. 'You do realise, don't you, my dear, that before long your father might need more full-time care?'

Rosemary nodded. He seemed better now since his fall.

But what about the next time? By the next time it might be too late.

'You know where to find me if you want to discuss things.' He lifted a hand. 'And any further problems, just phone the surgery.'

'Alright. Thank you. Goodbye.' Rosemary watched him climb into his old black Renault and drive away.

She let out a small sigh and went back into the bedroom. 'Everything OK, Dad?'

'Rosie.' He looked tired. 'What did he say to you, then?'

'Nothing much.' She smoothed the cover of the bed and flicked back the curtain. 'He said your blood pressure was fine. I'll make some tea, shall I?'

'I couldn't get much out of him either,' he said. 'They forget you have a mind once you hit eighty.' He coughed. 'Doctors. Treat you like a bloody imbecile.'

Rosemary chuckled. 'Doctor Martyn's not like that,' she protested. 'He's really kind.' But he had a point.

'Because I can get up, you know. I'm not just lazing around.' His breath rasped in his chest.

'Course you can,' she soothed. 'And we'll get you up later. Nothing wrong with having a little nap.'

He patted the bed. 'Come and sit by me for a bit. And stop looking so worried.'

'I'm not worried.' Though she was. And seeing him like this had made her worry even more. *And think of the future . . .* That's what Dr Martyn had said.

What did that mean? Full time care? A nursing home? She

couldn't imagine her father letting someone in to his house to wash him, shave him, change his sheets, and heaven knows what else if he wasn't capable of doing it himself. Mrs Briggs was one thing – that woman was an institution and she'd been here for ages. He knew her. He trusted her. But Mrs B couldn't afford to give them any more time and she wasn't strong enough to do any lifting. Neither was she a nurse. But nor could Rosemary see her father in a nursing home or retirement place. She shivered . . . She knew that many of them were very nice these days, and he had the money to choose a decent one. But he'd hate it. He belonged here in his own home, in their home. And he wouldn't want it to be filled with strangers.

'Pah, doctors . . .' He shifted into a more comfortable position, licked his dry lips. 'You don't want to let them worry you. I'll be on my feet in no time, you'll see.'

And if he wasn't? 'I'll make that tea,' she said.

'It's true I haven't been quite myself lately,' he mused, when she returned five minutes or so later. 'I've been thinking a lot about old times.'

'Old times?' she said. For a moment the bitterness resurfaced. Perhaps it was never that far away. 'The good old days in Burma, do you mean?' She put the tray down on the bedside table.

His serious gaze reproached her for her flippancy. 'Not so good during the war, love,' he said. He took the tea she handed him, the cup rattling in the saucer.

'Oh, the war . . .' She stilled it with her hand. 'It might be hot. Careful.' She took the plate from the tray. 'Biscuit?'

He shook his head.

'There were good times for you too,' she remarked. *Where are you going with this, Rosemary?* 'Before the war, I mean.'

'There were.' He met her direct gaze. ''Course there were.' Then he looked away and took a slurp of his tea. 'Ah, that's grand, love.'

She took her tea from the tray and sipped it, watching him over the rim of the teacup. One minute he seemed to know exactly what was going on, the next, off he'd drift into never-never land.

'But *we* had good times and all.' A small smile played around his mouth. 'You and me and your mum, didn't we, eh?'

'Of course we did,' she said. She thought back. She remembered him as a rough-and-tumble father who was always getting told off by her mother, always getting into trouble. He would take her out into the garden without her wellington boots on, so that they dripped mushy leaves and trod dirt into the pale green living-room carpet. And he would fail to bring her back from the seaside in time for tea. 'I don't know what I'm going to do with you,' Rosemary's mother would scold. 'You're like a child yourself, you are.' *Not always joking either . . .*

But most of the time . . . It had been her mother who looked after Rosemary, who taught her how to behave, who had brought her up to be whatever she had become. Her father had been busy with Fox and Forsters and his appearances were reserved for high days and holidays, not the everyday life in between. And she could remember hardly any times when the three of them were together and having fun. What good times? She must have frowned.

'No one gives you a manual, love,' he said. 'In those days, we had to make it up as we went along.'

And for the first time, Rosemary wondered. Had he wanted to have more of a share in her upbringing? Had he been excluded because he was too untidy, too careless? How had he felt being told off all the time? Helen had made of fun of him too. Sometimes even put him down. Had she been punishing him?

'She was a good woman, your mother,' he said, almost as if he knew what she was thinking. 'Thank heavens we had her to keep us on the straight and narrow, eh?'

Rosemary nodded. She thought of how she had felt when she'd lost her. Desolate. And yet at times it had been such a strain living up to all her expectations. Had he felt that too? She patted her father's hand. He must have felt that too.

CHAPTER 27

On Saturday morning, as planned, Ramon picked Eva up in his car and they drove towards Sagaing, stopping briefly at the Mahamuni temple. Sagaing was a highly religious site built on a hill, he told her, and she could see now that the green slopes ahead of them were studded with wooden monasteries and golden pagodas.

'Did you have a good day yesterday?' he asked pleasantly, as he changed gear to negotiate the hill.

'Yes, thank you.' It had certainly been full of treasures. But Eva decided not to tell him that; he might think that they were treasures which should stay in Mandalay. After her meeting with Myint Maw, she had emailed Jacqui to fill her in on the details and had received a reply straightaway. *Sounds good*, Jacqui had written. *Looking forward to seeing them*. Eva was confident she wouldn't be disappointed. Her boss had asked about Myint Maw too but Eva wasn't sure exactly what she wanted to know. *He's a bit shady*, she wrote back. *And he's never clear about provenance. But . . .*

'And your grandfather?' Ramon asked her.

'He's much better, thank you.' Eva had phoned again last night after dinner and spoken to her mother. 'Don't worry,' she had said. 'Just concentrate on what you have to do in Burma.' *What you have to do in Burma* . . . She wondered how much her mother knew about why she was here.

'And you?' Eva asked him. 'How are things at the factory?' He seemed very polite this morning and so she decided to reciprocate. He was wearing a black-and-yellow checked *longyi* and a white short-sleeved shirt which looked crisp and cool, considering the heat outside.

He nodded. 'Everything is good,' the hint of a smile touching the corners of his mouth. But not, she noticed, his eyes.

They passed a small wooden monastery and he stopped the car so that she could take a photo.

Eva decided to take advantage of his good mood. 'I've been thinking,' she said, when she'd climbed back in.

'Oh?' He raised a dark eyebrow, glanced in the mirror and drove on.

'About the chinthe.' She risked a look across at him.

He was focusing on the road ahead, which was narrow and steep with sharp bends. But now he was frowning.

'Do you really have a plan to get it back?'

Ramon let out a deep sigh. 'You are still thinking about that?' he asked. He didn't wait for her reply and he didn't look at her. 'I must tell you, Eva, to forget about it. You have done enough for our family in returning the other.' He braked sharply as a car came from the opposite direction. 'You can do no more.'

'But I could help,' she said. 'They don't know me. I'm not involved. I could at least—'

'No.' The car had passed and he drove on.

She blinked across at him. She'd had some thinking time since they'd last met. Couldn't she use what she was doing here for the Emporium as a cover? If she pretended she wanted to *buy* the chinthe . . . Wouldn't they be interested? They sounded very greedy. She suspected they would, if the price were right. And if she could draw them into the open, wouldn't they at least have a chance of getting the chinthe back?

'I know what you are thinking. But you must not become further involved.' And, once again, she was surprised by what sounded almost like tenderness in his voice. Taking his eyes off the road for just for a second, he pressed his palm on to hers in a swift and unexpected gesture. His hand felt so warm. 'You must leave it to me. You must trust me, Eva.'

Eva watched as he moved his hand back to the steering wheel. She would like to trust him, but he hadn't tried to get the stolen chinthe back before. Why would he do anything now?

'What will you do then?' she asked again. 'What are you planning? Can't you at least tell me that?'

He shook his head as the car continued to crawl uphill. 'It is dangerous.'

Which was all very well. 'But my grandfather—'

'They are dangerous.' His voice hardened. 'Do you hear me, Eva?'

'Yes, but . . .'

'We have our own ways of doing things here in Burma. I told you. You must not pursue this matter.' The road was getting even narrower and he bent forwards over the wheel. 'Please leave it alone, Eva.'

Eva sat back in her seat. But it meant so much to her grandfather to reunite the chinthes. She couldn't let him down. She couldn't just let it go, at least, not without a fight.

'Many Burmese people come here to Sagaing.' Ramon spoke in a clear voice, obviously determined that the subject be dropped. 'They spend weeks, months or even years in quiet contemplation.' He didn't look at her. 'Daw Moe Mya's grandmother, Suu Kyi, came here too at the end of her life.' He swung the car around a tight corner. On either side of them were traditional Burmese houses, simple but smart, tucked away behind bamboo fences and palm trees.

Despite herself, Eva's interest was piqued. 'How long did she live here for?'

'For the five years before her death. She ended her life here in Sagaing.' The car continued to crawl uphill. And they passed a golden pagoda, blinking in the sunlight from behind a thicket of trees.

'What was she looking for?' Eva tried to imagine.

'Enlightenment,' he said. 'She had been through much suffering. We call it *samsara*, *karma* is the force that drives it, the cycle of birth and death and the suffering therein.' He shrugged as if to lessen the intensity of his words. 'Many people come here to meditate and to live the right way, the non-harmful way, to find wisdom.'

Eva nodded. She could see that after the turbulent life Suu Kyi had lived, she would have wanted to end her days in peace and tranquillity. And she realised why Ramon had wanted to show her this part of Myanmar.

At last they came to the top of the hill and Ramon stopped by a golden temple.

'This is the highest pagoda,' he said. 'Shall we go in?' He shot her a broad smile.

The man's moods could change in an instant. But nevertheless, Eva got out of the car, put on her wide-brimmed hat, slipped off her leather sandals and followed him up the smooth dusty steps to the pagoda. And when she saw the view in front of her, her own frustrations instantly evaporated. The hill was cloaked with green and gold. She could almost feel a sense of quiet spirituality settling over her. This was it, she realised. This was what Myanmar and its people was all about. And it was something that she also longed for, for herself. That sense of peace.

'Where did she live?' she asked Ramon. He was gazing down the hill, past the bright pagodas and lush valleys, towards the wide silver curve of the Irrawaddy River and its two bridges, and he seemed lost in thought, as affected by the landscape as Eva, though he must have seen it many times before.

'You see the temple which looks like a giant cup?' He pointed, moving closer so that they shared the same sight line. 'Now go to the left.' He bent his head next to hers. She could smell the scent of him, oil and wood with the faintest hint of cardamom, and feel the heat of his dark-olive skin.

'Yes.' She followed his gaze.

'There is a tiny red-roofed building.'

'Like a Chinese pagoda?'

'A bit.' He smiled. 'That is the monastery where she lived her few final years. We can drive down and see it from the outside if you wish. But we cannot go in.'

She nodded. 'I'd like to.' It was her history too, she thought. Her grandfather was inextricably linked with Ramon's grandmother. They had moved apart for almost their whole lives, but it seemed that what they'd shared was somehow greater than that.

Beside the steps to the temple, a woman was selling *thanaka*, the traditional Burmese make-up. Eva paused and watched her pounding the bark it was made from.

'You try?' the woman asked.

Eva stepped forwards and the woman smeared some of the light brown muddy substance on to her cheeks. It felt cold and grainy. Unlike Western make-up, it wasn't rubbed in, it was more like a tribal marking. 'It will protect you,' the woman said.

Ramon smiled when she got back into the car. 'Very nice,' he said. He touched her cheek. 'It will make your skin soft.' For a moment their eyes met.

They drove down to the monastery and stood outside, absorbing the atmosphere of the place. Despite the exterior glitz, it was a simple building. In the yard, a line of saffron robes were drying on a rope strung between two coconut palms, and a mangy dog was sleeping in the shade. Someone was cooking a huge vat of food over an open fire and one of the young novices was sweeping the floor with an old-fashioned broom. Eva could see the long tables in the refectory where the shaven-headed young monks would go with their black rice bowls for their lunch.

'They fast after midday,' Ramon told her as if he'd followed her thoughts. 'That is when they study English language and Buddhist Scriptures.'

Eva remembered what Klaus had told her about the monks. 'Were you a novice?' she asked him. She couldn't imagine it somehow.

'Of course.' He nodded. 'For a short time. In our culture it is thought an important part of development to make your *shin pyu.*'

'Your . . . ?'

He smiled. '*Shin pyu.* It is the highest way to pay respect. To your mother, to Lord Buddha. That is what Buddhists believe.'

With some difficulty, Eva visualised Ramon with a shaved head and a saffron robe. But he wasn't the type, she suspected, to be content just being a scholar. He was a worker, a master-craftsman. And she guessed that he was a good businessman too.

'We have one of the highest rates of blindness here in Myanmar,' Ramon told her. 'Hundreds of thousands wait for cataract operations. There are charities. European eye surgeons come here to this monastery to operate and help us.'

'That's great.' They needed that sort of help, she realised. It would be a long time before the country would catch up on medical advances, before their people could expect their health to be looked after as a matter of course.

As Eva took a last look around the monastery buildings, she wondered about the woman who had lived here, the woman who had first received the special gift of the two chinthes from Queen Supayalat, the last queen of Burma. Suu Kyi, Ramon's great, great grandmother. She had wanted enlightenment. Would she also want Eva to try and get the chinthe back?

From Sagaing, they took a small ferry over the river to Inwa, where the roads were red dirt tracks and the people got around by horse and cart or bicycle. 'This was once the capital of Myanmar,' Ramon told her, 'from the fourteenth to the eighteenth century. For me, the place most represents the past and what we, the Burmese people, have come from.'

Eva sat in the back of the brightly painted cart, buffeted by cushions, as they rocked and rolled along the rutted track. And once again she thought she knew why they were here. It was indeed like going back in time. The fields unfolding beside her were still ploughed by bullocks pulling a wooden plough, the crops still picked by women wearing broad bamboo hats. And as they passed, the one and only tarmacked road was being re-laid by an old-fashioned steamroller and a posse of women, some of them looking far too old for this kind of work, Eva thought, watching them load gravelly rock into wide baskets which they carried on their heads before throwing it on to the wet sticky tar.

'Inwa is often completely flooded by the river,' Ramon told her, and she could see that much of the area was one big lake covered in floating white water lilies and backed by distant romantic pagodas, whose reflected shapes fluttered on the surface of the water like a landscape from a fairy tale.

Eva tried to take it all in. It seemed to sum up the feeling of being in the tropics. Paddy fields and banana plantations; bullocks on the road, tied to a tree; ruined temples and ancient wooden monasteries. The palm fronds and banana leaves were so green, the landscape so simple and uncluttered. On the far side of the lake, she saw a small group of women washing. They had unwound their *longyis*, pulled them above the collar bone, refastened them and were washing underneath, in perfect modesty.

This was what Burma must have been like when her grandfather lived here, Eva thought. Apart from the invasion of British clubs and accompanying paraphernalia, of course. Here, she was aware of what he must have loved about the land. The gentle wooded hills, the red earth and the paddy fields of rice. The golden temples, the warm air, that sense of peace.

The horse and cart stopped at an old teak monastery and Ramon jumped off the cart and held out his hand to help Eva down from the back.

'Look!' A little girl materialised at the bottom of the steps. She held up a necklace for Eva to admire. Like Klaus in Yangon, Ramon had told her she should ignore the souvenir sellers, but it was hard when she knew they had so little.

'It's very nice,' Eva told her. 'But my suitcase is full.' Which wasn't far from the truth.

'Very cheap.' The girl grinned.

Eva's heart melted. These children were so sweet but they shouldn't have to become street sellers at such a young age. 'How cheap?' She smiled back at her.

'Three million dollars?' The girl laughed. 'You are very beautiful and he is very handsome.' She pointed at Ramon, who shrugged and walked on. 'Three million dollars from the pretty lady for the necklace? It is made of watermelon seeds.'

Eva laughed too. 'That's too much for me,' she said. And she offered a thousand kyat, a little less than a British pound. Immediately she was besieged by children selling crayoned fans, beaded purses and jade bracelets and it took her several minutes to escape and wave them all away. Ordinary Burmese people, she thought. Would the political reforms in the country help them? Or would they become greedy as they tried to extract money from rich Westerners? She hoped that in Myanmar, things wouldn't move too fast.

Inside the cool dim interior of the monastery, the ancient teak carving almost took Eva's breath away.

'I thought you would appreciate this place,' murmured Ramon.

And she did. Every doorway, every piece of panelling was exquisite and everything from floor to ceiling was made of wood, so that its sweet and musty scent filled her nostrils, pervading all her senses. She could almost taste the wood on her tongue. A ray of sunlight poured through the open door like a laser, lighting up dancing dust motes and the shaven heads of the boy novices who were sitting in the corner, learning from one of their elders. But this only seemed to enhance the feeling of calm.

The interior was high and cavernous and on a raised platform sat a gilded Buddha. Eva was about to step up for a closer look, but Ramon touched her arm and pointed to a sign. Ladies apparently were not permitted on the platform. Eva shook her head at Ramon's meaningful look. Myanmar, she thought, had a long way to go. At the Mahamuni temple in Mandalay, only men were allowed to add gold leaf to the Buddha, Ramon had told her earlier today, with some relish, it had to be said. The knobbly Buddha not only looked impressive but his covering of gold was now apparently over six inches thick.

'And is that a rule decreed by Buddha?' Eva had asked sharply. Because if so, she hadn't heard of it. 'Or by man?'

'Who knows?'

Eva guessed that Ramon wasn't used to women questioning a tradition that had been in operation for centuries. Or perhaps he simply dismissed Eva as feisty, as if she were some circus pony, she thought grimly. But she had been brought up to question things. It was the only way that any of society's wrongs could ever be changed.

They moved into the bright sunlight outside the monastery, where the wood was faded and sun-bleached. Eva turned to Ramon. 'Will your grandmother bring the chinthe back with her when she returns to Mandalay?' she asked him. 'Or will she leave it in Pyin Oo Lwin?'

He frowned. 'Why?'

'I just wondered.' Together they strolled back along the weathered teak flooring. The truth was, that she was concerned.

'You wonder about things a lot,' Ramon observed. 'I do not think that she will let it out of her sight.'

They walked down the steps of the monastery and back towards the cart.

'Then she should be careful.' Eva took the hand he offered to help her back in.

He eyed her gravely as she settled herself once more against the red cushions. 'For what reason?'

Eva leaned forwards. 'Because she told me that the Li family live in Mandalay. They might hear that she now has the other of the pair. They might try to steal it just like they stole the other one.' Why couldn't he see that something must be done?

'They will not hear.' Abruptly, he turned, went round to the front of the cart and swung himself up next to the driver. The driver took the reins and the little horse with the pink flower in its harness trotted off.

Ramon sat stiffly in front, his back only inches from her. His mobile rang and he pulled it from his belt in an impatient gesture. He listened for a few moments, then hurled a torrent of fast and furious Burmese into the phone.

Eva glimpsed the expression on his face, it was thunderous. What was the problem? She thought of Maya. His grandmother was right, something was certainly troubling him.

Ramon let out a final curse and ended the call, shoving his mobile back into the belt of his *longyi*. It amused Eva that in this country which was in so many ways old-fashioned and behind the times, where it was hard to find an internet connection or an ATM machine, that even the saffron-robed monks and market traders could be seen with mobile phones.

'Trouble?' she asked tentatively.

He didn't look round. His back was straight and unyielding. 'It is the factory.'

'I thought everything was fine?'

'It is not.' He half turned and glanced back at her.

Eva was touched by the sadness in his eyes. She knew how important his father's company was to him. If he lost that . . . 'What is it?' she asked.

'The company is not doing well.' He shook his head in despair. 'How can we hope to succeed when our prices are undercut by so many unscrupulous companies?'

'Unscrupulous companies?' she echoed.

'How can we be appreciated? If we respect our workers and pay them a good living wage, if we respect the environment and buy only legitimately sourced timber . . . If we do these things, we must ask a fair price for our furniture, yes?'

Eva was surprised at the outburst. 'Yes, of course you must.'

Some children passed by on their bicycles, their books in a basket, woven Shan bags slung over their shoulders. They waved cheerily at her and she gave a quick wave back. But her attention was focused on Ramon. She was beginning to understand. 'Buying timber from sustainable forests is more expensive,' she murmured. The felling of trees must be regulated, just as it had been in her grandfather's day, and trees needed time to dry out before they were ready. 'If others don't do the same . . .'

'How can we compete?' Ramon's voice broke and he put his dark head in his hands. 'It is another order lost,' he muttered.

Eva's heart went out to him. She wanted to reach towards him, tell him it would all work out in the end. But something stopped her. He was so fierce, so proud. 'I'm so sorry,' she said. He couldn't compromise on his father's ethics and standards. There would be no other way for Ramon.

'It is not your concern.' He lifted his head.

This was what he had said to her before. Eva watched the children slowly disappear down the red dirt track by the lake. But this time she saw the dignity in the set of his shoulders and the tilt of his head and she knew she had caught him off-guard. But at least she had found out what was troubling him. 'How bad is it?' she asked.

'Bad enough.'

'And who are the people using the illegally felled timber and undercutting your prices?' she asked. 'Who's your main competition?'

He turned around until he was facing her. His eyes were hard, his mouth unsmiling. 'Those who produce poor quality goods and pay their workers a wage they can barely survive on,' he said. 'Those who make their money by damaging the credibility of other Burmese traders. Those who care this much . . .' He snapped his fingers. 'For our country and our forests.'

'Who?' Eva asked again. It couldn't be just one company, could it?

'The most unscrupulous company of them all,' he said, 'is Li's.'

Li's . . . Eva thought of what Ramon had shown her today: the Burma of her grandfather's time, the spirituality, the search for enlightenment. And she thought of the artefacts that Thein Thein and Myint Maw had shown her. The treasures of Burma. Soon to be shipped to the UK, to the Bristol Emporium and sold on. Was this her destiny, she wondered. To buy from someone else's culture, to follow someone else's lead? Or was there another path she should be taking?

CHAPTER 28

She stood by the bed, keeping watch over him. Blood pressure, heart rate, pills for this and pills for that . . . Lawrence was getting more than a little fed up with it. Life was more than that, surely? It always had been. Lying in this bed, struggling to think, struggling to breathe . . . That wasn't living.

But he remembered his life, his real life. All of it. Not just Burma, like she'd said. Not just the war and his life with Maya. But England too.

West Dorset, 1939

Lawrence had been in Burma almost two years when he got a long leave to go to England. *Home.* They all said it, at the club and the chummery. *You're going home, you lucky bugger.*

Lawrence had mixed feelings. Of course he wanted to see his parents and some of his friends, those who were still around. And he was tired, God, was he tired from the endless heat and rain and sun, from the logging, from the malaria that he'd shaken off only a few months before.

But . . . Burma was warm and vibrant and it had got under his skin. And there was Maya. Their relationship had grown into something that meant so much to Lawrence. When he was away from her, he longed, more than anything, to see her, to sleep with her, to feel the warmth of her silken body. But it wasn't just sex – he'd known that from the start. And it wasn't just passion, though the passion burnt and flared in him like nothing he'd ever known. It was also her quiet and her calm. It was the long conversations they had in the sweet dead of the night when they were alone, it was the touch of her cool hand on his brow, it was the serene expression in her dark eyes. It was love. That's what it was.

And in England . . . Yes, he missed that green and pleasant land. But England also meant Helen.

She'd written to him – he could hardly stop her from writing to him – and her little notes, affectionate and sweet, all held a subtext that Lawrence didn't want to acknowledge. He knew that she was waiting for him. And he knew that he should be honest with her. This would ultimately be to his advantage. If Helen knew that he was in love with another woman, a native woman at that, wouldn't she free him from this family obligation? Wouldn't she have too much dignity to want him when she knew that Lawrence could never think of her that way?

He'd tell her, he'd decided, face to face when he was on leave. It was the most honourable thing to do.

In the event, his leave had flown by.

'You've hardly seen Helen,' his mother pointed out, the night before he was due to return to Burma.

This was true. He'd flunked it.

'My fault, darling.' She'd hugged him and he'd smelt the familiar fragrance of her, the powder and the lipstick and the light, floral overtones of her cologne. 'I wanted you all to myself.'

He laughed. And he hadn't complained. It had been good to see her, and his father too, though he'd had more than one grilling about how long it would be before Lawrence returned to the family firm and stopped all this 'messing around in foreign parts' as he'd put it.

'But you must see her tonight,' his mother decreed.

'Of course.' Though he felt a dip of foreboding. He'd have to tell her tonight.

'There's a dance at the Assembly Rooms. You must take her.'

Lawrence had bowed his head. It was out of his hands once again. His mother was right. He must see Helen. But he hadn't intended to tell her at a dance.

He drank a large glass of whisky before he even left home. Dutch courage. *And God knows he'd need it.*

How had it happened? He hardly knew. They were outside, round the back of the dance hall, for Christ's sake. It was so bloody tacky. They'd danced and he'd drunk a lot. He'd felt sick and he'd needed some air. Next thing he knew . . .

It was the whisky. He should never have had all that whisky. 'Oh, God. Oh, God.' He put his head in his hands. His own breath stank. He wanted to die. He was sweating and he wanted to die.

Helen wrapped her slim white arms around him. 'I've always loved you, Lawrence,' she murmured into his shoulder.

'It shouldn't have happened. It was a mistake.' He remembered that day she'd kissed him at her parents' party when she was only twelve. He remembered other times too. Times when he should have stopped it, when he should have told her 'no'. They had never gone this far. And all those occasions had been before he went away to Burma. Before Maya. But now, it felt as if all those times had led inexorably to this moment.

Helen guiding his hands to her breasts, Helen lifting the hem of her dress, slipping the buckle of his belt. Helen's kisses. *Now, Lawrence . . . I want you now.*

'It wasn't a mistake,' she said. 'It'll be alright.' Already, she had adjusted her clothing. No one would know.

He thought of Maya. Oh, but it won't be alright, he thought.

'You're mine now,' Helen whispered.

Every sense and fibre in his body screamed 'no'.

'We should never have done it,' he said. He thought of what he'd intended to say to her. How could this have happened instead? How had everything gone so horribly wrong? How could he ever justify it? How could he explain? 'I should never have done it. Helen, I'm so sorry . . .'

'I don't want you to be *sorry* . . .' she fired back at him. Her lip curled. 'Why should you be sorry? And why should we wait?' Her eyes were like liquid in the darkness.

'Wait?'

'Till you come back from Burma. You know what I mean.'

Oh, God. She had got it all so wrong. 'Helen,' he said. How could he break it to her gently? 'I love you . . .'

'I know you do, darling.' She began once more to pull him towards her.

He resisted. 'But I love you like a sister.'

She laughed, a tinkle of a laugh that had always sounded forced to Lawrence and had always irritated him. 'Like a sister,' she echoed. 'I hope not, my darling. Not after what we've just done.'

He gripped her shoulders. 'Which was why we shouldn't have done it. Don't you see?'

'No.' Her blue eyes hardened. 'I don't see. I only know that we're promised to one another, you and me, Lawrence, and that we always have been. I know what I feel. And I know that you've just made love to me.'

'It was wrong, I tell you.' He was angry now and he pushed her away. They shouldn't even have gone dancing. He should have refused to take her. But it would have been impossible, his mother would have seen to that. So, he should have seen her, told her the truth, even gone dancing . . . But he should never have allowed her perfume and the music to seduce him in a weak moment. And he certainly shouldn't have drunk all that bloody whisky.

'How can it be wrong?' She was crying, hanging on to his arm and crying.

He felt like a total bastard. He was one. And he was a fool.

Acting like a sex-starved boy. Why couldn't he have been stronger? 'I'm sorry, Helen.'

'It doesn't matter,' she said. 'I wish you'd stop apologising. I'm glad we did it. And I don't care what you say, because I can see further than you can see.' And she wiped the tears from her face, suddenly composed. 'We've sealed our promise. You're mine now, Lawrence.'

The last day of his leave was a miserable one. Lawrence said goodbye to them all, Helen's parents (though he could hardly look her father in the eye), his parents and Helen herself.

'I'll write to you, Lawrence.' Helen was weeping. 'Come home soon. For good.'

And their parents, looking on fondly, clearly thought they'd come to some sort of understanding. Christ. How could he ever come back to Dorset now? Worse, how would he ever be able to get that night out of his head? Not only had he given Helen the very hope he had intended to stub out completely, but he had betrayed the woman he loved.

Lawrence had hugged his mother, waved farewell and boarded the steamer that would take him back to Burma, back to Maya's arms. But Helen's words still echoed in his head. And perhaps they always would. *'You're mine now, Lawrence. You're mine now.'*

CHAPTER 29

Eva dressed for dinner in a cream silk blouse and the embroidered indigo *longyi* she had bought in Yangon. She wore her velvety Burmese slippers, and around her neck, the antique pearls that her mother had given her on her eighteenth birthday. She took a thin silk wrap in case it turned chilly later. Not that there seemed much chance of that, she thought, as she stood at her bedroom window looking out into bustling Mandalay at night. She could see the illuminated golden dome of a nearby pagoda outlined against the black velvet of the sky, and the distant moat that encircled the Royal Palace. There was a crescent arc of moonshine and the stars were like sequins stitched on to the night.

Ramon smiled his approval when she appeared in the hotel foyer. He was dressed in linen trousers and a light shirt and jacket. It was the first time she had seen him in Western clothes and it took her rather by surprise. He seemed though to have recovered his composure since yesterday afternoon. She wondered how bad things really were and if he regretted telling her about the problems with his business. Surely the company weren't in danger of actually going under?

After they had left Inwa they had driven back to the city

and down to the port. Eva thought that she might perhaps take the boat when she travelled to Bagan. It was a long journey but it would be a good opportunity to see some more of the real Myanmar on the way. She'd collected the departure information from the office on the portside and walked down to where Ramon was standing rather disconsolately on the muddy sand looking out to the Irrawaddy. A barge was moving slowly along the river. She could make out the logo on the hull. A peacock in blue and gold.

'One of Li's boats,' he said.

She watched as it motored past. They had a lot to answer for.

'Shall we go?' Ramon asked now. He escorted her to the car, swung the passenger door open for her to get in and closed it behind her. He went round to the driver's side and climbed in. For a moment, he leaned in close. 'May I say that you look beautiful,' he murmured. 'I love that you wear our traditional *longyi*.'

'Thank you.' Eva smiled back at him. Yesterday, their outing together had been a bit fraught, this evening, perhaps they could both forget their troubles for a few hours, relax and enjoy.

In his Western clothes, Ramon seemed so different, almost not part of this Eastern landscape to which she had already become acclimatised. It unsettled her slightly and she looked away, out of the window, as they drove alongside the dark still waters of the moat.

'How do you feel about our country now that you are wearing our clothes?' Ramon teased. 'Are you getting used to it yet?'

'I think I am.' She was getting used to the white heat that lay so heavy on the city, to the constant thrum of the air-conditioning, to the heavy rain that was still falling once a day without warning, tumbling from the sky and turning the dust to mud. She was used to the hooting and bell-ringing of endless streams of motorbikes, trishaws, bicycles and cars and the street sellers squatting on broken paving slabs beside rickety stalls, frying noodles, rice and fish, sorting heaps of crimson chillies, lentils and tiny peanuts, and peeling giant *pomela* fruit, while the fragrances of dried fish, cloves and anise rose thick and pungent in the warm air. She was getting used to it and she was loving it. Myanmar, with its vivid colours of landscape and *longyi*, its raucousness and its calm, its intense flavours and fragrances, was a country of extremities. No wonder its people liked to smile. Many of them were poor, yes, but perhaps they were rich in the things that mattered more: in spirit, in their quality of life. After the grey November days she had left behind in the UK, Myanmar was like a hothouse bloom. 'It's everything I hoped for,' she told Ramon. 'And more.'

'Good.' Ramon nodded as they drew up outside the restaurant. He glanced across at her. 'There is just one thing missing,' he said.

'Oh?'

He got out of the car and came round to her side to open

262

the door. Eva took the hand he offered to help her out and felt the weight of the warm air settle over her once again.

Ramon turned to a boy selling flowers on the street corner, handed over a few notes and was given a string of tiny white blooms in return. Eva had seen similar street sellers at the temples; the Burmese bought garlands of flowers and fruit to lay at the feet of the resident *nats* of the pagodas and shrines. Nats, who must be charmed and appeased. In Myanmar almost everything had one.

'Jasmine.' Ramon held the blossoms out to her.

Eva sniffed. 'Wonderful.' She didn't care if he was trying to charm or appease her. Their scent was like honey, it sweetened the night air.

'May I?' And before she could even wonder what he was doing, he had moved behind her and she could feel his hands on her hair, which she'd worn loose tonight, deftly weaving the flowers through, as if she were a bride. 'There.' He stood back to survey the effect. 'Now you are a perfect Burmese lady.'

She laughed and put her hands to her hair. He had a gentle touch. She could feel the furry softness of the tiny white flowers and smell their scent, far superior to any bottled perfume.

'Shall we?' Ramon indicated the restaurant.

'Of course.'

A boy pulled the door open and Eva felt the light pressure of Ramon's hand on her back as he followed her inside.

She looked around. 'What a fabulous place.' It was colonial

in decor and style. The high ceiling had decorative cornicing and a teak staircase with a polished banister rail rose gracefully on the left side of the room. The walls were painted white, there were fat teak pillars from floor to ceiling and people sat in cane and wicker chairs at wooden tables laid with white linen cloths. The bar in front of them was a sheet of solid black granite.

Ramon spoke to a waiter who led them to their table.

'I wondered, would you like to visit my factory tomorrow morning?' he asked her when they were seated. 'Or do you have more antiques to inspect?'

Eva laughed somewhat warily. That was a tricky subject. She picked up the creamy linen napkin by her plate and spread it on her lap. 'I am seeing some more,' she said. 'But not till the afternoon. So of course I'll come. I'd be delighted.' Myint Maw had telephoned her earlier today at the hotel with the news that some more items had become available. 'They very good,' he had said. 'You come see tomorrow 3 p.m., yes?' But Eva couldn't help wondering where they had suddenly appeared from. She had put in a quick call to Jacqui before she'd come out tonight, but she'd had no idea either. *Go and see them,* her boss had advised, *take care and keep me informed.* Eva had spent the day wandering around the markets and antique shops of Mandalay, but had purchased very little. It seemed that to buy anything of quality, it was indeed a case of who you know. Jacqui was right then to stress the importance of their contacts.

They both studied the menu. A jug of iced water had been

put on the table by the immaculately dressed waiter and she poured them both a glass. 'I'm looking forward to seeing the furniture you design and produce,' she said.

He smiled warmly and she was reminded of that moment when he'd first opened the door to her at Pyin Oo Lwin. It transformed his face and she couldn't help noticing that he was attracting admiring looks from other female diners.

'We should order some wine,' he said.

'Wine?' Eva was a little surprised.

'But, yes. There is a reputable vineyard just outside Mandalay.'

'Really?'

'Really. It is run by a Frenchman.' His green eyes gleamed. 'They produce an excellent pinot noir which I recommend we try.'

The food was Chinese, and they ordered river prawns which arrived nestling in a ginger salad with sesame seeds, chicken with peanuts and fish steamed with lime along with various vegetable side dishes and rice. And Ramon was right. The wine proved to be delicious.

Conversation flowed easily between them, but although they talked about styles of furniture and wood, about English antiques and even about British colonialism, they hadn't yet touched on the subject that had come up at Inwa yesterday.

While they were waiting for dessert, Eva leaned closer towards him. 'I had no idea that the Li family also owned a furniture company,' she said. She tried to keep her voice nonchalant; this would certainly be another touchy subject.

Ramon ran a finger around the rim of his wineglass. He had allowed himself only one glass, she noted. After a moment, he looked up. 'Not just furniture,' he said. 'Statues, too. Wooden models, Buddhas, you name it. If they can make money out of it, they will produce it.'

'So they have a factory here in Mandalay? A showroom?' Eva wondered if she had already unknowingly visited it.

'Eva . . .'

Their dessert arrived, semolina cake with fresh coconut milk, a Burmese speciality, Ramon told her. Eva tasted it. It was very different from the unpalatable and bland substance she remembered from school.

'I'm not asking where it is,' she protested.

'Very well.' He dipped a spoon into the pudding. 'Then, yes. They do have a showroom – a shop – and there is a factory behind.' He narrowed his eyes. 'But you must promise me . . .'

'Yes?' She adopted her most innocent look.

'That you will stay away.'

Eva finished up her dessert. 'How can I go there, Ramon?' she asked. 'I don't even know where it is.'

They had coffee and Eva was surprised to see, when she looked at her watch, that it was almost midnight.

'I will take you back to your hotel,' Ramon said. He had paid the bill already and pretended to be offended when she offered a contribution.

Outside, the darkness enveloped them, but the air was balmy and still. Eva was aware of the scent from the jasmine in her hair. And of Ramon, as he opened the door of the car and she slid silently into the leather interior.

At the hotel, he walked her towards the foyer. But just before they reached the swing door, he drew her to one side. 'Thank you for coming to dinner with me tonight, Eva,' he said. His voice held a low intimacy. Gently, he touched her hair.

'You mustn't worry about the company, Ramon,' she said. She took a step closer, put a hand on his shoulder. 'I'm sure it will survive the competition and end up even stronger and more successful than before.'

'I have misjudged you, Eva.' He looked deep into her eyes. 'I thought you had come here to interfere, cause trouble and upset my grandmother all over again. But that is not true. You have only come here for the sake of your grandfather. I wanted to blame you for all sorts of colonial wrongs. I was mistaken.'

Eva waited. The tension was palpable between them she felt as if she were balancing on a knife edge.

'In a day or two, my grandmother will be coming here to Mandalay,' he murmured, drawing her closer, whispering into her hair. 'And when she does—'

'Eva!'

She spun around. Who would know her, here of all places?

A blond head and broad shoulders. An air of suave confidence. Klaus was halfway through the swing doors of the hotel. 'Hey, Eva! Hello!'

She felt Ramon stiffen beside her and take a step away.

'Klaus. Hello. I did try and phone you.' Eva forced a welcoming smile. She wasn't unhappy to see him, but his timing was atrocious. What had Ramon been about to tell her, she wondered. And what had he been about to do?

'I have only just checked back into the hotel. I was away for a few days, on business.' He came up to her and kissed her lightly on both cheeks. 'Sorry. I am interrupting, I think?'

Eva could imagine how it had seemed. 'Not at all,' she said politely. 'This is Ramon. Ramon, Klaus, we met in Yangon.'

The two men shook hands. Klaus's non-committal smile seemed friendly enough but Eva sensed Ramon's wariness. 'Yangon?' he echoed.

'We met in a café.' Klaus chuckled. 'And then I dragged Eva off to see the Shwedagon and to dinner.' He made it sound, she thought, like some sort of willing abduction. 'I wondered what had happened to you.' She saw him take in the *longyi*, the Burmese slippers, the jasmine in her hair. 'I see you have settled in, for sure.'

She smiled. 'That's true.'

'So what have you been doing since we last met?'

She wouldn't know where to start. 'I went to Pyin Oo Lwin,' she said, 'and met Ramon and his family.'

'And have you purchased many wonderful antiques?'

Eva wished he hadn't put it quite like that. 'I've seen some interesting artefacts, yes,' she said.

'Good. And I have the name of that contact I mentioned.'

'You will excuse me?' Ramon cut in. 'I will leave the two of you to talk.'

268

'Oh, but . . .' Eva realised she didn't want him to leave. Not now, not like this.

'No, no.' Klaus gave a playful little bow which seemed to irritate Ramon still further. 'It is I who interrupts your evening. We could meet tomorrow morning, Eva, if that is convenient? We can talk then.'

'Of course. Let's have coffee in the hotel bar. Will 10 a.m. suit you?'

'Perfect.' And Klaus gave a salute of farewell as he strolled away.

'I'm sorry.' But Eva realised as she looked at Ramon's face that the moment was gone. Could he possibly be jealous, she wondered.

Ramon frowned. 'I recognise that man,' he said.

'Klaus? Where from?'

'I am not sure.' Ramon strode to the swing door and opened it for her. 'And now, Eva, I must say goodnight.' He took a card from his jacket pocket. 'The address of our factory,' he said. 'For tomorrow.'

'Thank you.'

Eva wondered why she felt disappointed. Why did she feel she was on the brink of something, standing on a kind of dizzy edge and that the something kept being snatched away from her? From the hotel foyer, Eva watched him drive away with mixed feelings. She was drawn to him, yes, but she wouldn't allow herself to get emotionally involved. There was absolutely no point. And she was glad she was meeting

Klaus tomorrow. Another contact would be useful from the Emporium's point of view. And she'd had another idea about how to retrieve the stolen chinthe. This would give her an excellent chance to put her plan into action.

CHAPTER 30

Rosemary took a deep breath. 'Dad?' she said. 'I've been wondering.' Was he up to talking about it? Would he even remember? He was usually at his sharpest in the mornings, but . . .

'What, love?'

'Why did you tell Eva all those years ago that she could come and live with you?'

'When, Rosie?' There was the confusion again, the vulnerability that stopped her from being angry with him. But there were things she had to talk about, things she had to find out before it was too late.

'When I was planning to go to Copenhagen with Alec.' She willed him to understand. 'She was only sixteen. Why didn't you talk to me about it first?'

'Ah.' His gaze rested on her face for a moment as if he couldn't quite remember who she was. Then it drifted towards the window and the hydrangea bush outside – still flowering, though the blooms were faded and edged with brown.

Rosemary waited. She should be patient with him. Give him time. Nick used to make Christmas wreaths from the hydrangeas, the ivy and the holly in her parents' garden.

He was good at that kind of thing. Their Christmas tree at home had never been decorated with neat silvery trinkets like Rosemary's mother's tree. It had cones Nick had spray-painted with Eva, stained glass lanterns and angels from the workshop, Eva's own cotton-wool bearded Father Christmas with the lopsided grin. Soon it would be Christmas again, she thought. And what then?

'She seemed so sad,' her father said, just when Rosemary had thought he wasn't going to reply at all. 'She really didn't want to go.'

Of course she didn't. But that wasn't the point. Abruptly, Rosemary got to her feet, went to stand by the window. Her arms were tightly folded as if she could squeeze it all inside. Some hope, she thought. She tried to relax. It was raining, huge drops splashing on to the path and the bushes, smattering the window pane. 'Children never want to leave their friends,' she said. She unfolded her arms, ran her fingers around the gold bangle on her wrist that Alec had bought her. 'But they get used to it, that's the point.' She turned around. 'She would have got used to it.'

Her father blinked up at her.

Yes, and perhaps you should have said this to him at the time, thought Rosemary. How could she be saying it to him now? Look at him. He didn't deserve it, it wasn't fair.

'I felt sorry for her,' he said. He frowned. 'I should have spoken to you first, Rosie, but—'

'Sorry for yourself too, I should think.' There, that was it, out in the open. After all these years. And if he dared to say:

I'd just lost your mother, she'd . . . Well, she wasn't sure what she'd do.

But he didn't. 'Perhaps you're right, love,' he said. 'I hated the thought of you both going. My girls.'

His girls. Now that he'd admitted it, Rosemary wasn't sure what there was left to say. He'd hated the thought of them both going. That was a bit different.

'She was crying.' His eyes slipped into that faraway look that she had begun to recognise. 'She begged me. I said we'd have to talk to you first, but . . .'

'You didn't think I should have gone,' she said. Outside, the wind was blowing through the trees. She could hear its soft whistle.

'You had to do what you thought was right,' he murmured.

'But did you think it was right, Dad?' Even to herself she sounded like a dog with a bone. 'Did you think it was right?' She came back to the bed and sat down beside him. He was her father. She supposed she was looking for some sort of absolution.

'Aren't you happy, love?' he asked. He took her hand in his dry and papery grasp. Squeezed.

Rosemary looked down. She was as happy as she'd ever expected to be. But she wasn't sure that it was enough. She wondered if Alec thought it was enough. 'I wanted a new life,' she whispered.

'I know. I understand that. You went through so much, Rosie. You had to be strong.'

She stared at him. He seemed so . . . together, all of a sudden, so wise. 'I wasn't strong.'

'But you were.' And his voice held all the reassurance that her father's voice had ever held. 'You kept it together for Eva.' He sighed. 'No one could have asked for more.'

Except Alec, thought Rosemary. Except Alec and Eva and even Rosemary herself.

She patted his hand. She could see him tiring. And suddenly, everything that had happened back then, the fact that he'd offered to look after his granddaughter when she'd needed it, as if he hadn't already done so much, took on a different dimension. He had done it because Eva felt sad. He had done it to help them, because Eva had needed him to.

Rosemary slipped out of the room to let him sleep. She thought of how he had been there for them both after Nick's death, how he had pushed her into carrying on. She hadn't seen it that way, not back then. But of course, he had done it out of love.

She phoned Alec after work, brought him up to speed on what was happening with her father. And, all the time, another part of her was listening to what she said, as if watching from the living room ceiling. They were so careful with one another, so polite. Neither of them mentioned Seattle. It almost made the watching Rosemary laugh.

'Is what we have enough, Alec?' she suddenly asked.

'Sorry?'

'Is what we have enough? For you? For us?' That's what

she had been thinking. So why not break the habit of the last thirty years and say it?

'Not always,' he said. She heard his breathing, calm, considered. 'I thought it would be, but it's not.'

And Rosemary remembered what she'd said to him when he'd asked her to marry him: 'I don't know if I can . . .'

'Marry me?' he'd asked.

'No. I don't know if I can give you what you want.' *I don't know if I can give you a hundred per cent*, she had meant. *I don't know if I can ever stop grieving, stop thinking about the first man I married. I don't know if I can love you in the way you deserve to be loved.*

And Alec had said, 'You don't need to.'

'What about you?' Alec said now, as if they were having a conversation about the weather. 'Is it enough for you?'

'I don't know.' Seattle lurked like a shadow on the wall behind her.

'Then perhaps it's a good thing to have this time apart, Rosemary,' he said more gently.

'Yes.' Because she was trying, wasn't she, to let loose this constriction around her heart.

CHAPTER 31

This morning, through the hotel, Eva had booked her river boat tickets for Bagan. Her departure was scheduled for four days' time. It would be hard to leave, but she had more items to see for the Emporium and she was looking forward to visiting the famous temples of Bagan too. This would give her three full days there before she flew back to Yangon. She waited for Klaus in the hotel café. It was air-conditioned and slick, all black and chrome, a total contrast to the dusty streets of Mandalay.

Klaus arrived promptly at 10 a.m. He was dressed casually today in a blue short-sleeved cotton shirt and beige shorts and was carrying the same leather bag that she'd seen him with when they first met. His blond hairline was glistening with sweat. He must have been out already and Eva knew that, even this early, it was thirty degrees outside.

She greeted him with a kiss on both cheeks and waved at the seat opposite. 'Sit down. It's good to see you.'

'And you.'

They ordered coffee and chatted easily about the sights of Mandalay until it arrived, strong and sweetened with condensed milk, as was the custom. He caught her eye and they both chuckled.

'Here is the name of the contact I mentioned.' Klaus placed a business card on the table between them. 'I think he is a reputable trader. He may have some things that will interest you.'

'Thank you.' Eva glanced at the card and slipped it into her bag.

'And now.' He steepled his hands together and regarded her with a serious expression. 'May I ask you something a little personal, Eva?'

'Of course.'

'Are you involved with the man I saw you with last night?'

That surprised her. 'Romantically, do you mean? No, I'm not.' Although she wasn't sure she liked the question. She couldn't help noticing the sweat still on Klaus's brow from the heat outside, the damp blond hair pressing against his forehead. She felt like telling him it was none of his business, but perhaps he only had her best interests at heart. She took another sip of her coffee. 'Why do you ask?'

'And you met in Pyin Oo Lwin?' His blue gaze searched hers.

It seemed an honest gaze. Eva hesitated. But she wouldn't tell him the story of the chinthe. She remembered what had happened at the Shwedagon, her feeling that Klaus might be hiding something. She liked him, but she wasn't ready to confide in him. 'Yes,' she said. 'My grandfather knew his family when he was out here working in the timber industry before the war.'

'I see.' Klaus stroked his chin, which was clean-shaven and

smooth. He seemed to relax slightly. 'But you do not know him well,' he pressed.

'Not really.'

He nodded and stirred his coffee. He seemed pensive, not quite the Klaus she had met back in Yangon.

Eva looked at the hand holding the spoon. The back of it was covered with a blond down of hair. 'Is something wrong?' she asked.

'It was just that you looked . . . close,' he said. 'And I was a little concerned.'

Close? It was, she thought, rather more complicated than that. And why should he be concerned? 'Ramon's family have a teak furniture business,' she said, trying to lighten the atmosphere. 'He runs the company but he's still very hands-on from what I can gather.' A master craftsman was always a master craftsman; it was his life.

'Yes, I know his company.' Klaus frowned.

'You do?'

'Yes. Look, Eva.' He took a swig of his coffee. 'Please forgive me for interfering. And I realise that we have only recently met. But I think you should know . . .'

'Yes?' She waited.

'I do not fully trust him.' He sat back in his chair.

Eva felt a cold and prickly sensation on the back of her neck. 'For what reason?' she asked.

'He has dealings with a disreputable company,' he said. 'In what capacity I do not yet know. But I am certain that their business is not a legal one.'

'And I'm certain that you're mistaken.' Eva finished her coffee and put her napkin to her lips. 'Ramon's company is independent. And totally above board.'

Klaus raised an eyebrow. 'Maybe not as independent and above board as you believe.'

Eva shrugged. Perhaps Ramon had decided to join forces with someone in an effort to get the company out of trouble. How would she know? And, come to think of it, how on earth did Klaus know his business dealings? 'What does it have to do with you, Klaus? If you don't mind me asking?'

He raised both hands in mock defence. 'I have an interest in the company he is working with, that is all,' he said. 'Perhaps this Ramon is an innocent in—'

'What company?' Eva was getting a bad feeling about this.

'Li's Furniture and Antique Company,' he said. He leaned back once more. 'But you will keep that to yourself, I hope.'

Eva felt that hollow feeling of dread, right in the pit of her belly. 'That's impossible.' She shook her head. And yet somewhere inside she was also conscious of a fleeting sense of inevitability. It was almost as if she'd known what he was about to say. Li's seemed to be everywhere, lurking at the bottom of every ocean.

'Nevertheless, it is the case,' Klaus said. 'I am sorry if that is a disappointment to you.'

Again, Eva shook her head. She thought of the dark expression on Ramon's face when he had seen that boat at the port. It made no sense. No sense at all.

'Sometimes, Eva,' Klaus said, 'we see only what we wish to see.'

Was that true? Eva frowned. 'Where do Li's operate from?' she asked him. 'Where's this showroom of theirs?' She pushed away her coffee cup.

'You do not wish to know,' he said.

But there he was wrong. Eva most definitely wished to know. And she was more than a little fed up with being fobbed off by everyone. 'I'll ask at reception then,' she said. 'They must have whatever's the Burmese equivalent of Yellow Pages.'

Klaus leaned over the table towards her. 'Please be careful, Eva,' he said. 'That is all I ask.'

She nodded, waited.

'It's on Thirty-Sixth Street,' he said. 'Just before the junction with Eighty-Fourth. Ask any taxi driver.'

'Thank you, Klaus.' But Eva was confused. Could this be why Ramon was warning her away from them? Because he actually had dealings with the company? She couldn't believe it. But she would go there, she decided. At the very least she could see what the place was like, perhaps talk to someone or even start putting her plan into action. She didn't have much time left and she had to do something. She wasn't scared either. If you wanted anything doing you had to do it yourself. She owed it to her grandfather. And Eva was determined to find a way.

CHAPTER 32

Of course, Lawrence could understand that Rosemary blamed him, about Eva.

He closed his eyes. That bloody ceiling. He hated that bloody ceiling. Sometimes it was close. Sometimes it was far away. Sometimes it stopped him from thinking, from remembering. And he wanted to be clear. So much, he wanted to be clear.

He hadn't thought much about becoming a grandfather, not until after Rosie had met her Nick and he'd seen that love light in her eyes . . . 'It won't be long,' Lawrence had said to Helen. She wouldn't have it of course, told him he was a silly romantic fool. Perhaps he was. Perhaps that's why he could see it.

Nick had come to him, a decent young man – no money, but honest and hard-working – and told him what they planned to do, how they'd manage, how he intended to build up a business from scratch. And Lawrence had felt only respect for him. 'Good luck to you,' he'd said. 'Good luck to you both.' And he knew there'd been a tear in his eye. That was the way things should be. Lucky Rosie.

When their daughter was expecting Eva, Helen had fussed

around like women do. And he had thought it wouldn't make much difference to his life. A grandchild to spoil, that was all. He hadn't realised Eva would make him feel young again, that as she grew a bit older, she'd want to listen to his stories of the old days, and listen open-mouthed with such a look of wonder in her dark eyes that he almost felt he was back there. He hadn't imagined that he'd be asked to look after her in a way he'd never really ventured to look after his own girl, because now Helen tired so easily and wasn't good with disruption and noise. He'd never dreamt he would feel such love.

So when Rosie took it in her head to remarry and leave West Dorset, well, he'd thought his heart would snap like a dry twig. His two girls. Something had happened with Rosie, she blamed him for something, she was still wrung out after Nick's death. And when Eva, his lovely granddaughter, had come to him crying . . . What was he supposed to do? He could never say 'no' to her.

Lawrence shifted on to his side. God knows what time of day or night it was, because he didn't.

Most of all perhaps, he hadn't imagined that Eva would inherit from him his love of wood. The smell of it, sweet and deep in your nostrils, the darker rings of age and history, the feel of it, raw and sappy, smooth as satin on the inside, rough on the out. That there would be such a bond between them.

Upper Burma, January 1942

'You are very quiet,' Maya observed. She was wearing a cream silk *longyi* and it rippled as she rose to her feet and took the empty bowl from his place. But Lawrence noticed she didn't ask what he was thinking. Was it this that intrigued him about her? That she didn't need to know what he was thinking? That in fact she might already know?

'I was listening to the radio earlier,' he said. 'Catching up on the news.' He stretched out his legs. They were seated on low bamboo chairs on the verandah of her aunt's home and had just eaten a simple supper of noodles and *Ah Sone Kyaw*, stir fried vegetables cooked in a tamarind sauce. It was dark and clear, the stars sharply visible in the night sky, a perfect half-moon. Maya's aunt's house was more basic than her father's. It was made of bamboo and, like many of the traditional houses, was built on stilts. The furniture was plain and unsophisticated and this, too, was made of bamboo. The floor consisted of rush matting, but you still took your shoes off when you came inside.

'News of the war,' she said. She took a cloth to wipe the table and moved towards the back door.

'I want to enlist.' He hadn't meant to come out with it just like that. He hadn't fully decided, or so he'd thought. Clearly, he had. He remembered only too well sitting around the radio set in the logging camp with some of the other men on 3rd September 1939, glass in hand, listening to Neville Chamberlain telling them that once again the British were at war with Germany. Some of the men had wanted to book a passage west there and then, but there had been an immediate government order to block it. The British Empire had wide boundaries. Who knew where their skills would be most needed? It was far too soon to tell. But now . . .

She returned to the table. Observed him head on. 'You need to fight for your country,' she said. It wasn't a question.

'I can't not fight.' He was young, wasn't he, and fit? He couldn't do the work he did without possessing stamina. He had not yet received a call-up for military training. But it seemed like sheer cowardice to be out here in Burma living in relative peace while poor old Blighty was suffering from air raids and rationing and who knew what else. How could his mother be coping with that? He simply couldn't imagine her making do. And he was here being waited on by this beautiful woman while other men were fighting the enemy. Fighting, as Maya had said, for his country. *Your country needs you*. Lawrence wasn't a coward. He was more than willing to do his bit. But up till now he'd been playing the waiting game along with the rest. How long before it played itself out? How long before more countries got involved? Was this just the beginning? He feared so. Men were being enlisted into the Indian Army, the Burma Rifles, the Navy. It was time.

'You will return to England?' Maya asked him.

He examined the serenity of her face framed by her hair, almost indigo in the darkness of the night, lit only by the flickering lamplight on the porch. There was not a frown on her brow, not a flicker of anxiety in her eyes – or so it seemed. Like many Burmese people, she was Buddhist. But did she mind? He had no idea. Did she understand? Clearly.

Sometimes he believed she understood him better than he did himself.

And perhaps it was this that most drew him to her. On the level of language their communication was fluent but simple. But on a deeper level, there was a connection that made them as one. It wasn't sexual, as he'd realised long ago, though sex between them seemed natural and real, unfettered by convention. And it wasn't because she was different, other and exotic, though she was and he relished that too. It was, he realised, something in their twin souls. It was deeper even than love. It had scared him at first. But he had given himself over to it. It was, he thought now, a kind of peace.

England, Maya had said. For a moment he pictured the look of the docks when he had left last time. Last time . . . He tried not to think of Helen, though he could still see her in his mind's eye and she still wrote to him. Occasionally, he even wrote back: short, polite notes that said nothing and yet everything. But she didn't seem to understand what he was telling her, or she didn't want to. War had not yet been declared when he'd left the country. And yet there had been an uneasiness about England as if she might be preparing for it. He recalled the shouts and the whistles, the people rushing here, there and everywhere, boarding ships, standing on the docks with backpacks or suitcases, milling over the gangplanks, saluting, waving, shouting their last goodbyes into the grey skies and the murky sea. And he pictured his mother's face, her nod of encouragement. *This is what is expected. This is what you must do.*

'No,' he said to Maya. He spoke Burmese pretty well now. He knew the jungle and he had some understanding of the people. These skills would be appreciated in wartime situations. He had no military training, but Lawrence knew where he would be needed.

She poured him some green tea and he lit a cigarette. He drew in deeply, considering, and exhaled, watching the smoke spiral and disappear into the night. 'War is not only happening in Europe, my love,' he told her gently.

She looked up, startled. 'It will come here? To Burma?'

'I believe so.' He drew on his cigarette once more. He had heard rumours, you couldn't help but hear rumours if you kept your ear to the ground. The Japanese were already at war with Britain and, after Pearl Harbor, the United States of America. In his opinion they were on their way. 'The Japs are taking advantage of all the argy-bargy, no doubt about that.'

They needed to extend their boundaries. Japan, unlike Malaya and Burma, wasn't rich in rubber, oil or wood. In point of fact, when you looked at the history, Japan had long been after extending its power. They'd had an aggressive foreign policy for twenty years, since their invasion of Manchuria, and this had only fuelled their war machine. They had forces at the ready in Asia. They'd been fighting China and since the pact they'd signed with Germany a year and a half ago . . . Who knew how much else was going on behind the scenes? He had heard the Japanese described as a nation of fanatics. Maybe they were, although Britain had the fanaticism of Hitler to deal with at this moment in time. But he'd also heard that Japanese forward-planning was second to none.

Maya sat down opposite him and took his hands in hers. This was unusual. She, like many Burmese women, was not given to displays of affection. Often, she seemed strangely detached and unemotional. But he never doubted her love or loyalty. And more. Maya had set him free. 'They are striking while the enemy is looking the other way,' she said. 'Collecting the water while it rains.'

He smiled. 'I'm very much afraid that you are right.' Her hands felt so soft as they held his, so smooth where his were rough and calloused these days. He enjoyed the work and just the muted wooden tinkle of elephant bells could make his heart leap as he approached camp. Most of this was down to Maya, he knew that. And he had also long known that being in charge of a teak camp was a tough job, far from the white-skinned civilisation of an office job back in the UK. So how long did he have here, realistically? For how many years could he work here and survive the ravages of dengue fever and malaria and the rest, before he grew old before his time? This was not the job for a middle-aged man, only a young one. The company who employed him knew that, and Lawrence knew it too.

'So you will fight in Malaya?' Her eyes were wide. 'Or Burma?'

He brought her hand to his lips and kissed it. 'I will enlist with the Indian Army,' he said. 'Try to obtain an emergency commission. And then we will see how things develop.'

Another woman might have wept and begged him not to go. Another woman might have made him feel bad, as if he were deserting her. But Maya, of course, was different. And she had shown him the different possibilities for his life too.

So. It didn't matter how much he regretted what had happened, how bad he felt about Helen, and Maya too. Now, there was a war.

'You may never come back,' she quietly said. Her eyes were like the soft satin of the night sky. He wanted all his senses to sink into them and be lost.

'Perhaps not.' He released Maya's hand and held her face in his. 'But if I am alive, I will come back, my love.' And he meant it. God, how he meant it.

'Hush.' She put a finger to his lips. She did not believe in wasting words. She had a secret strength that had always drawn him, a dark strength of knowing. 'You do not have to give me your promises. You are a free man.'

They made love that night with a tenderness such as Lawrence had never known. Her dark and sinuous body seemed to wind itself around him in a way it never had before. Her hair, long and lustrous, trailed over his chest and his thighs, and her skin was silky to his touch, scented with a musky fragrance that seemed to take him to greater heights of passion.

'I love you, Maya,' he gasped as he felt himself climax inside her.

Her eyes were closed now, her brow smooth as a child's,

her lips slightly parted. 'And I love you, Lawrence,' she said
softly.

It was, he realised, as he drew the mosquito nets over their
bed and took her again in his arms, the first time.

CHAPTER 33

The moment Eva had said goodbye to Klaus, she grabbed her bag, left the hotel and took a taxi to Thirty-Sixth Street. She hadn't been here yesterday, but she found the showroom easily, though showroom was perhaps too grand a description for the rickety shop situated halfway along. It seemed to go a long way back and she saw that it was divided into two halves. One side was crammed with contemporary furniture, the other with what looked like old wooden artefacts. Dusty enough to be antiques. But . . . She decided to take a closer look. It was quite safe. She didn't even have to speak to anyone. She would look around and then work out her next move.

Outside on the street was a random collection of Buddha images, some made of stone, some wood. At first glance they looked worn and pretty ancient, it was true. She wet her finger with her tongue and traced it over the head of one of the wooden statues. The wood was dull and didn't have the richness of teak. And . . . She bent closer to take a sniff. It didn't smell of sandalwood either. A paler wood, sandalwood had a sweet sappy fragrance, even when dried and quite old. Teak, on the other hand, was deeper, it had more layers, more complexity.

She brushed some more of the dust aside. She'd hazard a guess that this was inferior wood, either felled much too early when it was too young or before it had been properly dried out. It could even have been recycled from some old or damaged furniture because the patina was uneven and inconsistent. Other pieces, she could see, had been none too cleverly distressed, discoloured, filed down in places. She ran her fingers lightly across the rough, amateur carving. It all seemed vaguely familiar. And it didn't take an expert to see what it was, or more accurately, she thought, what it wasn't.

Her thoughts drifted to Ramon. There was absolutely no way that he would work with these people. For one thing they had stolen his family's precious chinthe. And for another they represented everything that he detested in furniture-making and working with wood. As did she. Even if it were the only way to rescue his company from financial difficulties, even if it were the only way to retain his father's legacy . . . He wouldn't do it.

Eva edged past the Buddhas and into the dark, dingy shop, down a narrow aisle with shelves and glass-fronted cabinets on either side housing seated and reclining Buddha statuettes, elephants, horses and water-buffalo of wood, stone and perhaps even marble, and chinthes. Eva let out the breath she'd been holding. Chinthes of all sizes and types, some fierce-looking with snarling mouths, some proud, some grim-faced and indifferent. None, though, as charming or intricately carved as the chinthe her grandfather had given her to bring to Myanmar. And these were different in another way, too.

All these chinthes stood in pairs. Ready to guard the shrine of a seated Buddha, she found herself thinking. Ready to maintain harmony. Ready to protect a household.

'Can I help you? English, yes?'

Oh. Eva had been so lost in thought she'd almost imagined herself alone in the shop. But now she looked up. A small, Burmese man was standing, arms folded, beside her. He wore a stained *longyi* and a faded red shirt. 'Yes, I am.' She pointed to a chinthe in the cabinet. 'Can I see this one?' Though her stomach gave a little lurch of nerves. Ramon had said these people were dangerous. And he would be furious if he knew she had come here.

'Of course.' He produced a key from the ring on his belt, though whether the cupboards were locked to discourage theft or to imply that the contents were more valuable than they really were, she didn't know.

'I have a special interest in chinthes,' Eva told him.

His expression didn't change, not a flicker passed across it as he unlocked the door and swung it open. 'Which one?' he asked her. 'This? This?'

She pointed. 'What's it made of?'

'Teak.' He reached in, lifted up the chinthe in question and handed it to her.

That was very unlikely. It was too light in weight for a start.

'How old is it?'

He squinted. 'A hundred years maybe,' he said.

'How interesting.' If it was, Eva would eat her hat. It was

dusty, yes, but the carving was rough, the wood discoloured – possibly with chemicals – and there were some very suspect markings. It had probably been knocked up in their own factory less than a month ago. It wouldn't even fool an amateur.

So not only were the Li family common thieves, but they were also selling fake antiques. Eva's blood boiled. The distressing of furniture was commonplace. But passing it off as antique? That was illegal, crossing a boundary that was unacceptable – to Eva and to anyone honest who appreciated the value of true provenance. Old objects had a past, a history, which was part of their intrinsic value. So that you could sit on a Victorian dressmaker's rocking chair and imagine her taking pins from the little drawer under the seat, rocking and sewing in the lamplight. You could open an eighteenth century casket and guess what had been kept inside. You could wear a 1920s bead necklace and almost see a girl doing the Charleston. A genuine antique had generally been made by a craftsman with love and care. And it had a story. These people were fakers and forgers. They were dishonest. Criminals, even. She took a deep breath. Tried to hold back the adrenalin.

'You like?' the man asked. He didn't look as if he could care less.

'Not really,' she replied.

Once again, he shrugged. And it was that careless shrug that made something inside her snap.

'Because it's not really old, is it?' she asked him.

He blinked. 'It was bought in good faith, isn't it? As to age, I do not know exactly.'

And yet he'd been willing to let her believe it was a hundred years old a few minutes ago. 'So it wasn't made here?' She pointed to the back of the shop. She knew that she should stop, that it was extremely rash to stand here in the enemy camp making accusations. Klaus too had warned her to be careful. But she was so angry. Why should they get away with it?

'No, not made here.' The man almost snatched it back from her and replaced it in the cabinet next to its twin. 'It look old to me. Why not? I am no expert, isn't it?'

No expert? Didn't he work in an antique shop?

The man turned around and let out a stream of Burmese clearly addressed to someone who must be lurking in the darker recesses of the shop. Eva tried not to panic. 'Are you the owner of this shop?' she asked him. Though she knew he couldn't be. The owner of this place would have others to deal with customers who wandered in off the street.

'It is my family who own this business.' A different man spoke. He was walking towards them. His dark hair was slicked back from an unsmiling and unshaven face. His eyes were limpid, his shoulders drooped. He was also dressed in the traditional *longyi* but looked much smarter, his shirt clean and white. He glanced at her with a distinct lack of interest. 'What it is to you?'

Li. This was the moment when she should walk out of

the shop. But she had to make sure. 'Who are you?' she said instead.

'My name is Khan Li.' He gave a curt nod. 'And what make you think the chinthe not old? You are expert, is that it?'

'As a matter of fact, yes I am. I have a degree in antique restoration and the decorative arts.' Eva spoke before she had the chance to think about it. 'And I can certainly differentiate between genuine antiques.' She paused. 'And fakes.'

He didn't even flinch. They stood there staring at one another, but Eva refused to be intimidated. She would not back down. She knew that she was treading a dangerous pathway, but would a man like him really be that concerned about the shop's authenticity being challenged by an English-woman? She doubted it.

Sure enough, he looked her up and down with a sneer on his swarthy face. 'You make accusation, yes?' he said.

Even Eva wasn't foolhardy enough to rise to that one. 'No,' she said. 'But I'm surprised that you don't value your company's reputation more highly.'

'My company reputation?' He stared at her in amazement.

She supposed he couldn't believe it, some young European woman coming in here daring to lay down the law. But this, she felt, gave her an edge. She thought of Ramon when he'd confided in her the other afternoon, she thought of Maya and Suu Kyi and the stolen chinthe, she thought of her grandfather. She just couldn't stop herself. 'Don't you care about the credibility of antique dealers in Myanmar?' she asked him. 'How they are viewed by the rest of the world?'

He stared at her as if she were quite mad. And very probably, she was.

'What you want?' he growled. 'What it is you look for?'

Why would he assume she was looking for something? But his words gave Eva the opportunity she needed. It was heaven-sent. If she was ever going to flush him out into the open, she had to take it. She might never get another chance. Eva took a deep breath. 'I was hoping to buy something special,' she said. 'Something that is really old. That's my business, you see. I'm over here buying genuine antique artefacts for my company in England.'

'Something special, isn't it?' His eyes gleamed. 'Why you not say?'

Once again, his gaze flickered over her, top to toe. Eva shifted uncomfortably. It wasn't a pleasant feeling. But she could easily extricate herself from this situation at any time, she told herself. She knew what she was doing; this was her business. She would see what he had to offer and then she would leave. Simple.

'Come.' He beckoned her towards the back of the shop.

Eva saw that there was a desk and two chairs, one on either side. It felt a bit like venturing into the dragon's den and she hesitated. But she had to do it. For Maya and her grandfather, she had to do it.

She sat down. On the table was some paperwork and she recognised the stamped blue-and-gold peacock logo on the letter heading – the same logo she'd seen on the boat two days earlier.

'What kind of thing you want to buy?' Khan Li sat down opposite her and stared at her with his limpid gaze. It was unsettling.

'What do you have?' she hedged.

He called out something in Burmese. Eva fervently hoped no one else was going to appear.

'Some teak statuettes,' he said. 'Very old. Very unusual.'

'What kind of statuettes?' Eva couldn't believe she was sitting here talking business with Khan Li.

He shrugged. 'Robed Brahmin Priest blowing conch shell. Poona. Very good.'

And very expensive, Eva would guess.

'Water carrier, nats, ox-cart guardian. All very rare. All teak wood.'

'Can I see them?' It sounded like quite a collection.

His eyes narrowed. 'I not have them here,' he said, as if she were foolish to imagine this might be so. 'They special. But I can get them. If you want them, I get them.'

'I see.' What did he do, steal to order? He probably knew her own contact in Mandalay. They probably all knew each other. Heaven knows where they got all these artefacts from. Eva wasn't sure she even wanted to think about it. She sighed.

He leaned closer. Eva noticed the gold signet ring he wore, the dark hair from his chest curling over the top button of his shirt. 'What it is you want?' he asked again.

He was reading her like a book. Eva made a snap decision. It was now or never. What did it matter that five minutes ago she had let loose a tirade on fakes and forgery? Now, they were talking business. This wasn't the UK. Here, people didn't seem to get offended in the same way. Here, if the price was right, they would talk to anyone. About anything. She had to do it.

'My British client has an eighteenth-century decorative teak chinthe,' she said quietly. 'Very old and intricately carved.' She lowered her voice still further. 'With large ruby eyes.' There she'd said it. That should flush him out.

His expression changed. He looked decidedly shifty. He raised a dark and scraggy eyebrow and one foot jerked as if in a nervous reaction. But instead of answering her, he yelled out in Burmese again and this time a young girl wearing a red *longyi* and embroidered blouse appeared. He must have called for her before. She was carrying a lacquer tray, her face almost invisible behind a curtain of dark hair. On the tray was a teapot decorated with weeping willows and sampans in a lake, two tiny white cups and a plate of thin sesame biscuits. She poured out the green tea, handed a cup to them both, gave a little bow and disappeared.

He was rattled. Eva could see that he was rattled.

Khan Li offered Eva the plate of biscuits. Perhaps he was giving himself time to weigh the situation up, she thought. In his line of business he'd have to be careful, always on the lookout, always prepared.

'Your client owns one Burmese chinthe only?' he asked when a few moments had elapsed.

'He does.' She nodded. 'I see you have immediately grasped the point.' Flattery, she hoped, might help her.

298

'How big it is?'

She showed him with her hands.

'Carved teak?'

'Intricately carved, yes. Late eighteenth century.'

'With rubies for eyes, you say?'

'Yes.' There must have been quite a few. Burma had long been rich in rubies; gems had been mined for centuries and anyway, she hadn't told him how large the rubies were, or how rare. She hadn't told him where the chinthe had come from either. Its elusive provenance.

'But he is Englishman, yes?' he asked.

'Yes.' She threw caution to the wind. 'He is old. He lived here many years ago, before the war. He was very close to someone . . .' She tailed off. That was enough. She didn't want to overegg the pudding. 'He would very much like to own the other,' she said.

'Of course, yes.' He leaned forwards. 'But you know, I think, the value of such a piece?'

'Naturally.' Eva crossed her legs. She wished she were wearing something a bit more business-like this morning than her flowery wrap-around skirt and pink cotton blouse, but she hadn't expected things to develop quite so fast. This morning she'd planned to meet with Klaus and then visit Ramon's factory . . .

'And may I ask . . . ?' Khan Li's voice was smooth and pleasant – for the moment, Eva thought. 'Why you come to us?'

A good question. Eva bit into a sesame biscuit. She needed

299

some thinking time now. 'I have contacts,' she said. 'I had reason to believe you might be able to help me.' But perhaps she shouldn't be too specific? After all, the Lis had stolen the chinthe in the first place. She thought fast. 'My contact said that if any man could locate such a piece, it would be you.'

He frowned. 'And the name of your contact?'

Eva shook her head. 'I cannot say.'

He seemed to consider, but only for a moment. 'I am sorry,' he said. 'You have been misinformed, isn't it? This is not our speciality. We run a modest business. I do not think we can help you and your client.'

Eva hid her disappointment. So he didn't want to sell the chinthe. He wasn't as greedy as she'd thought. 'My client will be very disappointed,' she said. She sipped her tea. 'He is a rich man. He has owned the chinthe for many years and done much research on the provenance. But . . .' She shrugged. 'We will continue to look for its elusive twin.' She pushed her cup to one side and got to her feet. 'Thank you anyway.'

To her amazement, he chuckled.

Eva didn't get the joke. 'Sorry?' she said. 'What—?' His laughter scared her. *Had* she said enough? Or had she said too much? She thought of Ramon, and suddenly wished she hadn't come here alone.

'You or your client read too many novels, I think.' His eyes were hard now and unsmiling. But despite his calm demeanour, Eva sensed he was still on the alert. 'The selling and export of gems in our country is strictly regulated and controlled. I cannot help you.'

And as she shook hands with him and looked into those limpid eyes, Eva wondered. Had she misread the situation? Had she failed to take something else into account? It seemed so. She had taken a huge chance and walked straight into the dragon's lair. She could hardly believe she had done it. But it seemed that in the end, it had all been for nothing.

CHAPTER 34

Maya prepared for the journey to Mandalay. It was a mental preparation as much as anything. Eva's sudden appearance had been a shock, she felt quite dazzled by it all. Lawrence was still alive. Lawrence still thought of her. Lawrence had given his granddaughter the precious chinthe to be returned to her family where it belonged. And so there was something very important that she must do. She had made her decision.

As she organised her things – she might be old, but she was still capable, she would not be treated like a child – Maya let her mind drift back to the war, her war.

One particular peaceful April morning was branded into her mind. It was the first time she had heard the noise and it shattered the peace like nothing else on earth. She didn't think she would ever forget the sudden shriek coming from the sky outside.

'*Ba le?* What is that?' Maya's aunt had been confused. She turned from one side to the other, made to move towards the door of the house.

'Stop, Aunt!' Maya grabbed her and pulled her down. The shriek, high and inhuman, was the whine and whistle of falling bombs, followed immediately by the crashing explosions. Wide-eyed and terrified, they clutched one another. The earth trembled. *Lawrence*, thought Maya, as she often did. Where was he? Was he safe?

Maya and her aunt held fast. Maya could see the terror etched on her aunt's face. And it was not surprising. No one had expected this. Maya knew about the attack on Pearl Harbor, which had brought the Americans into both the war against the Japanese and a few days later the war in Europe, and she knew what Lawrence had told her about the Japanese invasion of Malaya and Thailand. She even knew that Japanese bombers had attacked Rangoon and, of course, that many of her countrymen had fled the capital and were travelling north upcountry. But somehow she, and most others she knew, had still not believed that they would be involved. They thought all the reports must be hugely exaggerated, they had imagined they would be safe here so far north of Mandalay; they had not felt the breath of the war coming closer.

When the low-flying Japanese bomber planes had let go of their load, they must have flown off to prepare for the next onslaught. Because there was more. Maya crawled from their hiding place behind the wooden sideboard. She put a hand to her mouth. She could see bodies strewn, injured and bleeding on the dusty ground, and that ground was stained with their blood. She could see an arm and, dear Lord Buddha, other dismembered limbs. Bullocks injured by flying shrapnel were bellowing in pain. Windows had been shattered. Bamboo huts and houses, even the stronger ones made of timber, had collapsed like dominos and were even now erupting into flames.

And then the planes returned and Maya crawled back to their hiding place. 'It is not over,' she whispered. It went on, hour after hour of ceaseless bombardment, the almost total destruction of the defenceless little town.

'It is market day,' her aunt whispered.

Maya knew what she was saying. If she had been in any doubt as to who were the heroes of this war – and in truth, she knew as all women knew, that there were no heroes, that war was a necessary evil that brought out as much cruelty and corruption as it did bravery and courage in the soldiers involved in it – this attack should have convinced her. For the Japanese bombers were not fighting the British here, although there were a few British living in the town. They were not fighting rebels, or even Burmese men who might rise against them. No. And the little town could have no military or strategic importance, surely? It was market day, as her aunt had said, and so the town was crowded with tribespeople selling fruit, fish, vegetables, woven goods. And the tribespeople tended to bring their families along for the ride. Largely then, they were fighting defenceless women and children. Those were the kind of heroes they were.

Maya's aunt began to weep and still the bombs were falling. When would it end? Maya thought of her father in Maymyo. Was he safe? Was he still talking of Japanese liberation? And if so, what would he say when he knew what had happened here on this day? He should know that the people he was looking to for granting Burmese freedom were capable of such things.

After what seemed like an eternity, the planes finally flew off, leaving nothing but an eerie silence in their wake. And then they heard the moaning, coming from the street. The moaning, the wailing and the crying. Once again, Maya crawled out from behind the sideboard and held her hand out to her aunt, helping the poor woman to her feet. She was distraught, clearly suffering from shock. Gently, Maya led her to an up-ended chair, righted it and sat her down. Somehow, Maya's aunt's house had survived the blasts, though the windows had shattered and, as she stood in the doorway, Maya could see that most of the houses in the street had been destroyed. The air was full of the stench of blood, the acrid smell of the explosions and the scent of scorched flesh, the street was lined with the charred remains of burned-out houses.

Maya's aunt came to stand by her side. 'Now what?' she whispered.

'Now we help to pick up the pieces.'

They proceeded to do what they could for the injured nearby, fetching dressings and binding wounds, bringing water to those who were probably dying, in order to ease their final moments on earth. Buildings were still burning and smoking. There was next to nothing left of Main Street where the Indian food shops were situated, now, it was just a row of charred shells. The small cinema had been destroyed and the shop that her aunt had always called the bits-and-pieces shop, because it sold everything you could need, was no more. The peaceful little town had, in a matter of hours, become one of mayhem and panic, noise and confusion, pain and bloody slaughter.

So many dead. And Lawrence? Was he still alive? '*Kador, kador . . .*' she muttered. Please, please let it be so. Maya liked to believe that she would know, in her deepest soul, if he were not. Was he at this very moment involved in the act of killing a man – a Japanese? Or was he one of the wounded, one of the dying? It was this thought more than any other that persuaded her to take the path she next took. How could she not?

Maya and her aunt ignored the corpses lying in grotesque positions on the streets, and concentrated on the survivors, helping to take them by barrow or on foot to the local hospital, which, miraculously, was still standing. It was a simple one-storey building made of brick and stone with a sloping zinc roof and it had always served the village well. But how would the small building and the limited staff cope with this?

'I would like to help,' Maya told the Scottish matron, who was clearly rushed off her feet and desperate. And the streets were still full of people wandering around in a daze or moving from one place to another in blind panic, often injured themselves, desperately searching for their loved ones or for a glimpse of some previous sanity. How many more of them needed to be in this hospital?

'It is dangerous,' the Matron said. 'Many people are leaving, if they are able. You should go too. The planes will surely come back.' She busied herself with the next patient, making her comfortable, preparing to tend to her wounds.

'Yes, we will go upcountry,' said Maya's aunt. 'We will be safe there.'

Maya turned to her. 'You must go, Aunt,' she said.

'Your father . . .' Maya could see the pain in her eyes. They both knew what he thought of this war, and what he thought of imperialism too.

'Perhaps he will come here,' Maya said. 'Or perhaps things will calm down and I can go and fetch him from Maymyo. We should be able to join you soon.' She had no idea though, if this were true.

Her aunt nodded. 'Very well,' she said.

Maya turned back to the matron. 'I'd like to stay and help,' she said. 'If you'll have me.'

'Bless you,' she said. 'We need to boil lots of water. And to stop the spread of disease we must start burying the dead without delay.'

And so . . . Maya's wartime nursing career had begun.

It was several days before she even had time to return to her aunt's house. There was very little worth saving, but some things might be useful, and these she gathered up to take back with her to the hospital. And then there was the chinthe. It was, she knew, her legacy and her security too. She tore a long strip from one of her *longyis* in the clothes drawer, and wrapped it up carefully in the fabric. She found an old trowel of her aunt's, went out to the red flowering *sein pan* tree and dug a deep hole in the dusty earth. She gave the chinthe one last kiss and put him in the grave. 'For safe-keeping,' she whispered. 'I will be back.'

And now, all these years later, the other had returned . . . Maya shook her head. The wonders of this world. And that was why she must do what she must do. It was a fair return.

CHAPTER 35

It was a relief for Eva to escape the stuffy, threatening atmosphere of Li's. How had she found the nerve to do it? There were beads of perspiration on her brow as she stood on the corner taking stock. She glanced back at the showroom, the furniture and the 'older' artefacts and she took a swig from her bottle of mineral water, as if she might rinse the feeling of the place away. She walked a couple of blocks to get her breathing back to normal and to think, dodging the broken paving slabs and avoiding looking at the sewer that ran, visibly, just below. She had taken a major risk with a dangerous man. She just hoped that Khan Li had written her off as deluded.

She stopped at an open-air bar on the corner for a quick coffee. It was sweet and milky as usual, but she appreciated the caffeine hit as she watched the traffic weave by, the metal on the cars and scooters shimmering in the heat haze that was downtown Mandalay. Outside the dingy shack next door, a public telephone was stationed rather bizarrely on a rickety table and beside this, on the pavement, some street vendors had set up shop under the shade of a tree and were squatting in a circle, eating their lunch from a tin. Perhaps it was her state of mind, but the noise and humidity were overwhelming.

Eva flagged down a taxi, got in and gave them the address of Ramon's factory. She sat back, relieved to feel the air-conditioning cool on her skin. But what would she say to him? Should she tell him where she had been? Confront him with what Klaus had told her? Eva sank further back into the leather seat. She would wait and see how things panned out, she decided.

Ramon's company, 'Handmade in Mandalay', was situated on the edge of town and so, although it was a factory, it had escaped most of the city's noise and pollution. The building was single-storey and made of wood and bamboo, and it was clear from the outset that it was mostly un-mechanised. Eva leaned forwards in the taxi as they approached. They might be having financial problems, but the place still seemed busy. A truck parked outside the building on the other side of the compound was being loaded with crates, presumably destined for shipping. A couple of men in flip-flops wearing *longyis* and loose shirts and carrying clipboards were talking by the factory entrance, another was taking some tools inside and several men were squatting as they worked on furniture on a wide terrace at the front.

Ramon was just coming outside. When he saw the taxi, he waved and came straight over.

'Eva, you made it.'

'Of course.' He looked happy to see her and, despite everything, this thought gave her a bit of a glow. She took the hand he offered to help her out of the taxi. And fervently hoped that Klaus had got it wrong.

Ramon spoke to the taxi driver and handed him two thousand kyatts.

'It's OK, I've got it.' Eva was fumbling in her purse.

'It is done.' Ramon waved her money away much as he had done after dinner last night, took her arm and led her towards the factory. His enthusiasm was obvious from the spring in his step. He was back in a red-and-black checked *longyi* and grey shirt this afternoon and Eva had to admit that it suited him. 'And now,' he said, 'I must show you what we produce.'

They began at the back of the factory. It was badly lit, the raw wood stacked on shelves up to the ceiling, the floor covered in shavings. 'This is where the process begins,' Ramon told her. 'The decisions of design have been made, the planks have arrived from the saw mill, we can now select the timber for each item of furniture.'

After this, she learnt, each potential piece – chests, cabinets, chairs, tables, some simple in design, some ornate – went on a journey through the factory, moving from one pair of practised hands to the next. It was about as different to what she'd seen at Li's as it could be.

It was a long process and everything was in a different stage of construction. 'Each piece must be sawn and planed using only traditional methods,' Ramon told her. Which explained the lack of mechanisation. Eva remembered what Ramon had said about his business ethics, about the importance of retaining the hand-crafted element in quality furniture. This was what they stood for. And practically the only bit of modern technology she spotted was the electric router, though the man wielding it sat shirtless and cross-legged on a plank of wood. Others squatted or crouched at their work, their dark hair matted with wood-shavings, their arms and legs bare and dusty. The sound of tapping, sawing and the occasional drone of voices filled the air.

'Some of our workers have been here for many years,' Ramon said proudly as they watched a man wielding an ancient saw. He was barefoot and stood on a plank, using his toes like a vice to help support the wood as he worked it. There was a real connection, she realised, between the craftsman and his materials, between the human body and mind and what he was making. It was humbling. It was how things used to be in the rest of the world too, she thought. Before production speed became the driving force. Before time was money. But where something was gained, something was also lost . . .

They picked their way past the low stools, mats and items of half-made furniture, and moved on to the next stage of the process.

'Who's this?' Eva paused by an old photograph in a frame on the wall. It was a black-and-white shot. A tall young man stood by an open topped British vintage car, one hand resting on it in a proprietorial gesture. He had longish dark hair, light eyes and Ramon's smile.

'My father,' he said. He straightened the frame. 'He began

this company in 1965. It was unusual in those days. A very brave step to take.'

Eva nodded. 'How old was he?'

'Only twenty-five.'

And Eva could hear the pride in his voice.

Ramon showed her how they used paper templates of most of their designs, which were then carved out with a chisel and a wooden pestle, working carefully with the grain of the wood. She watched his demonstration. Ramon worked with an easy confidence, his brown arms flecked with sawdust, his fingers applying the pressure, swift and sure. She could see the narrow blue veins on the inside of his wrist as he guided the chisel, in his hands the most delicate of tools. And she watched his face as he worked, observing his instant absorption in the job in hand, his eyes still and yet alert. A master craftsman, totally at one with his subject. An artist. Eva breathed in the scent of the wood, sweet and smoky, rich and mellow, sultry.

'We still have some of the traditional British hand-tools my father insisted were shipped over,' Ramon said. He pointed to the chisel. 'There is one. Also hand planes and saws. He thought British construction methods were the best and he taught some of our workers his own father's way.' He laughed. 'So now we have what you might call a fusion.'

East meets West, thought Eva. There were the hinges and the gluing and the cutting out for locks and handles. Sometimes there was delicate gilding work to be done. And then the final stages of staining, sanding and polishing. The final polishing of each piece was usually done outside and in daylight.

Much of the furniture was highly glossed. Which meant that it was coated with several layers of lacquer, each one left to dry, sanded down and polished until the piece positively shone. 'This is what most of our clients prefer,' Ramon told her. 'We cater mainly for the Oriental market, of course.' He leaned closer. 'Although, as I explained, we are hoping for that to change.'

Eva was aware that he had already begun shipping elsewhere. She just hoped that the little business wouldn't lose sight of its original values.

'What are these?' She picked up a small packet of coloured powder wrapped in cellophane from a whole stack lined up on a shelf. They looked like spices; turmeric or paprika.

'Dye.' He indicated the finished products: a set of dining chairs with long narrow spindles and curved backs in rich burgundy with gilded carving on their arms; a glass cabinet with ornate handles in the shape of swans in a teak so dark it was almost chocolate and a lamp-stand of light yellow wood, a delicate carving of a woman wearing a crown and a necklace of flowers carved on its base. Some were made of mixtures that had been subtly blended, and although the stained wood was not to Eva's taste – she preferred the natural shade of teak that was also very much in evidence – she had to admire the craftsmanship.

The golden teak wood was her favourite, a natural shade that had been hand rubbed until it shone. But there were also contemporary finishes such as lime wash and teak oil. The range was considerable and the pieces that emerged were breath-taking in their quality, workmanship and lustre. And they were so solid. Eva ran her fingers over the shiny surface of a table that was smooth as a baby's skin. But there the resemblance ended; these pieces were heavy. They were built to last.

'And what's the new development you mentioned?' she asked him, thinking about what he'd said when they were on the way to Mandalay.

'Ah.' He led her over to a far corner of the factory. Here, a carpenter was working on a different looking wood. Old wood, she thought. 'Recycling,' he said proudly. 'This is my new project. There will come a day when Myanmar must not destroy any more of its natural forest. And yet there are many neglected structures such as old cattle houses, derelict homes and bridges in our country that can provide old wood, good wood for the making of a different sort of furniture.' He picked up some old, very wide planking. 'We ensure that the wood is salvaged responsibly,' he said. 'And look at what we find. Its long seasoning time has given it good stability. It has weathered to show a richer heart within. Is it not beautiful, Eva? Look at the closeness and evenness of the grain. Does this piece not have a history?'

She nodded. Again their views were in unison. Why not use old wood to create new, rustic looking furniture with a unique character of its own? It was practical, environmentally friendly and creative.

'I am only beginning this idea for my company now,' he said. 'But it is, I think, the way of the future.'

But what about their financial problems? And what about Li's? It was impossible, surely, that Ramon could be involved with them. She thought of Klaus. If he could hear what she was hearing, if he could see Ramon's factory, then he too would realise how completely off the mark his accusations were.

'So what do you think?' he asked her at the end of the tour.

'It's very impressive.' She had seen the complete process involved in making a piece of hand-crafted furniture. It had been fascinating.

There was one room however, which Ramon didn't show her.

'What's in there?' she asked, pointing.

'Ah.' He seemed embarrassed. 'It is another workroom. Sometimes I go in there to work on a special piece.' He shrugged. 'But there is nothing in there at the moment to interest you.'

His secretive tone made Eva want to go in. She frowned. He had been so open as he'd shown her round his factory and yet now he had closed up again, albeit briefly. Why?

They had tea in his office and when he found out she hadn't had lunch, Ramon had a word with one of his female office workers who proceeded to conjure up *Pe Thee Thoke*, a salad with herbs and long beans, which proved delicious.

'Did you enjoy your coffee with your friend?' Ramon asked her, as he sipped his tea.

'Mmm.' Eva was non-committal. 'But he's not a friend, not really. I only met him in Yangon.'

'And you did not know him before?' Ramon seemed surprised, almost disapproving. His expression darkened.

She knew what he was thinking. But, 'It's different for Europeans,' she said. 'You're drawn together in a strange country.'

'So you are drawn to him, yes?' His brow knitted. 'In this strange country?'

Eva didn't like the turn the subject had taken. 'It's not like that.' She tried to explain, but in truth, she was beginning to feel some doubt herself. There had been that rather odd meeting at the Shwedagon. And now Klaus had tried to make her distrust Ramon. 'It wouldn't have happened like that at home,' she admitted. 'Or in Germany. But in Myanmar . . .'

'Strangers in a strange land.' He put down his tea-cup. 'Foreigners stick together.'

Fortunately, his mobile rang and effectively closed the subject. It was Maya. Like Eva with her grandfather, Ramon had forged such a strong bond with her, she could tell, made more so, no doubt, by having lost his parents. She heard him mention her name and his face broke once again into a smile. He was, she thought, such a mixture of a man.

He moved the phone from his ear. 'My grandmother has arrived in Mandalay,' he said to Eva. 'She asks if we will both join her at a local restaurant for dinner tonight?'

'That would be lovely.'

'She has something to tell you.' Ramon's eyes twinkled. 'I think you will be surprised – and pleased.'

More story-telling, Eva wondered? She hoped so. She couldn't get enough of hearing about the old Burmese days.

As Eva was just finishing her lunch, Ramon was called away and she sat alone in the little office for a few moments. One of his assistants came in to check something in the accounts book. He smiled and nodded to her.

'Do you speak English?' she asked him.

'Yes, a little.' He smiled again and bowed his head.

'You are happy working here?' she asked.

'Oh, yes.' He beamed. 'Mister Ramon is a good man, isn't it? A kind man. Yes.'

'I'm sure he is.' Eva smiled back.

'My brother, he work here too,' he went on.

'Oh yes?'

'He have operation for eyes, isn't it?' The man pointed to his own eyes.

'Cataracts?' she guessed.

He nodded. 'They do operation at monastery in Sagaing, isn't it?'

Eva remembered Ramon mentioning this on their day out. 'That's good,' she said. 'And he is better now?'

'Yes.' The man nodded furiously. 'Mister Ramon, he take him, he help family.'

'He took him to the monastery?'

'Yes, yes. Very good. Very kind. He pay him while he off

sick. He look after workers, isn't it?' He exited the room, still bowing and smiling.

Eva was thoughtful.

When Ramon returned, she got to her feet. 'I should be getting back to the hotel,' she told him. She had to meet Myint Maw at three and time was getting on.

'I will take you.'

'No, really. You've got so much to do here. I can easily—'

'I insist.' Ramon took her arm. 'Afterwards, I will return here for a few hours,' he said, 'and then pick you up tonight at eight.'

They left the building by way of the small front office door to the right of the warehouse area.

'I was talking just now to the brother of the man who had the cataracts,' Eva said.

'Oh, yes? Moe Zaw?'

Eva paused in the doorway. 'He told me you had paid the man all the time he was off sick.'

He shrugged. 'The family had need of the money. Any employer would do the same.'

She shook her head. 'I don't think so.' She glanced out at the terrace where men were finishing and polishing the gleaming furniture. 'Can the business afford to take on employees' health care?' she murmured.

He gave her a quick look. 'I can put my hand in my own pocket, Eva,' he said. 'It is not too much to do.'

They stepped outside into the blistering heat. So he had paid for it himself. No wonder his workers were loyal to him and his company. 'And the financial problems?' she said. 'The loss of orders?'

'We will overcome it.' Ramon flicked back the wing of dark hair. 'Just as my father overcame his problems. Our materials are not cheap. We have lost a few orders. So be it. I have to believe that our way is the right way. That we will be winners in the end.'

'I hope so.'

'And before you go, I have one more thing to show you,' said Ramon. 'It is over in the warehouse on the other side of the compound. It will only take a minute.'

'Very well.' Eva followed him to a small truck and climbed in beside him.

'We can do some more sightseeing tomorrow, if you like,' he said as they drove across. 'I could take an hour or two off. You must see the Royal Palace. It may be a replica, but it will give you an idea of the original.'

'I'd like that.'

As they got to the warehouse, a man came rushing out.

'Ah, Wai Yan.' Ramon introduced them. 'This is my warehouse manager,' he said to Eva. 'This is a family friend, Eva Gatsby.' They shook hands. 'Do you have the key to the garage, please?'

'The key, yes, pleased to meet you.' The man seemed a little nervous but produced a key from the ring looped into the belt of his *longyi*.

'Come.' Ramon led the way. He unlocked a door and flung it open. There was a car inside. And then she realised it was *the* car, the one in the photo. A gorgeous vintage car, all cream curves and red leather interior.

'Your father's car,' she breathed.

'It is a Sunbeam Alpine.' Ramon stroked the cream body-work lovingly. 'It was his prized possession. He had it shipped over here when he knew he would stay.'

Their eyes met and once again she felt it, that frisson she had felt in Pyin Oo Lwin as they had walked together towards Pine Rise, the roadside lined with the sweet scented blossom of frangipani. And that sense, last night, of feeling close to him.

'Ramon!' Suddenly one of his workers was at the warehouse door, waving his arms and gesticulating. The warehouse manager was beside him, tearing his fingers through his hair.

They looked at one another and laughed. It seemed they were destined to be interrupted.

'I can get a taxi,' Eva said. 'It's no problem.'

Ramon frowned. 'I will call a car for you. Excuse me for a moment, Eva.' He touched her face with his fingers. So briefly. But in that moment she knew. She wasn't mistaken. He'd felt that frisson just as she had.

Ramon stood in a huddle with the man who had just appeared and the warehouse manager, their voices rising, all talking at once, it seemed. They all sounded a little on edge, she thought.

Unnoticed, she wandered outside the warehouse and towards the truck still parked outside. So there was a spark and it wasn't just from the moonlight or the scent of frangipani. It was there in broad hot spanking daylight outside a furniture factory in Mandalay. Did that mean it was real?

She turned to look back at the factory building. It had taught her a lot about the man. He was a perfectionist and he was talented, for he had told her he still liked to get hands-on and she had observed that much of the furniture was designed and crafted by him alone. He cared about his work . . . She thought of the way he had run his hands over both the highly polished, finished pieces and the timber, raw, from where those pieces had begun. She thought of his expression when he'd been carving that piece of wood.

He cared for his employees. He loved his family too, especially his grandmother, and he cared deeply about Burmese trade and ethics. Eva wondered. How well did Ramon know the Li family and the business they ran? Would he be shocked if he knew how they were trying to hoodwink tourists, passing off old tat they'd artificially distressed as genuine antiques? But she couldn't tell him about it, not without admitting that she'd been there.

The sun was hot on her head despite the protection from her hat. Eva glanced at the old truck loaded with crates, wondered vaguely where the containers might be going. Japan, maybe, or China? She knew Ramon's dream was to export further afield, to expand, even set up a partner business elsewhere. Dreams . . . They could, she thought, be dangerous things.

She took a step closer. The door hadn't been closed properly and the wooden crate nearest to the back of the truck was clearly visible. She peered at the address label. Did a double-take. It couldn't be . . . She looked again. But it was. Her company's name *The Bristol Antiques Emporium* and their address in Bristol was written there, clear as day.

How odd. Eva frowned. But the Emporium was an antique company. Why would Ramon be sending a container of his handmade furniture out to them? And why on earth hadn't he told her? She had told him the name of her company, told him what she was doing here . . .

Eva ran her fingers lightly over the wooden crate as if it could tell her what was inside. And then she noticed something else. Under the stamp of the sender, 'Handmade in Mandalay', she could make out a different kind of marking, something that was familiar, something that made her blood run cold.

'Hey!' Wai Yan the warehouse manager was racing towards her. He looked furious. 'What you doing? Come away from there!'

Eva took a step back. 'Sorry,' she murmured. 'I was just curious . . .'

'You stay away!' He seemed quite threatening now as he brandished his clipboard, his face like thunder.

'What is going on?' Suddenly, Ramon was beside them. 'What has happened?'

The man muttered something in Burmese. He pointed to Eva, gesticulated at the truck, his voice seemed to go on and on in an incomprehensible stream.

Why wouldn't he stop talking? Suddenly, there didn't

seem to be enough air. Eva felt a wave of dizziness, her head was pounding and she swayed on her feet.

'Eva, are you OK?' Ramon's face swam in front of hers. His green eyes were concerned. Thankfully, the other man had stopped talking, though he was still standing there looking decidedly twitchy.

'It's alright, really.' She forced a smile.

'Your taxi is here.' He put an arm around her. Eva's first instinct was to shrug it off but she couldn't find the energy. 'I shouldn't have left you out here alone in this heat,' he was murmuring into her hair. 'I am so sorry. Take no notice of Wai Yan. I do not know what possessed him. He imagined you were stealing something.' He laughed.

'It doesn't matter.' She had only been out there for a few minutes. But her throat was parched and her lips dry.

'Are you sure you are OK?' He bent closer. 'You look as if you have seen a ghost.'

'I'm fine.'

Ramon opened the car door and helped her in, giving the hotel name to the driver and handing him a couple of notes. And this time Eva couldn't be bothered to protest.

He leant in, his eyes searching hers. But she couldn't even look at him.

'Later?' he said.

She nodded. 'Later.'

But as the taxi drove off and Ramon raised his hand in a wave goodbye, her head was reeling. What she had seen under the sender's stamp . . . Had it been some sort of a mirage from the heat? That distinctive blue and gold? No, it was real enough. It was the faded image of a blue-and-gold peacock, the logo of Li's Antique and Furniture Company. There was no doubt. Li's were sending stock to the Emporium. And they were using Ramon's company to do it.

CHAPTER 36

Rosemary took him in his breakfast. He was awake, but still looked a bit bleary. And old, she thought. And old.

'Morning, Dad,' she said, trying to sound cheery, although in fact she hadn't had a good night, outside the morning sky was leaden grey and she couldn't stop thinking about Alec.

'Oh.' He blinked at her. 'Hello, darling.' He frowned. 'For a second there, I thought you were—'

'I was what?' And then she realised. 'I was who?' Who was important in her father's life? Eva, obviously. Even Mrs Briggs, she supposed. She wasn't family, but she'd been helping them with cleaning for years and with cooking too since Rosemary's mother's death.

'Someone else,' he said. He looked lost. *Who, Dad?* But she didn't say it.

She helped him sit up, wrapped the old tartan dressing gown around his thin shoulders. When he was comfortable, she put the tray in front of him.

'Mm, porridge,' he said. 'I've missed that.'

'I tried to make it like Mother used to,' Rosemary admitted. Let it bubble for a few minutes, a swirl of honey, a flash of milk.

'Your mother always made the best porridge.'

She did something right then.

Rosemary rearranged the things on the bedside table. 'What used to be on here, Dad?' She had the sense of something missing. Like that old memory game with a tray and a tea-towel. It was elusive though.

He ate his porridge from the more solid edge, moving inwards. Tiny spoonfuls. Hardly enough to keep a bird alive, she thought.

'It was the chinthe.'

Of course it was. It had always been there. Rosemary's mother had hated it. *Evil little creature*, she used to say, and refuse to dust it. It was a small rebellion, but somehow Rosemary had come to think of it as malevolent too. When she was little and went into her parents' bedroom, she even used to snarl at it sometimes.

'How on earth did you persuade Mother to let you keep it there?' she asked lightly. All the rest of his Burmese souvenirs were relegated to the downstairs hallway where the light was dim and visitors might pass by the shelf, hardly noticing them. But the chinthe was the most iconic Burmese souvenir of them all. And Rosemary's mother must have seen it every night when she was about to go to sleep. No wonder she'd loathed it.

Her father put down his spoon. He'd only eaten about a quarter of the small bowl. But he exhaled with pleasure and she knew he'd enjoyed it. 'I didn't insist on very much,' he said.

She nodded. She understood. 'And where is it now?' But even as she asked, she knew the answer to the question.

'Eva took it to Burma.'

'I see.' Rosemary recalled what Eva had said in her email. Something that she was doing for her grandfather, wasn't it? But she *didn't* see. And suddenly, she couldn't bear it; he had confided in Eva and yet told her nothing. All these years. That she knew nothing of his Burmese days, apart from what she'd found out in those letters, apart from what she had imagined . . .

Rosemary took the tray off his lap and replaced it carefully on the bedside table. She passed him his tea. What if things had been different, she wondered. What if her mother hadn't deeply resented Burma and passed her own resentment on to her daughter? What if it had been Rosemary who had listened, enthralled to all those tales of a far-off place and far-off people, an exotic life that most people could only dream of? Instead of Eva?

She watched her father as he carefully sipped his tea. But that could never have been. Because . . . Rosemary realised that he was watching her.

'There was a woman,' he said. 'In Burma.' He reached for her hand. 'I'm sorry, love.'

'Before you met Mother?'

'No, not before that. There was always your mother.' He chuckled. 'I miss her, you know.'

'Me too.'

'You grew up together, didn't you?' she asked. 'You and Mother?'

'As good as.'

Rosemary listened to him talk. His voice was dry and thin, but the words rang true and she could fill in most of the spaces. She could imagine exactly how her mother had been, as a child, as a young woman. Demanding what was hers by right, refusing to take no for an answer, blindly believing that she could control everything and make him change. Make him love her . . .

It was part of her own childhood. *Of course you'll come to the shops with me . . . Of course your bedroom will be painted yellow . . .* Some people controlled by physical strength, some by mental domination. Her mother had controlled by her expectations, by her assumptions that there was a wrong way and then there was *her* way.

'I knew there was someone,' she told him when at last his voice faltered. 'But I didn't realise.'

'I had choices.' He nodded. 'I don't blame your mother at all. She did what she had to do. I was weak.'

'We can all be weak.' Rosemary squeezed his hand. She hated him talking like that. She wanted him to be as strong as the father she remembered.

'And Eva . . .' He stared out of the window as if he could see her there.

Rosemary waited. What exactly was Eva doing for him in Burma?

'She's given her back the chinthe,' he said. His eyes were

329

bright. 'It belongs with her family. It had so much history bound up in it, you see, Rosie.'

Rosemary nodded as if she understood, though she didn't, not really. She only understood that she'd wasted a lot of years without her father, blaming him for something that she should never have blamed him for. What had he done that was so different from what she had done – with Alec? Her father had not been able to give her mother one hundred per cent of his love, his life. But at least he had tried his best. Had Rosemary?

'Will you tell me about Maya?' she whispered.

He didn't seem surprised that she knew her name.

'If you want me to,' he said.

'Have you told Eva?'

'Some of it, yes.' He sighed. 'Some of it I don't even know myself. Not yet.'

Rosemary patted his hand.

'I'm waiting for Eva to get back,' he said.

And for an awful moment, she thought he meant *before I die*.

CHAPTER 37

Eva's head was still spinning when the taxi arrived back at her hotel. And she had to meet Myint Maw in less than half an hour. 'Can you wait for me, please?' she asked the driver. She would go up to her room, quickly get changed, collect her paperwork and the eyeglass she used to examine close detail and come straight back. And try not to think about what had just happened, she told herself, as she collected her key and took the lift to the seventh floor. Of Ramon and what she had discovered. Would he guess that she had seen what was in the truck? Probably. He must have thought she'd acted a little strangely. No wonder that warehouse manager had yelled at her like that. And yet . . . What *was* in that crate? And why in heaven's name was it being sent to the Emporium?

By 3 p.m. she was once again sitting in Myint Maw's stuffy little office. Thankfully, he had provided green tea.

'Miss Gatsby,' he was saying. 'I see this, I think to myself. I must show her. She must see it. She will not believe.' He shook his dark head, his entire scrawny body joining in the movement.

'What is it exactly?' Eva sipped her tea and wished she could summon up some enthusiasm. But it seemed her enthusiasm

331

waned in direct proportion to Maw's sense of melodrama. Unless the events of a very long day were getting to her at last.

Myint Maw made a big pretence of looking first to the left then to the right although the office door was shut and they were alone in the room. 'Doors,' he said.

'Doors?'

'Not just doors. No, no, no.' He waved a long finger in front of him. Leaned closer so that Eva could smell his slightly rancid breath and see the hairy mole once again at close quarters. 'Special doors,' he said. 'Intricate carving, yes, yes. Big doors. Old doors. Monastery doors.'

'Monastery doors?' She was sure they were very interesting, but . . . 'Where did they come from?' she asked. 'What happened to the monastery?'

Maw gave his usual expansive shrug. 'Restoration?' But he seemed to be guessing.

And here we go again, she thought. Temples that were no longer prayed in, monasteries with no monks or novices living inside. Didn't they care that the ancient treasures of Burma were being pillaged by the West? And then her shoulders sagged. What was happening to her? She was beginning to sound like Ramon. And yet now she knew that Ramon . . .

'You will see, yes, I will take you in my car.' Maw was nodding energetically.

And Eva knew that she had to be professional. She was here to do a job. She must at least see the doors.

They were in the back of another shop a few blocks away. And they were stunning.

'Solid teak, yes, yes,' said Myint Maw. 'Two hundred centimetre high.' His eyes widened and he nodded even more frantically. She couldn't imagine the cost of the shipping.

She took her time examining them. Burmese woodcarvers were so skilled even from an early period, and the carving was both intricate and flamboyant. The doors featured two guardians, *devas*, holding sprays of foliage, and had been created in the mid-nineteenth century, she estimated.

'Built by King Mindon, yes, yes,' Maw was telling her, circling the doors like a terrier, flinging nuggets of information at her over his shoulder. 'From Amarapura, yes, yes.'

Although not built by him personally, one would assume. Eva moved closer to examine the carving more carefully. The pilasters and pediments were rosettes, horn shaped projections known as *saing-baung* and the flames of *nat-saw*. These monastery doors were indeed, exquisite specimens.

'You interested, yes?' Maw nodded as though this could not be in doubt.

Which it couldn't, Eva thought. Because even if she didn't buy them, how long before some other Western dealer snapped them up? They didn't belong on a monastery any more. They were for sale, in a shop. It wasn't her responsibility where they had come from. *Damn Ramon*.

'How much?' And Eva began the difficult process of negotiating a price. It was hard to haggle about pieces such as these and impossible to even estimate how much they were worth to the Emporium. But that was part of Eva's job, and her responsibility. And Jacqui would, she knew, be so impressed.

An hour later, Eva was back at her hotel. She put a call through to the Emporium and when Jacqui answered, Eva told her about the monastery doors.

'They sound magnificent,' her boss said. 'Can you email me a photo?'

'Will do.'

'And the contact?' Jacqui's voice changed.

'Myint Maw?'

'How does he seem on second meeting? Reliable, would you say?'

Eva remembered how edgy he had been the other day when she had talked about provenance. How he had seemed surprised that she even cared. 'He never knows where anything's come from,' she admitted to Jacqui. 'Like these doors, for example.'

'But if they're for sale . . .' Jacqui's voice was crisp and confident. 'They can't be stolen goods, can they? And if they're genuine . . . ?'

'Oh, yes, they are genuine.' Eva wished she could express what was bothering her. It was that feeling that something else was happening that she knew nothing about. Only now, perhaps, she might be closer to finding out what it was. 'And, Jacqui, do we have dealings with a company called Handmade in Mandalay?'

'I don't think so. Why?'

'It's just that I saw a crate . . .' Eva wasn't sure how much to say. She wasn't sure how much she knew either. And she certainly wasn't sure about the Emporium.

'What sort of a crate? Is something going on, Eva? Look . . .' And her voice seemed to change. 'You will take care, won't you?'

'Yes, of course.' Eva was surprised.

'And email me – if there are any problems that is.'

She hadn't asked Jacqui about Li's. And Eva wasn't quite sure why not. She took her time over coffee in the hotel bar but there were still three hours before Ramon was picking her up for dinner and she didn't think she could stay here alone with her thoughts for all that time. She needed to go out somewhere, anywhere.

Seeing that crate in the truck had shaken her up and she needed to make sense of it all. What should she do? What could she do? The Emporium weren't doing business with Ramon's company. Why would they? They dealt in antiques. She thought of the blue-and-gold peacock insignia that had not been entirely obliterated by the stamp of Handmade in Mandalay. Which meant that the Emporium must be doing business with Li's.

Eva didn't want to think about that. She stepped outside the hotel lobby and was promptly accosted by a friendly trishaw driver.

'You want to go on a trip, lady?' he asked hopefully. 'I take you to Mahamuni temple. A good place. I very strong.' And he pounded his chest to demonstrate.

Despite everything, Eva had to smile. He was slight in build, but these trishaw drivers were sinewy and physically powerful. She'd often seen quite small men carrying two hefty tourists on their trishaws, one facing forward, the other back, their pedal–power truly impressive. 'I've been to the Mahamuni Temple,' she said. 'So, no, thank you.' It had been the same day Ramon had taken her to Inwa and Sagaing. Something she didn't want to dwell on. And yet he had pretended it was all so important, hadn't he? That she experienced the spirituality and the history. That she allowed Myanmar to touch something deep inside of her. And she had. She really had.

'The Royal Palace?' he persevered. 'You go there? It is close by.'

Eva considered. She had said she'd go to the Royal Palace with Ramon, and it was so connected with his family, to his grandmother's story . . . But now, everything had changed. Sooner or later, she'd have to confront him with what she'd seen. No wonder he hadn't wanted her to approach the Li family. He must know, mustn't he, exactly what they were? No wonder there was a back room in his factory that he hadn't wanted her to go in. It was unlikely that she'd be going anywhere with him in the future.

Eva glanced at the busy road. She couldn't walk anywhere, and it might be fun. 'Alright,' she told the driver. 'You're on.'

He frowned and shook his head. What now?

'You must ask me how much,' he told her.

Eva shrugged. 'OK. How much?'

'Five thousand kyatts there and back,' he said. 'This is good price.'

'Fine.'

Another frown. 'OK, lady, you drive a hard bargain. Four thousand it is.' And he grinned, revealing gappy teeth stained blood red and black from betel.

It was a ghastly sight, but Eva was getting used to it. Many of the Burmese didn't drink because it was against their religion. But Buddha had never said anything about betel. She climbed on board. Thought of her grandfather as she so often did. *Royal Palace, here we come.*

As Ramon had told her, the building was a replica since the original had been razed to the ground, and when they got there, after a nerve-jangling trishaw ride through the busy streets of Mandalay, Eva was disappointed. It was so different from what she'd imagined. Inside the city walls, it was a bit like being in the country, very green, with dirt roads and fields, which seemed bizarre after the griminess of the built up city outside. It felt peaceful but bare, with only the odd barrack-type building and a café shack breaking up the landscape and army personnel wandering around where once there must have been vibrancy, splendour, royalty and hangers-on. The palace was surrounded by lots of other tiered, red-roofed buildings. It was a maze. But what really dismayed Eva was that everything about the red pagoda palace looked so modern. It seemed to be such a cheap replica. And she'd seen more than enough of those at Li's.

Inside, however, there were old sepia photographs of Queen Supayalat and King Thibaw in their extravagant royal robes, jewels and crowns and Eva stared at these, letting her imagination run wild, thinking of how life had once been for them. Queen Supayalat looked as Suu Kyi had described, diminutive but strong-minded, her expression almost surly. King Thibaw looked meek and sweet as a lamb but terribly regal with his high cheekbones, arched eyebrows and drooping moustache. She supposed that it was impossible to reproduce that time of glory, though the copy of the throne, *Sihasana*, built on a high platform supported by sculptured lions was certainly golden and glorious enough.

Li's . . . As Eva began to look around the impressive Audience Hall where important visitors of a certain rank would have been received, she couldn't help thinking about them. They were sending a crate to the Emporium. But why? What was in it? And if it were anything like what she had seen in their showroom, then why on earth would the Emporium be interested?

She wandered through past the *Sihasana* and the array of golden caskets, lamps, even royal sandals and shoes made of solid gold, silver and decorated with rubies. Eva was getting a good idea of just how rich in gems Burma's Royal Family had been. Along with wood, gemstones had been Myanmar's chief source of wealth for centuries. And she supposed the

Royal Family would ensure that they kept the best for themselves.

Unless it wasn't Li's fake statuettes in the crate. It could be something else. The crate could be full of the kind of artefacts Khan Li had said he could obtain for Eva. But if so, wouldn't Jacqui have wanted her to authenticate those pieces while she was here?

There were few other tourists and Eva was grateful for the information boards written in English which gave her all the guidance she required. She had no need, she told herself, of Ramon. And where did he fit in? If the goods being sent by Li were above board – and, privately, Eva found this hard to believe – then why not send them direct from their own premises? She'd seen the cargo boat on the river. Why send them via another company? Why send them via Ramon? But there was only one answer to this that she could think of. They would send them that way to provide a front. And you only needed to provide a front when you wanted to hide something.

Pushing these thoughts away once more, Eva meandered through to the Hall of Victory, with the *Hamsa* Throne, complete with a model of King Mindon seated on it, and found herself replaying the scene of the British rout of 1885, the people of Mandalay plundering the riches of the palace while the British were stashing their first haul, and Queen Supayalat, Suu Kyi, Nanda Li and the two young princesses watched from their chamber with horror.

But she couldn't get Ramon out of her head. Did he know

what was going on? Did Jacqui? Was Ramon's business, with his father's good name and ethics, a front for something illegal? Something criminal? Could it be possible that this man who – *admit it, Eva* – she had begun to have feelings for, was, for all his fine talk about business ethics, working with the Lis and involved in something decidedly shady? Klaus had been right. Fakes and forgery. That was the impression she'd had when she visited Li's. But Ramon . . . Could she have read him so wrong? Had he simply pretended to be passionate about his family business, about the superior quality of the furniture they produced, about their use of the hand-crafted traditions so intrinsic to Myanmar? While all the time . . .

Eva was now in the Glass Palace. Its walls tiled entirely with mirrors, it was the shimmering hub of the Palace complex, situated exactly in the centre. The Glass Palace . . . How mind-spinning it must have been just to stand here . . .

Why would he do it? Was it for the money? Was it part of his scheme, his dream, to spend time in the Britain of his father? Or was all that a pretence, too? And what about her own company? Jacqui had seemed very keen to get her out of the country when all these shipments were supposed to be arriving and Myint Maw had been more than a little edgy. Eva remembered how surprised he'd been when she questioned his sources, and how he'd back-tracked about all the other stuff that he'd apparently sent them. How she'd been convinced that she was being told only part of the story. So what was going on?

At the end of the rabbit warren of adjoining rooms that

made up the Palace, Eva came to the Cultural Museum. Inside, were more photographs, of ambassadors who had visited the Burmese court and of the Royal Family. There was King Mindon who had apparently ordered the building of the monastery from which her latest acquisition for the Emporium had come, the King who had also founded the City of Mandalay and had it built at the foot of the sacred mound of Mandalay Hill, in accordance with the prophesies of Buddha. And there was another representation that Eva loved, a colour drawing of King Thibaw and Queen Supayalat sitting high on the Lion Throne in the Audience Hall, with hundreds of subjects bending and *shiko-ing* before them. No wonder the Queen had a superiority complex, thought Eva.

In the central aisle was a line of royal wooden carriages with old photographs so faded and indistinct, she could barely make out the royal figures in their glamorous jewelled carriage, harnessed to and pulled by bullocks. Some of the costumes were displayed in glass cabinets though: a sequinned and beaded tapestry robe studded with rubies worn by Queen Supayalat; the gold-threaded brocade of a Royal Maid-in-Waiting – maybe even Suu Kyi's, Eva realised with a jolt – embroidered silk and hemp, sashes and shawls. And there was the famous four-poster bed made entirely of glass. No replica, this was the real thing.

The real thing . . . Eva paused as she left the building and wandered back to the entrance on the outside of the Palace this time. In the distance, she could see the glint of a golden pagoda on Mandalay Hill. Visiting the Royal Palace had given her an insight into the story of the chinthes and Suu Kyi. But what about the Emporium and her own position there? And what about Ramon? She had trusted him and now it looked as if he was no better than all the rest.

And for the first time since she'd been in Myanmar, Eva felt very alone.

CHAPTER 38

When Lawrence woke up, he was sweating, really sweating, just like he had in those days and nights in that interminable heat, oppressive and heavy. For a moment he didn't know where he was. Could he be back in Burma? In that dark green uniform, those boots and puttees? No, he was old and he had never been back, though for so many years he had longed to. But perhaps part of him was still there, in the jungle in 1943, weary and footsore, marching up to twenty miles a day with a seventy-pound rucksack on his back, leading his mule over hilly and jungle terrain, down almost impenetrable muddy paths in monsoon, exhausted from the searing heat, sweating from the humidity, hot and wet enough to rot your boots, waking up every morning to a jungle growth of light green mould even on his own skin. Jungle warfare.

Lawrence shivered despite the warmth of his bed. How had they kept going? People talked of morale and courage. But really you just kept going because you had to. You were as dependent on your comrades in arms as they were on you. You couldn't let them down. He found out later they'd been called the forgotten army, thanks to some war correspondent, he'd heard. But at the time . . . Yes, there was a sense of isolation, a sense of marching to God alone knew where in a bloody evil terrain where typhoid or malaria might finish you off if the Japs didn't. They hadn't been forgotten by those who mattered, of course they hadn't. But their war wasn't the war in everyone else's minds and voices. Their war was more like a sideshow to what was going on in Europe.

How his shoulders had ached from carrying that pack. The puttees kept out the worst of the leeches. But his feet had suffered as much as everyone else's, blistered from the boots, thick, un-feeling, white-soled from the wet. His pack had held three grenades, meagre bedding, a mess tin and spoon, steriliser, salt tablets, rubber shoes and the little chinthe Maya had given him. *It had so much history bound up in it, you see.* He had said that recently, to someone.

He never considered leaving it behind though they all thought he was crazy. Others had pictures of their loved ones, well, he didn't need those; he could close his eyes and see Maya every night, clear as anything. And the chinthe would protect him, she'd said. Didn't that make it the most important thing of all? He'd carried a jack knife too, along with his gun, a length of rope and a water bottle. You tried not to drink it though. Not because it tasted brackish and of chlorine, though it did, but because you were rationed. Best to wait until you were desperate, with a throat parched and rough as sandpaper.

Lawrence remembered the food too, not so bad when the mules were carrying stocks or when the drops came through. Cans of stewed beef and carrots, bully and hard crackers, tinned fruit and condensed milk, rice pudding. But most of all he remembered the chilling sounds, stealthy footsteps that might belong to Japs in the pitch-black of night-time watch in the jungle, the whirr of a grenade, the crack of gunfire.

Lawrence thought of Eva. How long had she been in Burma? He wasn't sure of the days and nights like he used to be. When she first left, he had started counting. But then he lost track. What did she think of the place? And what did she think of Maya, his Maya? He had wanted to ask her when she telephoned, but he had been bowled over, utterly bowled over by the fact that his granddaughter had found her.

He had sensed that she was still alive. But . . . *You should have found out for sure*. Lawrence had always known this. He'd often wanted to tell Eva the whole story – she was the only person he could tell. A man didn't have conversations like that with other men. And then there was Rosemary . . . Once, she would have thrown a blue fit if she'd known her father had harboured longings for a woman other than her mother. And he couldn't blame her. But now? Things seemed different now. Eva, though, had the imagination and emotional intelligence to see how it could have been. They had always been close. And she would love Burma just like she loved wood, the feel of it: the rough and the smooth; the sweet and enticing forest-fragrance of it; the way it told its own age, its own story.

He shifted in his bed, avoiding looking at that ceiling. Something was telling him he'd been in this bed too long. The truth was that he had wanted to find out what had happened to Maya before now, had wanted to relive the memories and perhaps even meet again the woman who had stolen his heart. But he couldn't. He had committed himself to Helen and then he had fulfilled that commitment by marrying her. He had done it for his mother, for his dead father and because it was the right thing to do. Especially given what he had done. It was his duty. And that commitment, no matter how much he regretted it, meant he couldn't even take one step backwards to the past. That way would lead to something much darker than Lawrence could deal with. If he stepped back towards the past . . . He'd be done for. He knew it.

He closed his eyes. He was tired. Already, he was tired. After Helen's death, perhaps he could still have gone to find her. But something told him that it would be too late, that it would be wrong to intrude in her life now, so long after he had walked away from it. And then there were the politics of the matter . . .

Lawrence had told Eva many stories about his time in Burma. About the life on the streets where people crouched over open fires to cook their food, the spices smoking, rising and perfuming the air, the colourful bustling markets, the teak camps high in the hills built on stilts overlooking the River Irrawaddy and the elephants he had grown so fond of during his time there. He had talked about the wood, about the work, about the teak Buddhas and the golden pagodas of Mandalay, exotic fragments, he supposed, of what he thought of as his other life. His real life.

But he had never told Eva about his war. The war, he

didn't wish to remember. He'd seen men die from malaria and dengue fever and he'd seen comrades fall – too many of them. He'd killed men before they had the chance to kill him; you didn't think about it, you just made sure it was the enemy and then you fired. You ducked and you ran like blazes and you were glad that you were living another day. Some didn't, that was war. He'd seen blood and dismembered limbs and he'd walked away from it if there was nothing that could be done. He'd seen dysentery and disease and heard men going quite mad. He'd met women who had been tortured and raped, prisoners who had lived with only a handful of rice pushed through the bars of their prison cell to keep them going all day. He'd seen fear like he'd never imagined and he'd stared death in the face. Why would he want to remember such things?

But sometimes . . . The mind was a curious power. The mind and the memories could pick you up and toss you back there. Sometimes it was disconnected fragments, images that fast-forwarded through your brain. Sometimes you remembered every last detail. Back you went to the thick, cloying heat and damp of the jungle, back to the trenches, back to the stench of war. And you wondered how you'd got through it, just like Lawrence was wondering now.

Lawrence's emergency commission had taken him, on a train with no windows, to an officer training school in Mhow, India. Like Burma, this was a land of poverty. In the daytime there was plenty of action, even in training school. And more men were being trained as officers as the Japanese drew closer.

As he'd known it would be, it was a valuable asset to speak the language, to know the country and its people, even if one lacked military experience.

They woke at 4.30 a.m. Some of the lads were shaved in their beds by a barber and brought tea and biscuits by their personal bearer. It was laughable really, when you considered that they were preparing themselves for war. Lawrence always got himself up and ready for the 5.30 a.m. drill and weapon training that began the day. Especially after Maya, he couldn't bring himself to think of the natives the way a lot of the men did. Was it their right to be served? What gave them that right? There were many things he hadn't questioned when he first came to Burma. But since then, he had listened to Maya's father and others railing against colonialism and British rule. The Burmese wanted to be independent. Who could blame them? And was it for the British to decide whether they could control the in-fighting that made independence so fraught with difficulties? Lawrence didn't know. But he had come to think about these issues more deeply, had seen the other side of the coin. And it had left him feeling strangely disturbed.

At night, he used the light from the pressure gas butties to read and study the training manuals, details of weapons, drills, and soon Lawrence became an expert. But later, when the mosquito nets had been drawn over the bed and all he could hear were the crickets and the occasional far-off cry from someone in the village beyond, Lawrence thought of Maya. He thought of the seriousness in her dark eyes, the poise with which she walked around her father's house and the streets of Mandalay, the sleek sheen of her hair. And, worst of all, he thought of those nights spent close to her, drinking in her musky perfume and the faint fragrance of coconut oil, incense and sensuality that hung in the darkness, her supple body lying curled around his, her slender fingers tracing and trailing their way over his arms, his legs, his chest until he wanted to scream with frustration. Maya. In the day, he thought of his mother and sometimes he even thought of Helen. But in the night, always, he thought of Maya.

How was she? Where was she now? He had heard that the Japanese had carried out a series of damaging air raids on Rangoon and that people were fleeing and travelling up-country towards Mandalay and beyond. Would she be safe? In the depth of the night, Lawrence found himself praying for her.

In June the following year, Lawrence was commissioned into the Gurkha Rifles, with men recruited in Nepal from dependable tribes such as the Magars and the Gurungs, who'd already experienced crushing hardship. They were loyal, trustworthy and energetic; it was an honour to serve with them. Meanwhile, the Japanese had moved on. Their army had come up through Burma and was pushing India. The men were growing more restless, they wanted to be off, they wanted to be part of the war. Wingate's Chindits had done some damage to Japanese communications, having taken them pretty much by surprise, and now a force must be built to penetrate the back of the enemy and compel its retreat. This meant harsh jungle training to harden up the troops, build self-reliance and develop a knowledge of vegetation so that they could live off the land if needs be. There were many tricks. Some they learnt beforehand, some were instinctive or someone's bright idea, like the Gurkha who had the clever notion of catching lizards by putting a drop of Carnation milk in an empty tin. They'd used that a few times on the march, some of the little buggers weighed as much as half a hundredweight and tasted surprisingly good too.

Lawrence opened his eyes once again. Was it another morning or the same one? There was a shaft of light filtering through the curtain, reminding him that this was West Dorset and he should get up. *Mustn't let things slide*. He often said this to himself. He supposed he knew only too well how easy it would be.

He sat up slowly and reached for his dressing gown for it was chilly and he hadn't yet switched on the central heating. Sometimes it seemed almost a crime to be too comfortable, after everything.

At first, he thought as he tied the cord around his waist, the British had been slow and ill-prepared and the Japanese had made them suffer their worst military defeat for centuries. But . . . He chuckled to himself as he slowly made his way out into the hall and along to the kitchen to make his tea. None of that sweet char now. Now, he liked it strong and bitter. He looked around him. It was odd, but his kitchen seemed different and he couldn't remember coming in here for a while. He was feeling a bit wobbly. With some difficulty he groped his way to the rocking chair and sat down.

But once they realised what it would take to get going, the British had done it in style.

Because, despite everything, Lawrence remained a staunch patriot. Like terriers, the British forces were. There had been those who were little more than stuffy colonials and there were those who took advantage of the system they'd been born to. And then there were the others. The fighters. He straightened his back, heard the heating come on. Had he switched on a timer? Had he drawn the curtains? He heaved himself out of the chair and put the kettle on to boil. Sat down in the rocking chair again, just for a moment, and adjusted the red-tasselled cushion at his back. Had he taken advantage of Maya? He hated to think so. And yet . . . She had said he was a free man and it hadn't been true. He had never been free of her and he never would be. That was the sadness of it all.

In the dream-memory of his war, tramping through the heat of the jungle, his regiment had finally come to the end of the day's march. They had cut down banana leaves and bamboo to feed the mules – sensibly the animals preferred the latter, as if knowing they contained more roughage and less water – and they had unpacked them of the heavy burdens they carried: ammunition, reserves of food and the precious wireless of course, without which they wouldn't know what the hell was happening. Then they let them loose to graze. They had to look after the mules, they were more important than the men in many ways, especially when the air drops weren't getting through. The mules were their means of survival and the men got bloody fond of them too.

After they'd seen to the animals, they dug the slit trenches to protect themselves from the enemy, built their own shelter and laid out their sparse bedding, using the one blanket and groundsheet that each man carried in his pack. And they stayed on the alert. Two men stood watch in two-hour stags. Those bastards were never far away.

Lawrence thought he would collapse, from the heat, from the march, from sheer exhaustion. But he had dug because he had to dig. And as darkness fell he heard it: the whinny from a mule, the restlessness that could mean only one thing. The enemy approaching.

Where had they sprung from? Lawrence and his men were used to being taken by surprise. The Japanese were bloody good. In daylight, snipers sometimes stayed up the trees for hours; they had a roll of cloth round their waist full of cooked rice with bits of dried fruit and coconut, so the bastards weren't even going to get hungry. They always came down in the dark, though, to move position and to get drinking water as they only had small bottles. And they kept so bloody still. But when you spotted one, you knew there'd be others, so you had to spray the surrounding trees with a burst of Bren gunfire. That would bring the buggers down.

Lawrence crawled to the trench along with the rest. And as he peered over the edge, he saw him. A man. A soldier. Christ. His stomach lurched. The enemy.

Like lightning, Lawrence loosened the pin of his grenade, counted *one two three*, the longest three seconds he'd ever known. He chucked it and threw himself face down into the

352

trench. He tasted the dusty earth and he waited for the crump of the explosion. *Him or me*.

Now, Lawrence shuddered at the memory. The kettle was whistling and he got up to see to it, but his legs were so weak that he had to sit down again. *Oh my Lord* . . . He had no strength. He had no strength to remember.

In that moment he had thought of her too, of Maya. A man like this might have denied her food. He might have hurled abuse at her, hit her on the back of her head with the butt of his rifle, raped her, shot her. *Him or me*. In an ideal world, he should have been a man before he was the enemy, with a wife, a family perhaps. A man like this could even have been a friend. But there was no time to think of such things. And Lawrence had been close enough to see the whites of his eyes.

At 8 p.m., Eva was waiting in the hotel lobby when Ramon's car drew up outside. She was conscious of a feeling of dread in the pit of her stomach. She had even considered cancelling their date; she really didn't want to see him. But there was Maya to consider. The evening had been at her invitation. And besides, Maya had said that she had something important to show her. Eva thought of her grandfather. She simply couldn't not go.

The doorman swung the door open as she approached and Eva stepped out of the cool air-conditioning of the hotel into the humid early evening of the street outside. Immediately, she was conscious of the noise of the traffic, the dust, the smell of the food sizzling in oily cauldrons nearby.

'Eva.' Ramon had got out of the car and now he approached, bent to kiss her. 'You look lovely as always,' he murmured.

'Hello, Ramon. Thank you.' After some deliberation, she had chosen a simple long white linen skirt and loose shirt, which she was wearing with her velvet Burmese slippers and embroidered Shan bag. Her hair, she had swept and pinned up, and, once again, she was wearing her mother's pearls. Rather primly, she offered her cheek.

'Are you feeling better? Did you have a rest?' He was all solicitousness and concern. He opened the passenger door and Eva climbed in.

'A lot better thank you,' she said. 'My head's so much clearer.'

He gave her an odd look, but shut her door, walked round and got into the driving seat. 'And did you meet up with your contact?'

'I did, thank you.' His back was to her now. Hypocrite, she thought. He had given her such a hard time about buying antiques from Myanmar, when all the time he was involved in . . . What was he involved in exactly? And what was the Emporium involved in? She still didn't have a clue.

'And you?' she asked politely. 'How are things at the factory?' She could hear the barely concealed sarcasm in her own voice.

Ramon edged the car out into the heavy traffic. 'There is some good news,' he said.

'Really?' Crime obviously did pay.

'Yes. I have had talks with a man I know. He has agreed to become my new business partner.'

'New business partner?'

'I do some work with him already.'

Surely he wasn't talking about Khan Li? This seemed to confirm what Klaus had told her. She found herself clenching her fist and forced herself to relax. *Shoulders down. Look out of the window. Breathe.*

Ramon wove his customary expert passage between lanes

of traffic, hooting sharply to indicate his intention or where he felt someone ought to be alerted to his presence. 'But if I make him a partner,' he continued, 'then he will be more committed. I will have more spare time. And he will make a big contribution to my business.'

'Money?' she snapped.

He glanced across at her in surprise. 'Of course, money. This is business, Eva. I told you the position we are in.'

Yes, he had. But couldn't he see that money wasn't everything?

Ramon gripped the steering wheel more tightly. 'But not only money. Also his time, his professional input, his directional skills.'

Again, she heard in his voice that passion for his work. The difference now was that she couldn't believe in it any longer. And she certainly didn't see Khan Li possessing the qualities Ramon had mentioned.

'And what makes you so confident that this new business partner will retain the ethics that your father held so dear?' Eva asked him. The mention of his father might even make him think again, bring him to his senses.

Once more, he glanced across at her, though as Eva could see, the road was busy enough to claim most of his attention. 'Naturally, I chose with great care,' he said. Now it was Ramon who sounded cool. 'As you know, I share the ethos and beliefs of my father. I would not do anything that might compromise them.'

Eva had to refrain from snorting with incredulity at this

statement. Who on earth did he think he was fooling? Certainly not her, not anymore. 'And what will you do with all that free time?' she asked.

They were driving next to the Palace moat now and she fancied she could almost see the red pagodas in the distance, but perhaps not; they were so far away. All roads in the city still led to the Royal Palace, although the palace was not what it had once been. Neither was the noisy, dirty city that sprawled untidily around it. King Mindon, thought Eva, would turn in his grave.

'I think I told you I wish to develop the export side of the business,' Ramon said frostily. 'And that I wish to go to England and visit the place where my father was born.'

'Where was that?' Eva softened slightly.

'A place called Ilfracombe in the county of Devon,' he said. 'My father told us it was very beautiful there. He often spoke of the harbour.'

She remained silent.

'Do you know it?' Swiftly, he glanced across at her once more.

'I went there as a child.' She decided not to tell him that it wasn't far from where she had been brought up in West Dorset. What was the point? She had to remember what she'd found out about him. She mustn't let him get to her now.

They drew up outside a restaurant with lanterns strung around the trees outside. 'Is this it?' Eva made a move to get out of the car, but Ramon laid a hand on her arm.

'What?' She looked down at his hand, warm on her bare

357

skin, at the slender craftsman's fingers, calloused from working with wood. She couldn't look up at him, didn't trust herself.

'What is it, Eva? What is wrong?'

She looked out of the window, tried to maintain control. She might have known this would happen. She'd never been any good at pretending everything was fine when it wasn't. 'I went to the Royal Palace this afternoon after I left you,' she said.

'Oh?'

'I decided I'd rather go there alone.'

'That is OK.' He took his hand from her arm. 'I am not offended. But did something happen there?'

She shook her head. Now, damn it, she felt like she was going to cry. 'And before I came to see your factory,' she said, 'I went to Li's showroom on Thirty-Sixth Street.'

'You went to Li's? For the love of sweet Lord Buddha, Eva!' He sounded angry now, just as she'd expected. 'Why did you go there? Did I not tell you—?'

'That it was dangerous? Yes, you did.' But now she had discovered his ulterior motive. She turned to him. 'But, you see, I made a solemn promise to my grandfather to do my best to reunite those chinthes. It may not mean much to you, but for him . . .' She tailed off. How could she begin to explain how much it meant to her grandfather, how much Maya and his life here had meant to him? How the chinthe had become symbolic of that life and their love and their parting?

'Ah, the chinthes.' He slapped his palms on the steering wheel.

'Yes.' She took a deep breath. 'I had to do something. Don't you see? I'm not here for much longer, I don't have much time.'

'And do you imagine that I too do not yearn for my grandmother to hold those chinthes once again in her hands?' Ramon spoke quietly but his eyes glittered. 'Did I not tell you that I had a plan?'

'But you refuse to tell me what it is!' The man was so infuriating. Not that she even believed him. He would hardly hatch a plan to steal the chinthe back from a man he was about to make his business partner. Unless . . . Eva thought about it. Was that why he was shipping out their crates, not to make money but to try and get closer to them?

'Eva.' Ramon turned to her. He lifted her chin so that she was looking straight at him, at his green eyes, at the dark hair that flopped over his forehead, at the curve of his mouth. 'Can you not simply trust me?' he said.

If only. For a moment they stared at one another, eyes locked. But she couldn't do it, couldn't say it. Not after what Klaus had told her, and not after what she'd seen this afternoon with her own eyes.

He took his hand away from her face at last. 'I see that you cannot,' he said coldly.

'Well, what do you expect?' Eva was still close to tears, but she rounded on him. 'Aren't you about to make Khan Li your business partner? For heaven's sake! Is that likely to make me trust you? How could you? They're one of the unscrupulous companies who have got you into trouble in the first place. You know exactly what they are.'

'What?' He looked truly baffled. 'Khan Li? Are you mad? Why do you think such a thing?'

'Well, because . . .' But her words tailed off. She wasn't going to tell him what she'd seen in the blue truck, at least not yet.

He sighed. 'What happened there, Eva?'

'Nothing much.'

'So you will not tell me?'

She looked down. Twisted the daisy ring on her little finger. How could she tell him anything? How could she trust him with anything?

'Khan Li is the last person I would ask to be my business partner, Eva,' he said. 'The man who is to be my partner is a man I have worked with for many years. A man who has money, yes. But a man I respect.'

Before Eva could respond, Ramon's mobile rang and he answered it, speaking swiftly and softly in Burmese. 'We must go in,' he said to Eva. 'My grandmother is waiting.'

'Of course.' Could she believe him? He sounded convincing. But nevertheless, Eva reminded herself, there was no doubt that he was working with them in some capacity. Something else was going on.

She followed him as he strode through the door held open by a waiter, his tall figure giving off some of the tension that Eva too was feeling inside. He was wearing the traditional male *longyi* again tonight – she supposed his grandmother preferred it – with a crisp leaf-green shirt. But there was a hardness about him, a kind of suppressed strength that was scaring her. She shivered.

Ramon looked around, waved and then led the way towards the far corner of the restaurant where Maya was sitting. The place was traditional Burmese in layout and decor, with lots of bamboo and wood, the chairs and table a burnished chestnut laid with gleaming cutlery and linen napkins.

'Grandmother. Auntie.' He gave a polite little bow.

Maya and another woman were seated at a table set for four. Maya rose to her feet. She looked as serene and elegant as ever in a lilac silk *longyi* with a matching embroidered blouse. Her white hair was coiled on her head and she wore a necklace of jade. It was almost . . . Eva thought back to what she'd seen at the Royal Palace . . . a ceremonial costume. The woman beside her, now also standing, looked vaguely familiar. Had they met before? Eva wasn't sure, perhaps she had been at Maya's house in Pyin Oo Lwin? She'd slightly lost track of the relatives. Eva smiled at her and the woman smiled back.

Maya embraced Eva, looking into her face in that direct way she had. 'Eva, my child,' she said. 'Thank you for coming.' She turned to the woman beside her.

She was, Eva supposed, in her late sixties, her hair still dark but greying and smoothed away from her face. She possessed the same look of serenity as Maya and there was definitely a resemblance between them; she must be another relative.

'I told you I had something to show you,' Maya said,

almost impishly, her old face wreathed in smiles, her dark eyes bright.

'You did, yes.' Eva smiled back.

'But it is not a "something" to be exact,' said Maya. 'It is a "someone".' She indicated the woman beside her. 'This is Cho Suu Kyi.'

'Oh.' Eva looked from one to the other of them in confusion. 'You have almost the same name as . . .' Maya's grandmother. The loyal maid-servant to the Queen who had first been given the pair of chinthes by Supayalat.

Maya nodded. 'We do not always use family names here in Myanmar,' she said. 'But we often name our children after our ancestors, as well as according to the day on which they were born. It is auspicious.' Once again, she smiled.

Eva's mind was racing. 'I'm pleased to meet you,' she said to Cho Suu Kyi.

'Suu is my daughter,' Maya said proudly.

Another daughter? Ramon had called her 'Auntie'. So was this . . . ?

'Yes.' Maya took Eva's hand and then Suu's hand and joined them, one to the other, so that Eva's hand was clasped in Cho Suu Kyi's. 'Suu is my first daughter, Eva,' she said. 'Cho Suu Kyi was named after my grandmother who left me the legacy of the teak chinthes. I gave your grandfather one of those precious chinthes. And this is the child your grandfather gave me.'

CHAPTER 40

Maya said goodnight to Cho Suu Kyi and went to her room. The evening had, in the main, been a successful one. There was a problem between her grandson and Eva, she could see that, of course. Something, or someone, had come between them and they were not the friends she had hoped they would be. She was old. Perhaps she was growing fanciful. But somewhere inside had been a small spark of hope . . .

She had agonised long over whether to tell Eva about her first daughter, the daughter she shared with Lawrence, but had never shared with Lawrence. Telling Eva would be to tell him, and that would be hard. But the girl had come all this way to Myanmar. Not only that, but she had brought back the chinthe, which told Maya that Lawrence had never forgotten her. It gave her such joy – a joy she had thought she would never feel in her life again.

And then . . . Cho Suu Kyi had wanted to meet Eva too, and why not, for she was family? And so the decision had been made. She must give Lawrence the gift of knowledge of his daughter, a gift that might also bring some pain, she guessed. But so often in this world, happiness and pain combine.

Upper Burma, 1943

It was exhausting work and sometimes Maya felt almost too weak to stand. But the matron and her two other assistants worked tirelessly day and night and Maya did the same. Matron Annie taught her how to carry out simple medical procedures and she had always been practical and capable. She learned fast because she had to.

The Military Hospital nearby had lost almost all of its staff and so they took on most of the patients, transporting them by a couple of bullock carts, which had somehow been overlooked in the mass evacuation from the town. Refugees, the hospital saw more than its fair share. Thousands of them lined the roads to India, often dying by the roadside from malnutrition, malaria, dysentery or cholera, if not from their wounds. The hospital was full to overflowing. Mattresses were put out on the verandahs and makeshift beds in the storerooms.

Maya often attended to the soldiers who had been brought in. She would chat to them and ask them, if it were not too traumatic, to talk about their experiences. She always hoped she might, by some wonderful coincidence, hear something of Lawrence. And she wondered too, one day, would it be Lawrence who came here to the hospital? Or would he be cared for by another woman such as she? Silently, she thanked that imaginary woman from the bottom of her heart.

One morning, she had to rush to the sink when she was in the middle of dressing a soldier's particularly nasty wound. It had become infected. Matron Annie had already carried out one emergency amputation, though she was hardly qualified to do so. Perhaps she would have to do another.

When she returned, Matron Annie was standing by the bedside looking serious. 'I see how it is,' she said gravely.

'Matron?'

'Soon, you will not be helping any longer, is that not so?'

'I do not understand.' Though of course she did.

They completed the work on the soldier's injury and then moved away. The matron took Maya to one side. 'You are pregnant?' she asked.

'Yes, I am.' She held her head high. She had known it, a few weeks after he had first left. She had known it when the town was bombed. And she was glad. She was proud to be carrying Lawrence's child. She would always be proud.

'What do you want to do?'

Maya knew what she was asking. Did Maya want to get rid of it? Did she really want to bring a child into this world and at this time in this place? It was madness, was it not? 'I will have the child,' she said softly. 'But until that day and after that day I will work as much as I can, here at the hospital. I will not need much time off, Matron.'

Gently, the matron touched her arm. 'I should tell you that you are a fool,' she said. 'And you know all the reasons why.'

Maya bowed her head.

'But I cannot help but admire you for your courage.'

If she only knew, Maya thought. It was not courage. It was just that she might lose him and so desperately she wanted to keep a small part of him. And she could not kill what they had created together in love. It was not possible. She could not live with that.

'And it is good to think of the possibility of new life,' said the matron. 'When this . . .' And she gestured to the ward full of injured and dying men, 'is all around us.'

Maya's daughter was born in the middle of the night on a Tuesday. It was a warm night and a long labour and she was attended by Matron Annie herself, who held her hand and boiled the water, examined her, comforted her and encouraged her to push when it was the right time.

When Matron Annie finally handed her the baby girl wrapped in a thin cotton sheet, Maya touched the screwed-up wrinkly little face and she wanted to cry. After all this pain and all this bloodshed all around her, it was down to this. Death and new life, and she held that new life in her arms.

By the following day, Maya was on her feet again and working. Wards must be cleaned, medicine administered and wounds dressed. She had a baby girl strapped to her chest. Apart from that, nothing had changed.

One day, a colonel turned up at the hospital and spoke to Matron Annie and Maya. They were more or less running the hospital between them now; everyone else had left. He was in command of a special unit trained in bridge demolition and this unit had been detailed to carry out an extensive programme of bridge blowing which would, he said, affect everyone remaining in the town. The Japanese were close and the unit must delay their advance in order to buy time. The unit had also been ordered to take possession of funds from the nearby Government House to keep the Shan riches out of the hands of the enemy. Silver, rare jewels, bullion, the place was full of the wealth of the Shan princes, much of it deriving from the profitable opium trade, as Maya was only too aware.

She thought of her own Shan grandmother, Suu Kyi, and the pair of rare and decorative jewelled chinthes she had given her. Like so many families she knew, Maya had buried her treasure in that safe place where she knew she could retrieve it when the war was over. Her aunt had even sewn jewels into her clothes, hidden in the knot of her *longyi*. It wouldn't be the first time the Burmese had used their family jewels to barter and survive. And Lawrence's treasure . . . ? She could only hope that somehow the little chinthe brought him back to her safe and well when the war was over.

After the demolition, the unit would be pulling out and who knew what would happen to their town. 'You are British,' the colonel reminded Matron Annie. 'They may not spare you. And you . . .' He looked at Maya who was walking now with the baby tied to her back like a papoose. 'The child is very pale,' he said.

Maya felt a tremor of fear. She understood his meaning. The light skin of her daughter gave her parentage away. She would be an innocent victim, but her mother would be viewed as a traitor.

'You could both be raped or killed without further

thought,' the colonel told the two women. 'The Japs don't take any prisoners. Or at least they do, but they won't give you that dubious privilege.'

But would they be any safer upcountry or on the road to India? Maya and Annie exchanged a look. Maya had heard how many of the refugees were dying from disease and starvation. And there were so many bandit gangs on the loose. People were desperate. At least here there was kindness, there was shelter and there was food. Their hospital store was meagre, but they had condensed milk, which was vital for a mother with a young baby, there was vegetable soup, there were eggs, rice and flour and there were occasional hens and ducks donated by villagers and refugees. And here Maya could continue to work and nurse – she would feel she was doing something to help the war effort, to help her people and the injured soldiers too.

'I cannot leave my patients,' said Matron Annie.

'And I can make her skin darker,' said Maya. With mud if need be. Fortunately, the baby had inherited her mother's dark eyes and Burmese nose, she did not look like a European child, although Maya would swear already that she had Lawrence's smile. And Maya and Annie had become close; they had already been through so much. If anything happened to Maya, she was sure that Matron Annie would look after her baby.

'So?' said the colonel.

'I will stay here at the hospital,' said Maya.

'We both will,' said Annie.

★

368

Maya told Eva some of this story over dinner. Ramon and Suu had heard it before, of course. And the girl listened, clearly enthralled, looking from one to the other of them as if she could hardly believe it.

But there was one part of the story that Maya did not tell them. She didn't think that she would ever tell another living soul.

CHAPTER 41

In 1943, after their parting, Maya had given birth to a child. Eva's grandfather's child . . . Eva continued to roll the knowledge around in her head as Ramon drove her back to her hotel. What a bombshell. And her grandfather didn't know. Which meant that Eva would have to tell him.

The tension between Eva and Ramon, so palpable she'd almost felt she could cut it with her butter knife, had increased during the evening as Maya told her incredible story. It was a tale that held Eva riveted. Of her nursing, of how she had kept her and her daughter alive in an occupied and poverty-stricken country at war, while Eva's grandfather had been fighting in another part of the country, with absolutely no idea of his daughter's existence. Her grandfather had wanted to know about Maya's war experiences and it had turned out that Maya's war had been an awful lot more complicated that he could ever have guessed.

Her grandfather had left Burma and returned to Dorset, still not knowing. If he had known, Eva wondered, would he have stayed?

The streets of the city were much quieter than when they had left a few hours ago. The street sellers had cleared their stalls and gone home, leaving just the hint of oil and fried spices in the air, the shops were shuttered and the bars were closing up too. Very few people remained on the dark pavements, for there were no street lights and this, along with the rickety kerbs and loose, broken paving slabs, plus the fact that it was virtually impossible to cross the road, was why it was hard to walk anywhere in the city at night. 'It is a lot to think about, isn't it?' Ramon said, as they drew up outside the hotel. 'It was a shock for you, finding out about my aunt, Cho Suu Kyi.'

'Yes.' And it would be a shock for her grandfather too. How would he react? How would he feel when he found out he had a daughter he had never known about, never had the chance to acknowledge, living on the other side of the world in Myanmar? And as for Eva's mother . . . Eva shuddered at the thought of what she might say.

'Tell me about your mother,' Cho Suu Kyi had said over dinner, which had consisted of a selection of delicious curries and salads. She served a small portion of *Bae Tha Hin*, a type of Burmese duck curry, on to Eva's plate, along with some rice. 'My mother has told me much about my father, I almost feel I know him. But I would so like to know about my other half-sister.' She smiled at Ramon and then back at Eva. 'About Rosemary, your mother.'

So would Eva. She would very much like to know about her mother. But she couldn't say that to Cho Suu Kyi. Even so, she wasn't sure where to start. 'She lives in Copenhagen,' she said. 'My father died when I was seven.' Which was nothing compared to Suu's experience, she realised. She had never even known her father. 'She married again when I was seventeen.'

And I chose to stay in Dorset. She didn't say this though. It would only confuse this new family that she now seemed to be part of. It confused Eva too. She knew why she'd chosen to stay: her grandparents and Dorset were her security, their home her home. They had seemed like the only thing that was holding her family together. But she didn't know why her mother had left. Was it out of love for Alec? Or did Dorset represent everything that she'd held dear and everything that she'd lost?

'Do you think your mother would come over here to visit?' Cho Suu Kyi was so excited, her dark eyes shone. And Eva could see why she had immediately found her familiar. She had the dark eyes of Maya. But her cheekbones, her mouth, her smile . . . She had the look of Eva's mother, even of her grandfather too.

'I'm not sure.' Ramon had told her about *arnadeh*, a kind of over-politeness and extreme consideration for other people's feelings, which was part of Burmese etiquette. It was why they served food to their visitors rather than inviting them to help themselves and it was important to observe it so as not to cause offence. So how could Eva tell Cho Suu Kyi that her half-sister Rosemary had never wanted to know anything about her father's Burmese days? She simply hadn't been interested. To her, they represented her father's disloyalty. Or so Eva supposed. She didn't really know, since her mother wouldn't talk about it. But she'd have to talk about it now. And perhaps Eva could make her see that this lovely Burmese family weren't a threat, with the possible exception of Ramon, she reminded herself. They were part of her past, her story.

'Would you care for a nightcap?' Ramon wasn't even looking at her. His green eyes were fixed resolutely on a point in the darkness in front of him.

Nothing between them had been resolved, had it? They had reached a stalemate. And if Eva were going to take any action regarding the crate she'd seen on the truck, then she couldn't confide in him. He was, though it was hard to accept, looking at him now, the enemy.

But she'd been only too aware of that enemy as she'd sat at the round table in the restaurant, Cho Suu Kyi placed on her left and Ramon on her right. They were almost terrifyingly polite with each other. *Can I pass you more fish curry? Would you like some vegetable salad? May I refill your glass?* Which was almost worse than having a full-scale slanging match.

'Is everything satisfactory?' Maya had asked mildly at one point. 'Has something upset you, Eva? Ramon?'

'No,' they both replied. 'Absolutely not,' Eva added.

But Maya was a wise one and despite the celebratory nature of the evening, her expression remained a little concerned.

'He is a good man, my grandson,' she whispered to Eva when they said goodnight. 'But I hope you found out what was troubling him.'

Eva crossed her fingers. 'Not really, I'm afraid.' It wasn't up to her to blacken his name, no doubt Ramon could manage it entirely on his own.

And now he wanted to prolong the evening?

'I don't think that's a good idea,' she said. She was tired. And besides, what more was there to say? He had talked of trust. But had he trusted her, by confiding in her, by telling her his supposed plan? No. Perhaps, because there was no plan.

'Eva—'

'No.' She fumbled with the door catch. The last thing she needed was to be caught at her most vulnerable, especially after a night like tonight. And besides, there was so much to think about.

Ramon whipped out of the car, came round to open her door. He took her hand as she climbed out and pulled her into a close embrace so swiftly that she was there before she had the chance to wonder if she wanted to be there.

'I cannot pretend to understand,' he murmured into her hair. 'But I just want you to know—'

She pulled away, but not far enough. He was holding her quite firmly by the shoulders and he didn't seem about to let her go.

'Ramon . . .' The sense of him seemed to envelop her. She tried to remind herself of what he was, but when he bent his head and his lips met hers, she lost all that and just felt it. His lips, firm, demanding. His kiss. The scent of him – of wood shavings and polish and just a hint of cardamom. The heat of him.

It was the sort of kiss you could drown in. The sort of kiss you wanted to go on forever. But. She pulled away.

'Eva.'

But she was gone. Literally running. Through the door of the hotel, grabbing her room key from the desk, leaning on the button to call the lift, almost sinking into it when the door opened. Thank God it was empty. She closed her eyes. Ramon . . .

The lift stopped at the seventh floor and she got out with a sigh, wandered down the corridor, put her key in the lock and—

And the door was already ajar.

It swung further open. The next moment seemed frozen in time. Eva stood there, taking in the scene. A man – a stranger, small, dark, Burmese, was rummaging through the clothes in her chest of drawers, her things thrown around the room, on the bed, on the floor. In that split second, she must have gasped. Because the man twisted round to face her. They stared at one another. Eva felt her legs almost dissolve with fear. She hung on to the door handle. And then she opened her mouth to scream.

CHAPTER 42

Rosemary had gone out to get some shopping, but she hardly liked leaving him, especially after this morning's episode.

She shivered as she arrived at the supermarket car park and parked the hire car in a vacant space. And not just because it was such a cold day. It had stopped raining at least, but now there was a winter bite to the air that reminded her: time was getting on, she had to decide what to do. Seattle was still looming on her horizon. Hers and Alec's.

Her father had been in the kitchen slumped in the chair, the kettle whistling full pelt. That's what had woken her, of course. She'd heard the noise and thought for a minute it was a siren, ambulance or police perhaps. Then she'd realised it was coming from the house, to be precise, from the kitchen downstairs.

Rosemary had grabbed her bathrobe, pulled it on and run down there. The kitchen was steamy and she didn't see him for a moment. Just thought, *what the . . . ?* And snatching the oven glove from the Aga rail, took the kettle off the heat.

Now, Rosemary got out of the car, plucked her shopping bag from the back seat and went to get a trolley. They had to eat.

As soon as she'd turned around, she'd seen him. 'Dad? Dad . . . ?' And her heart had flipped over in much the same way as it had when she'd first arrived at the house and found him out for the count on the bathroom floor. But fortunately, this time he was just asleep, bless him, waking even as she raced into the room, muttering something about 'holding fire'. How he could have slept through that racket, she had no idea.

'What are you doing, Dad?' Fear made her voice sharp and she saw him flinch. 'Did you put the kettle on?' she asked in a gentler tone.

'It was a long, bloody night,' he said. 'You can get fed up of marching.'

Ah. So he was back in wartime, was he? 'So you thought you'd come and make a cup of tea, is that it?' She took his arm. 'Let's get you back to bed.'

He blinked in confusion. But he went with her, like a lamb.

Rosemary picked up a bag of salad and some fresh noodles. Perhaps she should ring the doctor again. Later this morning he'd been so much better though. After he'd freshened up in the bathroom, she'd taken in some coffee and read him out bits from today's paper. Sometimes they even tackled the crossword, but Rosemary had something else on her mind today. Then they'd chatted about this and that. Not what she wanted to hear about though. She wanted to hear about Burma.

'I read the letters, Dad,' she told him. She wanted to confess. And she wanted to know more. 'The letters you keep in the drawer.'

'Letters?' But she saw the understanding touch his eyes. She nodded.

'When?'

'I found them after Mum died.' She realised that something had shifted inside her, that she wanted to tell him now. 'I wasn't snooping. Just tidying up. And then I couldn't resist reading them. I'm sorry.'

'Ah.' He shook his head. 'I knew there was something.'

Yes, she thought. Something to pull you apart.

'Perhaps I should have told you about her,' he said. 'But it was all so long ago. And I couldn't, not without upsetting your mother. You are our daughter, love.'

Yes, she was. His coffee cup was rattling in the saucer and Rosemary steadied it for him. 'You didn't send any of those letters though,' she said.

'No.'

'Why not, Dad?'

He fixed her with his honest blue gaze. 'Because I was married to your mother.'

'But you needed to write them?' She wanted to understand. Nick was dead, so there was no point in writing to him. Or was there? She had always thought that if only she could communicate with him one last time . . . Then perhaps it would somehow clear the way for her future. She looked helplessly at her father. Would he realize what she was asking him?

'I did. It helped, Rosie.'

'Why did you ever come back here?' Rosemary whispered.

She didn't want to hound him or upset him when he was so frail. But it was a question she'd wanted to ask for such a long time. She understood how her mother had been and the pressure the families had put on him. But why did he succumb? The way she'd loved Nick she would never have let him go. 'Why did you come back and marry Mum? When you were still in love with someone else?'

'Ah, Rosie.' He looked at her full on. 'It was Maya's decision, not mine,' he said. 'At least . . .' And he seemed to be remembering something. 'I could have done more. I should have done more.'

'Maya knew how it was back here in England?' Rosemary guessed. She could picture them all, waiting for his homecoming. His mother, Helen's mother, anyone else who was left of the family when the war was over. Everybody wanting him to marry Helen.

He nodded. 'She knew most things.' And smiled.

'She thought it was your destiny,' Rosemary murmured.

He folded the newspaper she'd left on the bed, smoothing it with his gnarled old hands. 'She let me go.' He exhaled with some difficulty and she saw him wince with pain.

And you didn't want to let everyone down.

'But you never forgot her.' She patted his hand.

'No, I never forgot her.' His eyes seemed to glaze over, as if he'd slipped back to the past once again. 'It's like that with love sometimes. I think you know that, Rosie.'

Rosemary looked away, beyond him and out of the window. The days were getting so short now, she hated that, longed for the stretched out days of summer. 'I do, yes,' she said.

He came back to her then, just for a moment, and he held out his arms.

She curled into them, like a child, eyes closed, feeling her father's frail warmth, feeling his comfort. It still didn't take much to make her think of Nick. And Alec knew that too. Did he also know that she had never been able to give herself to him in the way she had so carelessly given herself to Nick? Of course he did. He had said as much, he had said that he would take what was left. *Just like her mother had* . . . But she knew that something had changed for Alec. It wasn't just her going away. It had been building, in her, in him. And sooner or later there would be an explosion, or as near as Alec would ever come to an explosion. And why not? It was hardly fair. Seattle, she realised, was that explosion.

'First love . . . It takes some beating,' her father said. Gently, he stroked her hair.

Rosemary nodded. She swallowed. He was right. First love took some beating. 'Hard on number two though,' she said.

'I reckon so.' But his voice was faint and she realised he was drifting off again. Back to sleep or back to the past. The two seemed entwined into each and every day.

'Hard on number two,' she murmured. She eased herself off the bed without disturbing him. Smoothed the quilt. Touched his hand. And left him to it.

At the supermarket, Rosemary paid for her purchases and

wheeled the trolley out to the car. She wound her cashmere scarf more closely around her neck. All these years she'd blamed him. And yet . . . How much better was she?

CHAPTER 43

'Ssh, lady!' The man swore, pushed past her and was gone, racing towards the stairs.

What the hell? 'Hey!' Eva yelled after his retreating back. 'Stop that man! He's a thief! He's—' But no one was listening; no one was around. And the man was already out of sight.

Eva ran over to the phone, quickly dialled reception. Her hands were shaking. The phone seemed to ring and ring.

At last someone answered. 'There was a man,' she said. 'He was in my room. I walked in and . . . He should be there any second. He'll be coming down the stairs or in the lift or—'

'Excuse me, madam,' The girl on reception spoke slowly and clearly as if Eva were either deaf or insane. 'Please repeat?'

Eva repeated. But she knew it was useless. By the time she got the message through, he'd be long gone.

'Was anything taken?' the girl asked her. 'Valuables? Jewellery? Money?' Her voice was friendly, but not overly concerned.

'I don't know.' Eva sat down on the bed. She felt . . . violated. She looked around at the disarray in the room. Fortunately, she carried all her money with her, and she'd been wearing her pearls and her diamond daisy ring. But . . . Who would have done this? Hadn't she been assured that there was very little crime in Myanmar, and especially against tourists? And how had he got into her room?

'Please check,' the girl said. 'I will send someone up. Please answer the door.'

The door, Eva saw, was still wide open. 'Yes. Thank you.' She got to her feet, hung up and strode over to the door. Slammed it shut and locked it. Leaned on the back of it, trying to control her breathing. When she saw him, she hadn't had time to be scared. But now, she couldn't stop shaking.

After a few minutes there was a frantic hammering on the door.

Eva flinched. She had made a cursory check of her stuff and even put most of it back in the chest of drawers. Nothing seemed to be missing. 'Who is it?' She could hear the tremor in her voice. Once more she felt the sensation of being alone.

'It's me, Ramon. Eva, are you OK?'

Ramon. Relief flooded through her at the sound of his voice. In that moment, he certainly didn't feel like the enemy. She unlocked the door and was immediately wrapped in his arms.

'What happened, Eva?' He sounded angry.

'There was a man.' Her voice was muffled into his shoulder. She took a deep breath. And a step away. She was unhurt. She had to regain control of her emotions.

'What man?'

'I don't know what man . . .'

Ramon spoke rapidly in Burmese to one of the hotel staff

383

now hovering behind him. 'You need some brandy,' he said. 'And water.'

'Thank you.'

'Come. Sit down.' He took her arm and led her over to the bed. 'Tell me what happened.'

She sat down and began to explain.

His expression grew darker and darker as he paced the room. A boy came back with a bottle of brandy and Ramon poured a generous measure into a glass. He handed it to her. 'But you are not hurt?' he asked. 'He did not touch you?' His hand rested on her arm.

'No, no.' In fact he had run away like a rat up a drainpipe. No one had been hurt, or even threatened. Someone had been ransacking her room, but that was all. Eva sipped the brandy. It slipped down her throat like a flame. She supposed she was just suffering from the shock of it.

Ramon turned on the bedside lamp and flicked the switch of the main light off so that the room was suffused with a warmer glow. Eva was grateful. Her eyes were hurting. 'Do you want me to call the police?' he asked.

'No.' She didn't want to involve the police. What was the point if nothing had been taken?

He swore softly. 'They will not get away with this.'

And how did he propose to find out who *they* were? A thought occurred to her. 'But what are you still doing here?' The brandy had revived her somewhat. Hadn't Ramon driven home after he'd dropped her off at the hotel? How had he even known there was anything wrong? Eva didn't like the direction in which her thoughts were heading. He wouldn't have had anything to do with this, would he?

He took the glass from her and refilled it. 'I was still outside in the car. Thinking.'

Eva nodded. She knew very well what he'd been thinking about. That kiss.

'And I was about to drive off when I saw a man running fast out of the hotel.' He handed the glass back to her.

She frowned. 'But why did you think he was anything to do with me?'

'I did not. Not at first.' He sighed. 'And then . . .'

'And then?' She swirled the rich amber liquid around in the bottom of the glass. The scent of the brandy was strong, but somehow reassuring.

'I thought I recognised him.' He looked across at her. His eyes seemed to gleam in the light of the bedside lamp.

Eva's throat went dry. 'Who was he?' But already, she thought she knew.

'I think it was one of Khan Li's men. One of those he asks to do his dirty work when he wants to keep his own hands clean.' Ramon went into the bathroom and emerged with a glass tumbler. 'May I?'

She nodded and he poured himself a brandy from the bottle the hotel had provided.

Eva recalled her conversation with Khan Li. So he had taken the bait, after all. She supposed it would have been simple to find out where she was staying. But what had he been trying to discover by having her room searched? The name of her rich client who owned a certain Burmese decorative and jewelled teak chinthe perhaps? Or something else? The chinthe itself?

'Eva . . .' Ramon came and sat down on the bed beside her. He seemed to be considering how to continue. 'I have told you these men are dangerous, yes?'

She nodded. 'Yes, I know.' And she knew that she should have been more careful. It had been too risky to go there alone, foolish to think that she could get the better of someone like Khan Li.

'And I am aware you do not fully trust me.'

She made no answer to this. There wasn't much she could say.

'But you must now tell me exactly what happened when you went to Li's showroom.'

Eva considered this. If he was as in league with Li's as she suspected, then it would be very easy for him to find out anyway. And even if she couldn't completely trust him . . . She couldn't believe he meant her harm.

So she told him, every so often taking a sip of the sweet mellow liquid that had done its job of calming her down and was now making her feel pleasantly woozy.

By the time she'd finished, Ramon was shaking his head in disbelief. 'I cannot believe that you said these things to Li, Eva,' he said. 'You were foolish. But also brave.'

She shrugged.

'And did you tell him the name of your hotel?'

'Of course not!' She wasn't entirely stupid.

'So tell me this,' Ramon said. 'Why did you stop trusting me?' He got up from the bed and now knelt beside her, his green eyes pleading. He had to be genuine, she thought. No one could be that good an actor.

'I saw a crate in the truck outside your warehouse,' she said. At least she should give him the right to reply. 'It was being sent to the Bristol Antiques Emporium.'

He frowned. 'But that is the company you work for, isn't it?'

She nodded.

'Impossible.' He got to his feet. 'I know the name of every company we deal with. You weren't well. You must have imagined it.'

She watched him as he stood at the window, saw him flick back his dark hair with that irritated gesture of his hand.

'I didn't imagine it,' she said.

'But why did you not mention this before?' He turned around to face her. 'I could have shown you your mistake.'

She shook her head. There was no mistake and nothing would convince her otherwise. 'Because of the logo I saw under your company's stamp,' she whispered. 'It wasn't your crate.'

He shook his head. 'Eva, it has been a long and difficult evening,' he said. 'There has been . . .' He spread his hands, 'a revelation. And now a man has entered and ransacked your room.' He smiled. 'You have drunk a lot of brandy . . .'

She got to her feet. 'It was a blue-and-gold peacock

insignia,' she said. 'I wasn't mistaken, I wasn't seeing things and I certainly wasn't drunk.'

He came closer, put his hands on her shoulders. 'A blue-and-gold peacock, you say?'

She nodded.

Abruptly, his hands dropped to his sides. He muttered something in his own language that she couldn't understand. 'It is late. You must be exhausted.' He turned from her, went over to the door. 'Get some sleep, Eva,' he said, more gently. He opened it. 'We will talk again in the morning.'

Eva felt a sliver of fear returning and he seemed to sense it. 'He will not come back,' he said. 'I will have a word with reception on the way out. For one thing, I want to know how he got into your room. After I go, make sure you lock the door from the inside. You will be quite safe for now.'

'And tomorrow?' She realised she wouldn't feel safe here anymore.

He put his finger to his lips. 'We will talk tomorrow,' he said. 'You must not worry. I will pick you up at midday.'

She nodded. 'Alright.' She was exhausted, it had been a long day and she could hardly think straight. She wanted to trust him, she wanted to rest her head on his shoulder and close her eyes. And when they talked tomorrow, she would, somehow, make him tell her everything.

CHAPTER 44

Maya lay in her bed that night but she did not sleep. It would come; it always came, she must be patient.

She had relived so much of the war sitting at the restaurant table tonight, and now she recalled that one experience which she had talked of to no one. It had happened in the hospital when Cho Suu Kyi was still a baby . . .

Upper Burma, 1943
Maya had jumped with surprise. She had been doing some sorting in the hospital storeroom and had not expected to be disturbed.

The man who strode into the room as if he owned it was immaculately dressed in the uniform of a Japanese officer. His boots were polished and rose to his thighs and he carried a large sword at his side, one hand resting on the hilt.

'Can I help you?' she asked. But her mind went into overdrive. She was thinking, as she always was, of Cho Suu Kyi.

'Show me what food you have,' he said stiffly. He had arrived with one other soldier this afternoon. She guessed that they were an advance party, sent ahead to reconnoitre the area. So far they had been civil to herself and Matron

Annie and even to the inmates of the hospital. But they had also been guarded. And she didn't trust them.

Maya bowed her head. In the corner of the room little Suu was sleeping and she didn't want her to wake and be noticed. If the officer looked closely, he might see and he might suspect. Maya could not risk it. However, neither did she want to give the Japanese their precious food.

She opened the cupboard. 'We have very little,' she murmured. Pray to Buddha that he did not find their emergency store of condensed milk, soup and rice. 'What we have is for the sick.'

The officer turned up his nose in distaste. 'Why do you stay here in this town?' His gaze roved around the room. 'A woman like you?'

Maya moved quickly, placing herself between him and the corner of the room in which the baby was sleeping. What did he mean, *a woman like you*? 'It is everyone's duty to do something,' she said. 'And I like to help the wounded.'

'British soldiers?' he sneered.

'Any soldiers.' She looked him straight in the eye. 'We have Indian soldiers here and Chinese. And civilians too. Refugees. We do not differentiate.'

'Then you are fools.' He spat. 'You should learn where you will be looked after. If you can nurse, we need you at our hospital, not here tending to traitors.'

Maya thought quickly. 'I am not a nurse,' she said. 'Just an ordinary woman doing what she can.'

His gaze raked her from head to toe. 'Not so ordinary.' He licked his lips.

Maya felt her throat go dry and her legs weak. She had been warned of this. They both had. When the colonel had left, he had given her a .38 pistol with which to protect herself and she had it even now, tucked into the belt of her *longyi* at the back, hidden under the loose blouse she wore. But would she have any idea how to use it?

'Come.' He beckoned her closer.

Maya took a small step towards him, though all she wanted to do was run. In the next room, the ward, she would be safe for a while. He would not try anything when there were other people around. But how could she run anywhere when her baby was in here? She could not leave her. And anyhow, she would not be safe for long. She understood the mentality of the Japanese soldiers by now and she knew how they felt about honour and respect. If she humiliated this man in any way, he would never forget it. He would seek her out and she and the baby would never be safe. But if she complied . . .

He reached out, tilted her chin, sharply, and Maya looked up and over his shoulder. *Do not wake, my child . . .* He ran his fingers over her blouse, lingering at the buttons on the neck and then down towards her waist and the belt of her *longyi*. What if he felt the gun? She thought her heart would stop beating. 'Not here,' she whispered.

He cocked his head, surprised. Maya guessed that many women would die rather than be raped, especially by the enemy. She wasn't sure she counted herself in that category. She felt differently about her own survival since she'd had her child; the survival of each was linked. But her first priority was to get him out of the storeroom.

But just as she thought she might have achieved her aim, just as she saw the desire flare in his eyes, and as he gripped hold of her arms, Suu whimpered in her sleep, half-waking, and he blinked, pushed Maya out of the way. He stared down at the baby. 'Your child?' he demanded roughly.

'Yes.' She nodded. Maybe now she'd have to please him. Maybe now she'd have no choice. *Lawrence*, she thought, *where are you now?*

She resumed her position in front of the baby and put a hand on his arm. 'What do you like?' She heard herself saying it and hated herself. But she had to stop him looking at the child.

Once again, his surprise showed in his eyes.

But she had made an error of judgment and she saw that straightaway.

'You are a tart?' He sounded quite dispassionate now. 'What do you do it for? Money? Food? Jewels?'

She should have been more subtle. She should have thought. 'I am not a tart,' she said, speaking more loudly than she'd intended.

'Just looking out for yourself, is that it?' He eyed her curiously in his detached manner, his lust seeming to have abruptly dissipated. Perhaps it was the sight of the little one. In Maya's limited experience, men didn't much appreciate being reminded that sex might be connected with child-bearing. 'Or are you looking out for the child?'

Dear Buddha, but he was sharp. Maya decided that honesty might be the best policy with this man. 'I need to protect her,' she said simply. 'She is innocent. She has done no wrong. And she is all I have.'

He pushed past her again and moved closer to the make-shift cradle. He frowned. 'This is your husband's baby?' he asked.

'Yes.' The Japanese, she reminded herself, were strong on honour.

'And your husband is of your race?'

'Yes.' Maya began to pray, silently. *Holy Buddha, keep us safe, let him not see . . .*

'And he is where?'

'He died in Mandalay.' She answered quickly, not giving herself precious time to think.

He pulled her roughly towards him. She could smell him. Rancid and sour. 'Shall I tell you what I think?' He leered.

'Yes. Of course.' With some difficulty, Maya maintained her dignity.

Once again he put his hand to the collar of her blouse. 'I think that you are a tart,' he said. He pulled sharply and tore open the thin fabric so that her breasts were exposed.

It was all that Maya could do to just stand there in front of him. She let out a small gasp, grabbed the remnants of her blouse and held them to her breast. But she could hardly hide herself from his greedy gaze.

His eyes narrowed. 'I think you have slept with a European.' He pulled the torn blouse away from her again. 'Which was a stupid thing to do. That child is half-white. There is no doubt.'

'It is not true,' Maya whispered. 'She is Burmese. It is not true.'

'Ah.' He leaned closer and tapped his nose. 'But I see that it is true. The child is half-caste.'

She watched his expression as he looked from her to the sleeping child. She watched it change from greed to distaste to anger. She knew that the Japanese had a reputation for thoughtless cruelty and indifference to the suffering of others. That was part of their philosophy and it was one of the characteristics that made them so dangerous, and such strong warriors, for they carried that philosophy through to their own rank and file. How could she save them both? It was a moment in time that seemed to freeze. She dared not speak, hardly even breathe. Annie would say that the entire Japanese nation should not be judged by the actions of some individuals. But all Maya could see was the man before her.

In an instant he moved two steps to the cradle and wrenched Cho Suu Kyi from her resting place. The child blinked, opened her mouth and wailed.

He held her at arm's length. 'You are a traitor.' His eyes had gone quite mad. 'You are a murderous traitor.' He was speaking to Maya but looking at the child with an expression of such pure hatred, it sent a cold sliver of fear through Maya's heart and mind. He was holding her baby as if he might fling her to the floor.

Maya made a snap decision. Her first instinct was to fly at him. But he was holding Cho Suu Kyi high and out of reach, and if she tried to wrest the child from him, Suu could fall, or he could simply push Maya aside and do what he wished. She had no option. The gun was in her hand before she could think twice.

She had taken him by surprise yet again and for a second he simply stared at her in disbelief. But pointing a gun at the man wasn't enough. She knew what he would do. She took aim with the instinct of a mother who knows exactly where is true. And she fired.

The explosion was deafening and she reeled back from the kick. Then she dropped the pistol to the floor, leapt forwards and, as he fell, she grabbed her child from his arms.

'What is happening here? What in God's name is going on?' Matron Annie was standing in the doorway. She looked from the Japanese officer who was clutching his chest, blood seeping from a wound, to Maya, huddled in the corner cradling her sobbing child. She looked at the pistol lying on the ground between them. She took a step towards Maya. 'The little one . . . ?'

'She is fine.' Maya let out a long breath, in a shudder. 'I had to do it,' she said.

'Yes.' Matron Annie dropped to her knees and felt the pulse of his neck.

But Maya knew already that he was dead. She had killed a

man. And suddenly she was shaking uncontrollably. *She had killed a man . . .*

'We must get rid of the body without delay.' Matron Annie's organisational skills came swiftly to the fore. 'Put the little one down. You must help me get him into the trench.'

Of course she was right. There was only one other Japanese soldier here at the moment and, with a bit of luck, he wasn't within earshot, but many more of them would soon be approaching. She could almost hear the sound of their army boots tramping through the jungle. And how many of them would see her baby and doubt Suu's parentage? How could she possibly protect her from them all? Maya could hardly bear to let go of Suu, not even for a moment. *She had killed a man . . .*

'First things first,' Matron Annie said briskly, indicating the dead Japanese soldier.

They took a leg each and dragged him out of the back door, checking the coast was clear before heaving him towards the small slit trench, leaving a trail of blood on the dusty ground. 'One, two, three,' said Matron and they hefted him in, watched the body fall to the ground, literally a dead weight, limbs splaying awkwardly to each side as it landed.

Maya realised that once again she was sobbing, wild sounds that seemed to come from somewhere else outside of her body. What had she done? She had never wanted to hurt anybody, it was against all the teachings to take a life. How could she have done it? And yet she knew how. She had done it because she and her baby were in danger.

'You had no choice,' Matron Annie said gruffly and placed a comforting hand on her shoulder. 'Come on. We don't have time for tears.'

And that was what they had come to, thought Maya. Having no time for tears.

Together, they collected firewood and kerosene, all the time looking out for the soldier's companion. 'He's probably looting the houses,' Matron Annie said with a shrug.

No doubt she was right. The Chinese soldiers who had come here only days before had been the same. They spoke of loyalty and they were supposed to be Allies, but all they cared for was what wealth they could find.

They piled the firewood over the body, working swiftly until they were both drenched with sweat, and then doused the wood with the kerosene. Although the flames caught and burnt the wood, the body remained virtually untouched, so they repeated the process again and then again until the body was unrecognisable. They piled on leaves and other rubbish and eventually the corpse burned and turned into a blackened mess that made Maya sick to the core as she looked at it. It could have been anything but it had been a man. Hurriedly, they dug up the earth and filled in the trench, raking over the soil and even the earth of the compound which had been stained with his blood. Maya knew they had to remove all the evidence or they would be dead for sure and it would all have been for nothing.

The Japanese were interested in total conquest of the Far East. A woman and a child, or two women and a child would not be allowed to get in their way. Their lives would mean nothing.

Maya made her preparations for sleep. She must put that experience behind her, as she had done so many times. Nevertheless, it haunted her and perhaps it always would. She prayed to the Lord Buddha that she might have to relive it no more. But how many experiences had Lawrence put behind him, she wondered. How much blood had stained his hands? She supposed that she would never know.

As she fell asleep she thought once more of Eva, that lovely girl and her grandson Ramon. What had happened between them? They were both unhappy, she could see. But it was not her affair. She would not interfere as her father had interfered between her and Lawrence, no good could come of that. She would wait and the right pathway would be revealed. That was the way that things must be.

CHAPTER 45

The following morning was as hot and humid as ever. After a somewhat disturbed sleep following the dramas of the night before, Eva got up late and went to the internet café to check her emails and send some more information to Jacqui. What else could she do at this stage but continue her work as planned? She was being paid by the Emporium to be out here, at least for part of the time. She still had the contact Klaus had given her to follow up, but she couldn't face that this morning. And it was too early now, but later she must phone her grandfather to tell him about Cho Suu Kyi. She wanted him to know. But how would he react? Would it be too much for him? Perhaps she should tell her mother instead, let her decide if he was well enough to hear the news, although she guessed it would be traumatic for her too. She decided not to tell either of them about the break-in, no need for them to start worrying over nothing. And she wouldn't send them any pictures of the family, not yet. She wanted to be with them, she wanted to see her grandfather's face.

Ramon was waiting for her in the lobby when she returned. 'Come to our house for lunch,' he said. 'I have something I want to show you.'

Not another long lost relative or vintage British car, she hoped. But she nodded and followed him outside. Perhaps now she'd find out the truth.

The house Ramon shared with Cho Suu Kyi and Maya was large by Mandalay standards, painted blue, pink and white, with a latticed balcony, blue shutters and a large verandah. The garden was small but there was a banana tree, a red flowering *sein pan* and some oleander and purple hibiscus. It was exotic and vivid and didn't seem to belong to the city at all.

Ramon showed her first into his own apartment which was an annex attached to the main building. The room they entered was small and almost bare, apart from an embroidered tapestry on the white wall, the depiction of a golden dragon, which made Eva give a little shiver. There was a low red chaise longue with blankets folded beside it, and the floor, she noted, was a gorgeous teak parquet. It was strange to be standing in his house, in his room.

Eva couldn't relax. She turned to him. 'Now will you tell me?' she asked. 'About the crate?'

'Ah.' He nodded. 'I spoke to Wai Yan this morning.'

'And what did he say?'

Ramon regarded her gravely. 'That he knew nothing about it.'

'But—'

'Hush, Eva. Please.' He made a gesture of invitation and led the way through to a small adjoining dining room where a low wooden table was set for tea. Around the table was an assortment of embroidered and beaded cushions, each one more vibrant than its neighbour. He indicated that they should sit. 'I saw the fear in his eyes,' he said.

What did he mean exactly? Eva waited.

'He knew something. He was scared. He did not want me to look in the warehouse, to investigate further.'

'But you did,' she breathed. She let herself sink into the cushions. They were very comfortable. She had known that man was hiding something, even when Ramon had first introduced him. She guessed that the warehouse was very much his domain. Ramon probably rarely even went over there unannounced. She exhaled with relief. Which might mean that he knew nothing at all about that crate.

'I did.'

'And?'

'I found another crate not belonging to us. When I examined it, like you, I could identify the blue and gold of the peacock insignia.'

Eva's eyes widened. 'What was in it?' she whispered.

'I don't know yet. It was sealed. Eva . . .' He grabbed her hand. 'It was also addressed to your company.'

She stared at him. She was still finding it hard to believe. Ramon didn't seem to be involved. *Thank God* . . . But what about Jacqui? What about the Emporium? And what were the crates doing in Ramon's warehouse?

'Can I ask you? Do you trust them? If that crate has been sent by Li's . . . We know what sort of a company he runs.'

Did she trust the Emporium? Eva didn't want to be disloyal, and despite their differences she had never doubted Jacqui's integrity, but . . . 'I don't know.' Miserably, she shook her head. Thought back to her conversations with their two contacts here in Myanmar, her sense that she wasn't completely in the know about what was going on, their edginess, Leon's reaction when he knew she was about to check the packaging of the shipment in Yangon. Not so much a string of coincidences, more like a string of similarities. A knotted rope, each knot leading to another section of the whole, each section unravelling the truth.

Ramon poured tea into the delicate white cups and passed one to Eva. Unlike the first room which had been so spartan, this room was painted in creams and reds and seemed almost opulent by comparison. And there was a faint scent of smoky incense in the air.

'Did you challenge your warehouse manager about the crate you found?' Eva asked him. She sipped the green tea. She had begun to develop quite a taste for it and she needed its calming influence right now.

'Of course.' His eyes positively glittered.

'And what did he say?'

'He denied any knowledge of it at first.' Ramon shrugged. 'And then he crumpled. He begged me not to tell them that I had found out what he was doing, he pleaded with me not to open the crate and he said that he had no idea what was inside.'

Eva raised her eyebrows. 'How many crates had he shipped out for them under your name?' she asked. She knew that Ramon must have gone through the same thought process as she had yesterday when she found out. And no doubt he had come to a similar conclusion: that his company was being used as a front for something that must surely be dodgy and possibly even illegal. She pushed the thought of the Emporium away for now. Whatever was inside those crates, his company's stamp was on the outside. And yet looking at him now as he sipped his tea, he seemed remarkably calm.

'It has been going on for several months apparently,' he said. 'Wai Yan promised this would be the last one, if I let it go.'

'But you won't let it go?' She stared at him. How could he?

Slowly, Ramon shook his dark head. 'I cannot. But neither can I trust him. So I let him think that I would.'

'We need to find out what's in the crate,' Eva murmured.

'Yes.' He frowned. 'And I do not have much time in which to do it.'

Because the crate wouldn't be left in the warehouse for much longer. Eva put her cup back on the tray. 'But why did he do it?' she asked. 'Why did he go behind your back like that?' She'd got the impression that Ramon was highly respected by his workers. It seemed a very odd way to repay him.

Ramon's mouth was set in a hard line. 'It seems that he is being blackmailed,' he said. 'There has been . . .' He hesitated. 'An indiscretion. He mentioned his wife who he loves very much.' His gaze strayed to a point beyond her and then returned to settle on her face. 'This is the sort of nasty game these people play, Eva. Men like Khan Li prey on people's

403

weaknesses.' Abruptly, he got to his feet. 'And so we must, as you might say, play them at their own game.'

Eva watched him as he walked over to the other side of the room and picked up a canvas bag that was lying there.

'So what will you do?' she asked.

'I am still considering my next move.'

She repressed a sigh. She knew he wouldn't be rushed. 'And what was it you wanted to show me?'

With a flourish, Ramon produced a parcel from the bag. He unwrapped the green tissue paper. Held it up triumphantly.

'Maya's chinthe,' murmured Eva.

He brought it over, knelt and held it out to her.

She took it. With her forefinger she stroked its carved mane. 'Did she bring it back with her from Pyin Oo Lwin?'

'That,' Ramon said, 'is good.'

'What's good?' Eva looked deep into the ruby eyes which had now replaced the red glass. Maya must have had them put in straightaway. It was odd knowing that they were rare, ancient and extremely valuable Mogok rubies. And yet . . .

'That you think this is my grandmother's chinthe,' he said. He was looking very pleased with himself.

Eva stared at him. 'But it's not . . . ?'

'The other one? No, it is not.'

'So there's a third?' Eva was confused. It certainly looked just the same. Although perhaps . . . She examined the eyes more closely. They were different from the rubies she had seen at close hand, she realised. Not so deep, not so intense.

'It is a replica.' Ramon took it back from her. He scrutinised it critically, holding it this way and that. 'I made it.'

'You made it?' Eva couldn't conceal her surprise.

'Yes.' He was trying to look modest now, but failing miserably.

And he had good reason. The wood was beautifully polished and exquisitely carved in the old primitive style. It was the work of a skilled master craftsman. Eva frowned.

'So the rubies are not real rubies?' She peered at them again. They were very convincing.

'Clever fakes.' He held the chinthe up to the light. 'They would stand up to the rough scrutiny of most people, apart of course from the scrutiny of an expert.'

'And you have aged it well,' she added dryly.

He shrugged. 'Everyone who makes furniture knows how to make wood look old,' he said. 'It is as simple a process as staining or polishing.'

Eva conceded the point. 'It's very good,' she told him. She was beginning to see what his plan might be. And presumably, he'd been secretly working on the carving of this little chap in the room in the factory which he hadn't shown her on his grand tour.

'I did a lot of it from memory after our chinthe was stolen,' Ramon admitted. 'And then you came along, Eva.'

She smiled. 'And provided you with the real thing.'

'Just for the finishing touches,' he admitted. 'Your timing was impeccable.'

'And you plan to swap them?'

405

He nodded.

She considered this. 'But how could you hope to do that? You're the last person they'd trust to get within spitting distance of the chinthe, given the history.'

He sat down again beside her. 'I have no hope of carrying out the substitution myself,' he said. 'But I hope that one day I will find someone . . .' He tailed off.

They stared at one another. His green eyes were warm. His lips curved into a slow smile. And it came to Eva, slowly but surely. She had no argument with this man. She could trust him. Because they were on the same side.

'I always knew that we could not simply steal the chinthe back,' he said. He stretched out his long legs. 'They would know who was responsible, there might be dangerous repercussions for my family and the matter would not be resolved.'

'That's true, I suppose,' Eva agreed. 'But it took you an awfully long time to come up with another plan.'

'Not really. My grandmother did not tell me the story of Suu Kyi, Nanda Li and the chinthes. Not until after my mother died. She said she was trying to protect me.'

Eva was surprised. 'So you didn't even know who had stolen it?'

'I did not. I think she imagined me too headstrong. She was afraid of me getting hurt. She thought I would charge straight round there and accuse them.'

Eva chuckled. And he probably would have. 'So she didn't tell you until she thought you'd grown a bit more sensible, is that it?'

He bowed his head, but when he looked up his green eyes held a smile.

'And that's when you started hatching your plan to carry out a swap?' It made sense, up to a point.

'Exactly.' He held the little chinthe at arm's length away from them. 'First, I had to find someone very accomplished at producing copies of Mogok rubies.'

'Which you seem to have managed.'

He laughed. 'Through a contact of Khan Li's,' he told her.

'But isn't that taking a huge risk? Mightn't he have told Khan Li?'

'No chance of that. They had a big falling out a while ago.' He gave her a knowing look. 'Most people fall foul of the Lis sooner or later.'

Eva didn't doubt it. 'And besides that, won't Khan Li be experienced enough to recognise them as fakes?' she asked. 'He must have seen a few rubies in his time.'

'You may be right.' Ramon frowned. 'It depends where they keep it, of course, and on the light. How often he picks it up to admire his little treasure.'

Eva was silent as she imagined this. She could almost see the gloating expression on Khan Li's face and she guessed that Ramon could almost see it too.

'And by the time he does realise,' Ramon said, 'or has it pointed out to him. By then it will, I hope, be too late.'

Because, she assumed, the chinthes would be far away. Or the Lis would have no idea whom among their acquaintances had done the swap. Though naturally, they would guess. It could work, she supposed. She tapped him on the arm. 'But how will you carry out the substitution?'

'That I do not know – yet.' He seemed deep in thought, his brow furrowed. 'But I know Khan Li. He would want to show it off. He does not keep it hidden away. I have already discovered that the original ruby eyes have been replaced in position. And if it is not hidden away . . .' He let this hang in the air between them.

Then it is up for grabs, thought Eva.

Ramon glanced at his watch. He jumped to his feet. 'But now,' he said. 'It is time for lunch.' He held out his hand and Eva took it. He pulled her to her feet and for a moment he kept her hand clasped in his, looked at her, in that considering way he had. Was he thinking about what he should do next? For Eva it was simple. She must phone her grandfather. And then she must, somehow, find out what was in those crates.

CHAPTER 46

Lawrence came to with a start, her cool hand on his brow. *Maya? Helen?* But of course he had lost them both. He struggled to wake. It was hard to prise himself away from the hospital; it clung like the sharp smell of iodine to his senses. He was there on R and R after a bout of malaria in the jungle, had been picked up by one of their light aircraft – a Dakota – carrying out a drop, brought back to India by a cheerful American pilot working double shifts and still with a grin on his face, bless his socks.

'How are you feeling, Dad?'

Rosemary. 'Just tired,' Lawrence croaked. 'Bad night.'

Too much to think of on those deep dark nights, sleeping under the mosquito net, listening to the sounds of the nurses changing shifts, discussing their reports and who needed what treatment the following day. A far off whistle from a train. The snoring of men in the ward, their sleep heavy from drugs, their occasional moans of pain, their nightmares. They all had those. And the sweats. A fever that seemed to carry him off to god knows where. The delirium.

He heard the sweeper climb the stairs and walk past, drunk as usual, humming to himself, smelling of alcohol and *bidis*, those cheap Indian cigarettes. It seemed a lifetime since Lawrence had been in India, at the jungle training camp in Rawalpindi, nipping down to Cooper's for coffee and a cake.

'There now, it'll pass,' said the nurse with the kind smile.

And she was right. Lawrence had been one of the lucky ones.

He wrote to Helen while he was in hospital. He still had the birthday card she'd sent him, tucked in his pack. He reached for it now. It had a picture of a gate and a lantern on it. *Your gateway to happiness*, it said. It had seemed bloody ironic to Lawrence, even then. But she had tried her best. *Happy birthday, my darling,* she'd written in her neat sloping hand. She'd remembered. And the least he could do was write to her occasionally, she deserved that much.

'I hope this finds you well, Helen,' he wrote. And as he re-read the words he sent a silent thought to Maya. *My love, my love.* 'I'm recovering in hospital from malaria, and am better now. They say war is glorious . . .' He stopped. That, it could never be. What was glorious about men falling by the wayside with disease and fever? They called that queasy dip in your stomach the thrill of battle. Some thrill. 'But it isn't,' he wrote. Stark but true. 'How was your Christmas? I hope you got something good to eat.' The politeness of his own words to a woman he had grown up with, who was practically a sister, to whom he had once, so wrongly, made love, shocked him.

Christmas . . . In the jungle, Christmas Eve had been a rare rest day. They'd spent it hunting and one of the chaps had nabbed a forty-inch-long Burmese black squirrel. It was bloody good, and they'd disturbed a flock of pea fowl that almost tasted like turkey if you closed your eyes and crossed your fingers.

Lawrence hardly knew what else to say to her. He could tell of the men and the marching, the true conditions of war, but she would only worry. He could tell her of the politics. But he had never discussed politics with Helen and it seemed bloody pointless now. Leave the politics to them in charge, he thought grimly. *They'll do us.*

He was unable, however, to forget about what she called his promise. *You're mine now . . .* Would she hold him to it? Was it even a promise at all? This was war and all the normal rules of behaviour went out of the window. Or did they? Wasn't a commitment still a commitment, even if it were unspoken? His pen hovered over the paper. 'Give my love to Mother when you see her,' he wrote instead. His father was dead. Christ, so many were dead. He had received the news in a letter from home that had taken months to reach him. In truth, he felt that he had hardly known his father and perhaps this was why he found it hard to grieve; his mother had dominated his childhood and his life since, until Burma. 'I think of you both often.'

They wouldn't mind that it was short, if they ever got it. He could hardly imagine that they would get it. It seemed a miracle that a letter could travel so far in wartime when all around was in chaos and turmoil.

The nurse took his temperature. 'You'll be out of here soon,' she said cheerfully, shaking the thermometer.

'Can't wait,' he laughed. 'Back to the jungle, eh?' What a prospect.

He stretched out in the narrow bed. How often did they have to change the sheets here because of the malaria and the dengue fever? But . . . Ah. The feel of the sheets around him. The softness of the bed after the hard ground of the jungle terrain . . . Even in the midst of his delirium, it had felt like heaven. And soap. The sensation of clean skin, he'd almost forgotten how it felt. It might have been exciting to rough it in the early days; they were marching to war, to victory, it seemed. That camaraderie around a section brew up. There had been moments and friendships he'd cherished.

But now the marching seemed interminable and victory still a long way off. Forty-five minutes every hour tramping through the jungle, driving the mule, hoping he was sure-footed enough to help show you the way, fifteen minutes rest. Not that the mules got any rest, it wasn't worth unpacking them for such a short time, poor buggers.

Some of the lads got fed up and tried to slip bits and pieces of their own load on to the mules. But Lawrence wasn't having that. 'Shape up,' he'd said. 'There's a limit to what they'll carry.' And he wasn't going beyond it. Those animals worked hard for the men and they'd be treated right.

Two days before he'd gone down with the fever, he'd lost him, Gallop, his faithful and strongest mule who'd been with him all the way, the best leader they possessed.

Lawrence had named him. 'Hope he bloody doesn't,' one of the men had said, getting a laugh.

He hadn't galloped but he always knew where he was going. The mule needed to be shod, Lawrence knew this and he had some spare shoes ready in Gallop's pack. But they also needed to cross the river and soon. He didn't show he was worried: it didn't do to show you were worried, or they'd all be in a funk. Lack of confidence saps confidence: if you don't feel brave, just look brave, that was as good. Once they got to the other side they'd be safe – relatively – and there was a paddy dried out to grass where the animals could graze for an hour or two before being rubbed down and picketed for the night. He could see what looked like a mass of yellow flowers in the marshes too. But as they got closer, he saw that his eyes had been playing tricks again. And he saw them disappear, because they weren't flowers but frogs, noisy as hell, each one the size of a man's fist. If they could catch some they'd be good for tonight's meal, he reckoned.

Last time they'd crossed a river, Lawrence had swum across first, blown a whistle, which he'd blown at feeding time in training, and then the mules had crossed one by one in a wavering line, Gallop leading the way, each driver holding on to a mule's tail. But this was the Irrawaddy, swift, muddy and cold. This time the river was deeper and wider, and Lawrence knew it well. He thought of all the times he'd used its power to transport the timber from upcountry down to Rangoon and he thought of the time he'd been stuck away from camp when the monsoon and the freak floods had hit. They'd never make it across here and they couldn't risk blowing whistles either, the enemy was too close.

They had a brief confab and decided. They'd use an eight-mule ferry, built in situ. Swiftly, they got to work. Lawrence's raft building experience from the logging came in useful, but this was something they'd also practised in training.

Soon, it was ready, and they began to cross, the ferry going back and forth. But Gallop was slow because of his leg, so he was one of the last and the sniper appeared from nowhere. The bullet came with a crack and with a yelp, he was down. Christ.

Jap. They were bloody effective in the jungle. How many times had they left gaps for the British troops to go through before closing the box? It was their military calling card, you might say, bloody devious too. But rumour had it they were using up their ammo and food. Meantime, British and American pilots were flying double hours to provide supplies for their men. They'd caught Jap off balance, it was said. Used observation patrols to go out and discover his concentration points, to break up attacks before they were launched. They were getting him out into the open and they were winning. But when would it end?

Now, Lawrence felt the tears wet on his face. He'd cried then too, cried for that mule who'd worked so hard on the march, plodding on, never kicking, never complaining. That animal could see a trail where a man could see bugger all. He was intelligent too. Mules could be stubborn but they were bloody strong. Gallop had never liked elephants but apart from that nothing would faze him, he wasn't one of the skittish ones.

Yes, Lawrence had cried for Gallop. So bloody what? He'd done it in private though, emotion had no part in war. Men died, animals died and more would follow, that was the nature of war and there was nothing more to be said. You got yourself up, you ate, you marched, you went to sleep: you carried on. Some called it the British stiff upper lip, not so popular these days, of course. But without it . . . Lawrence didn't think they'd have got through.

Two days later, he got the fever. But the march would be going on without him and he knew he'd be back. Someone would take him.

'Don't cry, Dad,' she said. 'Please don't cry.'

He squeezed her hand. 'I'm sorry, love,' he said. He couldn't seem to stop himself returning to the place. Did she realise?

'Eva will tell you all about it when she comes back,' she soothed. 'I've made you some nice soup for lunch. If you eat it up, you'll be strong enough to listen.'

Strong enough to listen.

It was almost as if she knew.

'Will you tell me about it?' Rosemary asked him. She had brought him lunch on a tray and was sitting with him while he ate. Lawrence wasn't hungry, but he was having a few mouthfuls, just to keep her happy.

'About what, love?'

'Mandalay.' She leant to pull his dressing gown closer

round his shoulders. 'It sounds so romantic, doesn't it? Bet it wasn't like that during the war though?'

She was trying. He knew how hard she was trying. And it had certainly been a shock to Lawrence when his men finally reached Mandalay that day in April. 'It was in ruins when we got back there,' he said. Though for a moment he'd imagined the city was as it had always been. 'It was criminal really. We knew it would never recover its former glory.' It had broken his heart.

'The road to Mandalay,' Rosemary said. 'What happened when you got there?'

Over the past days, weeks, months, they had marched on their own particular road to Mandalay. The war in Europe was long over and yet still their war went on. 'The Japanese were fanatics,' he told her. 'They never knew when they were beaten, would never accept defeat.' Lawrence and the Gurkhas had passed so many of their dead bodies, the jungle and mangrove swamps were full of them. Men who would not be taken prisoner, who would rather die in the jaws of a marsh crocodile. Men who would not give up. Tough in training and brutal, even to their own.

'Was the war in Europe still going on?' Rosemary asked.

'No, love.' Lawrence pushed his bowl away. Not that a little thing like that mattered to the Japanese.

He remembered VE day.

'We were in the jungle when we heard,' he told her. 'I'm not sure exactly where, but I bet you I could still find the co-ordinates on a map.' It was about 5 a.m. 'There was a signaller up a tree with an aerial wire picking up the BBC News no less, being relayed through All India Radio, Delhi.'

Rosemary smiled. 'Incredible.'

It was. All of a sudden the man let out a whoop.

'Jesus, soldier!' Lawrence was about to tear him off a strip but he didn't have a chance.

'The bloody war's over,' the signalman yelled down to them. 'We've done it. It's only bloody over.'

And then they were all whooping, even Lawrence, and the men went wild, shooting off their rifles towards the direction of the enemy, at random really. Rifles, Brens, mortars, the air was thick with the sound and smoke of gunfire.

Lawrence let it go on for a minute before he realised. 'Hold up!' he yelled. 'Enough!' They might have won the war in Europe, but this war was still going and they needed the ammo for more important targets.

Even so. It gave them hope and they marched bloody hard that day. They were winning this war too. The welcome drone of the big Dakotas circling in was becoming more frequent, the sight of those planes glittering in the sun as they banked and unleashed their canvas bundles of rations and ammunition into the drop zone, to hit the ground with a resounding thud, bouncing and careering over the paddy field, a few more delicate items fluttering down with the aid of small white parachutes billowing in the breeze. Confidence was returning. They might be weary and mere shadows of their former selves. But the enemy was on the run.

'And then you reached Mandalay.' Rosemary took the tray

from the bed. She sat down again and held his hand. 'At last. You got back there.'

'The outskirts of the city were easy to occupy,' he said. 'But Mandalay Hill was built up with brick and concrete buildings and honeycombed by tunnels and passages like you wouldn't believe.' He took a thin and rasping breath. His lungs seemed so weak these days. 'The area outside was open with no cover and the town was surrounded by a moat.' How big was the enemy's force in the city? They had little idea.

'So what did you do?' She was a quiet listener. She didn't listen like Eva did, wide-eyed and wondering. She listened calmly; she was taking it all in, as if she wanted to absorb his history.

'I took a few men and climbed up the city walls by ladder at dusk.'

'Dad!'

'I was careful. We did a quick recce of the straight grid of the main streets. Then we saw what had happened.'

'What was it?'

'The Japanese had left.' He patted her hand. 'They'd deserted Mandalay. In secret.' But much of the fort was already in ruins; the palace was half-destroyed by artillery fire and the old pavilions had been razed to the ground. The railway station was no more than a charred shell, the lines trailed with the mangled remains of coaches and engines. The streets that had once been full of Burmese people going about their business, market traders, bullock carts, saffron-robed monks begging for food and alms were almost deserted and the shops were empty too. Or bombed.

But despite the devastation, Lawrence had felt something leap inside him. Was it possible? No. She wouldn't be here. She couldn't possibly be here, not after so long. She wouldn't have stayed through it all, she must have set out like so many others for India. She could be a pilgrim, she could be a refugee, she could be dead. Nevertheless, he looked for her everywhere he went.

Some Burmese had remained in the city. And where did their loyalties now lie? It was a complex situation, Lawrence was aware. Some of them had given allegiance when it was demanded, whether to British or Japanese, it hardly mattered; they simply wanted to survive. Others had remained loyal to their British *thakins* whom they had served for perhaps as long as three generations and whom, Lawrence liked to think, had been fair masters. The hill tribes especially and those living in remote villages near the jungle had helped the Chindits and others hide from the Japanese, given them food and even guided them so that they could accomplish their missions of attacking the enemy routes of communication. Some, indeed, had died for it.

Then again he knew what Maya's father had believed, that Burma had a right to be independent, that the Japanese effort could justifiably claim Burmese support if it were to rid them of the yoke of imperialism. Perhaps Maya now thought the same. Perhaps she had even nursed Lawrence's enemy at one of the hospitals the Japanese had set up. Perhaps she'd been forced to. He'd heard that some women had been shot rather than allowed to nurse a British soldier. But he wouldn't think of that now.

Of course, things hadn't gone quite the way the new Burmese Independent Army and their supporters had expected. Anybody could see that the Burmese government installed by the Japanese were mere puppets and that the country had exchanged one master for another. Worse, this was a more brutal master, so much so that many Burmese had reverted to their previous loyalties, taking the side of the British once again, helping them finally expel the Japanese from Burmese soil.

Some of those who had stayed had been employed by the Japanese, as stenographers in their civilian offices running trades such as *saki* and ice-cream making. Lawrence talked to a few people. They'd been treated fairly, they said. The pay was low but had been supplemented by luxuries such as soap. The worst thing by far had been the surprise police raids. Always they were looking for hidden documents and for spies. Had that happened to Maya, Lawrence wondered.

He asked after her. But even those who knew her didn't know where she had gone.

And they couldn't hang around. Once Mandalay was taken, it was a race to retake Rangoon before the monsoons started up again. They couldn't give the Japanese the chance to re-group, they needed to keep up the impetus with the full force of aircraft, trucks and infantry, not risk getting stuck in a swamp in the middle of nowhere with the mozzies and the leeches and no help to hand. So . . . 300 miles, one road and the Japanese on either side. Afterwards, they called it the mopping up of Southern Burma. They knew they were beaten, but the enemy didn't recognise the word surrender.

And we made it.

'Are you tired, Dad?' she asked him. 'How about a little nap?'

'Good idea, love.' He could hardly keep his eyes open. He'd get up later. No harm done. Because that was just about the end of it. The war, his war, was over.

Lawrence returned to Mandalay as soon as he was able, though the post-war demobbing took longer than he'd expected. He hadn't weighed much more than seven stone when the war ended, but he was getting stronger with every day. He was released from military service and now he could return to his previous employer. Or could he? What was he looking for? Maya? His future?

Two letters had arrived for him c/o the company. One was from Helen.

She couldn't wait to see him, she wrote. *When will you be back?* She would count the days, she promised. *Every day I think of you. Every night I relive the last time we were together* . . . Lawrence threw the letter to one side. She wanted to remember. He longed to forget. *Coward.* He had been through this war and never thought himself that, and yet that was what he was.

How had things changed so little? How come everything – after this war – was exactly the bloody same? He might not wish to remember, but he had made a commitment to her, and wasn't he supposed to be a man of honour?

Lawrence paced to the other side of the dusty wooden verandah. Had he put down roots here in Burma or had he not? Did he want to return to Dorset? Or could he see himself permanently living here? He looked out over the hot and dusty ground. He was staying with a family he had befriended when he first returned to Mandalay. They had not known Maya and her father, but they were sympathetic to his cause and he had confided in them in part about her. And as for returning to his previous employer . . . Things were different now, he learned. The company Lawrence had worked for were finished, at least as far as logging in Burma was concerned. There was talk about re-establishment in the forests of Tanganyika and British Guiana, but it wouldn't be for him. One thing he knew, his work with timber was over. But was his life here over too?

It was dusk and nothing more could be achieved today. He should eat, try to relax, leave his decision till the morning. But . . . *A man of honour.* Did a man of honour leave the woman he loved and let himself be seduced by another, a woman who trusted him, whom he thought of more like a sister, for God's sake? Did a man of honour then marry that woman, a woman he did not love?

'*When you are home,*' Helen had written. '*Then our life together will truly begin.*'

Truly. Truly, it filled him with dread. She had not said how she felt about her father dying, she did not really say what she felt about him. But she had waited for six long years. He owed her.

Even so, today, like every other day, Lawrence walked the streets and looked for Maya. Every day more refugees were returning. And what would he do if she came? He could not answer that question.

The second letter was from his mother.

'How I have survived this terrible war, I shall never know,' she wrote. And Lawrence had to smile, for he could hear her voice saying it. 'But I have and now you must come home.'

Lawrence sighed. Typical black and white. Typical Mother.

'We need you. The company needs you to rescue it.'

She seemed to have considerable expectations of his skills. How would he rescue the family firm? Lawrence knew nothing about stock broking. He had never cared to know.

And then came the emotional twist she'd always been so good at. 'You owe it to your father to do this. He and Helen's father spent their whole lives working for the company's success.'

Which was true. But did that mean the son had to follow the father? What about the son's pathway? The son's destiny? Could he not choose his own?

'I need you,' she wrote. 'I need to see my son again, to see with my own eyes that he is alive and well, before I can believe it.' On the other hand, how could Lawrence deny her that? It had been seven years.

'And Helen needs you too. You made a commitment to that girl, Lawrence. I know it. Her father is dead now and you must take his place and look after her. It's the right thing to do. If you do not return, her heart will be broken.'

Because of course, his mother knew. Lawrence had never been able to hide anything from her. She had known about Maya, or at least that there was someone, on his last leave before the war. She knew her son. She always had, and that was why she had first let him go.

Days went by and Maya did not come. He delayed his return. Weeks passed and still he stayed. He asked after her and her father; no one knew where they were or what had happened to them. So many had got to India and might never return. So many had died in the trying.

He went to the house in Maymyo. It was a depressing visit. The house was still there, but shut up. Perhaps it had been requisitioned during the war, perhaps others had lived there, Lawrence had no idea and no one seemed able or willing to help him. Or perhaps there was no information to pass on. Much of the town had disappeared though, destroyed by bombs, and only a skeleton community remained. How long would it take them to recover, Lawrence wondered. To restore even half of the town's lush beauty and architectural grandeur? Nature would recover in time, but most of those buildings were lost and now would be lost forever.

He stayed for three days at Pine Rise, his old place of refuge, which had also survived the bombings, bar some damage to one side of the house and shattered windows and doors. And he remembered that last time he'd been there in March 1942, just before he was called up for action. He remembered a per-

424

fect day with Maya when she had given him the gift of the little chinthe, he remembered the photograph that one of the lads had taken. He remembered that last evening in the club, it was crowded because you could still get whisky there, when you couldn't in the shops. It was rationed though, they filled a glass barrel early every evening to limit the supply. Otherwise you'd hardly know there was a war on: there was still dancing at the club and even strawberries and cream for tea. And he remembered saying goodbye to the woman he loved.

But now he could stay no longer. If Maya were still alive and still in Burma, she would have come to Maymyo if not to Mandalay as they had agreed. He had to face it. He had lost her. And perhaps it was for the best.

Lawrence booked his passage. Another three weeks passed and still she had not returned to Mandalay. He tucked the little chinthe in his travelling bag. He'd keep a part of her though. He'd always keep a part of her.

He wrote to his mother and he wrote to Helen. He had no choice.

'I'm coming home.'

CHAPTER 47

They had lunch with Cho Suu Kyi, a clear soup with herbs and leaves followed by *Pa Zun Thoke*, salad with prawns. Maya was resting, Suu told them.

Eva made the most of her time with her, encouraging Suu to talk about her childhood and her life in Myanmar. Maya was linked to her grandfather by their love. But Cho Suu Kyi was actually related to Eva. She was her Auntie, well, half-Auntie, if such a thing existed.

She was just a baby and so did not remember the war, she said, though her mother had told her some stories. 'But after the war, I was happy.' Her expression was serene. 'Before my mother's marriage, we lived with my grandfather.' And it was clear that this arrangement had suited everyone. The family were not as well off as they had been before the war, but Maya's father had resumed his business interests as a broker in the rice industry and Maya brought in some money by doing fine embroidery work, a skill she had developed before she even met Lawrence and which she was able to pick up again after the war. They managed well enough to keep both a modest house in Mandalay and retain the one in Maymyo, which Eva, and her grandfather before her, had visited.

'We have some pieces of my mother's work here in the house.' They had finished lunch and Cho Suu Kyi got up to show Eva a vibrant embroidered silk tapestry in silver, gold and red threaded silk on a background of black velvet, which had been framed and hung on the wall. It was of a golden temple with two silver chinthes guarding the gate, their eyes red as rubies. And it was the work of the same skilled needlewoman who had embroidered the dragon tapestry in Ramon's quarters, Eva realised.

'And there is the quilt. You must see the quilt.' Cho Suu Kyi went to fetch it. It was sewn from multi-coloured patchwork squares, each one having an image from Myanmar embroidered within: there was a ruby of course, a golden temple, an orchid and a chinthe, to name but a few.

Eva fingered the delicate material. 'It's very fine,' she said. And it must have taken a long time to finish. But she wasn't surprised. Maya's patience was etched on her face and Suu, her daughter, had the same look about her. Not for the first time, Eva wondered if it was their religion, their upbringing or their character that gave them such a sense of acceptance and peace. She thought of her own life back in the UK, of her grandfather, who was becoming so old and frail, and of the Emporium. Whatever was going on there, did she want to spend the rest of her working life following other people's rules? Or did she want to work for herself, find her own pathway? Eva thought of Sagaing and the enlightenment people sought by going there. She needed to recapture her dream, the dream that had inspired her to do her degree in the first place, the dream that was about the scent of teak wood and the history of past lives.

Suu nodded with enthusiasm. 'Even now, my mother works most days for an hour or two,' she said. 'She says that her work gives her purpose and pleasure. She would not like that to end.' She smiled. 'But she often asks one of the young ones to thread the needle.'

Eva smiled too. How different would Maya's life have been if she had remained with Eva's grandfather? She didn't know. She just couldn't imagine it. But the fact that Maya could still undertake such work was a testament to her health, as well as her ability. She was not the kind of woman who would ever give up. So why had she given up on Eva's grandfather? Or had he given up on her? Eva was determined to find out.

'And then my mother met Ramon's grandfather.' Cho Suu Kyi put a hand on Ramon's arm. 'And he made her happy, I know.'

Ramon's Burmese grandfather, Eva discovered, had a small but successful business managing a tobacco factory, and it was clear that he had been more than willing to take on Cho Suu Kyi as his own.

Eva couldn't help thinking that perhaps Maya had enjoyed a more fulfilled personal life than her grandfather had had in England. He had never said a word against her grandmother to Eva, but there had always seemed to be something missing. Maya might have married primarily for the security of herself and her daughter, but she had married a good man and it had clearly developed into a rewarding kind of love. Eva was glad. And she was sure that her grandfather would be glad too.

'And they had a daughter,' Suu continued. 'Ramon's mother.' One of the younger girls had brought tea and now she poured the stream of green-gold liquid into the tiny porcelain cups with no handles.

'Who met and fell in love with a furniture maker from Devon.' Eva smiled. 'Thank you, Suu.' She took the cup that was passed to her.

'Exactly.' Ramon smiled too as he took up the story. 'My father's business did well in Burma. My family were able to build this house.' He sipped his own tea and looked at Eva across the rim of the tea cup. It was a disconcerting look. Perhaps, Eva thought, it was easier to know what you wanted to do in life when you were following in the footsteps of your mother or your father.

She looked at the smiling face of the woman sitting across from her. 'But you never married, Suu?' She hoped it wasn't too personal a question.

'No.' She looked down. 'I became a teacher and I was content in my job until I retired. But I never met a man I wished to marry.'

Eva nodded as if she understood, but she wondered how difficult it might have been for an Anglo-Burmese woman back in the early sixties. The streets of Myanmar were full of mixed races – she'd noticed this from the first – but back in the fifties when Cho Suu Kyi was growing up, it might not have been so easy. And how had Suu felt about the man who had unknowingly abandoned her, Eva's grandfather?

'Will you tell him about me?' Cho Suu Kyi asked, as if she had read her mind. She offered more tea.

'Of course.' Eva nodded and pushed her cup a little closer. He had a right to know. She was planning to phone him this afternoon. She didn't add that he had been ill, nor that she was worried about how her mother would take the news. But both these things were never far from her mind.

Suu glanced at her. 'But like my mother, he is very old now, I think?'

'He is.' Eva sighed. 'He would not be able to travel . . .' She tailed off. She didn't even know if Cho Suu Kyi wanted to see him, if she had forgiven him.

'Perhaps one day I can make a visit to England.' Suu looked down. 'If it is meant to be,' she said quietly.

If it is meant to be . . .

Eva took her hand. 'He'll be so happy to know about you,' she said.

Suu looked up, her eyes bright with tears. 'And he will forgive my mother for not telling him?' she asked.

'Oh, yes.' Eva was sure of that much. 'He'll understand. I'm sure he would forgive her anything. If he had known about you . . .' She squeezed her hand. 'He would have loved you.'

Suu nodded. She seemed to be hanging on Eva's every word.

'And if he could possibly come and see you, he would.'

She just hoped that she was getting the message across to this woman, who must still feel so abandoned.

'Thank you, Eva,' she said serenely.

Eva leaned closer towards her. 'He is a good man,' she assured her in a whisper. 'He would never have wanted to leave you.'

'I have been thinking,' Ramon said, on the way back to Eva's hotel.

He had been rather quiet at lunch, clearly still mulling it over. And yet he hadn't seemed in a hurry to get back to work this afternoon. Could that be because he wanted to spend more time with her? Eva thought of the look he'd given her earlier. 'About those crates?'

'Yes.' His eyes were fixed on the road ahead, his brown hands loose on the steering wheel.

Eva watched him, stapling the image into her mind, so that she could conjure it up whenever she wanted to in the future. She wasn't sure quite how she felt about him, but she certainly wasn't ready to forget him.

'It makes me very angry,' he said. 'That they have dared to use my name, my father's company, in this underhand way.' He glanced across at her as if considering how much he should say.

And for the first time Eva wondered, was he doubting *her* integrity? She couldn't blame him. After all, the crates were being sent to her company. 'I know,' she said. 'It's unforgiveable.' She hesitated. 'But what do you think is inside? Fake

431

antiques?' It seemed the most obvious thing, given what she had seen in Li's showroom.

Ramon frowned and braked at the road junction. She could almost see his mind moving up a gear. 'Perhaps. But what sort of fake antiques can they be?'

He was echoing her own thoughts. 'Forged antiques can fetch a lot of money in Europe,' Eva pointed out. 'An ancient Buddha that once stood in the temple of Pashmina, you know the sort of thing.'

He laughed and indicated right by hooting and swinging the steering wheel around sharply. 'Pashmina is a shawl, Eva. Even I know that. But . . .'

'But?' She looked across at him. It sounded like a big 'but'. His features were concentrated, still on the problem rather than on the road, she guessed, though Ramon continued to weave the car in and out of lanes as deftly as ever.

'You are right, of course.' Now, Ramon turned left on to the road Eva always called the moat road, lined with trees and a walkway, the wide waters of the moat glinting in the afternoon sun on the other side of the railings. 'Perhaps that is all it is. And perhaps Li tries to implicate us because his family continue to hate my own. But still . . .' He let out a sigh, 'I would like to see.'

So would Eva. She would very much like to see. She had wanted to see inside those crates for a long time.

'And so . . .' Ramon pulled in to the kerb outside her hotel. 'There is only one possible thing to do.'

'Yes,' she breathed. And she knew what that was.

A group of men were squatting outside a shop doorway, playing *mah jong*. Beside them, a woman had set up a stall selling some sugary confection fried in oil. Eva could sniff it in the air. She was always tempted by the street food, and a couple of times she'd tried it, restricting herself to things that looked relatively safe and identifiable.

'Thanks for the lift.' She undid her seat belt. Earlier, he had asked her if she wanted to change hotels, or even come and stay at the house. There was plenty of room, he'd said, and Maya would be delighted, even though it was officially against the rules for a tourist to stay in a Burmese home. But Eva had turned down the offer. If she changed hotels, they'd soon find out where she was – if they were still following her. And if she went to stay at the house . . . Well, Ramon would be rather too close for comfort. She didn't want to get anyone into trouble. And why should she be driven underground? She wouldn't give them the satisfaction.

'Come.' Ramon got out of the car and went round to the passenger side. He opened the door. 'I will escort you to your room.'

'There's really no need,' she said.

But he wasn't taking no for an answer, so she followed him into the hotel, got her key from the desk and called for the lift.

'And how do you plan to find out what's inside the crate?' she whispered to him as they stood side by side. 'If your warehouse manager is always there keeping a watch on it?'

The lift arrived and they got in. 'He must go home some-time,' he said.

'And if the crate is sealed?'

He turned to face her. 'Anything that is sealed can be unsealed, Eva. Anything that is closed can be opened.'

For a moment, Eva wondered if he was even talking about the crates at all. Conscious of his proximity, she moved away, towards the far corner of the lift. She closed her eyes for a moment, breathing him in, it felt like. Even when he hadn't been at the factory, he smelt vaguely of freshly sawn timber and oily wood polish. 'When will you do it?' It was very melodramatic. But there was no going back, not now.

The lift was pinging its way up the floors. Finally it reached the seventh and the doors hissed open. 'It will have to be soon.' He strode out of the lift and she followed him. 'Tonight.'

'Of course.' If they left it any longer, the crate would be taken away for shipping. But her heart leapt. At last, things were happening.

She waited meekly while he inserted the key in the lock and flung the door open. He strode in, glanced in the bathroom, looked around the room, which, thanks to the chamber-maid, was pristine and tidy, and seemed satisfied that it was empty. 'I will go back to the factory,' he said. 'And when it gets dark—'

'Why when it gets dark?' She looked up at him. 'It's your factory. Why can't you just open up the crate in broad day-light?'

'No.' He frowned. 'It is better under the cover of darkness. Who knows who might be watching? Who knows who cannot be trusted?' He walked over to the window and surveyed the vista of downtown Mandalay, his arms folded. Not for the first time, Eva wondered what he really felt for this city and how much he wanted to stay.

'Take me with you.' She joined him at the window. 'I want to be there when you open up the crate. I want to see what's inside.'

'Impossible.' He glanced towards her and then away. 'It is far too dangerous. This is not work for—'

'A woman?' she challenged.

He shrugged. 'I will not put you in any more danger. That is all.'

Eva sighed. 'How can it be dangerous? It's your warehouse. All we have to do is slip in, open up the crate and take a quick look inside.'

His expression was inscrutable. He shook his head. 'Not "we", Eva. "I".'

'But I'm already involved.'

'No.'

'And you need my expertise. I can tell you—'

'No.'

She sighed. He was really very stubborn. 'Well, I'm coming anyway,' she said. 'I'll get a taxi as soon as you've gone. I'll stay there, out of sight, until it's dark.' She glanced across at him but there was no response. 'I'm going to be part of this, Ramon.'

435

Finally, he looked at her and she thought she saw the ghost of a smile turning the corners of his mouth. 'OK.'

'What?' She stared at him.

'I said OK. In England, it is different for women. I know that already. My father warned me.'

'Warned you?'

He raised both hands as if asking for mercy. 'No more arguments, please,' he said.

'No more arguments,' she agreed. After all, she was the one who had got them into this predicament. If she had only trusted him instead of rushing over to Li's . . . But it was hard to trust someone who was so secretive and who seemed to be living in the Dark Ages as far as women's liberation was concerned. He had an awful lot to learn.

'You will leave the hotel at sunset and not before,' he said. 'Walk two blocks before you get a taxi by the moat. Come straight to the warehouse door and I will let you in. Knock three times. Tell the driver not to wait. Can you do that?'

'Of course I can do that.' Eva bridled at his tone. He'd given in, but she knew he didn't like it.

Ramon moved towards her, his dark hair flopping over his forehead. She reached out, brushed it back gently with her fingers. It was almost an unconscious gesture. She held his gaze. But they both knew what it meant.

'So I will see you later, Eva.' He put his fingers on her mouth, then tilted her chin and brushed her lips with his. He still did not look away.

'See you later,' she whispered.

And she stood at the window while he went down in the lift and left the building. She stood there until he had got in the car and driven away. Until he was out of sight.

CHAPTER 48

'Eva? Is that you?' The phone line connection was fragile. Ironic, thought Rosemary. Something she would work on. 'How are you, darling?'

'Fine. Absolutely fine.' Eva sounded tired, but there was something else. A suppressed excitement.

'What's happened?' Rosemary glanced towards the open living room door. But he was sleeping. Sleeping or drifting. She'd left him with Mrs Briggs this morning, while she went out for a walk. She had to get some air, escape, just for an hour, and despite the chill wind she'd chosen to go to the golden sandstone cliff above Burton. She loved it there, it had been one of hers and Nick's special places. She tramped along the grassy cliff-top. The sheep were out grazing in the shorn November fields and she could see the grey church tower of the village beyond, the broad olive sweep of the ocean on the other side. *I'll come again tomorrow*, Mrs B had said. She seemed to know that while Rosemary didn't need her to cook or clean, she needed something else.

'You'll never believe it,' said Eva. 'How's Grandpa?'

Fading away, thought Rosemary. *Fading away before my very*

eyes. 'Not strong,' she said. 'Looking forward to seeing you, of course.'

'I don't know whether or not to tell him.' She heard Eva catch her breath. 'I don't want to give him too much of a shock. If he's not feeling strong, I mean.'

Tell him what? Rosemary sighed. 'You'd better tell me then.' She was her mother. 'Is it about Maya?'

'Oh.'

'He's told me about her.' Rosemary sat down on the piano stool her father kept by the phone table. She remembered her mother having it re-covered in this chintzy rose pattern over the old green velour. Funny, the things you remembered, the things you could visualise as if you'd seen them yesterday.

'How did that make you feel, Mother?' Eva asked. 'Are you alright?'

'Of course.' Rosemary spoke quickly, before she had a chance to consider. She ran her finger along the bevelled edge of the stool. 'It was a long time ago, Eva. It was well before he married your grandmother.' Though they both knew. Time had very little to do with it.

'Good.' Eva sounded decisive. 'But you'd better brace yourself, Ma.'

Brace herself? The thought of a plane journey filtered into her mind. *Get ready. Prepare.*

'For what?'

'Grandpa and Maya . . . Well, he didn't know, of course. She kept it a secret all these years.' Eva's voice held a note of wonder. And respect, Rosemary noted.

'Kept what a secret?' *Out with it, girl.*

'After Grandpa enlisted, Maya found out she was pregnant. She gave birth to their daughter during the war.'

Eva paused and the silence seemed to echo down the phone line. All of a sudden the connection was clear, uncluttered by all the things that didn't really matter.

'A daughter,' Rosemary said.

'Yes.' There was another beat of silence between them. 'Are you OK, Ma?'

Something fluttered inside her. Trepidation? Excitement? Disbelief? 'Yes.' She took a deep breath. 'I'm OK. Tell me.'

'Her name is Cho Suu Kyi. I met her yesterday. Maya introduced us. I had no idea either.'

'But how old is she? What's she like?' Again, Rosemary looked towards the door.

'She must be in her late sixties, I suppose. She's quiet and serene. Really quite lovely.'

A daughter, thought Rosemary. Maya and her father. So her father had two daughters. 'What does she look like?' she whispered. Or did she mean who? She couldn't imagine.

'Brown eyes. Dark hair. Greying. She has Burmese features. But the shape of her eyes is different. And actually . . .' She paused. 'She looks a bit like you.'

'Oh my gosh.' Rosemary blinked. She was still trying to take it in. Burma. His other pathway. Their parallel world.

Eva let out a low laugh. 'She was desperate to find out about you,' she said.

'Really?' Rosemary felt quite weak. Lucky she was sitting

down, she thought. 'What did you tell her?' *That your mother had left you when you were sixteen?*

'That you lived in Copenhagen. About Dad. About Alec.'

Goodness.

'You have a half-sister, Ma,' Eva said. 'Don't you think that's rather wonderful?'

'Well . . .' She wasn't sure what to think. But the surprising thing was, that 'wonderful' was in there somewhere. She'd always wanted a sister, she thought. And all these years . . .

'And Grandpa . . .'

'Heavens, yes.'

'Grandpa has another daughter.' Eva lowered her voice. 'A daughter living on the other side of the world.'

'Yes.'

'How do you think he'll take it?'

Rosemary frowned. 'He'll be pleased,' she said. 'Thrilled.' After all, Maya had been the love of his life and, much as she hadn't wanted to accept that, it was a fact and there was nothing she could do about it. She thought of Nick. You couldn't help who you fell in love with. This Cho Suu, who-ever she was, was a child born from love. Which had to be special.

'But he's missed out on all those years. He won't blame Maya will he, for not telling him?' Eva asked.

Oh, Eva, Eva, it was so long ago. And she didn't think her father was capable of blame, not now, when he was so frail. 'I'm sure he won't, darling,' she said. And there was some-thing ironic, Rosemary thought, in the fact that no sooner had she found that bond with him, no sooner had she discovered her own father . . . That he should gain another daughter.

'Will you tell him?' Eva asked. Suddenly, she sounded like a child again. Rosemary thought of this daughter of hers, who had been so irrepressible, so independent and who had somehow grown up estranged from her. How she wanted to get to know the real Eva, the Eva who probably still was strong and independent, but who was vulnerable too.

'He should be told,' Rosemary murmured. 'Of course I'll do it.'

'And as soon as possible.' Eva's voice was urgent now. 'That's why I phoned. I didn't want to leave it until I got back. Just in case.'

In case it was too late, thought Rosemary. *Oh, my heavens . . .*

'I'll tell him.' She straightened her shoulders. 'Don't worry, darling. First chance I get.' *When I think he might understand what I'm saying,* she meant.

'Good.' Eva sounded a little surprised. 'Thank you.' Rosemary guessed she'd been expecting the phone call to be much harder than it was. And that's what she had done all these years, she thought. She had made her daughter's life harder, not easier. Not intentionally. She'd only been after damage limitation, she'd done what she had to do. But nevertheless. That's what she had to live with now.

'And everything else?' Rosemary forced a normality into her tone that she didn't really feel. 'Is everything else alright?'

Eva exhaled loudly. 'There's a lot going on, to tell you the truth,' she said.

'With your work?'

There was a pause. 'I've got a suspicion that by the time I get back I won't have any work.'

'Why on earth not?' Rosemary felt a jolt of concern.

'It's a long story.' She sounded a little despondent. 'And it isn't over yet. But . . .'

'I worry about you being there on your own,' Rosemary said. The country was still such an unknown. And an awfully long way away.

'I'm not completely on my own.' There was a different note to her voice now.

'Oh?' Rosemary was intrigued.

'Maya and her husband had a daughter too. She married an Englishman who came over here in the sixties.'

'Quite a coincidence,' murmured Rosemary. Like mother, like daughter. So often, that seemed to be the way.

'And they had a son, Ramon.'

'Oh, yes?'

'He's been showing me round a bit. He's been very helpful, supportive.'

'Mmm?'

'He's really nice, Mother.'

Rosemary didn't have a problem reading between the lines. Eva was telling her that she had become somehow attached to Maya's grandson. *Oh, my Lord*. She didn't know whether to laugh or cry. But so long as someone was keeping an eye on her.

'I have to go now, Ma.'

'Take care, darling.' Half of Rosemary's mind was on her father. Could she make him understand? But the rest was with her daughter in Burma. 'Please take care.'

Eva felt as if she'd side-stepped into a James Bond film as she slipped out of the hotel at sunset, walked a couple of blocks and crossed over to the wide and glimmering moat. The sun had dipped low behind the buildings and the sky was suffused with a deepening blush of red and grey. Another stunning sunset in Myanmar.

But Eva had other things to think about tonight. She was wearing close-fitting cotton jeans, sandals and a long-sleeved T-shirt to discourage mosquitoes. And she wanted to be able to run. She'd followed Ramon's instructions and had taken a circuitous route to the moat, dodging in and out of shop doorways, past the street sellers and market traders, whose stalls were piled high with crimson chillies, peanuts and pungent, colourful spices, swathes of fabrics in cottons and silk, patterned, embroidered, beaded. But she hadn't been tempted to stop and linger. She was on a mission and the adrenalin was rising high. She was pretty confident she hadn't been followed, but she couldn't be sure.

She waved down a taxi and gave the address of Ramon's factory, forgetting, as usual, to barter. By the time they arrived at the familiar building, dusk was drawing in. Eva got the taxi to drop her off by the main entrance and then walked quickly up the dusty track that led to the factory, forcing herself not to break into a run. She looked from left to right. There was not a sound to be heard, not even the faintest brush of the breeze through the thick clumps of bamboo and palm trees lining the track, and not a soul to be seen. And the building, as she'd expected, was in darkness.

She crossed the compound to the warehouse and knocked softly three times, trying not to think about what she would do if Ramon weren't there. There was no sign of his car, but then he'd hardly leave it at the front for anyone to see. She'd let the taxi go as he'd told her to. Her mobile didn't work in Myanmar and, anyway, she didn't know the numbers of any taxi-cabs. She thought she saw something – a bat? – flapping around near the roof. She shivered.

No one answered the door. Eva tried not to panic. She was miles away from anywhere and, with no streetlamps, it wouldn't be easy to walk back to civilisation either. Still . . . She thought briefly of the conversation she'd had with her mother earlier. A good conversation. She'd sounded so different.

She leant against the door. 'Ramon,' she whispered. She knocked again, three times.

As if by magic, the door creaked open at last. Thank God. She slipped through the opening.

'I thought I heard someone out there earlier,' Ramon said. He peered into the gloom. 'I was watching when you arrived, but there was nothing suspicious.'

446

'Good.' He shut the door behind her and Eva's eyes began to adjust to the light. Ramon was also dressed in jeans and a T-shirt and he was holding a large crowbar.

She gasped. He looked very menacing.

'It is to open the crate,' he hissed. 'Come on. It is through here.'

Eva followed him, stepping carefully past all the obstacles. The warehouse was strangely eerie in the near darkness, crates and packed furniture stranded here and there, the beam from Ramon's torch flashing briefly over them as they passed through. The scent of wood, newspaper and cardboard filled the air.

'Can't you switch the lights on?' Eva whispered. It was all very cloak and dagger.

'That is not a good idea, Eva. The lights could be seen from outside.'

He stopped, handed her the torch and when she shone it down, she saw a crate that had been separated from the rest. She directed the beam to the stamp of Handmade in Mandalay. And closer still . . . She could just make out the blue-and-gold peacock insignia half-hidden underneath.

'The dancing peacock was on our country's flag,' Ramon said sadly. 'And before that it was on King Mindon's silver coins. It is a disgrace for that company to abuse our heritage in this way.'

Eva couldn't agree more. But perhaps now was not the time. 'Let's get on with it,' she suggested.

'OK. Here we go.' Ramon lifted the crow bar and began to

lever the crate open while Eva continued to direct the beam. Breaking the seal was a simple enough matter. But the top of the crate was firmly fixed with nails and what looked like bits of old tin cans for reinforcement. Even so, Ramon worked quickly and in less than two minutes, he had prised off one of the planks of wood. Eva caught her breath.

'What was that?' He stopped. 'Did you hear something?'

She shook her head. 'It was probably the wind. Or bats.'

'Now we have it.' He eased open the crate. It was full of shredded paper. He dug his hand in and pulled out a package wrapped in newspaper. He looked up at Eva who was still standing, the torch-light directed at the crate. 'Yes?'

'Yes,' she breathed.

'Stop what you are doing, please.' The voice came from the other side of the warehouse.

The broad beam of a searchlight swept over them. Eva felt completely exposed. *What the . . . ?* Khan Li, was her first thought. But no, Khan Li wouldn't be speaking English for a start.

Ramon jumped up from where he'd been squatting by the crate. 'Who is there?' he demanded. 'You are trespassing. This is my property. Come out where we can see you.'

She heard the sound of footsteps coming closer. One pair of footsteps. One man.

'This crate. It is yours?' the man asked.

She knew that voice. There was a dryness to it that she recognised.

'That is my business,' Ramon growled.

448

'And mine too, I think,' the man replied.

With a click, the lights came on.

Eva stared at the man with his hand still on the switch. 'Klaus,' she breathed. What on earth was he doing here?

'You . . .' Ramon muttered a curse in Burmese under his breath. 'How did you get in?'

Klaus switched off the spotlight. 'Hello, Eva,' he said. 'Ramon. It was a simple matter to get in through the door. You must improve your security, I think.' His voice seemed to echo around the half-empty warehouse. 'And the crate . . .'

'It's not our crate,' Eva said. 'Otherwise, why would we have come here in the dead of night to break into it?' She didn't feel so scared anymore. This was Klaus, for heaven's sake.

But Ramon was glaring at him. 'This is my warehouse,' he said. 'What are you doing here? Why are you asking us all these questions?'

Klaus looked from one to the other of them. 'You say this is not your crate . . .' he began. 'May I ask you then, why you are so interested in it?'

'What is it to you?' Ramon was still bristling with anger. He took a step forwards, but Eva put a restraining hand on his arm.

'It's a long story,' she said. She was still trying to work out where Klaus fitted into all this.

'I am listening.' He folded his arms.

'Are you working for Khan Li? Is that it?' It was all she could think of. Klaus had admitted that he knew him.

'Most certainly, no.' Klaus reached into his jacket and flashed an identity card at them. 'I am part of a German investigation team,' he said.

'Police?' snapped Ramon.

He shook his head. 'We are professional, yes. And we work for a private individual. But now, we work alongside the Burmese custom authorities.'

Eva and Ramon exchanged a glance.

'So you're investigating Khan Li,' said Eva. She felt a wave of relief wash over her.

He raised an eyebrow and nodded.

'Then switch off the lights,' Ramon said. 'There may still be someone watching.'

'There is no one watching,' said Klaus. 'They have all left.'

Once again, Ramon muttered something uncomplimentary under his breath and Eva couldn't blame him.

Klaus turned to him. 'And you?' he asked.

'Me?'

'You are working for Khan Li, yes?'

Ramon swore again. He tore his hand through his hair.

'No, of course he isn't.' Eva had begun to grasp the situation.

Klaus looked disbelieving. 'Then why does the shipment go out from your factory?'

'I was not aware it did,' Ramon said. 'Until yesterday. My warehouse manager . . .' But he tailed off. Eva guessed that even after what the man had done, Ramon would make every effort not to get him into more trouble.

Klaus was still regarding him appraisingly. And of course it looked suspicious. Hadn't she thought the same thing herself? 'Have you been keeping watch on the factory?' she asked Klaus.

'I have.'

'Were you watching when I arrived?'

'Of course.'

Again, Ramon made a move towards him, and again Eva put a hand on his arm. 'To see what happens to these crates?' she asked.

'Exactly.' Klaus came closer, looked down at the crate. 'We have been following their progress,' he said. 'We have gathered the material and evidence we need. There are people who are very interested in what is happening here. Not only German people.' He nodded. 'Burmese too. Not everyone is corrupt.'

'Of course not everyone is corrupt,' Ramon said.

'And the man at the Shwedagon?' Eva asked. Had he given information to Klaus? He had certainly been paid for something.

'The man . . . ? Ah.' He nodded. 'You are very observant, Eva. And yes, he is a man who has been of some help in our investigations.'

How many more of them were involved? Eva could see it was a bigger enterprise than she'd ever suspected. 'Perhaps,' she suggested, 'we should all see exactly what's inside.'

Klaus frowned. 'I confess that I was not expecting this development,' he said. 'We do not wish to alert people too soon. It is a delicate matter. But when I saw that you two . . .'

Clearly, he remained unconvinced. She waited. It was blatantly obvious that she and Ramon were not involved in anything other than finding out what was going on.

'You must be tempted,' Eva said. The crate was already open.

With that, Klaus seemed to make up his mind. 'Why not?' He gestured to Ramon.

Ramon shrugged, but picked up the package wrapped in newspaper still on top of the crate.

They both watched as he uncovered a small wooden image of Buddha. There was nothing remarkable about it. It looked much the same to Eva as hundreds of others she'd seen at Li's, badly distressed and made of inferior wood, roughly carved, looking nothing like the antique it was presumably pretending to be.

Eva glanced at Klaus. 'How did your client get involved with all this?' she asked. Though she could guess. The questions she was trying to ignore were rather closer to home. Why would the Emporium be interested in this stuff? To what extent were they involved? And where did that leave her?

'All this?'

'Fake antiques.' It was, she had to admit, a disappointment.

Klaus raised an eyebrow. 'They have been exporting to Germany,' he told her. 'Many questions have been asked.' But his eyes were on the wooden Buddha in Ramon's hands. 'May I?'

Ramon handed it to Klaus, who turned it this way and

that, weighed it in one hand, shook it, examined it as if he were looking for something specific. 'Perhaps we must dig deeper,' he suggested.

Soon, they were surrounded by wooden Buddhas, elephants and chinthes scattered on the warehouse floor, all made of the same inferior wood with tacky coloured glass eyes. 'Should we keep going?' she asked.

'Yes, of course,' said Klaus. 'We keep going simply because most people would stop.'

She saw what he was getting at. But what was he hoping to find?

They reached the next layer and Eva unwrapped a small wooden tiger. It didn't look much different from the others. Apart from . . .

'Please, Eva?' Klaus was looking over her shoulder.

Eva handed it to him. 'Now it begins to make sense,' he said. He removed a handkerchief from his pocket, spat on it and rubbed.

All at once, Eva knew exactly what was going on. It was so obvious. So simple. It wasn't about fake antiques at all. This . . . This was what it was all about. The wooden tiger was of the same quality as the other pieces so as not to arouse suspicion from any custom officers who might be checking. But one thing was different. They had stolen the idea from the historic little chinthes.

Ramon squeezed Eva's hand. The wooden tiger had large, striking and quite perfect crimson eyes. Even in the artificial light from the bulb above, they glowed.

'Rubies?' Eva whispered.

'Rubies,' agreed Klaus. He whipped an eyeglass out of his shirt pocket and examined the tiger's eyes more closely. 'Just as I was expecting,' he said.

CHAPTER 50

'You have a daughter. Another daughter.'

These words kept running in and out of his brain and Lawrence tried to make sense of them. Like a mountain stream, they tripped down from his consciousness, sometimes clear, sometimes picking up assorted debris on the way, winding and flowing towards the source. Only what was the source?

He sighed and tried to get more comfortable in the bed. So much of his life seemed to consist of this now, attempting to make sense of things that were happening, things that were being said to him. Sometimes he took it in. He always tried to take it in. Then he'd hear a voice whispering: 'Did he hear me? Do you think he heard me?'

And he'd want to shout: 'Yes, I heard you! You can talk to me. I can hear you.' But he couldn't. He couldn't shout. And although he had heard – he really had – already, he'd lost the sense of whatever it was that had been said. He tried to catch it, pull it back. He tried to prise the meaning out of it as if it were nothing more than a tin of sardines and he'd simply lost the key. He tried to grasp it. But it wasn't always possible. Not anymore.

Sometimes it stayed with him, for seconds, minutes, hours,

a day . . . Sometimes it vanished. Gone to gossamer, lightly floating away like a forgotten dream, like fairy dust. And just as bloody elusive.

'What's elusive? Dad, what's elusive?'

He must have said it out loud.

'Did you hear me? I was telling you about your daughter.'

'Rosie,' he croaked. She wasn't making any sense. 'You're my daughter. I've always loved you.' Tears were pricking at his eyelids, though whether this was due to frustration or what had happened with Rosemary, he couldn't say.

'Oh, Dad . . .'

He couldn't say either precisely what had happened with Rosemary or where he'd gone wrong. Though he knew he had. But he was sure that, very recently, he had understood and tried to put it right. That was all he could do now, try to put it right. And he had the feeling that she'd been trying too. He could also say, for certain, that he'd always loved her. And it'd be true.

He felt her cool hand on his brow. So sweet, so calming. It'd be true.

The past, now, that was another thing. It revealed itself to him every day and every night with such clarity. Those pictures in his head, flickering behind his eyelids, sleeping or waking, there was less difference now. Technicolour. Pure cinema.

He was young then and bold. He was with Maya, watching her at night time when the moon was hanging low like a cradle in the sky and the night was so clear you could count the stars, every one. She let down her hair and unwound the jasmine flowers from its dark sleek coils, their perfume filling the air with the sweetness of honey, the intoxicating richness of opium. She slipped off her blouse and untied her *longyi*. She let it shimmer down to her ankles as she took his hand and stepped out of it, into his arms. His arms. He'd been a lucky man.

'You have a daughter.'

The day before his ship was due to sail, Lawrence ran into an old neighbour of Maya's father, an Indian businessman. He could hardly believe his luck. But was it too late?

'Did they get to India?' he asked him. 'Did they survive? Do you know?' He had always felt that she was alive. It was almost as if he could feel her there, by his shoulder, whispering sweet words of support and love.

The man gave him rather a shifty look. 'They never went to India,' he said.

'Oh?' Lawrence's heart sank. Was she dead then? 'Do you have news?' he whispered. His legs felt weak as if they could no longer support him.

'Last I saw of them, they were living just north of Maymyo,' the man said.

In the heat, Lawrence could feel himself losing focus. 'How long ago?' he asked.

The man frowned. 'Just before it all ended,' he said.

Before it all ended . . . Lawrence knew what he meant. Less than six months ago then, Maya had been well and living with her father just miles from Maymyo. His first feeling was one of relief. She was alive. It swept over him like a cooling shower, sheer joy. But . . . Why? Why hadn't she returned to Mandalay?

'Thanks,' he said gruffly and turned away.

His second thought was to cancel his passage, to travel back to Maymyo, go to the village and find her, have it out with her: why in God's name hadn't she come to meet him as they'd always planned? Wouldn't she want to see that he was still alive, if nothing else? His next thought was rather different. Clearly, she didn't want to. She no longer cared. The war could change people. He knew that better than most. And Maya? She wanted him to return to Britain. She had lost her love.

A sense of rejection and a burning anger, frustration, really, at the amount of time he had wasted here in Mandalay trying to find her when she was living tucked away just out of sight, took Lawrence on to the steamer and out of Burma on the ticket he had bought.

It was only on the long journey back to England staring into the depths of the endless churning ocean, that he had more time to reflect. Not turning up in Mandalay, not seeking him out to see that he was well and had survived the war, was completely out of character for the woman he loved. Even if her circumstances had changed, or her love had died, she would still have come to tell him. He remembered the chinthe, still in his pack. No. There was only one reason why she hadn't come, and that was because she hadn't trusted herself to come. He knew he was right. She had been trying to make it easy for him, he realised, thinking of what she had once said to him about promises. She had decided to let him go.

'You have a daughter.' The voice spoke again. Rosie.

'You're my daughter,' he whispered. Why couldn't she understand?

'Another daughter.' Her voice was more urgent now. 'Maya had your child. Many years ago. Her name is Cho Suu Kyi.'

Another child? Another daughter? Maya?

And a vision came to him of that same time just after the war when he'd left Rangoon and returned to Dorset. It hadn't happened, had it? But it could have. It was a vision of Maya, his baby daughter in her arms. And Maya was waving goodbye.

You have a daughter. Another daughter. These were the words that stayed with him, imprinted on his mind. He thought that now, he might remember those words forever.

CHAPTER 51

The following morning Klaus had arranged a rendezvous in a small backstreet café whose proprietor he knew and trusted and where they would have complete privacy. There were things they must discuss, Klaus had told them. It seemed that he had decided they didn't pose a threat to his investigation and that he could trust them. He needed their help too. He had asked Ramon to keep the crate in the factory for now, as it seemed the safest place, and they had repackaged and resealed it so that no one would suspect it had been tampered with. Within the next few days, he promised, everything would be resolved. He also guaranteed that the watch on the factory premises would continue.

Ramon had reluctantly agreed. As he said to Eva on the way back to her hotel, what else could they do? They had uncovered no more rubies, but they had to allow Klaus and his investigative team to follow the crate to its destination. And Eva knew only too well where that was. The Bristol Antiques Emporium. Her own company. It didn't bear thinking about.

'But how come Khan Li isn't still having the factory watched?' Eva asked Klaus after they'd ordered coffee from the female proprietor. It seemed unlikely that Li would let two of his precious rubies just sit in Ramon's warehouse without standing some sort of guard over them.

'I think I can explain that one.' Ramon leaned forwards. They were sitting at a round table on rickety chairs. In fact, the whole place was rickety and looked as if it could be blown down by the nearest ogre. But the floor was swept and the place seemed clean. 'According to my warehouse manager, nearly all the crates went out the day before yesterday. But that one was left behind. There was a small drama.' He smiled across at Eva. 'When Eva spotted one of the crates on the truck, and this provided an unintentional distraction. My manager decided that rather than tell Khan Li what had happened, he would keep quiet and simply send the final crate on later.'

Wai Yan wouldn't want to risk upsetting Li, Eva surmised. He wouldn't want to risk him carrying out that threat to tell his wife what he'd been up to. An indiscretion, Ramon had said. Eva wouldn't put it past Khan Li to have set a honey trap for the unsuspecting warehouse manager. And more fool him for walking into it.

'Following that distraction, it must have been easy to lose count of the crates being loaded into the truck,' Ramon continued. 'To assume they were all safely out and on their way and to cease the observation of the factory.'

'That must be it.' Klaus nodded.

He and Ramon seemed to have reached what Eva could only suppose was an uneasy truce. At least, to have accepted that they were both on the same side.

They paused in their conversation for a moment as the proprietor brought out three cups of milky coffee.

'For how long have you been watching my factory?' Ramon's eyes glittered, but his voice did not betray any emotion. Eva knew how hard it was for him to hear that his good name had been used in this way.

'For some weeks,' Klaus admitted. 'Our team has been watching their every move.' He shook his head. 'But I confess I did not expect the next move to be made by you, Eva.' He turned to her.

Eva shivered. She had been quite vulnerable there. It was a good thing that Klaus had turned out to be a friend and not an enemy.

'And you have still not explained to me how it is that you are involved,' he added.

Eva shrugged. 'It's a family affair.'

Klaus murmured something softly in German.

'What was that?' Eva asked.

'I said, perhaps not so much a family affair, as an affair of the heart.' He glanced knowingly at Ramon.

Eva flushed. But perhaps it was best that he thought that, for now.

'And you have suspected the Lis for some time?' Ramon asked, tactfully changing the subject. He took a sip of his coffee.

'Yes, we have. I am sure you know that Burmese rubies have been smuggled out illegally from your country for many years.'

'Of course.' Ramon nodded.

'At one time, ninety per cent of the entire trade was carried out illegally without regulation, now only fifteen per cent, I believe.'

'I did not know the figures were so high,' Ramon murmured. He glanced across at Eva. She too was somewhat taken aback.

'And naturally, the most precious and rare examples are much sought after in the German market.' Klaus pulled his coffee cup closer and eyed its milky depths with some suspicion.

'Are the ones in the tiger's eyes precious rubies?' Eva asked. They had certainly looked like it. Their colour was rich and full, almost blue-red, and they had a heat and a depth about them that reminded her of the rubies in the chinthe.

'I think they are Mogok rubies, yes,' Klaus said.

'How much are they worth?'

Eva wasn't fooled by the casual way in which Ramon put this question. The stones, after all, were still on his premises.

Klaus considered. 'It is hard to say without examining them more closely. But they are less than three carat, I am sure. Maybe thirty thousand US dollars each on the open market.'

Eva was stunned. She'd known they were lovely, but . . . She looked across at Ramon. He too seemed surprised, though less so. 'How do you know so much about rubies?' she asked Klaus.

'I have always had an interest in gemstones,' he said modestly. 'But for this case I have done much research. And . . .' He spread his hands. 'The more research I do, the more my interest, it grows.'

Eva nodded. 'And you can tell they are from Mogok just from the colour?' Mogok, Ramon had told her on the way back to her hotel in the car yesterday, was the city where most of the mining for Burmese rubies took place. They called it the Valley of Rubies. It was two hundred kilometres north of Mandalay, foreigners were rarely allowed in and the first rubies had been discovered there in the Stone Age. They had become more or less a royal monopoly, he had explained. All the best stones went to the crown, hence the Burmese chinthes with the famous Mogok ruby eyes that had been given to Suu Kyi back in 1885.

'From the colour, yes.' Klaus's expression grew dreamy. Not only did he know his subject, but he really loved his rubies, thought Eva. 'But also from the lustre and the tone. The best rubies even change colour according to the time of day, the weather, the location. They are very hybrid, very complex. And if the stone is natural there may be an inclusion, a blade of a crystal, a delicate shimmer of light. We call this the silk. It is, you might say, nature's own fingerprint.'

'But why would your client object to receiving such a magnificent stone?' Ramon asked. 'I'm surprised he wants to put a stop to it at all.'

Eva could see what he meant. And all the time there was a market, there would be illegal exportation.

'This way there is no regulation and also no export tax

to be paid by the seller.' Klaus took a sip of his coffee. 'We do not know the provenance of the stones, maybe they have been stolen and are worth much less, of course. More importantly for us, not all the rubies have proved to be of the same quality. My client has been, he thinks, taken for a ride, as the English might say.'

Ah. Khan Li must have got greedy and seriously underestimated his client, Eva thought. But of course there could be no come back if the stones had been illegally exported in the first place. She drank some of her own milky coffee, which she had grown used to during her trip. In fact she found it quite comforting with all this talk about jewels and thieves.

'But this is a crime against my country.' Ramon sat up straighter. He frowned. 'It is us who should be pursuing them. Not you.'

'Yes, of course.' Klaus picked up a teaspoon and stirred his coffee thoughtfully. 'And I told you we were working together. Though we must tread carefully in that regard.'

Ramon nodded. Eva guessed they were referring once again to corrupt officials. Myanmar had lived for so long under the yoke of a repressive military regime, the kind of regime where corruption and greed could flourish. The people wanted 'The Lady' Aung San Suu Chi and her democracy party to come into power and introduce changes and reform. But Eva suspected that true democracy would be a long time coming.

The proprietor of the little café brought over a small plate of shortbread biscuits and left them on the table with a nod and a smile. She had placed a curtain over the door to discourage customers; in effect it was a secret meeting.

'My team will be taking care of the men at the other end, in Germany.' Klaus helped himself to a biscuit. 'You may be sure of that. But we did not want them simply to be replaced by new contacts. We needed to track down the source.'

'And not only in Germany.' Eva sighed. She had been through this in her head over and over since she'd first seen the crate addressed to the Emporium. She thought back to that moment. At first she couldn't accept it, despite the overwhelming evidence. Then she'd concluded that her own company was involved in something she despised: the buying and marketing of fake antiques, of forgeries. But it hadn't made sense, even then. Here she was in Myanmar meeting their contacts, examining Asian artefacts, authenticating goods on their behalf. Why bother if those contacts were corrupt? If those artefacts were forgeries? And besides, she knew what the Emporium sold. Genuine antiques; anything that wasn't authentic was weeded out at an early stage and sold off to a second-hand furniture dealer. They had ethics, they had integrity. Or so she'd always assumed. So what was going on?

She'd known something wasn't right, if only from what had happened since she'd been out here. The edginess of her two contacts, the back-tracking from Myint Maw, his attitude when she had questioned the provenance. But this . . . Finding the rubies had changed the picture entirely. This was big, this was something completely beyond her experience. Because the Emporium was involved in illegally importing rubies from Myanmar. And they were about to be found out.

'At least two of the crates were being sent to my own company in the UK,' she told Klaus. 'I can still hardly believe it, but . . .' She didn't need to say more.

Klaus nodded. 'We have contacts in the UK too,' he said. 'I am sorry, Eva, but I must confess that when we first met . . .' He sighed. 'I had been informed that you were in Yangon. We knew that you worked for the British company that was under investigation. But we did not know in what capacity.'

She stared at him. 'You mean you engineered our meeting?'

He spread his hands. 'I had no choice. But I liked you immediately. I was sure you were not involved, you can be certain of that. I even tried to warn you, if you remember.'

About Khan Li and Ramon, that was certainly true. 'And when you saw me going into the warehouse last night?'

He nodded. 'I assumed I had been mistaken at that point. I assumed you were involved after all and that my judgement, it was unsound. You were looking very guilty.'

Eva remembered the surreptitious knocking on the warehouse door. How she had slipped inside. The fact that they hadn't even put on the lights . . .

'I thought you an excellent actress,' Klaus said. 'Until I saw what the two of you were doing. As you pointed out, why would you be breaking into your own property? I knew then that you two were innocent, that you had stumbled on the truth.'

'But what should I do now?' Eva asked. She could hardly

go back to Bristol and pretend that everything was fine when her boss was about to get arrested for gem smuggling. She didn't even want to contact Jacqui by email. But she was still working for her, she had promised to keep in contact and in two days' time she was going to Bagan to examine more pieces that were for sale. She would have to do something.

Klaus frowned. 'Do you know who is responsible?'

'Not really.' She shook her head. Then she remembered how resistant Leon had been to her examining the packaging of that shipment. Jacqui had never really confirmed that, had she? She remembered Jacqui's questions and how she'd repeatedly told her to take care. She remembered the row between Jacqui and Leon too, before she left for Myanmar. Was it possible that Leon hadn't wanted her to come here at all? That he realised she might find out what was going on? 'But I have an idea,' she said. She told him what she knew.

'I will take it from there,' said Klaus. 'Do not worry. By the time you return . . .'

He didn't have to finish the sentence. By the time she returned, she would be looking for another job. Whether Jacqui Dryden had known what was going on or not, the Bristol Antiques Emporium would be finished. 'I'll have to resign,' she said.

'But not until you return to the UK, please, Eva,' said Klaus. 'We do not want to risk alerting them, not at this stage.'

'Very well.'

Ramon put his hand on hers, sending a signal of silent

sympathy. 'And what happens next?' he asked. 'To Khan Li, I mean?'

'I do not want to frighten him off too soon,' Klaus said. 'I have been trying to get close to the man.'

Eva shuddered. 'Why?'

Klaus spread a napkin on the table and pulled a pen from his shirt pocket. He made a drawing.

'A spider's web?' said Eva.

'Indeed.' Klaus drew the spider right at the centre. 'The more you can find out about him, the more easily you can capture him and his entire world. So you tantalise him. With a fly perhaps.' He drew a fly on the outside of the web. 'And out he comes to investigate. Out of his safety zone, you see? And then . . .'

'You move in for the kill?' suggested Ramon.

'Exactly.' Klaus screwed up the napkin and tossed it to one side. 'I posed as a buyer. I had to prove I had the necessary finances, I had to give evidence of my credentials, they were very thorough.'

'Yes, they would be.' Eva recalled her own rather pathetic attempt to do a similar thing.

'And how close did you get?' Eva could see where Ramon's thoughts were heading.

'What do you mean?'

'For example . . .' Ramon was unable to keep the excitement from his voice. 'Did Khan Li ever invite you to his house?'

'Yes, of course.'

Eva and Ramon exchanged a swift, conspiratorial glance. A rich buyer. How could Khan Li not want to show it off to him? But Klaus wouldn't help them, would he?

Ramon leaned forwards. 'Have you seen the chinthe?' he whispered.

'The . . . ? Ah.' Klaus tapped his nose. 'Yes, I know the piece you mean. It is a beautiful item. Very old, very rare stones. Pigeon-blood rubies as they are known, not after the blood of the bird, but the colour of the whites of their eyes. That piece is a master, an absolute master. And of course . . .'

Eva could see his mind working out the link, the resemblance to what they had found in the crate.

'Yes, they showed it to me.' Klaus finished his coffee and pushed his cup aside. 'That kind of man will always want to display what he owns to the rest of the world, I think.'

'I agree.' Ramon fell silent.

'It is only a pity,' Klaus said, 'that it is not part of a pair.'

Eva and Ramon exchanged another complicit glance.

'But of course it is not for sale,' said Klaus. 'It is far too fine. The price . . . We are talking a great deal of money here. It is part of your national heritage that piece, I think?'

'Did you wonder where they had obtained it from?' Eva asked, shooting a glance at Ramon. He shrugged and nodded.

'Yes, I did,' Klaus admitted. He looked from one to the other of them. 'But I did not want him to become suspicious of my motives. And so I did not ask.'

'It's part of the long story I mentioned last night,' Eva told him. 'It's the reason I got involved in the first place.'

470

Klaus sat back in his chair. 'As I said before, I am listen-ing . . .'

'When I knew I was coming to Myanmar,' Eva began, 'I told my grandfather. He used to live here, you know. And he asked me to do something for him.' And between them, taking up the story when the other left off, Eva and Ramon related what had happened since the chinthes had first been given to Suu Kyi by Queen Supayalat at the time of the rout of the Royal Palace.

Klaus listened gravely, nodding from time to time. When Eva got to the bit about flying to Myanmar with the chinthe in her travel bag, he gaped at her in astonishment and then laughed so much he almost choked.

'It is so very interesting,' he said when they had finished. 'And naturally the pair – they should be together, as you say. But why are you telling me all this? How do you imagine I can help you?'

'Anyone who gets close enough to Khan Li to be shown that chinthe,' Eva said, leaning forwards, fixing Klaus with a gaze of entreaty, 'would be close enough to take it and return it to its rightful owner.'

Klaus laughed. 'Even if I could take it, Eva, and I might do it just to please you, you know'. He patted her hand. 'All hell would break loose. You would be in considerable danger. They might even stop you from leaving the country. And as for you . . .' He glanced at Ramon. 'Your family would never be safe.'

He was right, of course. The copy Ramon had made was of excellent quality. But was it good enough?

'You should tell the police.' Klaus addressed this to Ramon. 'You should perhaps have told them when the chinthe was originally stolen.'

Why hadn't they? Maya had insisted it was because she had no evidence of ever owning it, but Eva wondered. Had Khan Li or one of his associates got to one of Maya's household just as he had got to Ramon's warehouse manager? He had certainly found out somehow, where the chinthe was kept and that the family were not taking it with them to Maymyo.

'You know as I do, that would not work,' Ramon said. 'Men like Khan Li have too many contacts. And besides, we have no proof of ownership. It is our word against theirs.'

'Plus the fact that you now own the other chinthe once again,' Klaus said. 'But you are right about the police. They are idiots and usually in someone else's pay. What you need is a professional.'

'Like you,' said Eva.

Klaus shook his head. 'Do you not think they would notice their precious chinthe is missing?' He laughed. 'Though I would love to deprive them of it, for the personal satisfaction alone.'

Ramon pulled his bag towards him and took something out. Eva knew what it was. 'Can I trust you?' he asked Klaus.

'Of course.'

Ramon looked at Eva. They had gone so far. This might be their last chance. 'I think we can,' she said.

He nodded as if satisfied. 'I have a plan, Klaus,' he said. 'If you can go round there one more time before the family are exposed as the criminals they are . . .'

'Yes?' Klaus watched with interest. 'I think I can do that. They are waiting for me to make a decision about a certain gemstone I might buy.'

'Perfect. And when you go . . .' Ramon unwrapped the replica chinthe and handed it to Klaus. 'I want you to take this.'

He stared at it. 'But . . . ?'

Ramon leaned closer. 'It is not what you think,' he said. 'Please allow me to explain.'

CHAPTER 52

On today's walk round the lake at Mangerton Mill, Rosemary was on her mobile talking to Alec. It was almost, she thought, as if their previous conversation hadn't taken place. They skirted carefully around their danger zones, reverting to the politeness that had always served them well.

She had told him already about Eva's revelation. About Maya and that fact that she had a half-sister she'd never known about.

'That's amazing,' he said. 'How does that make you feel?'

Which was, she had to confess, getting a little bit close to that danger zone. 'Confused,' she admitted.

When she'd returned to Dorset less than two weeks ago, she had come because she needed to think about things, because she wanted to see her father, take stock. Rosemary looked around her at the smooth lake, the water ever so gently buffeted by the breeze, at the trees now a burnished copper and gold, the grass already cloaked with crumpled leaves. She'd never really admitted to herself why it was so necessary to come back here in order to think about these things and consider her future, but it was. Sixteen years ago she'd wanted nothing more than to escape from this landscape

that held her so firmly in the painful grip of the past. But now
. . . She seemed to need it in order to make sense of who she
was, what she needed, what she had to do. Was it her roots?
Her childhood? Her marriage to Nick? She didn't know. But
while she'd been here, the vice-like grip of the landscape in
which she'd grown up had relaxed into something that was
still holding, but was now comforting too. A place where she
felt grounded and complete. A sanctuary. She realised with a
dip of panic that she didn't want to leave.

'And your father?' Alec asked. 'How did he take it?'

Rosemary couldn't help smiling. 'He was confused too.
Actually, I'm not sure that he took it in, not properly. A
couple of weeks ago he must have felt that he didn't have any
daughters. And now he's got two.'

'He's still not quite himself then?'

'Not really.' Or perhaps he was himself. He was living far
more securely in the past than the present, telling her long,
rambling stories about his days in Burma, about Maya and the
war, about his family, Rosemary's family, and his obligations.
Perhaps he was more himself than he'd been for a long time.

'His mind's still wandering,' she said. 'But every so often
he comes back to me and the here and now and he grips my
hand – he's so strong still, it's astonishing – and I look into his
eyes, Alec and . . .' She felt the tears welling again. They were
never far from the surface these days.

'And?'

'And I know that somehow everything's alright between
us again.'

475

'I'm glad,' he said. 'Really glad for you.'

It was hard to believe, Rosemary thought, that so much had happened since she'd left Copenhagen. But what about Alec? She surveyed the leaves on the path in front of her. It hadn't rained in the last couple of days and as she stepped forwards they crunched under her suede ankle boots. The scent of autumn, crisp and fungal, was in the air, the spiders' webs, spun between blackberry bushes, glittered in the weak sunshine. 'And what's been happening with you?' she asked.

'You mean, have I said "yes" to Seattle.'

Rosemary left the path and ventured on to the grass, still damp from the morning dew. The moisture began to seep on to the suede of her boots, darkening the tan. 'I suppose that I do.' Seattle, she thought.

'If I said "yes" to Seattle . . .' He paused. 'Would you come with me?'

That was a big question. But was it the right question? On the other side of the lake was a man with a toddler. They had a plastic remote-controlled boat and the man was stepping down into the reeds to launch it. Rosemary thought of her own child, Eva, and she thought of her father. He might not be with them very long; she knew in her heart that he was fading fast. But Eva . . . Alec was her husband. But, 'I can't leave her again,' she said.

There was a heartbeat of silence between them.

'She's a grown woman, Rosemary. She's not a child anymore.'

'I know that.' The child on the other side of the lake clapped delightedly and, together, father and son followed the progress of the boat as it chugged determinedly out into the centre of the lake.

'And you have your own life to lead.' He hesitated. 'We have our life. Don't we?'

'Yes.'

She heard him sigh.

'But I can't leave her again.'

There was a pause. 'I understand.' Nevertheless, she heard the impasse in his voice. And that was the thing with Alec. He always had understood. He had understood her grief over Nick and so he had never challenged it, never made her feel that it was time to move on. If he had forced her to confront it, she sometimes thought. If he hadn't simply accepted her for what she was . . . So, what? Was she now criticising him for being too compliant, too kind, too understanding? That was hardly fair. And yet only when someone really challenged you, could you discover where you stood.

The little boat was on her side of the lake now, heading for a tangle of rushes. There was a brief flurry of rudder and leaves, and then it choked and came to a standstill. On the other side of the lake there was a commotion and she heard the little boy begin to wail.

Gingerly, Rosemary stepped down on to the little beachy bit of the lake which had a damp sandy bottom and a few tiny pebbles. If she went a little further and reached out . . .

Her leather-gloved hand came into contact with the stern of the boat, she gave it a little push. And it was freed. She stepped back. Looked down at her boots. Ah, well. Over on the other side the man waved a thank-you and the little boy gave a whoop of delight. And the boat chugged on back to home straits.

'Rosemary?' said Alec.

'I'm still here.' She had gone with him to Copenhagen. She had lived the life he wanted to live, she had taken the escape route he offered her. 'What do you want, Alec?' she asked him. 'Do you want to move to Seattle?' It sounded large and alien. But Copenhagen had seemed that way at first.

'It's the way forward,' he said. 'As far as the job's concerned. And they won't wait forever.'

But was it the way forward for them? 'The job isn't everything,' she murmured. There was family too. A family she was only just beginning to rediscover. Alec could stay where he was. Why did everything have to change?

'Things always change,' Alec said softly.

Rosemary realised she must have spoken aloud.

'The job isn't everything, no, but things always change. If you're strong, you can accept change, go with it, benefit from it.'

If you're strong, you can follow your heart, she thought.

'If we're strong,' he said.

Rosemary realised what he was saying. This was the time when he was going to push her, when he was no longer going to be kind, compliant, understanding. 'So you have to do it?' she asked. 'You'll go to Seattle?'

'It's such an opportunity,' he said. 'What reason do I have to say "no"?'

CHAPTER 53

It was Eva's last night in Mandalay. During the day, she had gone to view the archaeological finds in the Cultural Museum and had visited the famous Angkor Chinthe, which was as impressive as she'd hoped. She had also finally met up with Klaus's contact in Mandalay, though there seemed little point. If the Emporium were finished, it would no longer need any contacts in Myanmar, whether dubious or not. But the man was pleasant, seemed honest enough and she kept his contact details. *You never know,* she thought.

The night before, Ramon had taken her to Mandalay Hill at sunset and to one of the famous puppet shows. And now, she was leaving on the river-boat for Bagan tomorrow, to fulfil the terms of her contract for the Emporium and to see the famous temples on the plain of Bagan before she flew back to Yangon and the international airport from there. And so . . . This would be her last evening with Ramon.

She had been invited to have dinner with Ramon, Maya and Cho Suu Kyi, but before this, Ramon picked her up in the car and drove her to Amarapura, once the capital of Myanmar, but now almost part of Mandalay's urban sprawl.

'Look.' He stopped the car.

In front of them a procession of ponies was approaching, decorated with red and gold garlands, wild flowers wound in their manes. On top of every pony sat a young boy in a crown and silk robes, holding flowers and strings of golden bells. An adult attendant walked alongside each one, holding a parasol over each boy's head. 'What's happening?' But even as she asked, Eva knew what this was. She had seen versions in the temples of Mandalay and Yangon. It was *shin pyu*, the Buddhist equivalent of a first communion. After this ceremony the boys would live for a time as *phongyis* with shaven heads and saffron robes, begging for alms and studying the Buddhist scriptures.

'Shall we?' Ramon was getting out of the car and Eva followed suit.

Behind the ponies came a lorry crowded with people. In the centre of the open truck a young girl was dancing. Ramon held Eva's arm. 'This is a *Nat Pwe*,' he murmured, his voice soft in her ear. 'A Burmese dance-drama to celebrate the occasion of the *shin pyu*.'

Eva watched, intrigued. The girl was about ten years old and wore a *longyi* and an embroidered blouse of shimmering red and gold. And she moved fast as a flame; leaping, arching, flexing, twirling, her palms stretched back towards her wrists, her tiny feet in red satin slippers flicking up the hem of her *longyi*. Her ebony hair swung up and out and around like a curtain of silk and the red and gold fabric moved with her, flashing in the early evening sun, a streak of arcing movement, a tongue of fire. The girl's face glowed and her eyes were dense, lost in the drama of the dance. Until at last she paused, placed her palms together, head bowed and came to rest. It was enthralling.

They watched the small procession until it disappeared up the road behind them. 'Beautiful,' murmured Eva. She was glad that she had seen it, but the road seemed so quiet and empty now that the procession had gone. And she wondered if she would feel like that when she finally left this country. It had touched her grandfather with its magic and now, sixty-five years later, it had done the same to Eva.

They got back into the car. 'I am taking you to the famous U Bein Bridge,' Ramon told her, glancing across at her with a smile. 'The longest teak bridge in the world.'

Eva sat back, relaxed for once in his company. After all the drama of the last few days, it was good to be almost a real tourist for a change. Even though the shimmer of those rubies in the wooden tiger's eyes was never far from her mind. And whatever else they had done – and she was yet to discover the full extent of it – she knew that she couldn't forgive Jacqui and Leon for letting her come here, for putting her in such a potentially dangerous position and for allowing her to become involved.

'Who was U Bein?' she asked.

'The mayor of the time,' he said, accelerating smoothly. She knew they were close to the river now; in her heart she just felt it. 'He had it built with teak planking left over when the Royal Palace was moved to Mandalay.'

Everything, Eva thought, seemed to come back to the

Royal Palace sooner or later. It may have been moved and taken over and destroyed. But it still lived on. A bit like her grandfather's feelings for Maya, she couldn't help thinking.

And suddenly, there it was before them, the bridge stretched high over the wide river, the tall teak upright stilts reflected and glimmering in the surface of the Irrawaddy. The planking was strung loosely between the teak posts like a xylophone. More people were beginning to arrive, but at the moment there were just a few stragglers weaving across the bridge, and a group of monks, their saffron robes billowing gently in the breeze. It was quite a spectacle.

Ramon parked the car. 'Come,' he said.

And once again, she got out of the car and followed him.

At the bridge, they began to walk along the planking. Eva's steps were tentative at first; there were cracks in the wood and planks missing so you had to watch your footing. And the old wood had of course been repaired in places; with so many visitors, the work must be ongoing. It wasn't very wide and there wasn't much in the way of a handrail, the sides were mostly open. Eva stayed in the middle, trying to ignore the way the bridge undulated gently with the movement of people walking over it. It was a long way down to the River Irrawaddy.

'What do you think?' Ramon offered her his arm and she took it gratefully. He was dressed in a black *longyi* and shirt tonight, and he cut quite a dashing figure, his body moving with the gentle rhythm of the bridge, balanced and sure-footed.

'It's very special.' They paused and looked down into the rippling Irrawaddy, at the sampans helmed by men in conical bamboo hats, at the huge expanse of river and sky beyond. The clouds had built and the sun was sinking lower in the sky. Tomorrow, she would be on this river, Eva thought. Sailing towards Bagan.

'Have you heard from Klaus?' Eva asked Ramon. She had hoped that the matter of Maya's chinthes would have been resolved by now. Ramon had already told her that he'd had another meeting with Klaus in the back street café and that more information had changed hands. It looked as though Khan Li and his accomplices would be incarcerated for a long time once charges were brought, but Klaus was waiting, still gathering his final evidence. And once Khan Li was brought to justice, Eva had the feeling it might be even harder to get back the little chinthe. The family would close ranks. It would disappear, perhaps never to be seen again.

'Yes, I have heard from him.'

'And?'

'And he is having dinner with them tonight.'

Eva glanced across at him, at the inscrutable face she had become strangely accustomed to. They both knew what this meant. Ramon had given Klaus the replica chinthe. He would try to make the swap tonight. Eva shivered. The last supper, she thought. And it would be the same for her. Tomorrow, she'd be gone.

'You are cold?' He put a protective arm around her.

'No.' It was a warm evening with just a slight breeze.

But Eva was happy for him to leave his arm where it was. She wouldn't be enjoying the proximity of him for much longer.

There had been no further intimacy between them, no kisses, nothing to make her think that she meant anything more to him than a friend. And perhaps that was as it should be, because tomorrow she would be gone. And yet . . . With each day that passed, she seemed to grow closer to him.

They walked on in silence as the sun dipped lower and the trees on the little river islands became skeletal silhouettes. The sun was hazy now, half-hidden behind the clouds, sending a warm and gauzy glow on to the teak bridge and the water. Eva had experienced the sunset from the Shwedagon Pagoda in Yangon, from the road to Maymyo and, most spectacularly, two nights ago from the top of Mandalay Hill. But this, Ramon had promised her, would be the best. Saving the best for last, she thought.

'Will he tell us how he got on?' Eva asked. It would be wonderful to have some good news before she left, something she could tell her grandfather.

'I am sure he will,' said Ramon. 'If all goes well, there will be no further need for secrecy.'

Eva nodded. 'Good.' She was fortunate, she realised, that since her abortive attempt to lay a trap for Khan Li and since the ransacking of her hotel room, she had been left alone. Whatever happened now, it was up to Klaus. He had many more contacts, information and manpower at his disposal. But she liked to think that she had at least played a part.

She turned to Ramon. 'Who do you think found the first ruby in Mogok?'

He raised an eyebrow. 'They say it was an eagle.'

'An eagle?'

He smiled, warm and lazy. 'Long before the Buddha walked the earth, the north of Burma was inhabited only by wild animals and birds of prey,' he said.

'Yes?' And Eva moved in a little closer, their heads together as they walked along the rickety planking. How did he know she loved these sorts of stories?

'One day a huge, old eagle flew over the valley. On the hillside he saw a big piece of fresh red meat, bright and shining in the sun. He tried to swoop down to pick it up, but the meat was hard and he could not dig his talons into it. At last he understood: it was not meat at all, but a sacred stone, made of the fire and blood of the earth itself. The stone was the first ruby on earth and the valley was Mogok.'

'Is that true?' she asked him.

He shrugged. 'We do not question such stories,' he told her. 'We simply listen and we interpret.'

Another lesson to learn, thought Eva. The British had first colonised Burma, imagining that they could teach them so much, that they could bring progress in education, medicine, transport and material wealth. But as they imposed their will, their changes, their ways and their Imperial Rule on to these people . . . Had they ever stopped to think about what they could learn from the Burmese nation? Had they valued Burmese ways and Burmese culture – and not just for material gain? She thought that her grandfather had, she hoped that he had. He had, after all, fallen in love.

And what had she learnt? Eva thought of what Ramon had told her about Burmese culture and artefacts, the bitterness on his face as he had railed against those who had plundered Burmese wealth in the past and present. And she made a decision. She would not be responsible for taking any more Burmese artefacts away from the country, no matter how reliable the provenance. It was too easy to say that there would always be other antique dealers who would do the same. She was only responsible for own actions. She would go and see the temples, but, contract or no contract, she would not be buying anything for the Bristol Antiques Emporium in Bagan.

They stopped again, three quarters of the way across the bridge. The Irrawaddy had darkened now, the sky was suffused with red and indigo, the sun a ball of liquid fire sending a red torchlight streaming on to the water below. Despite the other people still on the bridge, there was a tranquillity about the setting that made Eva want to just stand there and absorb. She wanted to be able to remember this moment, this location, this exact and pure feeling, when she was far away. Ramon had been right. This was the best place to experience the Myanmar sunset. On the old teak bridge on the Irrawaddy river with this man by her side.

Ramon stroked Eva's hair from her face. 'This is an extraordinary place,' he whispered. 'Somewhere you might bring a lover.'

They were so close. Their arms and hips were touching, their faces only inches apart.

'You can bring them to the bridge to look down into the river,' he said.

Eva looked down. In places the water seemed deep and she couldn't see the bottom. In other parts, it was shallow and brackish with the little marshy islands that seemed to be used for duck farming. She watched the ducks waddling in a long line to form a group almost under the bridge.

'Or you can take them out in a boat,' he murmured, his voice hypnotic. 'It is the best view of the bridge, from the river.'

And she could see that this would be so. The U Bein was stark, rough and uneven. And yet the wooden bridge in its simplicity had blended into the natural landscape and become part of it, as it had indeed once been.

'And what about you?' Eva asked, stealing a glance across at him. All this talk about lovers, what exactly was he trying to tell her?

'Me?'

'What will you do?' When all this is over, she meant. When she had gone home.

He looked past her into the depths of the Irrawaddy. 'I will work at turning things around for my business,' he said. 'And I will continue pursuing my dream.'

His dream. The orange globe dipped towards the water, slowly sank into the horizon, washing the sky and the River Irrawaddy with its golden red flare.

His dream was to expand his family business, while keeping all its values intact. His dream was to travel, especially to the land of his father, and maybe even set up a business there in the UK. But dreams, well, they were just dreams, weren't they? You couldn't pin them down.

'But surely you must stay here and look after your grandmother,' Eva said. 'Won't she need you?' She knew that she was fishing.

He just turned to her. 'Perhaps,' he said.

Eva stared into the reddening sky. In a few weeks everything she had seen – every golden temple and saffron robed monk, every teak monastery, the *nat pwe*, even Myanmar itself, this river, this bridge, this man . . . Would those too all feel like a distant dream?

CHAPTER 54

For Eva's last supper, a feast of traditional Burmese food was served up by Cho Suu Kyi and Maya.

Ramon was quiet. Perhaps he, like Eva, was imagining Klaus, at dinner with Khan Li and his associates, maybe even at this precise moment performing the swap. He hadn't told them precisely how he intended to carry out the plan, but he had seemed quite confident.

'Leave it to the professionals,' he'd said as he'd left their clandestine meeting at the backstreet café. 'I assure you that I will do my very best.'

Under the table, Eva crossed her fingers. It was possible that tonight the two chinthes would be reunited and back with Maya where they belonged. If all went well . . .

'When you visit Bagan,' Maya was saying, as she forked more rice and fish curry with tomatoes on to Eva's plate. 'You must visit the Ananda Temple. It is a masterpiece of Mon architecture. There are four teak Buddhas there, each one facing a different direction. Two are originals.' She smiled, but Eva thought she was looking tired. 'It is my favourite temple in Bagan,' she added wistfully.

'And you must do a tour of the temples by horse and cart,' Cho Suu Kyi added. 'It is the only way.'

Eva looked across at Ramon. His eyes were sad. Was he remembering their visit to Inwa when they had taken a horse and cart together and visited the wooden monastery and the ruined temples? Or was he thinking of their imminent parting?

After dessert of fresh melon, papaya and a kind of sweet rice pudding, tea was poured according to the custom and they sat around chatting.

The knock at the door made Eva jump. Ramon glanced across at her, swiftly got to his feet and went to answer it. He returned with a package in a small box. 'For you, Grandmother.' He handed it to her, exchanged a complicit glance with Eva.

She wondered, could it be?

Eva watched Maya's face as she eased open the box.

'What is this?' she breathed. Slowly and carefully, she took it out. It was the other chinthe, the lost chinthe, the chinthe that was an exact twin of the one Eva had brought to Myanmar.

Eva beamed across at Ramon. 'He did it,' she whispered.

'Who did it?' Maya looked from one to the other of them. 'How can this be?'

'Never mind, Grandmother.' Ramon bent closer and murmured something softly to her in Burmese. 'Let us celebrate. A glass of our very best wine.'

'I will get it.' Cho Suu Kyi got to her feet. Eva knew that

although the women of the family kept to the Buddhist rule of no alcohol, they still kept wine in their house for Ramon and for visitors.

'I truly do not know what to say.' Maya was still staring at the chinthe. Her face was old and lined, but her eyes, in that moment, looked like a girl's. 'Can this really be him?' With her finger she stroked the carved mane, smoothed a fingertip over each of the magnificent ruby eyes. Even from where she sat, Eva could see their unmistakeable lustre and shine.

'It certainly can.' Ramon went to fetch the other chinthe from the shrine where he stood, now that the family had returned to Mandalay. He placed them side by side on the table.

'They are restored.' Maya's eyes filled with tears.

Eva and Ramon accepted a glass of sparkling white wine from Cho Suu Kyi and all four of them spent some time admiring the two rather extraordinary and special chinthes who, against the odds, had been reunited at last. Her grandfather would be so happy, thought Eva. If only he could be here now. It hadn't been easy and she'd needed a lot of help from Klaus and Ramon to succeed in her task. But they'd done it. She admired the rubies. They were quite breathtaking.

'Each ruby is perhaps twenty carat,' Ramon said casually.

'And they're from Mogok?' Eva asked. 'Pigeon-blood rubies?'

'Of course,' he said. 'They are from the Royal Jewel Box after all.' And his eyes gleamed.

492

'My grandmother told me that Queen Supayalat had an unrivalled collection of gems,' Maya added. 'As did the King.'

'Oh, yes.' Ramon laughed. 'Have you heard of the Nga Mauk ruby, Eva? It was named after the man who discovered it.'

She shook her head. 'No. What happened to it?'

'The story goes that at eighty carats, it was King Thibaw's prized jewel,' Ramon said. 'But it disappeared soon after the King and Queen's exile.'

'Who took it?' And Eva found herself wondering, first the chinthes and now this. How many other precious jewels had been looted from the palace or even lost and never returned?

'Opinion differs,' Ramon shrugged. 'Some say it was one of the Queen's maid-servants.' He smiled at his grandmother. 'Some say it was looted by one of the guards. And some . . .' He looked at Eva. 'Some say that it was stolen by the British colonel in charge of the exile and that it later turned up in Britain, in Queen Victoria's royal crown, no less.'

'Really?' Nothing would surprise Eva. Everyone seemed to have wanted something from the last Burmese King and Queen.

'The Nga Mauk is worth a small fortune,' said Ramon. 'And even these two little chinthes are—'

'Far too valuable for me to keep,' Maya said.

They all looked at her in surprise.

She nodded. 'They have not brought happiness, only bitterness and jealousy and parting.'

'Perhaps because of the manner in which they were first given,' suggested Ramon. 'It was a time of greed and betrayal.'

'You are right, Ramon.' She smiled. 'Through no fault of their own, they have caused pain. As it was in the original story. And so I have decided to give them on permanent loan to the National Museum,' she said. 'All the treasures of the Royal Palace – at least those that have been restored – are there. They will be safe and protected in its custody. And people may go to see them. They are an important part of our Burmese culture and heritage. It is where they belong.'

Ramon nodded. 'That is a good idea, Grandmother,' he said. And to Eva: 'Would your grandfather approve?'

'I think he would.' Eva smiled. 'But I also think you should write down the story of Suu Kyi and Queen Supayalat and the Chinthes with the Ruby Eyes. And I'll do an English version as well, if you like, before I leave. And then,' she said, 'everyone who sees them will know what really happened.'

Maya bowed her head. 'An excellent idea, Eva,' she said.

When the time came for Eva to leave, Ramon slipped out of the room for a moment, while she said goodnight and goodbye to Maya. It was surprisingly hard to leave this serene looking woman who had meant so much to her grandfather and still did. But she knew that Maya was tired and must rest. There had been a lot of excitement for one evening.

'I understand now,' Maya said, 'what was troubling Ramon. And I also understand how you have helped him.'

Eva blushed. 'Not really,' she said.

494

'And if there is ever anything you wish for . . .' She let the words hang.

'There is one more thing I'd like to know,' Eva admitted.

'Yes, Eva?'

'Why didn't you tell my grandfather about Cho Suu Kyi?' she asked. 'Why didn't you tell him that you – and he – had a child?'

CHAPTER 55

Why didn't she tell him that she had their child . . . ? It was a good question. Maya knew that both Eva and Lawrence deserved to hear the truth.

Upper Burma, 1944
Somehow – she hardly knew how – Maya remained with Annie at the hospital and they continued to nurse the sick, through the Japanese occupation and then the rest of the war. Maya could only hope that her aunt was safe, though she heard nothing. But she grew more and more worried over the whereabouts and health of her father. She had heard that some refugees were living in ramshackle huts made of palm leaves and bamboo in a small village near Maymyo, surviving from what they could forage, snare and grow, and she prayed that he was one of them and that he was safe. There was little freedom of movement, she could not go to him with a child to look after and she did not want to leave Annie. Together, they had managed to guard and protect Cho Suu Kyi from further Japanese curiosity and, in truth, Annie had been right: not all the soldiers were callous and cruel, others held them in some respect and it was this that kept them safe.

But one day she was given the chance to try and find him. There was a Japanese journalist with whom she and Annie had formed a good relationship after Annie had nursed him through a bout of malaria. He spoke fluent English, having been educated at mission schools in Japan and Canada and, more importantly, he was not one of those who believed in the Japanese conquest of the Far East. He was sympathetic and he was kind, even procuring rations of food for them when they were short. As a journalist, he enjoyed considerable freedom of movement. And he was on his way back to the headquarters for war correspondents, which was not far from Maymyo.

Before she left, there was something that Maya had to do. She returned to her aunt's old house and she dug up the little chinthe that she had buried there for safe-keeping near the red flowering *sein pan* tree. It took a while, she kept thinking that perhaps she was in the wrong place, but eventually she found it, still wrapped in the piece of fabric torn from her own dress in which she had buried it. The fabric was rotting and the dirt had got in but with a little polish from a rag, the chinthe's eyes gleamed as bright as they ever had. She could not leave without it. Who knew how long it would be before she could return? For now, she would take her chance and the chinthe would travel with her.

It took some persuading for Annie to join her. But everyone said it was becoming increasingly dangerous for a white woman to remain here in the village and since most of her patients no longer needed her and a Japanese hospital had been set up nearby, she finally agreed. Their Japanese friend provided them with the white armbands worn by reporters and settled them and Cho Suu Kyi on cushions in the back of the truck.

It was a long and uncomfortable journey along cratered and bumpy roads, but worst of all was the sight of so many refugees, some of them barely able to drag one foot after another, often diseased, all emaciated. And what were they heading for? Almost certain death, sooner or later. It nearly broke her heart.

It was July and unbearably hot in the truck. Maya's head was pounding, she felt dizzy and her eyes kept losing their focus. But every time she felt that she must surely pass out from the heat and the discomfort, Annie squeezed her hand and seemed to give her the strength to stay alert. And she must stay alert. Who knew when they might be stopped by the Japanese military or attacked by one of the gangs roaming the area? And she had her daughter to care for. At least they had some water, though Annie rationed it with care, ensuring that they all had enough to ease their sore throats and cracked lips.

The sight of Mandalay, when it came, almost finished her. The beautiful city was in ruins, almost totally devastated by bombings and explosions. The Palace of the Kings was full of Japanese soldiers. First British and then Japanese, she found herself thinking. Not since the time of her daughter's namesake had the palace belonged to Burma. The streets which had once been filled with noise and laughter, thronged with her people, with bullock carts, street sellers, craftsmen and monks in saffron robes begging for food and alms, were almost empty. There was an air of bleak desolation hanging over the city she had loved.

Maya was tempted to ask if they could drive to her old home, but she didn't dare. She wasn't sure she wanted to see it, because she knew what she would find. And they must press on to their destination. 'One day,' she breathed as they drove out of the city. 'One day I will return.'

After fourteen hours, they arrived at the village near Maymyo where they had decided to start their search. The refugees were living in ramshackle conditions, crowded, several families to a house, each of which had obviously been built from anything they could lay their hands that could provide shelter. And they were clearly starving. There was a sense of hopelessness in their dark eyes. They didn't know what to do and they didn't know where to go.

'Have you seen or heard of my father? His name is Sai Htee Saing.' Maya lost count of how many times she said these words.

Finally, a woman nodded. 'He was here,' she said. 'He moved on, to the next village, I think.'

Maya's heart soared. He was alive then! And off they went to the next village where conditions were only slightly better. More of the houses here had survived, but they had been abandoned, looted and were now housing families of refugees. 'Have you seen or heard of my father? His name is Sai Htee Saing.' The search went on.

'Does he play the piano?' an old woman asked her.

'Well, yes, but . . .' Maya was at a loss.

The woman pointed. 'The white bungalow at the end,' she said.

It was perhaps incongruous, considering his anti-British sympathies, that her father should be living in a colonial bungalow left by a British family who had simply locked the doors one day and left. But there he was.

Maya ran to him and at last in his arms she let herself weep. For he was thin and gaunt, but he was alive and she had found him.

'But who is this?' He was looking curiously at Annie, who was holding Cho Suu Kyi in her arms.

'This is my friend, Matron Annie,' said Maya.

'And her child?' her father added. 'How sweet she is.'

Cho Suu Kyi looked up at him and she beamed. It was clearly love at first sight.

Maya took her from Annie. 'My child,' she said. 'This is your granddaughter, Cho Suu Kyi.'

Maya and her father, Annie and Suu remained in the village until after the war ended. Annie's nursing skills soon came into play when people discovered her profession, and in turn this helped the little family to survive. Maya and Annie even took to using some of the old native remedies, taught to Maya by an old woman in the village, which meant foraging roots and herbs from the nearby jungle, some proving more effective than others. It wasn't easy, though, to get enough food.

The black market flourished, Japanese currency was almost worthless and they were increasingly dependent on gifts of eggs, rice or scrawny chickens from patients who often had nothing else left to give.

At first, Maya's father was wary of Annie. After all, she was British, and, having expected the Japanese to liberate the Burmese from British imperialism, here he was living with what must have seemed like one of the enemy. Only now though, was he realising that the second master of his beloved Burmese people was more cruel and much less forgiving than the first.

'But will her presence not inflame any Japanese soldiers who come into the village?' he asked Maya. 'We must put our own survival first, especially now that there is the little one to think of.'

Maya tried to persuade him that this wasn't the case, that in fact the Japanese had tended to treat Annie and Maya in exactly the same manner. 'And you have no idea, Father,' she added, 'how often Annie has put Suu and me first.'

What eventually changed his mind was Annie's generosity in treating anyone and everyone who needed her nursing skills, regardless of nationality or situation, and the way she had with Cho Suu Kyi, his granddaughter. That was what really made the difference, Maya thought.

And then news reached them that General Aung San, who had been made Commander-in-Chief of the Burmese National Independence Army, had changed allegiance, that he was no longer fighting with the Japanese and that he was supporting the British in driving back Japanese forces. He was not happy, it was said, with the Japanese treatment of Burmese soldiers, he had first responded to the Japanese in 1942 for the sake of Burmese independence, not to help Japan take control of his country. And had he also begun to doubt that Japan would win? Whatever the truth behind his decision, the British were gaining ground and the Japanese were staring defeat in the face.

'So be it,' Maya's father said, bowing his head.

Maya was aware that this news was another blow. They had received no word and believed her aunt, like so many others, had died as a refugee. And now this. Politically, her father had always supported the Nationalist Minority Group and General Aung San had certainly inspired some of his anti-British sympathies. 'Never mind, Father,' she said. 'It is for the best.'

'We will wait for Burmese independence,' he told her. 'That is all that matters. And it will come.'

And the end of the war would come, too. Rumours were rife that the British were advancing and would arrive soon. Let it be very soon, Maya prayed. Everyone was getting nervous, Burmese, British, Japanese alike. Air raids intensified as the British got closer and Maya began to worry that they might actually be killed, albeit accidentally, by their new liberators. But the air raids were concentrated on the railway, and their little village was spared. Soon Maya could almost smell it, the air of change. It was just a matter of time and once again, she started breathing his name with a new hope, that soon they would be reunited once more. *Lawrence* . . .

And then it really was over. A convoy of British and Ghurkhas arrived, a column of bullock-drawn carts led by two British officers on horseback. Maymyo had been taken and another force was heading for Mandalay. This convoy had broken away from the main platoon, travelling over little-known mountain tracks used by opium smugglers, catching the Japanese garrison to the east of their village unawares.

The people in the village were delirious with delight. 'We are free! We are free!'

Maya held her daughter close in her arms. And she prayed.

'Will you go back to Mandalay?' Maya's father asked her some weeks later. 'Will you try to find him? See if he is still alive?' It was the first time he had mentioned Lawrence since she and Annie had arrived here.

'I believe that he is,' she said. 'I feel it.' It was against the odds, she knew. But she did feel it, in her heart, and she was certain that the bond between them ran so deep that if he had perished, she would know. She looked up at the little decorative teak chinthe with the ruby eyes. Once again, he was guarding their Buddha in the shrine, once again he was on show, where he belonged. But what of his twin? Had he guarded Lawrence as well as she had hoped?

'It is unlikely.' Her father's expression was grave. 'And if he is still alive . . .'

'What, Father?'

He avoided her gaze. 'If he is still alive, he will have changed, my daughter,' he said. 'That is what war does. It changes everyone.'

Maya thought about this. Yes, he was right. War did change everyone. A man, or woman, could not witness a friend or comrade's pain and suffering, could not kill or maim, could not live in the conditions which Lawrence, as so many, must have lived, and not change. 'But that does not mean . . .' She faltered.

'That he no longer wants you? No, it does not mean that.' Her father reached out and patted her hand. 'Of course it does not mean that. Any man would want you.'

'And so how can what there is between us be wrong?' she asked. Her father had not said it was wrong. Indeed, he had never suggested it was wrong, even back in Mandalay before the war. 'Everyone has the right to do what she or he must do' had always been his watchword, the philosophy he lived by. He believed in individual independence as strongly as he believed in Burmese liberation.

'It is not wrong,' he said sadly. 'But you are from two different cultures, my daughter. Two different countries. And those countries have a relationship that has never been . . .' He hesitated. 'Equal.'

Maya digested this. She was aware, of course, that many British men had taken native Burmese women for their mistresses before the war. She and Lawrence had often discussed it. And she knew that those mistresses never dreamed that their lovers would stay with them, let alone marry them.

They were there to provide pleasure and comfort for their British masters who happened to be far from home. It was an accepted situation, by Burmese and British alike.

'But it is not like that for us,' Lawrence had told her, holding her close. 'For us, it is different, it is real. You know that, Maya, don't you?' And she had known it, she had told him she had known it. It disturbed her that her father hadn't known it too.

'It was not like that for us, Father,' she said, trying not to sound reproving. 'You know he loved me.'

'Yes, he loved you.' Her father left her side and wandered past the piano which had apparently been here when he moved in and which he still sometimes played, but not so often these days. He lightly ran his fingers over the keys, then walked slowly towards the window of the bungalow in which they still lived. Who would claim it now? Would someone simply return one day and tell them to go?

'Then why shouldn't we be together?' Maya asked.

He sighed. 'Because life and love is not just about two people whose worlds collide, my daughter,' he said. He stared out of the window, almost as if she were no longer in the room. 'It is about their backgrounds, their experiences, their cultures, too.' He tightened the knot of his *longyi* and straightened his back, as if he had come to a difficult decision. He turned to face her. 'It could never work between the two of you. For a short time, yes, your lives did collide. But now . . .'

Maya flinched. Was it over? Was it possible that Lawrence

no longer felt the same way about her? She too stared out of the window and into the distance, past the bright yellow flowers of the *ngu wah* tree in the garden outside, to the shacks and makeshift homesteads that had been built on the red earth by refugees. Her father had been lucky to find this place. He was still thin and gaunt and had a racking cough that worried her. But he was alive and now they were all safe at last.

She sighed. But was he right? Would their different cultures and backgrounds make it impossible for her and Lawrence to share a future? She could hear Annie at the other end of the bungalow talking to the baby in that sing-song way she had, her Scottish accent always able to sooth the child somehow. Was that all it had been between her and Lawrence? A collision?

'If it was just a collision,' she murmured. 'It was a very powerful one, Father.' Powerful enough to make her believe that they belonged, one to the other. She had always believed it, from the first moment they met. That belief had kept her strong throughout the war. At her lowest points, when she was in pain, terrified, or half-starving, at the time when she had killed a man, against everything she held dear, that belief had helped her through. 'I love him, Father,' she said. 'And I think that he will still love me.'

Her father turned from his stance by the window. 'If you love him enough, Maya,' he said, 'you will let him go.'

Maya let out a cry. 'I could not,' she whispered. She couldn't even think of it.

'It would be a sacrifice, yes.' Her father took a couple of

paces towards her. His dark eyes were fierce. 'But think not just of yourself,' he warned. 'Think of Lawrence. And think of his family too.'

'We are his family.' Maya was sobbing now. How could he be so cruel? 'Me and Cho Suu Kyi. We are his family.'

Her father came back to her side, cradled her in his arms as if she were a young girl again. 'You are Burmese,' he said. 'I am your family. But Lawrence has family back in England. Think of them. They have not even seen him for so many years.'

Maya could feel her tears wet on his shirt. Despite herself, she thought of Lawrence's mother. And then she thought of Helen.

'You told me there was someone else,' her father said. 'You can pull back the leg, but not the committed word.'

An old Burmese proverb. 'Yes.' She whispered the word. She had hardly dared think of her. Helen, whom Lawrence had been promised to. Helen, who was a white British woman and everything Maya was not. Helen, the woman everyone expected him to marry. And why not? Wasn't she from his world?

'Perhaps now that the war is over, if you are right and he has survived . . .' Her father let the words hang. 'You should allow him to return to her.'

Maya was silent. She had always told Lawrence that she wanted nothing from him, especially his promises. She looked up at the little chinthe standing in front of the shrine. But she had given him the other, to protect him from harm and return him to her arms. And she had believed they would be together.

Her father followed the direction of her gaze. He nodded. 'It takes a great deal of strength to turn your back on your past,' he said. 'On your family and your promises. On your country and your upbringing. To begin again in a strange land after you have lived through a war.'

'He could do it,' Maya shot back. She sat back on her heels. If Lawrence had lived through this war, he could do anything. And she would be by his side. She would help him.

'Yes, he could do it,' her father agreed. 'But would he thank you for it?'

Maya did not answer this. She did not know what to say.

'Or one day would he turn and look at you and think. *If not for her . . .*'

If not for her. Maya couldn't bear it. If he ever looked at her that way . . .

'He might be prepared to give up a great deal for you, my child.' Her father reached out and stroked her hair. 'His English life, his chance of promotion, perhaps even his career. But do you want him to? Do you expect him to?'

No, she did not. She never had. But she could not believe that now, after this terrible war, it would still be criticised or frowned on. To marry a native woman. If it was acceptable to bed one, why not acceptable to make her your wife?

A sound came from the kitchen. Maya got to her feet and straightened her *longyi*. 'There is our daughter,' she murmured. 'What of Suu? Does she not have the right to know her father? To live with him? To love him?'

'Yes, there is your daughter.' Her father drew away from her, his expression thoughtful. 'She is lucky to have escaped detection.'

'Detection?' But Maya knew what he was saying.

He turned back to her. 'She is neither one thing nor the other,' he muttered.

'And yet her features are more Burmese.' Fortunately for them all. Maya had continued to darken Suu's pale skin with a paste she made from bark and this had been sufficient for no one else to comment on her parentage. But in recent weeks Maya had let this practice slide. Could Cho Suu Kyi not now be who she was? Would she have to hide forever?

'Yes, that is true.' Her father frowned. 'But if it is known that she has a British father . . .'

What was that supposed to mean? 'Other children are of mixed race,' Maya began. Where there had been mistresses, there would be children. Would it really be such a disadvantage to Suu, having an English father?

'The British will have to leave Burma,' her father said. Once again he went over to the window. 'Their time is gone. What we need now is the freedom to rule our own country.'

She knew what he was thinking. Anything the British might have done for them was nothing; he believed that they had only ever done it for themselves. And perhaps this was true. The British would not want to lose a land with riches such as theirs.

'But it will not be easy.' He turned back to her. 'And it will not be easy for Suu. Trust me, my daughter. I cannot say how difficult her life will be.'

Maya thought about this conversation all evening and deep into the night. What she wanted more than anything was to be reunited with Lawrence, presuming that he was, as she fervently believed, still alive. She wanted it almost more than life itself. And yet . . .

In the early hours of the morning, she got up to look at her sleeping daughter. Would Lawrence think that she had trapped him? She could not bear that. What was best for Suu? What was best for Lawrence, the man she loved? What should she do, so that the two people she loved most in the world could be happy?

'So you didn't go back to Mandalay?' Eva asked.

'Not for six months.'

Eva raised an eyebrow. 'Six months?'

Maya smiled sadly. 'No man will wait forever, my dear,' she said. Six months might not seem very long, but it was what she had agreed with her father.

'If it is meant to be, it will survive six months,' he had said, when they had next discussed the matter. 'Stay here for six months. Think it over.'

It was perhaps the longest six months of her life.

'I thought it was for the best,' Maya told Eva.

Their eyes met. Maya didn't say more. This young girl, the

granddaughter of the man she'd never stopped loving, under-stood. She could see it. It was, perhaps, a sacrifice she should never have made. Only six months. But life went on.

In 1947, the entire Burmese Cabinet under Aung San had been assassinated and this was a blow her father hardly recovered from. Aung San had eventually secured Burmese independence from the British, but for what? Her father became faded and diminished, from politics as much as from his experiences in the war. As for Maya, she had met San Thein, her husband, and her life had been good enough. Not earth-shattering perhaps, but he had been a kind man, a hard-working man who had done his best for them all under the harsh regime that followed. It had all been so far from her father's hopes and aspirations, she thought sadly, and she almost thanked the Lord Buddha that he had not lived long enough to witness the worst of it.

And if she had ever wondered about Lawrence and what she had given up . . . Which she did. Oh, how she did. She could satisfy herself that she had done what she thought to be the right thing – for Lawrence and for Cho Suu Kyi.

CHAPTER 56

'Shall we have a last drink together before I take you back to your hotel?' Ramon murmured, as he and Eva finally left the house.

She turned to him, surprised. 'In a bar?' She had already stayed longer than she'd intended. But it had been worth it, to find out the truth.

'I was thinking of somewhere more private.' He raised an eyebrow, gestured towards his own apartment.

'Yes, let's.' Eva didn't even want to resist. It would at least put off the moment of parting. And she didn't want this evening to end.

She followed him inside.

But he walked right through the reception room and out of a door the other side on to a sheltered verandah with a bamboo roof. He held the door open for Eva.

She stepped through. Let out a small gasp. 'It's beautiful.'

The verandah was lit with a warm amber glow from two lanterns, one placed by the door and the other on a wooden table next to two cane deck chairs. Soft oriental music was playing and, as she looked up, Eva spotted the discreet speaker up in the corner on the wall. On the table was a bottle of champagne in an ice bucket with two glass flutes set beside it on a black and gold lacquer tray. Beside this, was a shallow ceramic bowl filled with water and floating hibiscus and jasmine flowers.

She turned to him. 'When did you do all this?'

'I took a moment to come out here earlier.'

Eva smiled. He'd certainly set the scene. She sat down on the chair he indicated. 'What a lovely idea,' she said. It was so very special. Did that mean that the time they'd spent together had meant as much to him as it had meant to her? She hoped so.

He shrugged. 'I wanted some time alone with you, Eva.'

'And why would you want that?' She watched his slender fingers as he loosened the cork in the bottle.

'Eva?' He stopped what he was doing and looked at her. 'Are you flirting with me?'

The cork popped, they both laughed and Eva quickly held up the two glasses for him to pour. 'Should I be?' she asked.

'Probably.'

They clinked glasses and he sat down in the chair next to her. 'To you and your grandfather,' he said.

'And to the chinthes.'

'Long may they live in the National Museum.' He smiled.

'Hear, hear.' At first, Eva had been surprised by Maya's decision, but now she realised that it made perfect sense. The family would no longer have to worry about owning something so valuable that might be stolen. And the chinthes could remain with all the other treasures from the Royal Palace, as part of Myanmar's history and heritage.

'Eva, when I first met you,' Ramon said, 'I may have been a bit unfriendly.'

'Just a bit.' She smiled back at him.

'The truth is that from the first moment I saw you standing there outside our house looking all earnest and asking to see my grandmother . . . I thought you were quite lovely.'

Eva felt a warm glow and it wasn't just from the champagne. 'You disguised it well,' she murmured, and took another sip. On top of the wine she'd already drunk this evening, it was going straight to her head. But it didn't matter. She was quite sure of what she wanted.

'But I also distrusted you,' he said. 'To suddenly appear in the way you did. And with the chinthe . . . It all seemed so unbelievable.'

'Yes.' She could see that. She watched as a huge dark moth fluttered around the orange glow of the lantern. The night outside was as still and the darkness as dense as she'd ever known it here in Myanmar. They were tucked away at the back of the building, with no houses in sight, no lights and no signs of civilisation. The fragrance of the flowers gently floating in the bowl wafted up to her, mingling with the dry citrus sparkle of the champagne.

'It seemed at first that you were only here to take from our country, our culture.'

Eva bowed her head.

'And then . . .' His voice tailed off.

She looked across at him. He seemed thoughtful. 'And then?'

'And then, when I realised who you were and what you were . . .'

Eva considered this. That she was the granddaughter of the Englishman Maya had loved? She supposed that was what he meant. That she was there to bring them their family's chinthe, to meet them and to listen to their stories, rather than ask for anything in return perhaps? Or did he mean something quite different?

'But it turned out by then that you distrusted me,' he said.

She nodded. Very true.

'And so we travelled full circle.'

'I suppose that we did.' Eva wasn't sure that she had ever felt such a sense of peace. She leant back in the cane recliner and closed her eyes. The oriental music played gently on as if it were caressing her senses. This might be her last magical experience in Myanmar, she thought. And she would make the most of it.

'Even so.' His tone changed. 'I have tried to resist you, Eva.'

And I you, she thought.

'Especially now, seeing you lying there in that chair looking like some sweet-faced angel.'

'Really?' Eva opened her eyes. She'd never been called an angel before.

He was staring at her, leaning forwards and looking very serious. The dark wing of his hair had flopped again over his

515

forehead and again she reached out to brush it back, just as she had once before.

He caught hold of her wrist. 'You are leaving my country very soon,' he said.

She nodded. 'Yes.'

'You live in the UK. You belong to a different world.'

She couldn't argue with that. Eva waited.

'And yet,' he said.

'And yet,' she whispered. She knew exactly what he was thinking. Hadn't she been thinking the same thing these past days?

'And yet I feel that I cannot let you leave without telling you.'

'Telling me what, Ramon?'

'That I have begun to care for you.' He brought her hand to his lips and kissed it, not taking his eyes from her face. 'And I cannot let you leave without knowing what it would feel like to touch you, to kiss you once more, to feel you so close to me that nothing remains between us. Nothing at all.'

'And I you,' she said simply.

Ramon got up from his chair and he held out his hand to help Eva to her feet. She stood there in front of him, very close, and she looked up at him, recognised the desire in his eyes.

'Eva.' He held her face cupped in his hands.

When he kissed her, it felt good and it felt right. It began as a gentle kiss but as she responded to him, she could feel his urgency and answered it wordlessly with her own. He smelt of wood and wax polish with that faint scent of cardamom and he tasted of champagne. His skin was smooth under her fingertips, his hair silky to the touch. His kisses became more demanding and their bodies cleaved together. Yes, she thought, she knew exactly what she wanted.

He led her into the adjoining bedroom and slowly, one by one, taking his time, he began to remove her clothes and she, his. He unbuttoned her blouse, she, his shirt. Their eyes met. She slid his shirt from his shoulders. Under the cotton fabric his chest was brown, muscular and almost hairless, his shoulders lean but strong. He unzipped her cotton skirt and she felt for the knot of his *longyi*. His hips jutted out and she ran her fingers gently over them and felt him shiver. He clutched her buttocks closer to him and then his hand was inside her bra, gently caressing her, the other hand unclasping the hook and eye. She nuzzled her lips into the softness of his neck, tracing the shape of his collar bone and he bent to kiss her bare shoulder.

'Ramon . . .' And then they were on the bed, pulling at the remainder of one another's clothes, passion overtaking them at last.

Later, much later, for the light of dawn was creeping through the window and Eva knew she must have slept, Ramon hiked himself up on one elbow. He stared down at her.

She looked at him, ran her fingertip along his collar bone, smiled lazily.

'There's so much I want to say to you, Eva,' he breathed.

She put her finger on his lips. 'Don't say it. Don't say a word.'

'Why not?' His green eyes seemed dark in the half-light. His hair was unruly, his lean brown body flexed and smooth.

'Because we may never see each other again, Ramon,' Eva forced herself to say. It had been a magical evening, but the night was over now. Soon it would be morning, reality would set in, and she would be gone.

'Do not say that,' he muttered.

'But it's true.' Dreamily she smoothed his hair from his eyes. 'You live in Myanmar and I live in the UK. And we both know that long-distance relationships never work.'

'But if we were determined for it to work . . .' he said.

She shook her head. It was sweet of him to say, but she had stayed here last night fully knowing that she would probably never see him again. She had stayed here last night because, like him, she had needed to feel him, love him, even if it was only to happen once. Only once, but she would never forget it, never forget his touch.

'I would like to say that one day . . .'

'Please don't,' she murmured.

'Don't what?'

'Don't encourage me to hope,' she said.

He stroked her hair, bent down and kissed her lightly on the lips. Now he tasted of night time, she thought. Night time and dreams. 'You are right. I cannot make any promises,' he said.

'I know,' she whispered.

*

An hour later, after they had dressed and showered, Ramon took her back to her hotel.

'I have something for you,' he said, as they drew up outside. 'A souvenir, to remember us by.'

'Oh.' Eva felt bad. She had nothing for him. She hadn't thought, hadn't expected . . . And she didn't need anything to remember them by.

'I made it myself.' He handed her a small intricately carved teak Buddha. 'It is not old.' He shrugged. 'But perhaps you will like it.'

'I love it.' Eva ran her fingertip over the carving. 'Thank you so much, Ramon.'

'Just remember,' he said gravely. 'He must always be the highest in the room.'

'Of course.' She smiled.

'And so . . .'

'No more goodbyes,' Eva said. In front of them, weaving down the road were two men on a scooter, a mattress held vertically between them. Only in Myanmar, she thought. 'Just kiss me once and then I'll walk away.'

'You won't look back?' he asked.

'I won't look back.'

How could she look back? That would mean Ramon would see her tears.

CHAPTER 57

Rosemary was giving her father a shave. 'Mustn't let your-self go,' she told him as she gently massaged the shaving foam into a lather over the grey stubble.

'You're right, love.' He sat up in bed, good as gold. The doctor was coming this afternoon, just to take a look at him. But Rosemary knew there was nothing any of them could do. The light was fading. Her job now was to make every-thing as comfortable as possible for him.

As she carefully manipulated the razor, Rosemary was aware of his gaze, fixed on her face. 'Alright, Dad?' she asked. He wasn't talking so much about Burma now. He wasn't talking about anything very much.

'Where's Alec?' he asked.

Rosemary was so surprised that she stopped shaving for a minute. 'Alec?' She rinsed the razor in the bowl on the bed-side table.

'Your husband.' He gave her a look.

She smiled, resumed the gentle strokes. 'He's still in Copen-hagen,' she said.

'Waiting for you to go back to him.'

'Don't talk,' she warned him. 'No, he's not really waiting. He knows why I'm here. He's happy for me to be here.' For the moment, she thought.

Her father gripped her wrist. Rosemary stopped what she was doing. Waited.

'Don't make him wait too long, Rosie,' he said.

'I won't.' She made her voice light. Little did he know. Alec wasn't waiting for her to return to Copenhagen. He was waiting for her to say yes to Seattle, to say yes to them. Which was, apparently, one and the same thing. *But not for me*, she thought. As she'd already realised. It was the wrong question. And both questions might need a different answer.

He relaxed his grip and she finished off. Put the razor in the bowl beside the bed to rinse it, took his blue flannel and gently wiped his face. It was perhaps the most intimate thing you could do for a man, shaving him. She still remembered when she was a girl, watching her father standing in front of the bathroom mirror, his face covered in shaving foam, sweeping the razor in confident strokes from neck to chin while she watched goggle-eyed, amazed he didn't cut himself to shreds. She remembered the scent of that shaving foam too, it was here now in the bed-room, sweet and soapy, with a hint of lemon.

'You love him, don't you?' her father wheezed.

Really, she could hardly believe it. These moments of lucidity might be few and far between, but when they came he could cut himself, he was so sharp. 'Course I do,' she said.

'Not like it was with Nick though, eh?' His eyes were actually twinkling.

She nudged him, patted his face dry with the towel. 'No, not like it was with Nick.'

'You put that man on a pedestal,' he said.

'Hardly.' Rosemary took the bowl into the bathroom and rinsed it out. She returned for the towel. He was still looking at her in that way. She sighed and sat down on the bed. 'What are you trying to say, Dad?'

He nodded. 'That you idealised his memory.' He got the words out with some difficulty. 'I know that's what you did. I did it myself with Maya.'

Rosemary wasn't having that. 'Nonsense,' she said sharply.

He closed his eyes. 'Ah, Rosie,' he said.

While he was sleeping, Rosemary thought about it. He'd written to Maya, hadn't he, though he'd never sent any of the letters. It was a connection that had helped him somehow.

She sat down at the kitchen table with a sheet of notepaper she'd found in the bureau.

My darling Nick,

she wrote.

If you are watching me, if you have ever watched me, you will know how much I miss you. You'll know what a terrible mess I made of things with Eva and with my father, too. And of course you'll know about Alec.

She paused. Shivered, despite the heat of the Aga.

I saw it — marrying him — as a way out of the life I had in Dorset without you. But it wasn't fair, was it? She sighed. *And neither was it a way out.*

My father told me earlier, in one of his more lucid moments, that I had romanticised your memory, idealised you. He did that too, with Maya, he said.

Rosemary thought about this for a moment. She had denied it instinctively; it had seemed like an attack. But it was true.

The truth is that our love was special, and so was his with Maya. She understood that now. *But it's over, Nick. It wasn't over when you died, but it's over now.*

Rosemary took a deep breath. This wasn't easy. But then it never was easy to let go. *I tried to pretend that it wasn't over, but I'm not going to pretend any longer. I loved you but now it's over and I want you to set me free.*

Rosemary read the letter through. It was what she wanted to say. But, 'I'm sorry, Nick.' She fetched a bowl and the box of matches, struck one and held the letter over the flame. It curled, caught alight and she dropped it into the bowl, watched it flare briefly and then turn to ashes.

When Mrs Briggs arrived, Rosemary went out, back to Burton Cliff. It was cold, but she parked at the end of the no-through road and sat on the bench at the top of the grassy cliff, looking down. She wrapped her warm cashmere scarf more closely around her neck. She was wearing her thick coat, cord jeans and walking boots. To one side, she could see the old hotel and the sandstone path leading down to Hive Bay, to the other, the cliff-top walkway that led through to Fresh-water. And the sea stretched calmly out towards the horizon, the tide gently rippling, gleaming grey-green in the limpid autumnal sun. She had come here twenty-six years ago to scatter Nick's ashes. And this was another sort of goodbye. There was a moment when you had to discharge the past. And move on.

It was time. Rosemary got up from the bench and walked closer to the cliff edge. A young couple were strolling along the path, hand in hand. He paused, pointed out to her the church tower in the distance, in the village, beyond the river. It was a walk Rosemary and Nick had done so often, strolling along the top of the high golden cliff, down to Freshwater where the river emerged from a bank of tiny pebbles that had formed an island before it flowed into the sea. Then over the stile and back along the river bank, past the bridge, along the lane with the allotments and what used to be the Dove Inn. Back through the field and up the hill to the cliff top. If Nick were anywhere watching over her, he was here.

'No one should be second best,' her father had said.

This had been their special place. She had never come here with Alec. She had excluded him, just as her father had unin-tentionally excluded her mother. She supposed it had been their way of trying to keep it special. But . . . She groped in her bag for the little tin with the elephants on. Elephants were for remembering. And she would never forget.

She opened the lid. 'Bye, Nick,' she murmured. 'See you.'

She tipped the tin. And the ashes of her letter fluttered in the breeze, on to the pathway, on to the sandstone cliff. Some, she hoped, would make it down to the ocean below. Rosemary stared out to sea, almost thought she could glimpse the shimmer of Nick's smile shifting gently with the tide.

She stood there for a moment, watching, then she groped in her bag for her mobile.

He answered on the third ring. 'Alec?'

'Rosemary? How are you?'

'Not so bad.' She held the phone closer. 'I just wanted to speak to you. I wanted to hear your voice.' Here, she thought. Here in this place.

'Where are you?' She thought she heard his voice catch. Had he been thinking of her? Had he been wondering what to do?

'On top of a cliff.' She smiled. 'Surrounded by fields and sheep and seagulls.'

'Lucky you.'

'Can you hear the gulls?' She held the phone up. 'And the sea?'

He laughed. 'Yes, I can.'

'I miss you, Alec,' she said.

'I miss you too.' She heard the emotion in his voice. And she realised how unusual it was for them both to say those kinds of words. Words of love.

'Are you alright, Rosemary? I mean, your father . . .'

'Still the same. And I'm fine.' At least, she thought, I will be.

'I have to decide by tomorrow,' he told her.

She remembered what he'd said. Had she given him any reason to say 'no'? 'I can't come back to Copenhagen, Alec,' she said. 'I know this will be hard for you to hear. But I need to stay in Dorset, at least for a while.'

'For Eva?' His voice sounded very bleak. Rosemary knew she was hurting him. Sometimes it seemed that was all she had ever done. And yet she'd never wanted to.

'For Eva and for my father,' she said. 'But also for me.' The words tumbled from her in a rush. 'When I married you, when I came to Copenhagen, I was running away, Alec. Away from what had happened here and what the place meant to me. But running away from my emotions too. I thought I had to escape. I thought the most important thing in my life was self-preservation.'

'But it wasn't?'

'No, it wasn't.' Rosemary took a deep breath. 'The most important thing in my life was love.'

For a moment he was silent. 'So you regret marrying me?' His voice was thin. He sounded an awfully long way away. Rosemary knew she had to be honest with him, but she also had to get it right.

'Never.'

'Never?'

'I still don't.'

'And love?' He sounded sad.

'I love this place.' Rosemary opened her arms as if she

could hug it close to her. The sandstone cliffs, the pebbles of Chesil Beach, the cold and grey English Channel. 'I love my daughter and I love my father. And I love you.'

'So you've decided not to come to Seattle then, Rosemary?' His words cut through her like a winter wind.

But . . . Honesty. 'I'm sorry, Alec,' she said. 'But I can't.'

When she ended the call, Rosemary realised she was crying. Big fat tears rolling down her cheeks. She didn't reach for a tissue or wipe them away. She just let them come. She didn't know if she was crying for Nick or for her father or for Alec. It didn't matter. She just needed the release. She had to let it go.

CHAPTER 58

Eva was surprised to see her mother waiting for her at Arrivals. She'd emailed and asked her to organise a taxi; she knew the last thing she'd feel like doing after a long flight was travelling by train all the way from Heathrow to Dorset. But there she was, smiling, looking . . . Different, she thought.

'Eva.'

'Hello, Mother.' They kissed a little awkwardly. Eva was wary. Her mother had been so warm when they'd spoken on the phone. But it had been a while since they'd been face to face.

'How was your flight?' Rosemary's smile was encouraging and seemed genuine enough.

'Fine. How's Grandpa?'

'Not good,' she said. Her expression changed. 'I'm afraid to say that he's deteriorated a lot since you left.'

Eva's shoulders sagged. Just as she'd thought.

Rosemary patted her arm. 'Come on then, darling.' She took Eva's case and headed towards the exit and the car park. 'You'll see him soon. He'll be so happy you're back. You will come to the house before you go back to Bristol?'

'Of course.' Bristol. Eva wasn't looking forward to Bristol. 'Is Grandpa . . . ?'

'You'll see for yourself.' She turned around. 'But I should warn you, darling. He keeps slipping in and out of consciousness. Sometimes he's quite lucid . . .' She paused, and put her arm on Eva's. 'But other times, to be honest, we're not sure how much he hears, how aware he really is.' Her eyes filled.

'Oh, Ma.' Eva thought of how he'd been not much more than a month ago when she'd told him she was going to Burma. Frail, yes, but definitely still with all his faculties intact. *Slipping in and out of consciousness?* Shouldn't he be in hospital then? Shouldn't someone be doing something more for him? She looked helplessly at her mother, who was paying their car parking ticket at the machine.

She tucked the ticket into her bag. 'The doctor says he's comfortable.' And Eva saw her swallow back her tears. 'He's doing all he can for him. And he's in the best place, at home.'

'Good.' Then her mother's arm was around her shoulders. She hadn't felt that for a long time.

'We must be strong,' she whispered. 'We mustn't let him see.'

'Yes.' Eva nodded. 'I'm sorry. You're right.'

'Come on, darling.' Her mother's voice became brisk as she took hold of the case and again led the way towards the lift of the car park. Eva noticed as she followed her that her blonde hair was longer and less neat. That was new too.

'You said "*we're* not sure" how much he hears?' she asked, hurrying to catch up with her. 'Is Alec over here too?'

Something flickered over her mother's blue eyes. Her expression changed. 'I meant Ida Briggs and the doctor. Both of them have been marvellous.' She shook her head. 'No, Alec's not here. Just me.' She pressed the button and they waited for the lift.

'And . . . Ma?' She had to know.

'Yes?'

'Did you tell Grandpa? About Cho Suu Kyi?' This revelation had become, in its way, the most important part of the journey she'd made. The lift arrived and they both got in.

'Yes, I told him.' There was a silence as the lift winged them up to the second level of the short stay car park. The door opened and their eyes met, briefly, before Eva's mother scanned the level for the car. 'There it is.' She hurried over and unlocked it. Presumably it was one she'd hired for her stay here, Eva thought, since her grandfather no longer owned a car.

She followed her over. 'And what did he say?'

'Not much,' Rosemary told her. 'But he seemed to take it in. Finally.'

Her mother had opened the boot and Eva helped her heave in the case. Telling him couldn't have been easy for her, Eva thought. But there had been no other way. And it looked as if her worst fears had been realised. Now might have been too late.

But if her mother was upset, then she hid it well as she bundled Eva's hand luggage in with the case and shut the boot with a decisive clunk.

Eva slipped into the passenger seat. She was glad her mother had come to pick her up. It felt good to sit back and let her take over. But it wasn't just that of course.

Her mother started up the engine and put the car into gear. She turned to her. 'You'd better prepare yourself, Eva, darling,' she said. 'We think he's slipping away.'

Slipping away . . . Her grandfather had always been her rock. She didn't want him to slip away. Couldn't bear the thought of losing him.

Rosemary drove out of the airport terminal. It was drab, grey and industrial but they were still on the perimeter of the airport and Eva could see another plane landing, more passengers returning on a long-haul flight back to the UK. Even after just a few weeks away, everything here looked alien and strange. There was no colour, no red earth or vibrant flowers, no market stalls or street sellers. And it was so cold. Her mother had turned up the heating in the car, but Eva still had the shivers. She thought of those last days in Bagan, exploring the temples on the grand plain with an ever increasing sense of loneliness. She didn't want to think of her last night with Ramon. And she didn't want to think about her grandfather slipping away.

'Thank you, Ma,' she said.

'For what?'

'For telling him. For picking me up from the airport. For being here.'

Rosemary turned to her and smiled and Eva noticed her crimson-painted fingernails, her jewellery: gold, expensive, under-stated. Her jacket was gorgeous too, the softest of brown leather and her sweater was cream cashmere, which she wore with chocolate coloured trousers. Smart, thought Eva. But almost jarring to the senses after the simple white cotton blouses and embroidered *longyis* of Myanmar. After the poverty. They'd led such a different life, hadn't they, these two half-sisters? If it weren't for the unmistakeable resemblance between them, it would be hard to believe they were related.

'That's OK,' her mother said. 'It was my pleasure.'

Eva sneaked another glance at her. 'It must have been a shock for you too,' she ventured. 'Hearing about Cho Suu Kyi, I mean.'

'It certainly was. All these years thinking I was an only child . . .' But her mother didn't seem to want to say more. She glanced at Eva and then away.

'So tell me about your trip,' she said encouragingly as she took the motorway. 'That's if you feel like talking. But there's plenty of time. Rest if you want to rest.' She smiled.

Softer, thought Eva. That's what she was. Easier. For once in her life, she felt she didn't have to be walking on eggshells around her. After her father's death for as far back as she could remember, her mother had been so tense that Eva was afraid if she hugged her, she might snap. So she hadn't hugged her. She supposed she had responded to the vibe, kept her distance, confided in her grandfather rather than her mother. But what about the times before that? When she and her mother had cuddled and were close, when her mother had read Eva those bedtime stories about lions in the meadow and foxes in the fields in her low, sing-song voice, her laughter bubbling like fizzy lemonade? When her father had been working late and they'd stayed up to watch TV together, when her mother let her help bake gingerbread men. She hadn't forgotten those times. She'd thought of them on the way to Burma, on the flight, images of her childhood had fluttered like story-flags through her mind.

Once she started talking, it was hard to stop. Eva told her mother about her Myanmar impressions, the people she'd met, and even about Maya, though she didn't dwell on how much time she had spent with her; there was no point in rubbing salt into the wound. And then she told her about the rubies, the stolen chinthe and how Klaus had eventually got it back.

'My God, Eva,' Rosemary muttered under her breath as they eventually came off the motorway and headed towards West Dorset. 'I can't believe all this happened in less than four weeks. Are you alright, darling? It all sounds very dangerous.' She turned to look at her, her blue eyes full of concern.

'You sound just like Ramon.' Eva swallowed. She missed him already. He had phoned her at her hotel in Yangon before she flew back, but it had been a difficult conversation. She was leaving Myanmar and he was staying. What more was there to say?

'Ah, yes.' Rosemary raised her perfectly plucked eyebrows. 'Ramon. He seems to have had quite an effect on you.'

'He did.' Eva thought of the little carved Buddha in her

cabin bag. And she had a sense of déjà vu. She stared out of the window. Although the roads were clear, there was still snow on the hills.

'And?'

'And nothing.' Eva wasn't sure she wanted to be having this conversation. 'I'm British. He's Burmese. Well, half-Burmese anyway. We live in different worlds. There is no "and".'

'But there might have been?'

Eva shrugged. 'Maybe.' He had said he'd keep in touch. But she didn't know whether they would. Sometimes to keep in touch was even harder.

Her mother reached out and patted her hand. It was clearly an unconscious gesture and yet to Eva it was so unusual that it took her a moment to register it. 'If it's meant to be . . .' Rosemary said.

Eva stared at her. Wasn't that exactly what Cho Suu Kyi had said about seeing her father? *If it is meant to be*. And since when had her mother become so philosophical?

On both sides of the road now, the Dorset countryside stretched out around them as if it might enfold Eva in its arms. Green hills and lush valleys, the triangle of the distant ocean. The sky was still grey, but, as Eva watched, a shaft of feeble wintry sunshine peered through the clouds. Eva smiled. Another creature entirely from the sapping sun of Myanmar. She turned to her mother. 'And how about you?' she asked.

'Me?' Rosemary kept her eyes on the road.

'Yes. You seem pretty laid-back about my visit to Myanmar, all of a sudden. But I know you've always hated the place.'

'That's true.'

And now that she'd been there, Eva thought she understood why. 'So what's changed?' she asked.

'Let's say that while I've been looking after your Grandpa, I've had an awful lot of time to think,' she said.

'Oh yes?' Eva waited for her to elaborate. What had she been thinking about? The past? The present? The knowledge that she had a half-sister?

Rosemary glanced across at her. 'You and I have got a lot of catching up to do, darling,' she said. 'But there's plenty of time for that, too.'

Which sounded as if she intended to stay for a while. Eva relaxed into the passenger seat. But not plenty of time for her grandfather, by the sound of it. And so she willed the remaining miles to disappear. She wouldn't be going back to Bristol, not yet. She was going back to Dorset. Because she needed to see him now. She needed to get home.

CHAPTER 59

It was evening. Rosemary had lit the fire and they'd moved her grandfather into the lounge on the settee so that he could lie and look into the flames as they talked.

The doctor had been in earlier, and although he hadn't been so good when Eva first arrived, her grandfather had seemed to rally this evening. At last he seemed able to talk to her, able to listen to what she had to say.

She knelt beside him on a cushion on the floor, her mother sitting opposite in the floral armchair with the antimacassars Eva's grandmother had always insisted on.

'Well now, Eva, my dear.' He spoke softly, his pale blue eyes fixed on her face. 'How was she?'

Eva glanced up at her mother but she just smiled in a way that told her it was alright. Whatever her own feelings, she must have decided to put them aside, for her father's sake. 'She's very well.' Given her age. But Eva decided not to tell him how tired Maya had looked that last night in Mandalay. Tired but still peaceful, she thought.

'Ah.' He nodded as if this was the news he'd been waiting for. 'And was she pleased when you gave her the chinthe?'

'Pleased, yes. And very surprised.' Again, Eva glanced at

her mother. Before they went into the house they'd agreed not to tell him all the details. It might be too much to know that his granddaughter had been breaking into shipment crates and trying to inveigle her way into the homes of criminals, not to mention getting involving with illegal antiques and stolen rubies.

'Good, good.' He stared into the flames as if mesmerised.

'And I showed her the photos I took with me,' Eva added. She could see now why Maya had seemed so interested in that photograph of Rosemary. She'd been comparing Lawrence's daughter with his other daughter, she'd noticed that family resemblance right away.

'Did you take many photos while you were out there?' her mother asked.

Eva sat back on her heels. She'd already put them on to her laptop. 'Would you like to see?'

'Of course,' said Rosemary.

Her grandfather blinked at her and nodded.

She went to get her laptop and located the file, setting it up so that all three of them had a clear view. The first pictures were of Yangon, then Maymyo and then the orchids and Kandawgyi gardens.

'And who's this?' asked Rosemary. The picture was of Ramon. It caught him half in reverie as he examined a particularly stunning purple orchid, half indignant that he was being photographed unawares.

'Ramon.' The picture brought the memory of that afternoon back sharply into her mind. 'Maya's grandson,' she told her grandfather. 'He showed me around Maymyo and Mandalay.'

Her grandfather frowned and nodded. 'Ramon,' he said, as if committing the name to memory.

When she got to the picture of Maya, looking sweet and serene and white-haired, standing outside the house in Maymyo – the house that her grandfather had visited all those years ago – he caught his breath. 'She's hardly changed,' he murmured. And his head sank back onto the cushions.

Eva and her mother exchanged a small smile.

'She says hello,' Eva told him. 'And she asked me to give you her love.'

He nodded, as if he already knew, as if he already had her love. 'Did she have a good life?' he asked. 'Was she happy?'

'Yes, she did. She was.' That had certainly been Eva's understanding. And she recalled that this was what Maya too had wanted to know, *had he been happy? Had he been loved?* Maya might have regretted her decision, but if so she showed no sign. She had shown only acceptance; she had made the best of it. 'She married a good man,' Eva told her grandfather. 'And they had a lovely daughter.'

'And my daughter?' His voice was faint. 'My other daughter?'

So he had understood. Over in the armchair, Eva was conscious of her mother's silent presence. 'I have a picture of her,' she said. She clicked on it and her face filled the screen. 'Cho Suu Kyi,' she said.

Her grandfather and her mother stared at the image in

silence for a few moments. At last her grandfather nodded. 'She looks very fine,' he said. 'She looks . . .'

'Serene,' Eva's mother supplied.

'She is.' Eva looked appraisingly at her mother. 'And don't you think she looks a little like you, Mother?' she asked.

'Oh, she does,' her grandfather said firmly.

'A little.' A small smile played around her mother's lips.

'Maya wanted to tell you about her, Grandpa.' Eva willed him to understand. 'And she never wanted to lose you. But . . .'

He nodded. 'She thought it best to let me go,' he said.

Exactly. He knew the woman. Perhaps he had never doubted her. Eva moved on to the next photograph of Maya and Cho Suu Kyi together. 'Maya's husband brought Suu up as his own,' she told them. 'He looked after them both very well.'

'I'm glad.' Her grandfather reached out and squeezed Eva's hand. 'I'm glad they had a good life. As I did,' he added. He gave Eva a look. *Be patient with your mother*, it seemed to say, *try to understand.*

She did understand. And her mother too, Eva thought, was doing her best to understand. She moved on to the next pictures of the Royal Palace and other sights of Mandalay. There was the gaudily painted horse and cart which had carried she and Ramon around Inwa, the golden pagodas of Sagaing Hill and the glorious Mahamuni, covered in knobbly gold leaf by all his followers; a visual reminder of her entire journey. 'And the chinthes,' she said. 'Reunited at last.'

539

'Ah.' Her grandfather leaned closer.

They stared back at the camera lens with dignity, heads proud, eyes glittering. 'And here they are in the National Museum in Yangon.' Because Eva had taken another photo of them when she visited the museum the day before she left Myanmar. They were already installed beside an information board which told the story, in Burmese and English, of how Queen Supayalat had given them to her loyal maidservant Suu Kyi in thanks for looking after the princesses and how they had now been given on permanent loan as a precious relic of Burmese culture. Beside them, was an old photograph of the King and Queen, the pair of chinthes unmistakeable, each one on an arm of Supayalat's throne. You couldn't, Eva thought, get a more reliable authentication than that.

Lawrence peered at the photo more closely. 'They look very grand,' he commented. 'And in a museum too.' He chuckled. 'Who would have thought it, eh? When one of them's been in the jungle and even to Dorset and back.'

Eva caught her mother's eye. She shrugged.

Eva leaned closer. 'The eyes of the chinthes are rare Mogok rubies, Grandpa,' she whispered.

He stared at her, then back at the laptop screen, then into the flames of the fire. 'Rubies?' he breathed. 'She gave me rubies?' He laughed, his chest heaving in an effort to get breath, but the laughter turned to a wheeze and then a cough. 'Rubies,' he muttered. He glanced at Eva. 'You know I've always admired an adventurous spirit, my darling,' he said.

'But I do hope you were careful.' And, once again, his eyes seemed to glaze over.

Rosemary got to her feet. 'Time for bed, Dad, I think,' she said. 'All this excitement. It's exhausting.'

Eva helped her support him and they got him into the bathroom and then to bed.

When Eva leaned over to kiss him goodnight, he gripped her hand. 'Did you like it, my darling?' he asked her. 'Did you like the old country?'

Eva smiled. 'I loved it, Grandpa. It was just as you always told me.'

He nodded, as if satisfied. 'And have you thought?' he asked her. 'About what you'll do next?'

Eva was surprised. She hadn't said anything. But it was almost as if he knew. 'I think so.' She hadn't quite thought it through, not yet. But she had a good idea. First thing tomorrow she was going to write her letter of resignation. And, in the circumstances, she hoped they would allow her to leave with immediate effect. But she was going to talk to Jacqui too, she'd decided. She would phone her tomorrow.

'I'm pleased to hear that.' He patted her hand. 'And he seems like a nice enough boy,' he said. 'Maya's grandson and my granddaughter. Well, I never . . .'

Eva smiled. He'd only seen a few photos of Ramon, but he'd still picked up on it, the old rascal. Her mother needn't worry. Grandpa was as sharp as he'd ever been.

He nodded. 'You'll come into some money soon, my dear,'

he whispered, his voice drifting. 'Think carefully about what you want to do with it.'

'Oh, Grandpa.' She didn't want to think about that at all, because of what it would mean.

'And thank you.' His eyes fluttered open and then closed. 'Thank you for taking Maya's chinthe back to Burma for me.'

'That was about the longest period of lucidity he's had since I got here,' Eva's mother said as they sat back in the lounge together, Eva on the settee this time. 'As if he were saving it up for your return.'

'Maybe he was.' She wouldn't be surprised.

'And what else was in the National Museum, darling?' her mother asked. 'It sounds a remarkable collection.'

'Yes, it was.' Despite being incomplete. Eva stared into the fire. The logs, burning orange, sparks flaring with red flames reminded her of the treasures she'd seen there. 'Gilded furniture studded with jewels,' she said dreamily. 'The Queen's couch — gold filigree with jade; the King's day bed — gold filigree with diamonds; a carpet woven of strips of silver.' She took a deep breath, remembering. 'Jewelled caskets decorated with elephants' heads. Royal costumes and state attire.' Their wide sleeves were threaded with gold lace, the body petalled with tiny bells and stiff with sequined rubies, the lapels embroidered with images of the peacock and the hare. 'Golden goblets, pitchers and salvers and betel boxes on dragon stands.'

Rosemary laughed, in her voice a note of wonder.

But Eva wasn't finished yet. 'Lacquered incense jars. Silver spittoons, swords and scabbards. A jewel-encrusted saddle, a hand mirror bordered with gemstones. Rings and bracelets and necklaces of silver, gold and jade, of diamonds and deep red rubies.' She smiled. 'The riches of Mandalay.'

'All taken from the Royal Palace,' murmured her mother. 'By the British, the Japanese, the Chinese, and by the Burmese themselves by the sound of it.'

'Yes.' Incomparable riches, in terms of precious metals and gems. How could a country that was so rich, also be so poor? Some of those riches, at least, had now been returned. But those weren't the only kind of riches the country owned, thought Eva, despite the poverty of many of its people. It also owned something even more precious. It owned riches of the heart.

In the morning, Rosemary knocked lightly on Eva's door and came in with a cup of tea. She sat on the edge of the bed and Eva knew.

'He's worse?' she asked.

'You'd better come in,' her mother replied.

Eva got up, put on her dressing gown and went into her grandfather's room to say goodbye.

CHAPTER 60

After her father's funeral, there was a reception back at the house, but one by one his friends and neighbours went home and just Rosemary, Eva and Alec were left.

'Thanks for coming,' Rosemary said to Alec. They were carrying bowls, plates and glasses from the living room back to the kitchen where Eva was clearing up and stacking the dishwasher. He had only arrived last night and they hadn't really had a chance to talk. Rosemary didn't know what he was going to do. She only knew that she was grateful for the support today. Her father's death had hit her harder than she ever would have expected.

'I'm your husband,' Alec said. 'Of course I'd come.'

Rosemary put glasses on a tray and took them into the kitchen. But what about Seattle? What about his ambition and his job? She returned to the living room and began stacking tea plates.

'Thank goodness you came back here when you did,' Alec said. He came closer, gently rested his hand on her arm.

'Yes.' She had made her peace with him, she had said goodbye, she had even come to comprehend the difficulty of the decisions he'd had to make, the pressure he'd been under and the effort of making a go of his life here in the UK with her mother. And the fact that he'd always loved her.

Alec's hand moved to her shoulder. Rosemary looked up at him. 'Put those plates down a minute,' he said.

She did as he asked. Turned to face him. What next? What would he tell her? She knew that she could manage alone, if she had to. She had made the decision, and she wouldn't go back on it.

He held her face in his hands. Looked straight into her eyes. 'Did you mean what you said the other day on the phone? When you said that you missed me? When you said that you loved me?'

'Of course I did.' Rosemary tried to smile but she wasn't sure that the right muscles were working. No doubt it was a very lopsided affair.

'I hoped so,' said Alec. He seemed to be searching her face for a clue.

Rosemary tried to give it to him, as much and as honestly as she was able. And surprisingly, she seemed more able than she'd expected. *How could you mend a marriage that had never been perfect?* You could start again, that's how.

'So I did some asking around.'

'Asking around?'

'To see what was available over here in the South West.'

'A job?' She was trying to take it in.

'A job.' He pulled a face. 'I'm not quite ready to retire yet, you know.'

'Me neither,' said Rosemary. She had already started

looking. She didn't want to be dependent on Alec, she had to do something for herself. Some sort of secretarial work perhaps, even working in the right kind of shop. She craved the personal contact. In Copenhagen, she'd been lonely, she realised.

Then it struck her what he was telling her. 'You'd come and live back here?' she said. 'To be with me?'

'I would.' He seemed very sure all of a sudden. 'You're my wife, after all.' His brown eyes twinkled behind his glasses.

'But what about Seattle?'

'Do I really need another challenge at my age? That's what I've been asking myself. And besides . . .' He pulled her closer.

'Besides?'

'You gave me enough reason to say "no",' he said.

Later, Rosemary and Eva went out together to scatter Lawrence's ashes in the garden he loved. 'In the spring, I think we should plant him a magnolia tree,' Eva said. 'In his memory.' And she squeezed her mother's arm.

'Yes, let's do that.' Rosemary turned to her and they shared a complicit smile.

Winter had now arrived in earnest and the lawn was still crisp with frost. The pond had iced over too and their breath warmed the air in gasps of steam as they made their way to the bench. Two weeks had passed since the morning he'd died, after his burst of energy following Eva's return. And Rosemary could understand, now, how he'd summoned up those final reserves in order to find out what he'd been waiting for, to listen to what Eva had to tell him: that the chinthe had been returned to where it belonged; that Maya was well and had been happy; that she had never stopped loving him and had given birth to their daughter. It was like that sometimes. And when he was ready to go . . . He had gone.

In those two weeks, Rosemary and Eva between them had dealt with the awful administrative aftermath of death, which was the last thing you felt able to cope with when you'd lost a loved one.

'Where do you think?' Eva asked. In her hand was the urn containing his ashes.

More ashes, thought Rosemary. Another goodbye.

They had decided on the garden because he had loved it and lived here most of his life. From here, by the bench, he could see the raspberry canes he'd planted when he and Helen were first married, the crazy paving path he'd laid for Rosemary to run along when she was a little girl, and the pond where he'd grown purple irises and a sunshine-yellow waterlily.

Rosemary had brought a spade. She stuck it into the ground but it was rock-hard and resistant. 'Maybe we should have waited till the spring,' she said ruefully, resting her arms on the handle.

'Let me have a go.' Eva passed her the urn and took over.

In less than two weeks it would be Christmas. 'Will you spend Christmas here, with me?' Rosemary asked Eva, watching her daughter as she pressed in the blade, dug in with her heel, levered up a few miserable grains of earth and frost.

Alec wanted to go straight back to Copenhagen and start making arrangements for their move.

'I'd like to spend Christmas here – with Eva,' she had told him. 'I'll come back to Copenhagen for New Year. Will you join us – just for a day or two?'

'I'll do my best,' he said. 'But we've got plenty more times ahead, you and I.' He tilted her chin and dropped a light kiss on her lips. 'You're right. It's more important that you stay and keep Eva company. She needs you. You need each other.'

And Rosemary didn't have to be told just how lucky she was. To have him. To have this second chance, with Alec and with Eva.

Eva stopped her digging and turned to her, surprised. 'Of course I will.'

'Good.'

They both looked down at the ground. 'We're not getting very far,' Rosemary said wistfully.

'Tell you what . . .' Eva picked up the urn and took the lid off. She looked at Rosemary. She nodded. Eva up-ended it and scattered the ashes randomly into the winter air. 'To freedom,' she said.

'To freedom.'

They stood for a few minutes in silent contemplation, both saying their farewells in their own way. It was a good end to a life, Rosemary thought. To be free.

'Are you going back to Bristol, darling?' she asked Eva as they made their way towards the house. She rubbed her gloved hands together to keep warm. She knew that Eva had left the Emporium. She'd only returned once to her flat to collect some things which she'd brought back in her old red-and-black Citroen, since then she'd stayed at the house. But Rosemary didn't know her daughter's long-term plans. She just knew that in these two short weeks, they'd grown an awful lot closer. It would take time. You couldn't undo years of growing more distant in a fortnight. But it was a start. A good start. She wondered if her father was watching, if he knew.

'Only to pack.'

Goodness. She and Alec both. Rosemary felt a jump of panic.

'I've given notice to the landlord,' Eva told her. 'I'm moving out.' She opened the shed door and replaced the spade on the hook just inside.

'But where will you go?' Rosemary heard the jaggedy gallop of her own breathing. Not to Burma? Was it all going to be for nothing? Was Eva leaving, just as Rosemary was coming home?

'I'm going to make my life back here in Dorset,' Eva said. She shut the shed door with a clunk and replaced the padlock. 'I love it here.' She turned around, waved her arms to encompass this little part of it. 'There's nowhere else I'd rather be. It's where I belong.'

Rosemary felt the rush of relief. 'So you'll stay here?' Her father had left Eva the house as well as a good deal of money.

Rosemary had her share too, but her father had known Eva needed it more.

'I'm not sure. For a while, yes.' Eva turned to look at her. 'What about you, Ma?' Her tone was non-committal, but Rosemary wasn't fooled.

'We'll look for a place not too far from here,' she said. She led the way back into the house. 'By the sea. And we might go away on a trip somewhere.'

'A trip?' Eva looked curious. She shut the back door behind them and began to pull off her boots.

'Mmm.' In her leather bag Rosemary had Cho Suu Kyi's email address, set up and sent on to Eva by Ramon so that she could keep in touch with her English family. Rosemary was planning to write to her half-sister.

'She's always felt as if she were abandoned,' Eva had told her.

Much more abandoned than Rosemary had ever been.

And so, yes, she would write to her. She would tell her that their father had tried his best and that he'd been a good man. She would tell her that although he'd been unable to meet his other daughter, she would like to. If that would be alright.

Rosemary had tried all her life, especially after finding those letters, to shake off the thought of Burma and her father's time there, a world she had felt excluded from. But through Cho Suu Kyi, she was no longer excluded. She was linked to it, as was Eva. It was a part of her, because it had been a part of her father and she no longer wanted to pretend otherwise.

'Thanks for coming back, Ma.' Eva squeezed her arm.

Rosemary squeezed back. She was determined not to lose her daughter again and this time it was for keeps.

CHAPTER 61

Eva was in the process of restoring an Art Deco dressing table to its former glory. She had bought it from a dealer in the local market. Usually she only bought privately or at auction, but this piece had tempted her. It was a warm June day and she had flung open the double doors of her workshop-cum-studio to welcome the spring sunshine.

The dressing table was colonial in style and it reminded her somehow of Myanmar and her journey there. Much had changed in the six months since her return. Eva knew that her decision to live here in Dorset, her conviction that this was where she belonged, was due in part to what she had learnt on that journey. As was her decision to set up her own antiques restoration business. She missed Leanne and a few other friends, but she had contacts here too, it was where she'd grown up after all. And it was a good place for her new venture; the local antiques and vintage market attracted customers from all over the country and abroad and the area was developing quite a reputation for quality antiques at fair prices. As for furniture restoration, it was what she had always wanted to do and what she'd been trained for, but it was her grandfather's legacy which had enabled her to put it into practice, by buying a large unit which would house her workspace, selling space and a small office and where she could be her own boss. She was lucky, she knew that. She had managed to recapture her dream – the dream that had inspired her to do her degree, the dream that had the scent of teak wood and the history of past lives as its beginning and its end. She was following in her grandfather's footsteps. And she was moving towards, she hoped, that elusive sense of peace.

She already had a small staff of two, a couple, Kim and Jon, who helped out with the buying and the transporting and looked after the place when Eva was away. But like Ramon, back in Mandalay, Eva enjoyed being hands-on. Imaginative restoration of a piece of history was what she enjoyed the best. She had learnt the skills at uni: hand-finishing furniture, veneering and marquetry restoration; the conservation of upholstery and textiles. And now she was putting them into practice. The business, Gatsby's, was still in its infancy, but, like a proud parent, Eva was nurturing it every step of the way.

Last night she had gone round to her mother's for supper. She and Alec had bought a small cottage in Burton, the place her mother had always loved. The conversation had turned to Burma. Much to Eva's surprise, her mother and Cho Suu Kyi were now emailing one another regularly, and her mother and Alec had a trip to Mandalay planned for November.

'Have you heard from Suu lately?' Eva asked as they sat relaxing in the small sitting room.

'About a week or so ago, darling.'

'And did she say anything? About anyone?'

'Only that they were all well.' Her mother shot her a look. 'Have you heard from Ramon?'

'He emails occasionally.' Eva shrugged. 'But I don't encourage it. And I think he's more or less given up.' The last message had been three weeks ago. Three weeks and one day, to be precise. She had finally answered it last week, but she hadn't told him very much. *I'm fine. Working hard. Busy life . . .* That sort of thing.

'Why don't you encourage it?' Rosemary frowned.

Eva would have thought it was obvious. Her mother was sipping red wine and looked more contented than she'd ever seen her. She had grown out her neat blonde bob and wore her hair loose and free. She still looked stylish and elegant but was more likely, these days, to be found in a waxed jacket than a tailored one and green waterproof boots rather than calf leather and heels. She worked part-time in a local solicitor's, but she also kept chickens and was growing organic veg in their rambling cottage garden.

It was late and Alec had already gone to bed, pleading an early works meeting the following morning, hence this conversation á deux. 'He'll never be able to retire,' Rosemary had said as he went, a note of laughter in her voice. 'There's always some new project. I'll have to drag him away kicking and screaming.' But Alec had only laughed back at her and rumpled her hair. Things between them, Eva could see, had changed.

'I don't see the point,' she said, elaborating, since her

mother had raised an eyebrow and was clearly waiting for her to continue. 'We should both be free to get on with our own lives.' And she was getting on with her own life. Work kept her busy; it wasn't easy to set up a new business and take the step of becoming self-employed.

Eva had emailed Ramon to tell him of her grandfather's death. He could decide, she thought, whether or not to tell Maya. And he had a written a note of sympathy back. A week or so later, he had emailed to tell her that Khan Li and his corrupt associates had been arrested and would be charged. *I thought you would like to know*, he wrote. *His business is to be wound up*, he added. *It has been exposed as a discredit to Myanmar.* The way would be clear for reputable companies, like Ramon's, to trade legitimately with the rest of the world and progress, Eva thought, without unfair competition. And she was glad for him. He dealt in new furniture, she in old, but their values had always been the same.

It had been a strangely formal email, cool and distant, so maybe he felt the same way as she did. Eva wasn't sure she could deal with that sort of formal communication with him, as if they had never been lovers at all. He had big plans for his business, he wrote. As always. Big plans, thought Eva, but plans that didn't include her. Hadn't he said that because of his father he had a yearning for all things British? So why not include a fling with an English girl? She still had the little Buddha he had made for her; she would keep it forever. But as she'd told him before, a long-distance, email relationship was never going to work.

She had heard from Klaus too, that things had been taken care of on the European side. They had intercepted the crates and by the time Eva had tendered her resignation, he had passed on all relevant information about the Bristol Antiques Emporium to the authorities. Eva's phone conversation with Jacqui soon after her grandfather's death had not been an easy one.

'You know what's happened, I suppose?' she had said. 'I presume that's why you're leaving.'

'I'd rather not say,' Eva told her. The last thing she wanted was to get drawn into this sort of discussion. 'But I wanted to let you know. If not face to face because of my grandfather's death . . .'

'I understand.' And there was an empathy in Jacqui's voice that she didn't think she'd heard there before. 'And I apologise, Eva,' she said. 'I had no idea of the extent of what was going on. I knew there was something. But by the time my suspicions grew . . .' She sighed. 'I would never have wanted to put you in danger.'

Eva believed her. Whether or not Leon had initiated a relationship with Jacqui Dryden because she owned the Emporium was not Eva's concern. But Jacqui had been an honest antique dealer, of that she was sure.

These things will go on, Klaus wrote. *All we can do is continue the fight, Eva.* Less than a month later her friend Leanne had sent her a newspaper cutting reporting that the Emporium had closed down. And Leanne had done a bit more digging. Apparently Leon had been charged with handling stolen goods and illegal importing. And Jacqui . . . Eva did not know what had happened to Jacqui. She only hoped that she'd been able to start again.

But Eva, too, was continuing the fight in her own small way, for the future. She'd already formed GADA, the Genuine Antique Dealers Association, to support ethical trading in antiques, to create professional standards and to encourage dealers to buy and sell only genuine and authenticated pieces. This way, if they bought through dealers who belonged to the association, consumers could be sure, or as sure as possible, what they were getting for their money, with some sort of guarantee of authenticity, and with all available information provided about source, age, provenance and collection history.

Genuine dealers had already begun to show interest in GADA and Leanne, who had a background in marketing, was helping her spread the word. Hopefully, this would discourage outfits like Khan Li's from trying to fob off their fake Buddhas and chinthes and from being able to sell them on as genuine artefacts of Burmese history. Whether it was misrepresentation or just plain forgery, such activities would be considered illegal, as was the theft of any object which could be considered part of a country's heritage and cultural history. As far as Eva was concerned, GADA would strongly condemn any such action and would support law enforcement to forbid and eradicate it from the antiques trade.

Ramon and his passion for ethical standards and practice had started her on this pathway, she realised. And it had been reinforced by her other experiences in Myanmar. Eva wanted to bring the integrity and sense of history back into antiques. She wanted it to be a creditable and respected profession once again. She couldn't do it single-handedly, but as time went on, the more people in the business who supported her ideals and joined her association, the more chance she would have of making it a reality. But this didn't mean she no longer dealt with Asian artefacts. In fact the contact she'd made through Klaus did sometimes purchase antiques for her and she could always be sure of the provenance.

She thought of the replica chinthe Ramon had made out of his recycled ancient teak. That was a forgery too, of course. But she didn't feel it was hypocritical. Sometimes, the end justified the means.

'It was a healing journey, the one you made to Myanmar,' her mother said thoughtfully.

'Yes, you're right.' Though Eva hadn't fully realised it at the time. It had been healing for her grandfather, who could now be at peace; for Eva, who had finally seen for herself the Burma of all those childhood stories; for Maya, who'd had her family legacy returned to her. And for Rosemary, who had found the strength to understand, forgive and let go.

Eva thought of the way her mother had held her the morning after her grandfather had died. Her mother. It had been a healing journey for the two of them too, because Eva was getting close to finding her again. And there was no one else, she thought, who could hold her quite that way.

*

In the workshop, Eva glanced up as a man entered, a cap pulled down over his head.

'Morning,' she called.

'Morning,' he replied.

She let him browse. Eva loved the fact that people wanted to look around the studio, watch the repairs in progress, run their hands over furniture lovingly restored and polished and hopefully sometimes wanted to buy. Her prices were competitive, the pieces were hand-picked and everything was restored after considerable research and with meticulous attention to detail.

'I have something to sell.' The voice cut into her reverie.

She looked up, but couldn't see him. 'Oh yes?' For a moment, she felt a jolt of fear, but that was ridiculous. This was a lovely June day, it was broad daylight and they were in a studio in the middle of town. She wasn't in Myanmar now.

'What is it?' Though Eva didn't generally make purchases from people who came into the shop. The best pieces, she had to say, were somewhat more elusive and hard to find.

'A pair of chinthes.'

She gasped.

He stepped out of the shadows, came towards her, almost unrecognisable because of the hat.

Eva got to her feet, her polishing cloth still in her hand.

As he drew closer, she saw that he looked much the same, though more anglicised in that hat, black jeans and a leather jacket. He leant on the desk which she used as a counter.

Raised a dark eyebrow. 'They have very nice carving,' he said. 'And ruby eyes.'

'Ramon,' she breathed.

'But why didn't you tell me you were coming over to the UK?' she asked him half an hour later when they were sitting in her office, a cafetière of coffee between them. She couldn't stop staring at him, she was still getting over the shock.

'I wanted to surprise you.' He smiled.

'You did that alright.' She poured the coffee. Her hands were shaking and she hoped he wouldn't notice. 'How on earth did you find out my address?'

'Easy.' He shrugged. 'You are Eva Gatsby and you come from this town in West Dorset, is that correct?'

'Of course. But—'

'I Googled "Gatsby" and a website came up. *Gatsby's Antique Restoration.* Is this someone else, I ask myself. Or is this Eva? What are the chances?'

She laughed. 'I suppose it was pretty obvious.' She passed him his coffee. 'But why are you here, Ramon?'

He took off the hat and laid it on the desk next to his coffee cup. 'I told you I had big plans.' He shot her a reproachful look.

'The plans being . . . ?'

'To set up a sister company in Europe,' he said. 'I will keep the business in Mandalay. But I want to expand. Maybe even trade worldwide.'

'As your father wanted to do,' she murmured.

'Exactly.' His green eyes shone. He picked up the photo of her father on the bench in the garden, which she kept on the desk, alongside the one of Eva and her mother making a daisy chain, taken at the same time by her grandfather. 'Your father?' he asked.

Eva nodded. Everyone said they looked alike, not just in colouring but in her features too.

'Same dimples.' Ramon ran his fingers over the picture.

Eva tried not to blush.

'And your mother?' He picked up the other photo.

'Yes. My father was watching us make a daisy chain.' She shrugged. The photographs might not mean a lot to anyone else, but to her they represented the family past that she had lost. And they were special, because they too were a pair.

Ramon stared at them for a long time.

'And will you come and go between the two business premises?' Eva tried to make her voice casual. 'Between Europe and Mandalay?' She was trying not to analyse it. But what did this visit mean exactly? He hadn't said a word to make her think that anything had changed. And did she even want to hope? Seeing him here in Dorset, in her own workshop, just as she had once been in his, she wasn't sure what she felt. Perhaps she was still in shock.

'I will have overall responsibility of the two, yes,' he said.

'And how is your grandmother, Maya?' Eva asked. But she knew the answer almost as soon as she spoke.

His expression changed. 'It was only a few days ago.'

'I'm sorry,' she murmured.

'She rests,' he said simply. He bowed his head. 'She rests in peace.'

'Like Grandpa.' Maybe they were even resting together.

They looked at one another and then away.

'More coffee?'

He nodded and she poured.

'So, where will you—?'

'I wanted to—'

They both spoke at the same moment, both laughed uncertainly.

'You first,' she said.

'I wanted to write to you, Eva.' He reached out and took her hand. 'But there was too much to say.'

She nodded. Was this his way of trying to tell her it had all been a mistake?

'I told you once that I could promise you nothing.'

She nodded again, trying to smile, but feeling miserable inside. 'And I told you I didn't want your promises,' she reminded him. Just like Maya hadn't wanted Lawrence's promises. But that didn't mean . . .

'What were you going to say?' he asked gently.

'I was going to ask you where in Europe you were planning to set up your business,' she said brightly. Though it was an effort.

'Here,' he said.

'In Britain, you mean?'

'Here in Dorset,' he said. 'As close to you as possible. If that is OK.'

She stared at him.

'It will need someone here to set things up,' he said. 'And of course that person should be me.'

'Of course.' She beamed back at him, she just couldn't help it.

'And now, I think, I can make you that promise,' he said. 'If you will let me.'

Eva got up to stand next to him and she gently brushed his dark hair from his brow as she had done before. 'I'll let you,' she said softly.

'Your emails . . . ?' He took hold of her hands and got to his feet.

'There was too much to say.'

He nodded. 'I hoped that was it.'

Eva looked up at him. Was he really here? She could hardly believe it. And was he going to stay?

'Those chinthes that brought you and me together must be as powerful as my grandmother always believed,' he whispered.

'I think you're right.' And then she was in his arms again and his lips were on hers. Tasting as warm and golden as Myanmar itself and of the stories of her childhood, that had so long ago wound their way into her heart.

ACKNOWLEDGEMENTS

Thanks to my tirelessly supportive agent, Teresa Chris, whose intuition and 'eye' I greatly respect and to my talented editor, Jo Dickinson, and all the team at Quercus, especially Kathryn Taussig and Margot Weale. Jo and Teresa have helped me to mould this once unwieldy novel into its present shape and condition, and I am very grateful.

Thanks to the Sams family: Dee for her support; Mervyn and Jean for kindly lending me the memoirs of the late John Sams, in which he wrote about his time in the Gurkhas, training and then fighting in Burma. For John – Gallop, the mule! Thanks to Bill Johnson, who has delighted our Alston Hall writing group with his memoirs of his war in Burma and who was kind enough to read and comment on a section of the novel for me. And most importantly to my husband's father, the late Peter Innes, who fought in Burma in the Chindits and also worked in the timber industry there. Some of his Burmese artefacts are now in my husband's possession – including, of course, two chinthes. Although I have used aspects of John and Peter's lives and experiences in the novel, I must stress that Lawrence's story is entirely fictional and that none of the characters relate to any of their acquaintances, friends or loved ones!

My late mother-in-law, Hazel Innes, also acquired many books about Burma, which I have used in my research, notably Sue Arnold's autobiographical *A Burmese Legacy*, Helen Rodriguez's autobiography *Helen of Burma*, H.E.W. Braund's account of Steel Brothers and Company Ltd in Burma, *Calling to Mind* and Alan Carter's *Last Out of Burma*. *Helen of Burma* was particularly invaluable to me in writing about Maya's war. Again, my characters are not related to any real people I have read about here, many details have no doubt been absorbed into this story, but it is fictional and my own.

Of other books I have read during my research, the ones that stood out were *The Glass Palace* by Amitav Ghosh, which allowed me to dip fictionally into the world of the final Burmese dynasty in 1885 — and thanks to Claire Zolkwer for recommending this book to me — and of course George Orwell's wonderful *Burmese Days*. The story of the Ngau Mauk ruby is apparently a true one and was derived from information on the internet, as was other material about Burmese rubies and chinthes.

Thanks to my husband's 'Burmese family' especially Suu Suu and Tin Mya and the others we met during our stay in Myanmar in November 2012 such as Ben, the driver who took us to Maymyo. And to other people we met and talked with there who may have made a contribution, thank you too.

Grateful thanks as always to Alan Fish, who read and commented on an early draft of this novel. And to my husband, Grey, who listens to every scene I read to him and always finds something useful to add. As I have said before, he is the best travelling companion a writer can have and a good problem solver to boot. Thanks to my daughters, Alexa and Ana, for answering random queries about language, music and things technical and for their unflagging support of my books. And to my son, Luke, for information about Copenhagen and computer scientists. Thanks to June Tate for her 'riches of the heart'. Finally, thanks to friends who have supported me during the journey of this novel and to readers who take the trouble to contact me to tell me that they enjoy my books. And to anyone I have forgotten. Thank you all!

The Creative Landscape

Rosanna Ley lives in West Dorset. Here she writes about the relationship between landscape and creativity . . .

There are little hotspots all over the world to which groups of creative people are drawn. But why? Surely it's not simply a question of contacts and existing artistic infrastructure – though clearly this helps. Is it something to do with landscape? And if some landscapes provoke more creative responses than others, which kind does it for you?

In the west country of the UK we can do wild and bleak or cute and scenic. We get a lot of rain – but this is why the grass is always greener. There are more writers, musicians, potters, artists, weavers, sculptors and glass blowers here than anywhere else in the UK. And tourists of all nationalities brave our English weather and come in their thousands to visit our galleries, exhibitions, mills, shops and craft centres. But what is it about the landscape that inspires creativity?

Is it perhaps the sense of history? Age can certainly give a landscape a vibe – Lyme Regis, Charmouth and the Jurassic Coast of Dorset have a sense of history which literally clings to the fossilized rocks, the cliffs and the beaches. Roman roads and ancient forts abound. In the novels of Thomas Hardy, Dorchester provides an artistic legacy too – of the writerly kind.

Visitors are equally inspired by the golden sandstone cliffs of West Bay – as recently featured in ITV's crime drama Broadchurch. Following Broadchurch, visitors (known locally as 'Broadies'!) have flocked to West Bay to see for themselves those amazing, towering honey-bricked cliffs

Or is it perhaps the tranquillity of a natural landscape – be it coastal, woodland, upland or riverside – which appeals to the creative mind and feeds our desire to get back to nature and away from the noise, turmoil and stress of busy city life?

Sometimes, walking along the vastness of Chesil Beach, you feel solitary, humble, affected by Nature. It's liberating.

Artists here in Dorset often talk about the quality of the light for painting. The rocks range from the orange sandstone of West Bay through to the Blue Lias of Lyme; where there is light there is always shadow.

As for Fuerteventura . . . There is a late-afternoon light that tints the landscape with a deep yellow and turns the sand (and blonde hair!) an unearthly golden green.

Whatever the personal response to landscape, it seems that this is a relationship and a dialogue between individual and place. Landscape brings out the creativity in us all. It encourages us to reflect, express ourselves and even to change our thinking.

Landscape might offer a glimpse of memory and the past – as it does for Ruby in my second novel when she first sees the turquoise lagoon in Fuerteventura, otherwise known as the 'Bay of Secrets', which became the book's title. It might even offer a glimpse of the future.

I always felt I belonged to West Dorset. It's my 'soul home'. And I'm always happiest writing where there is a sea view. It may be in my local cafe in West Bay with the high bank of ginger pebbles and the waves right beside me, the harbour and the sandstone cliffs beyond. Or in Fuerteventura on the Playa de Castillo watching the surfers ride the wild waves. It might be a tranquil summer day or bleak mid-winter. The sea lets me dream – it does it for me every time.

Discover

ROSANNA LEY

'Elegant storytelling at its best . . . the gentleness and authenticity of Rosamund Pilcher, with its strong sense of place, family and friendship. What a winning combination!' *Veronica Henry*

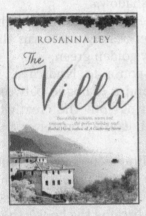

When Tess Angel receives a solicitor's letter inviting her to claim her inheritance – the Villa Sirena in Italy – she returns to her mother's homeland, only to discover some long-buried family secrets.

Six months after her parents' shocking death, journalist and jazz enthusiast Ruby Rae has finally found the strength to move on. But as she tries to do so, she unearths a truth her parents had kept from her all her life.